Outstanding Praise for *A World of Curiosities*

Instant #1 *New York Times* Bestseller
One of *The Washington Post*'s Best Mysteries
and Thrillers of the Year
One of *CrimeReads*' Best Psychological Thrillers of the Year
One of Barnes & Noble's Best Books of the Year
One of *Library Journal*'s Best Books of the Year
One of *The Globe and Mail*'s Top Ten Mysteries of the Year
One of *People*'s Best Fall Books
One of AARP's Best Fall Books
One of *Bustle*'s Most Anticipated of the Month

"Simply outstanding."   —*The Christian Science Monitor*

"[Penny] leaves you feeling better about the world once you've
finished."   —*The Guardian*

"The eeriest Gamache novel yet, *A World of Curiosities* is also one of
Penny's most intricately plotted and harrowing."
                                                        —*The Washington Post*

"A fine balance of humane values, spellbinding prose, Dickensian rev-
elations, and nail-biting suspense."   —*The Wall Street Journal*

"Dive in."   —*People*

"*A World of Curiosities* is an irresistible read."   —*Tampa Bay Times*

"*A World of Curiosities* [is] action-packed."   —*St. Louis Post-Dispatch*

"Another superb achievement."   —*BookPage* (starred review)

"A narrative tour de force."   —*Booklist* (starred review)

"Virtuoso."   —*Publishers Weekly* (starred review)

"The darkness in this intricately plotted story forces readers to search
for contrasting moments of hope."
                          —*Library Journal* (starred review and Pick of the Month)

ALSO BY LOUISE PENNY

The Madness of Crowds

All the Devils Are Here

A Better Man

Kingdom of the Blind

Glass Houses

A Great Reckoning

The Nature of the Beast

The Long Way Home

How the Light Gets In

The Beautiful Mystery

A Trick of the Light

Bury Your Dead

The Brutal Telling

A Rule Against Murder

The Cruelest Month

A Fatal Grace

Still Life

LOUISE PENNY

—

A WORLD OF
CURIOSITIES

MINOTAUR BOOKS
NEW YORK

For Hardye and Don Moel

Published in the United States by Minotaur Books, an imprint of St. Martin's Publishing Group

A WORLD OF CURIOSITIES. Copyright © 2022 by Three Pines Creations, Inc. All rights reserved. Printed in the United States of America. For information, address St. Martin's Publishing Group, 120 Broadway, New York, NY 10271.

www.minotaurbooks.com

The Library of Congress has cataloged the hardcover edition as follows:

Names: Penny, Louise, author.
Title: A world of curiosities / Louise Penny.
Description: First edition. | New York : Minotaur Books, 2022. | Series: Chief Inspector Gamache novel ; 18
Identifiers: LCCN 2022033302 | ISBN 9781250145291 (hardcover) | ISBN 9781250145314 (ebook)
Subjects: LCGFT: Detective and mystery fiction. | Novels.
Classification: LCC PR9199.4.P464 W67 2022 | DDC 813/.6—dc23/eng/20220715
LC record available at https://lccn.loc.gov/2022033302

ISBN 978-1-250-14530-7 (trade paperback)

First Minotaur Books Trade Paperback Edition: 2023

10 9 8 7 6 5 4 3 2 1

CHAPTER 1

⁓

O h, *merde*."
    Harriet looked in the mirror, her toothbrush hanging out of her mouth. It was the first of June and she'd forgotten to say, *rabbit, rabbit, rabbit.*

She said it now, toothpaste foaming on her lips, but had the sinking feeling it was too late. The magic wouldn't work. And if there was any day when she needed magic, it was today.

"*Merde.*"

"It'll bring you good luck, little one," Auntie Myrna had assured her niece when she'd taught her the incantation. "It'll protect you."

That had been years ago, but the rabbit habit hadn't wholly taken. Most months Harriet remembered, but of course this month, when she needed it most, she'd forgotten. Though she knew it was probably because she had so much else on her mind.

"Shit."

Did she really believe repeating *rabbit, rabbit, rabbit* made a difference? No. Of course not. How could she? It was a silly superstition. There was nothing actually magical about those words. Where did it even come from anyway? And why "rabbit"?

It was ridiculous.

She was an engineer, she told herself as she prepared for her morning run. A rational human being. But then so was her aunt. Did Auntie

Myrna even do it? Or had it been a joke the timid child had taken to heart?

Setting aside the absurdity of magical incantations, Harriet marshaled her rational self and entered the day.

Everything will be okay, she said as she ran through the warm June morning. *All will be well.*

But Harriet Landers was wrong. She really should have repeated *rabbit, rabbit, rabbit.*

It was the beginning of November when the Chief Inspector first saw Clotilde Arsenault. He pulled his field jacket closer around him and knelt beside her, like a penitent at some awful altar.

Do you want to hear my secret?

"*Oui*," whispered Armand Gamache. "Tell me your secret."

He heard a snort of derision behind him and ignored it, continuing to stare into the worried eyes of the dead woman at his feet.

The head of homicide for the Sûreté du Québec had been called away from Sunday breakfast with his young family. He'd flown hours northeast from his home in Montréal to the shores of this godforsaken lake to kneel beside the body that now bobbed in near-freezing waters. She was shoved half ashore by the gray waves that were growing increasingly insistent by the minute.

Whitecaps had formed out at the center of the lake, and even in this fairly protected cove, they bumped up against the woman, moving her limbs in some mockery of life. As though she'd decided she wasn't dead after all and was about to rise.

It added a macabre element to an already morbid scene.

It was a bleak day. The first of November. A wind blew in from the north, bringing with it the promise of rain. Perhaps sleet. Perhaps freezing rain. Even snow.

It frothed up the already tumultuous lake, creating waves on the waves. Shoving the dead woman ever forward, offering her to Gamache. Insisting he take her.

But he couldn't. Not yet. Though all he wanted to do was haul her further onto the rocky shore. To safety. He wanted to wipe her face dry and close those glassy eyes. And wrap her in the warm Hudson's Bay blanket he'd spotted in the back of the local Sûreté vehicle that had driven him there.

But he, of course, did none of those things. Instead, with immense stillness, he continued to stare. To take in every detail. What could be seen, and what could not.

It was hard to tell her age. Not young. Not old. The water, and death, had slackened her face, washing away age lines. Though she still looked worry-worn.

She obviously had had good reason to worry.

Blond hair, like string, was plastered across her face. A strand touched her open eyes. Gamache could not help but blink for her.

He didn't have to guess her age, he actually knew exactly how old she was. Thirty-six. And he knew her name, though they hadn't yet searched her body for ID, and no formal identification had been made.

She was the woman reported missing by her two children a day earlier.

Children now orphaned.

"Photographs?" he asked, looking across at his second-in-command.

"Taken," said Inspector Linda Chernin. "Scene of Crime has searched the immediate area. Teams are on the lake and moving along the shoreline, looking for where she might've gone in. We're waiting for the coroner before we move her, *patron*."

Behind him there was a pfffft and a muttered "*Patron*. Kiss-ass."

Inspector Chernin's lips thinned, her eyes hardened, and she made to get up to confront the agent, but a look from Gamache stopped her. Just.

Harriet ran through the bright, cool June morning, keeping to the center of the dirt road out of Three Pines.

She glanced this way and that, always aware of her surroundings. Aware of the thick forest, and what might be hiding in there. Bears. Moose. Rabid foxes. Bloodsucking ticks with Lyme disease.

Bigfoot. The murdered kid who now murders other kids.

She smiled, remembering the silly ghost stories told around the village bonfires. But still, she picked up her pace. Harriet had spent much of her life running. And now, in her early twenties, she was running faster and faster. Further and further. Away.

"Injuries?" Gamache asked.

From his vantage point he could see none, though the coroner would be able to tell them more. He hoped.

"Here." Inspector Chernin pointed to the side of the victim's head.

Gamache leaned across the body for a closer look. As he did, a shadow blocked out what little sunlight penetrated the pewter clouds.

"Do you mind?" he asked, glancing over his shoulder. When the shadow withdrew, he bent closer.

A crushing blow had caved in that side of the woman's head.

"It could've been postmortem," said Chernin. "From what her kids told the local cops, she'd been drinking and was depressed."

"You're thinking suicide?" asked Gamache, sitting back on his heels, aware that his legs were growing numb from a combination of the kneeling and the cold.

A gust of wind blew spray from the lake onto his face. He turned his back, protecting not himself but the dead woman. It was not necessary. It was instinct.

Behind him he heard another snort, this time of amusement.

"Suicide? Are you kidding? She was a drunk and whored around from what I hear, but she didn't kill herself. That's obvious. Though who'd have blamed her? I'd off myself too, if I were her. Fucking waste of space."

Gamache had a few quiet words with Inspector Chernin, then rose. He slowly, deliberately, turned to face the unfortunate young man.

Had the agent been more astute, had his head not been quite so far up his own *derrière*, had he not been so intent on self-destruction, he might have noticed the look in Chief Inspector Gamache's eyes.

"Come with me, please."

Gamache reached out, and the agent braced for the inevitable shove. But it didn't happen. Instead, the Chief Inspector simply indicated a rocky outcropping, away from the activity.

Once there, Gamache stopped, turned, and after regarding the young man for a moment, he finally spoke. His voice was deep, calm. Quiet. But it held more force than any screaming the agent had heard his entire life. And he'd heard a lot.

"Agent Beauvoir, don't you ever—"

"—Wonder what would've happened if your father and I had never met?" asked Jean-Guy Beauvoir.

He looked across the tub at his wife, Annie, who was bathing their infant daughter, Idola. Then he went back to trying to put a sweater on a squirming Honoré, who was eager to get out to play on the village green with his friends.

The fact the child's best friend seemed to be the deranged old poet Ruth Zardo both amused and slightly worried his parents.

"You mean had Dad never found you languishing in the locker of that Sûreté detachment in the middle of nowhere?"

"I mean when he recognized my brilliance and begged me to help him solve the most difficult murder ever."

"Anywhere," said Annie, who'd heard this before.

"In the world," agreed Jean-Guy.

He released Honoré, who sprang out of the room, thumping down the stairs and outside, banging the screen door behind him.

"The lady in the lake," said Annie.

"*Oui.* And by the way, I wasn't actually in the locker."

"Only because you were too big to stuff in there."

"Because I was too tough. And still am." He bent closer to his daughter, smiling. "Daddy's big and strong and won't let anything ever happen to you, right, *ma belle* Idola, Idola, Idola."

As Idola's father held her flat, saucer-like eyes, she laughed. With abandon.

She was so like her mother that way. A light and easy heart.

"Dad did mention your contribution that day," said Annie, toweling the child dry. "But it sounded more like 'shit-head.'"

Jean-Guy laughed. "Sûreté code for brilliant."

"Ahhh. Then you are definitely luminous." She heard a snort of amusement as he turned and looked out the window at the village of Three Pines.

Harriet Landers let herself into the New and Used Bookshop and tiptoed up the stairs.

She needn't have bothered. Auntie Myrna, in her signature huge caftan, was already up and in the kitchen of the loft, brewing coffee. Her partner, Billy, beside her, frying eggs and bacon.

Harriet had smelled it when she'd opened the door to the bookshop and thought it might be coming from the bistro next door.

An emerging vegan, her kryptonite was bacon and eggs. And real cream in her coffee. And croissants. She was too afraid to ask Sarah the baker if there was real butter in them.

It seemed her magical thinking, while not extending to incantations, did extend to croissants.

"Ready?" asked Billy, after they'd finished breakfast.

Harriet had showered and dressed, and made up the sofa bed in the living area.

She took a deep breath. "Ready."

Auntie Myrna, unconvinced, folded her into her arms, and whispered, "It'll be all right. We'll be there. You look beautiful."

Harriet smiled, and didn't believe a word of it.

Jean-Guy had his back to the bedroom and was looking out the window at the peaceful little Québécois village.

Annie could see that he was no longer in the bedroom of her parents' home in Three Pines. He was standing on the frigid shores of a lake that had just thrown up a corpse. The memory was never all that far away. And it was never really a memory.

That day had changed everything.

It was the day a disgruntled little shit of a Sûreté agent had met the distinguished head of the most successful homicide division in the nation. It was the day the man who would become Annie's husband had met her father.

What would have happened had they not met? What would have happened had the lady in the lake not been killed? Had her father not chosen to investigate it himself?

What if he had not gone into the basement of that far-flung Sûreté detachment? A place not flung quite far enough.

Why had he? There'd been no reason. Chief Inspector Gamache hadn't even been to the scene of the murder yet. There was no evidence housed down in the basement of the detachment. Only a surly young agent, discarded and forgotten.

And yet, Armand Gamache had.

Because he had to. Because, Annie Gamache knew, it was fated.

From the bedroom window, Jean-Guy watched their five-year-old son pause, look both ways, then run across the dirt road and onto the village green, where a bunch of boys and girls were kicking a soccer ball. The skinny boy gave every appearance of being impetuous, even reckless, while in fact being quite cautious. Not fearful, but careful.

He was like his father that way. Filled with piss and vinegar and caution.

An elderly woman and a duck watched the children from a nearby bench. Honoré ran up, gave them both a quick kiss, then turned and tackled another kid.

Even from the open window of his in-laws' home, Jean-Guy could hear their shrieks of laughter.

Ruth, watching from the bench, shook her head in mock disapproval, then took a swig from a mug of what might contain coffee, though no one would bet on it.

Despite the laughter and fresh sunshine and the promise of warmth in the young June morning, Jean-Guy rubbed his hands together and drew his elbows into his sides.

The memory of that November morning by the forlorn lake had

called up a chill. A cold that had settled into his bones, into his marrow, all those years ago had never really left.

But it wasn't just the past that had resurrected the chill. It was the present, what was going to happen on this shiny day. So many years later.

"*There's always another story*," whispered Jean-Guy. "*There's more than meets the eye.*"

His gaze shifted from the children and the poet to the solitary man walking around the perimeter of the village green. As a guard might. Not to keep criminals in. But to keep those inside safe from an outside world that could not always be trusted. But the truth was, this man, who had no business or reason to trust, actually did.

Jean-Guy knew that, as head of homicide for Québec, his father-in-law had seen things no human should witness. Day in. Day out. The corpses had piled up. Armand Gamache had seen the worst that people could do. Acts that would harden most hearts and turn a good person cynical, despairing, and finally not caring.

And yet Gamache seemed impervious, almost blind, to the horrors, even while investigating them.

When Jean-Guy, as his second-in-command, had finally pointed out the dangers his blindness posed to his team, to the citizens he'd sworn to protect, the Chief had sat him down. Leaning forward, his elbows on his knees, his fingers intertwined, Gamache had explained.

Yes, Jean-Guy was right. He'd seen the worst, truly terrible things. They both had. But he'd also seen the best. They both had.

He held the younger man's eyes, inviting him to set aside for a moment the great brutality that existed and to remember the acts of greater courage. Of integrity and decency. Of self-control.

Of forgiveness.

Not by moral giants, not performed by superhumans. These were men and women of human size and proportion. Some were cops. Many were not.

What blinded us, he told Beauvoir, were the horrific acts. They threatened to overwhelm and obscure the decency. It was so easy to remember the cruelty because those left a wound, a scab that hid the rest. Hid the best. But those appalling acts, those appalling people, were the exception.

"You need to remember that, Jean-Guy. The blindness you mention isn't believing in the essential goodness of people, it's failing to see it."

Jean-Guy Beauvoir listened and nodded but wasn't convinced. Which wasn't to say he thought the Chief was soft. Anything but.

Gamache was clearheaded, even ruthless when necessary.

While he hated guns and didn't wear one in the normal course of his day, Gamache did not hesitate to use the weapon. When necessary. Aiming and firing with an astonishing precision for someone who loathed firearms.

Ghosts followed the Chief Inspector, haunting him even on this bright June morning. And yet, for all that, Armand Gamache remained a hopeful, even happy, man.

He'd chosen to spend his adult life tracking killers, looking into the minds of madmen. Exploring the dark caverns and fissures where acts of murder were born and raised, nurtured, protected, and sent out into the world.

While Gamache had become an explorer of human emotions, Jean-Guy Beauvoir was the hunter. They were a perfect, though unequal, team.

Watching his father-in-law toss a slimy tennis ball to Henri the German shepherd, Jean-Guy was under no illusions who was the leader. He'd follow him anywhere. And had.

And had. Almost. Anywhere. Almost . . .

Again, he felt the chill.

Henri bounded after the ball, followed by old Fred, who never stopped believing he had a chance of getting there first. And finally tiny Gracie, found on a rubbish heap by Reine-Marie. And brought home.

Gracie might, or might not, be a dog. The smart money was now on guinea pig, with hedgehog a close second.

Armand knelt and picked up the ball Henri had dropped in the muck at his feet. The dog's tail wagged so furiously it shook his whole body. Then Armand kneaded Henri's ears, no doubt whispering that he was a good boy.

Though he needn't have gotten so close. Had Jean-Guy whispered it from the second-story bedroom window, Henri would have heard.

The shepherd's ears were so enormous they were capable, the villagers suspected, of picking up transmissions from outer space. If there was alien life, Henri would be the first to know.

Then Gamache kissed Fred on the top of his smelly head, patted Gracie, and, standing back up, he tossed the ball again. Then continued his Saturday morning stroll through the sunshine.

A happy and content man. Trailed by ghosts.

It had taken Jean-Guy years to figure out how Gamache managed to hold on to his equilibrium, his humanity, when so many fellow senior officers had seen their marriages fall apart. Who'd taken to drink, to drugs, to despair, to cynicism. To corruption. To turning a blind eye to violence, their own and those of their officers.

Every day Armand Gamache commanded a department that hunted the worst that humankind offered. All day, every day.

And he took the most gruesome task on himself. To break the news to the families.

He absorbed the unfathomable grief as the world collapsed on top of these husbands, wives, fathers, mothers. Children.

With his words, he crushed these people. Killed these people. They were never, ever the same. They now lived in a netherworld where the unthinkable happened. Where the boundaries would now forever be proscribed by "before" and "after."

This Armand Gamache did.

How he carried the sorrow and responsibility and still remained hopeful had baffled Jean-Guy for years. But now he knew.

He could do it because at the end of each brutal day, Armand Gamache returned here. To the tiny village of Three Pines. That existed on no map. That sat in a hollow surrounded by forests and mountains. As though in the palm of some great hand.

Every evening, he returned here to Reine-Marie.

He sat in the bistro and sipped a scotch and listened to the stories of their days. Clara the painter. Myrna the bookstore owner. Ruth the poet and Rosa, her foul-mouthed duck. Gabri and his partner,

Olivier, would join them by the fire, or out on the terrasse on warm summer evenings, their voices mingling with the trill of crickets and the gentle murmur of the Rivière Bella Bella.

Monsieur Béliveau and Billy Williams and Sarah the baker and Robert Mongeau, the new minister, and his wife, Sylvie, and any number of other friends would be there.

All having discovered a village only ever found by people lost.

Every evening Armand Gamache was reminded that goodness existed. And every morning he drove away, to face the horrors. To roll away the stone and step inside the cave. Secure in the certainty that no matter what he found, he could always find his way back home.

There was, though, to Beauvoir's knowledge, one boulder that Gamache refused to move. One cave he would not enter.

Yes. There was one person, one mind, Armand Gamache feared.

CHAPTER 2

D on't you ever—" the Chief Inspector began to say.
    The softly spoken words cut through the wind and roar of
crashing waves and landed in the younger man's ears as though whispered directly there.

"—talk like that—"

Agent Beauvoir braced for the Chief Inspector to say "—*to me, you
stupid, arrogant little shit.*"

But instead . . .

"—at the scene of a murder. That isn't a body, that isn't a corpse,
that isn't a puzzle. She's a human being whose life has been taken.
Stolen. I will not tolerate that sort of language, that behavior."

Spray from waves beating against the rocks stung their faces, but
while Beauvoir winced, the Chief Inspector never flinched. Never
turned away. His deep brown eyes never wavered, never left Beauvoir's.

With every word the man uttered, the young agent grew more and
more perplexed.

More and more afraid.

Screaming, yelling, threatening he understood, even went out of
his way to provoke.

But this? It wasn't just a foreign language, it was alien. As though
the man in front of him had appeared from some strange world unknown to Beauvoir. He understood the individual words, but their
meaning eluded him.

And then it got worse.

"We have a duty," the Chief was saying. His voice steady, never rising above normal level, even as the wind whipped around him and lake water coursed down his face. "Sacred or otherwise, to the murdered person and those who love and care for them. Part of that duty is to make sure their humanity is preserved. Do you understand, Agent Beauvoir?"

Don't say it, don't say it. Do. Not. Say. It.

"What I understand, sir, is that you're a laughingstock, a joke, in the Sûreté."

Stop. Stop. For God's sake, stop. He's not the enemy.

And yet it felt like he was. Gamache was threatening, in his soft, even gentle voice, all Jean-Guy's defenses, fortifications that had taken a lifetime to erect.

"Your department is made up of all the garbage no one else wanted. They're the only ones who'll work for you. You don't even wear a gun. You're a coward. Everyone knows that."

Word after word, like a shotgun blast to the chest, he aimed at this senior officer.

It was, of course, suicide. But necessary. A panicked effort to push away what now seemed inevitable. That this man would breach his walls. Would see inside. And so, Beauvoir lashed out. Wildly. Saying the most insulting things any cop could hear. Any human could hear.

He braced for the counterattack. But none came. The older man just stood there, his face gleaming with lake water, his hair, just touched with gray, tousled in the wind.

Around them the other agents, members of Gamache's team, had stopped to watch. Some must have moved to intervene because the Chief Inspector made a subtle gesture to stop them.

Jean-Guy raised his voice to be heard above the ruckus of the waves and the wind and the water drumming against their clothing, as though nature was trying to drown him out.

"Only a fool would follow you."

What happened next shocked and terrified the young agent. And changed his life.

Armand Gamache strolled through the early-morning sunshine, past the three soaring pines. Past the bench, where Ruth raised her middle finger in greeting.

He smiled at the elderly woman and continued on, past his grandson, already caked in mud. Past Monsieur Béliveau's General Store and Sarah's Boulangerie. Past Olivier's Bistro.

The door to the bookshop opened, and Armand turned to greet his friend and neighbor Myrna Landers.

"Big day," Armand said to her as they continued the walk together. "Can we give you a lift?"

"Thanks, but I'll take my own car. I'm driving Harriet in."

Myrna studied her companion. His hair, curling slightly around his ears, was almost all gray, though he wasn't yet sixty. The lines down his face were accentuated in the morning light. Creases and furrows made from worry, and sorrow, and pain. One, a deep scar by his temple, was made from something else entirely.

Not for the first time the retired psychologist wondered who'd decided to name that part of the body the temple. No doubt some man who worshipped information. Thinking that the brain was the temple where knowledge was housed.

But she knew, as did her companion, as did the dogs, and Gracie, trotting beside them, that anything worth knowing was kept in the heart.

Armand turned to her. "How're you feeling?"

"About today? Nervous for Harriet. She's almost sick with anxiety. Panic attacks."

Armand nodded. He was nervous too, though not for Harriet. He told himself it was ridiculous. Nothing bad could happen.

Reine-Marie came out onto their front porch and waved. Breakfast was ready.

As he smiled, Myrna was reminded that the deepest creases down his face were made by laughter.

"Will you join us?" he asked.

"Already had mine, but *merci*."

She accompanied him to his front path.

It was promising to be not just warm but hot. Perennials were well along, the lupines and vibrant red poppies and irises were in bloom. Peonies that had survived the winter kill were budding out. The maples and wild cherry trees in the surrounding forest were in bright green leaf.

"Fiona will be there today," Armand said casually. "I had confirmation last night."

Myrna's lips compressed and she took a deep breath. "I see. You asked the families? The survivors?" Though she knew he had.

"Yes. I met with them ten days ago. Walked them through it and left the final decision up to them. It's been many years since it happened."

"Yesterday," said Myrna, and Armand knew she was right.

If it had been Annie, it would still feel like yesterday. Like today. Like this minute.

"I spoke with Nathalie Provost last night," he said.

She was, Myrna knew, the spokesperson for the victims and families. The public face of a national tragedy.

"They've agreed."

"I'm not sure I would have. Still, you must be pleased." Myrna's voice was flat, noncommittal.

Armand hesitated and stared out at the village green. "There's more."

Myrna gave a small, unamused laugh. "Of course. There's always more. Let me guess. He'll be there too. The brother."

"We can't stop him. She wants him there."

Myrna nodded. They'd known that was a risk. Still, how bad could it be?

Upstairs, Jean-Guy was wondering the same thing as his mind went back to that November day.

News of the discovery of a body in the frigid waters of Lac Plongeon had filtered down to the basement of the remote Sûreté detachment. Agent Beauvoir guessed it was probably the missing woman.

A real case. A real body. And the incompetent, jealous fuck-faces upstairs were keeping him out of it.

Agent Beauvoir sat on the stool, guarding bits and pieces of evidence from petty crimes that would never get to trial. He consoled himself by once again mentally composing his letter of resignation from the Sûreté and in the process telling them what he really thought. Not that he hadn't already.

That's what had landed him in the dim basement.

And yet, and yet, despite repeated mental drafts, Agent Jean-Guy Beauvoir hadn't yet taken that last, irrevocable step.

As for Captain Dagenais, Beauvoir composed, a more stupid, incompetent asshole, dumb-as-fuck commander would be impossible to find—

Steps. Someone was coming down. He was used to the captain's heavy footfalls, but these were different.

And then the man had appeared.

Chief Inspector Gamache stood in the doorway. Like some apparition. Beauvoir rose from his stool and felt his cheeks begin to color, as though he'd been caught doing something he shouldn't.

Here was the head of homicide, in the middle of nowhere. In fact, he was in the basement of nowhere.

How could this be?

Of course. The body in the lake. Gamache had come up himself to investigate. No doubt having heard what an incompetent, shit-for-brains, dumb-as-fuck officer was in charge.

The man in the doorway was in his late forties, tall, not heavy but sturdy. His Sûreté-issue coat was open, and Beauvoir saw he was wearing a shirt and tie. A tweed jacket. Gray flannel slacks. No gun.

He looked, Beauvoir thought, more like a college professor than a man who chased killers.

The Chief Inspector cocked his head and smiled. Very slightly.

"*Bonjour*. My name," he said, coming forward and holding out his hand, "is Armand Gamache. And you are?"

"Beauvoir. Jean-Guy. Agent." He had no idea why he'd suddenly started talking backward.

"I'm here to investigate the death of the woman whose body was found by hikers. I presume you know the lake?"

"*Moi?*" said Beauvoir. Jean-Guy. Agent.

"Answer the man, you cretin," said Dagenais. Gamache turned and must've given the captain a look because he backed up a step and remained quiet, though his expression spoke volumes as he glared at his junior officer.

Don't embarrass me. Don't fuck this up.

"*Oui.* I know it."

"*Bon.* If your captain has no objections, perhaps you can drive me there and help with the investigation. It's good to have a local officer."

Dagenais's brows shot up. "Are you sure, sir? We have other—"

"No, this agent will do. *Merci.*"

Agent Beauvoir smirked at his captain as he followed the Chief Inspector up the stairs, through the small station, and out the door. For Gamache to have chosen him meant only one thing, Beauvoir realized. His brilliance must be known even at headquarters.

At the car, Dagenais took Gamache aside.

The wind was picking up, causing a swishing sound in the thick pine forest. The captain hunched his shoulders as he spoke.

"Be careful of him. He's trouble. I was just writing an evaluation, recommending he be fired."

"Why?"

"Insolence. But it's more than that. He's angry. Discontented. And that sort of thing spreads."

Gamache agreed. Infighting among men and women with guns was a disaster, especially if their anger and resentments spilled out onto a defenseless population.

He'd seen it happen. And yes, it often started with a single malcontent.

Gamache had heard rumors of irregularities at this detachment, which was why, when the report of a possible homicide came in, the Chief Inspector chose to investigate it himself.

He glanced at the young cop getting into the driver's seat. Then at Captain Dagenais.

This Agent Beauvoir had been banished to the basement for a reason. It was where the malcontents were placed. And yet, and yet . . .

He looked into the car just in time to see Beauvoir give the finger to his fellow officers. Gamache sighed. And yet, and yet . . .

As they drove toward the scene of crime, the Chief Inspector gave the young agent instructions. What to do. What not to do.

"Do you understand?" he asked when his words were met with silence.

"I do. It's all pretty obvious."

Beauvoir waited for the rebuke for this insolence, and when none came, he smiled. He had the measure of this man. While he was certainly senior, there was nothing remarkable about Chief Inspector Gamache. Beauvoir suspected he was in the presence of a product created by the Sûreté PR machine. A solid, dull, trustworthy figure designed to win the confidence of a gullible public. Nothing more.

Beauvoir had heard rumors while in the Academy that this man didn't even wear a gun. What sort of cop wasn't armed?

A coward, that's who. A weak man who depended on others to do the dangerous work.

A few minutes later they turned off the secondary highway onto a rutted and potholed dirt road. A few jarring kilometers down they finally arrived at the lake.

It was, even to Gamache, who had seen a lot of wilderness, a desolate place.

Low clouds clung to the thick forest. There were no homes, no cabins, no lights. No docks or canoes. Few came here, except bears and deer and moose. And murderers.

Agent Beauvoir went to get out of the car, but the Chief Inspector stopped him.

"There's something you need to know."

"Yes, I know. Don't disturb the evidence. Don't touch the body. You've told me all that."

Pathetic dumbass.

"There are," said the Chief, unbothered by what he'd just heard, "four statements that lead to wisdom. Do with them as you will."

Beauvoir sat back in his seat and stared at the Chief Inspector. *Do with them as you will?* Who talks like that?

But, more than that oddly formal phrase, no one in Beauvoir's experience had ever strung together more than three words without saying "fuck," or "*tabarnak*," or "*merde*." Including, especially, his father. And his mother, for that matter. And they sure had never mentioned *sagesse*.

Wisdom.

He stared at this older man, not far off his father's age, but as unlike his father as humanly possible. This man spoke so softly that Jean-Guy Beauvoir found himself leaning forward. Listening.

"I'm sorry. I was wrong. I don't know." As he listed them, Chief Inspector Gamache raised a finger, until his palm was open. "I need help."

Beauvoir looked into Gamache's eyes, and in them he saw something else that was new. That was unexpected.

It took him a moment to place what it was. To find the word to describe the look. And when he had it, the blood drained from Beauvoir's face, from his extremities. He felt his hands grow cold, and was suddenly light-headed.

What he saw in those eyes was kindness.

It was terrifying.

He practically fell out of the car in his haste to get away from this assault on his defenses. He didn't understand this man, those words, that look, that threatened his carefully constructed fortress.

Though he wasn't the only one surprised by the encounter.

Armand Gamache had gone down to the basement because he knew that was where the outliers were kept. He needed a local cop, and who better than one who was either the instigator of the trouble at the detachment, or who was not involved at all? An agent banished to the basement because the others did not trust him.

Once down there, he had not expected to recognize this wretched young agent. He'd never met the man before, Gamache was certain of that. And yet, there was a familiarity. Like unexpectedly running into someone from the distant past.

But Captain Dagenais was almost certainly right. There was a meanness about this Agent Beauvoir. Something lean and feral. Something dangerous.

This young man was trouble and troubled.

And yet, Gamache recognized him. And that had shocked the Chief Inspector.

Later, on the side of the lake, when Agent Beauvoir had let fly that barrage of insults, loudly enough for every other living human and most wildlife to hear, Gamache was forced to rethink.

He must have been wrong. Had made a mistake. It was a trick of the mind. A déjà vu. Without the déjà. Or the vu.

On that rocky shore, the spray hitting his face, Armand Gamache stared at Jean-Guy Beauvoir and was faced with a choice. One that would decide both their fates, their futures. Though at that moment Armand Gamache had no idea just how profoundly.

Should he do what was obvious, sensible, and rational and send this insolent young agent, surely a liability to the Sûreté and a danger to the public, back to the detachment? Where he would soon be fired. And good riddance.

Or.

"You're incompetent," Beauvoir was shouting, his voice rising above the crashing waves. "Stupid. And stupid is dangerous. You'll get them all"—his arm swooped around, his finger pointing toward the men and women on the shore—"killed, if you're not careful."

Over Beauvoir's shoulder Gamache saw Inspector Chernin step toward them, her face filled with fury. But a look from him stopped her. Barely.

His eyes returned to Beauvoir. He'd had enough. He was about to tell this ridiculous agent to go back to the station. Hand in his weapon and badge. He was done.

But instead, Armand Gamache found himself saying, "*Behind the corpse in the reservoir, behind the ghost on the links / Behind the lady who dances and the man who madly drinks.*"

His voice was so soft Agent Beauvoir wondered if he'd really heard it, or if it was an illusion. Some trick of the wind and waves.

This was the Chief Inspector's response to a verbal attack? To being called a coward in front of his own team? Instead of lashing out, the man was quoting some poem? He really was weak, a coward.

And yet, this response was far more terrifying than any insults the Chief might have hurled back.

Agent Beauvoir stood there, at a loss. Lost. Petrified. With force of will, he turned away and faced the lake that had just coughed up a corpse.

"Under the look of fatigue, the attack of migraine and the sigh." The voice, now seeming to come from inside Beauvoir's head, continued. Unrelenting.

"There is always another story / There is more than meets the eye."

Chief Inspector Armand Gamache reached for Beauvoir's sleeve, holding his arm firmly. Not painfully, but as one might hold a drowning man to prevent him from going under.

"It's all right," he said. "Things aren't always as they seem. It'll be all right, son."

Then he smiled.

The cold water pelting Jean-Guy's face tasted inexplicably salty. With those words and that grip on his arm, Beauvoir felt something shift inside him. It was as though in that instant Armand Gamache had not just breached but shattered his defenses. And stood now in the wreckage of Jean-Guy's young life.

But instead of recoiling, Jean-Guy felt drawn to this man, this stranger. Felt his DNA attach itself to him, like a mariner lashed to the mast in a ferocious storm, to keep from being swept overboard.

Jean-Guy Beauvoir felt totally vulnerable, but he also felt safe for the first time in his life.

Though he also recognized, in that moment, that it came at a price. If the ship should founder, he would go down with it. That was the deal. His life and future were now bound, inexorably, to this man. And probably always had been.

As he looked out across the lake, Jean-Guy Beauvoir sensed something else.

The approach of a ferocious storm.

CHAPTER 3

~

After hosing down Honoré and finishing a Saturday morning breakfast of banana-filled crepes with crispy bacon and maple syrup, Annie, Jean-Guy, and the children headed to the car for the drive back to Montréal.

Armand held Idola while Reine-Marie kissed her daughter and Honoré. Then she turned to her son-in-law. "See you later?"

"Absolutely."

He sounded far more enthusiastic than he was. The last thing Jean-Guy wanted was to sit in a stuffy auditorium on this fine June day and listen to speeches. While Annie and the kids went to a barbecue with friends near their home in Montréal.

He was doing this for Armand. Jean-Guy needed to be there in case this was the day something stepped out of that blind spot.

Armand kissed his granddaughter, then handed her back to Annie and turned to Honoré. Kneeling down to eye level, Armand opened his arms. The boy raced forward, plowing into him. Though prepared, he almost tipped over, and realized it would not be long before the boy actually tackled him.

Honoré, once free of the embrace, rifled his grandfather's pockets, where he found a wintergreen mint in one and a licorice pipe in another. Their parting ritual.

As they drove out of Three Pines, past the tiny church and the bench on the brow of the hill, Jean-Guy looked in the rearview mirror.

Reine-Marie was waving, but Armand had drawn in his elbows and hunched his shoulders against a chill no one else felt.

Except Inspector Beauvoir.

Maybe the Chief wasn't so delusional after all. Maybe he could see what was coming.

There is always another story, thought Jean-Guy. *There is more than meets the eye.*

After getting into her dress, bought solely for this occasion, Harriet looked in the mirror.

You can do this, you can do this, you can do this.

She took several deep breaths, holding them, then slowly exhaling. As she'd been taught to do when she felt overcome with anxiety. Then she looked around to make sure she was alone.

Harriet Landers was nothing if not careful. It was a point of pride, as she'd watched the reckless behavior of her fellow students. Though as she'd seen them going to parties, getting high, heading to Cuba and Mexico and Florida for March break, Harriet had begun to wonder if "careful" was really the word.

Bending down quickly, she reached into her knapsack for the special gift for her aunt. She felt its heft in her hand and knew Auntie Myrna would be surprised.

By the time Armand and Reine-Marie had found parking and got to the auditorium, the place was throbbing as hundreds of parents and friends greeted each other. Barely believing this day had finally come. When they could stop writing checks.

Though they all suspected that day never really came. But the big obligation was done.

Their children were graduating from university, and with a degree that might actually get them a job.

How well Armand and Reine-Marie remembered sitting in similar auditoriums watching first Daniel, then Annie take their degrees.

But this event, in this university, evoked far more complex feelings.

Armand's eyes swept the crowd, observing, noting. The proud

parents and grandparents. The bored and resentful younger siblings, glancing toward the windows. And the sunshine.

The Chief Inspector's practiced gaze took in the professors in their gowns, the Chancellor in his ceremonial robes, chatting with parents. The technicians onstage, preparing to begin.

But his eyes kept returning to the large young man standing by the door. He wore jeans and a hoodie and was unlike anyone else there.

Dark hair in a bun. A small growth of beard. And a bulge—was that a bulge under his sweatshirt?

Gamache started forward just as a uniformed officer went up to the man. Armand watched. Alert. Prepared.

Then he stopped and smiled with relief.

The younger man was a plainclothes officer, assigned by the local Montréal police. He looked over at Gamache and brought his hand up in a subtle salute.

Gamache nodded. Then continued his survey of the auditorium.

It was a scrutiny born of long years of practice. And necessity. Crowds were always, for a cop, problematic, and never more so than here. Today.

While he'd spent part of that morning remembering the early days with Beauvoir. Jean-Guy. Agent. Now, as he walked through the milling crowd, Armand remembered his own early days in the Sûreté. And the first time he'd come here to the École Polytechnique, the engineering school for the Université de Montréal.

He'd been in the final week of a placement in the Montréal ambulance service, training with a senior paramedic. Though already a graduate from the Sûreté Academy, and having applied to the Criminal Intelligence Division, he'd volunteered for this extra training while waiting to hear about his first placement.

It had been a cold day in early December. He'd just bought a plane ticket to visit his godfather, Stephen Horowitz, in Paris. He'd be flying out Christmas Day. It was the cheapest flight he could find.

Armand and his supervisor were packing up at the end of their shift when the call came through.

There was an incident at the École Polytechnique. That was all.

No other information. Armand looked at the clock on the station wall. It was almost six p.m.

"Come on, Gamache," she said. "Let's go. It's probably nothing. A drunk student. I'll buy you a beer later."

They went.

She was wrong.

It was December 6, 1989. And it was not a drunk student.

"*Bonjour*, Armand."

He turned, startled. "Nathalie!"

They embraced, then examined each other. There was gray in their hair now. And lines down their faces.

It was what happened naturally when people were allowed to grow older.

Nathalie Provost had been a young engineering student when they'd first met.

She was going about her day, going to her classes near the end of the semester as they prepared for the Christmas break. When it happened.

Armand was not that much older than she was. Than all of them. When they first met. When it happened.

Nathalie looked around the crowded auditorium before turning to Reine-Marie and hugging her too. Old friends by now.

"A beautiful day," Nathalie said, and they knew she meant more than the fine spring weather.

"It is," said Reine-Marie.

"I hope you're staying for the reception."

"We wouldn't miss it."

Just then Myrna arrived. She was hard to miss in her exuberant caftan of bright pink and lime green. Reine-Marie waved her over. She moved through the crowd like an ocean liner and docked beside Reine-Marie, who introduced her to Nathalie.

"Landers," said Nathalie. "Any relation to Harriet?"

"My niece. I take full credit for her brilliance."

Nathalie laughed.

Myrna's eyes went to the stage, where a huge bouquet of white roses sat in a vase on a table. Nathalie's eyes followed.

"We must never forget," Myrna said.

"No danger of that," said Reine-Marie.

"I hope you're right," said Nathalie. "But I'm not so sure. We see how easy it's becoming to move backward and call it progress. No, we need to do more than just not forget. We need to remember." She studied the woman in front of her. "Myrna Landers. You're the psychologist."

"Retired."

"Not completely," said Nathalie. "I read the report Armand asked you to write about Fiona Arsenault. You supported her taking her degree today." Nathalie looked more closely at the woman in front of her. "You look uncomfortable. Is something wrong? Was your report not accurate?"

"No, no, it was accurate. As far as it went."

"Meaning?"

"Meaning I guess I wish the issue hadn't come up." Myrna shot Armand a look. "It's difficult. Psychology isn't an exact science, unlike engineering."

"And even then, buildings and bridges still collapse."

There was an awkward silence as Nathalie Provost twisted the thin ring on the little finger of her right hand.

When Agent Gamache and his supervisor had arrived at the École Polytechnique that December evening, they found chaos.

The sun had set, and the place was lit with the glare of headlights bouncing off banks of snow and hitting the imposing engineering building.

Exhaust from emergency vehicles hung in the frigid air.

Gamache's supervisor told him to stay by the ambulance while she tried to find out what had happened. What was still happening. She came back none the wiser, but considerably paler.

"There're tactical units outside the building," she told him. "They're armed."

"But they haven't gone in?"

"No."

The information they did pick up was contradictory and garbled. Even a newly minted Sûreté agent knew the one thing to avoid in an emergency was this. Confusion. But it too hung thick in the air.

There was a lone gunman inside, they heard. There were two gunmen. Three. A gang of them.

He was dead. He was still shooting.

Students started running from the building, shouting for help. Gamache and others on the scene moved forward, wrapping the dazed and panicked young men in blankets and checking for wounds as the senior cops peppered them with questions. Digging for, desperate for, solid information.

And still the tactical squad waited. For what?

Finally, the word came. The gunman had shot himself. There were multiple casualties. They could go in.

Armand and his supervisor moved quickly through the outer doors, not far behind the armed cops, and were immediately hit by a thick wall of sound. Screams of pain. Cries, pleas for help. Orders shouted by the police.

And not just orders. There were warnings now.

There might be another attacker hiding in a classroom. Armed. Maybe with hostages.

Classrooms might be booby-trapped with nail bombs.

Armand's heart was pounding, his eyes wide. He tried to control his breathing, to remain calm. To keep his mind clear. To remember his training.

But there was a shriek inside his head. *Leave. Leave. Run away. Go home. You shouldn't even be here. Go.*

He'd never known fear like this. Never knew such terror existed.

At each classroom, he expected to see the man. The gun.

At every door he threw open, he braced for the impact. Of bullets or nails. Of splintered wood and shards of glass.

Then, when that didn't happen, when the room was empty except for overturned desks and chairs, he moved on. To the next door, the next classroom. Down, down the long hallway, he and his supervisor ran. Following the screams. Throwing open doors. Scanning. Every detail preternaturally sharp and clear.

Then, finally, they found them. Lying against the wall of their classroom. The bodies. Of the dead and wounded. It was suddenly very quiet. The wounded had no energy left to call for help. To even moan in pain. They were just trying to keep breathing.

He went to the first person clearly alive, though bleeding heavily.

"What's your name?" he asked as he knelt beside her, his eyes and hands moving quickly over her blood-soaked clothing. Trying to find the wound.

"Nathalie," she whispered.

"Nathalie, my name is Armand. I'm here to help." He pulled bandages from his kit. "Where does it hurt?"

She couldn't tell him. She was numb, going into shock.

He found one wound. Two. Three.

This woman, barely more than a kid, had been shot four times.

He put a compression bandage on the worst of her injuries, talking the whole time. Forcing his voice to be calm. Telling her she was going to be fine.

"*Ça va bien aller.*"

Repeating her name.

She was shivering. Nathalie. Her lips turning blue. Nathalie. He took off his coat and laid it over her.

As he worked, he asked her easy, mundane questions to keep her conscious. Blood was running into her eyes from a head wound. He wiped it away, but her eyes had closed.

"Where do you live?" "What courses are you taking?" "Stay with me, Nathalie."

Armand stayed with her, holding her hand sticky with her own blood, calling for a stretcher. Yelling for a stretcher.

"*Ça va bien aller*, Nathalie."

A stretcher finally arrived minutes, what seemed like hours, later. She gripped his hand as they took her from the classroom.

His supervisor grabbed his arm and shouted, "Come on. Move. There're more."

Armand had to yank his hand free as Nathalie disappeared into the hallway. And he moved in the other direction, searching for survivors.

It was only after half an hour and more victims that his supervisor, bending over one of the bodies and checking for a pulse that was no longer there, had turned to him, her eyes wide.

"Women. My God, they're all women."

Armand looked around. He'd been so busy just functioning, trying to help, trying to keep the horror and terror at bay, that he hadn't noticed.

She had seen what he'd missed.

The gunman had only murdered, only wounded, only targeted women.

The fourteen white roses on stage represented each young woman murdered that day, thirty years and a stone's throw away from where they now stood.

The killer had separated out the men and told them to leave. And then he'd shot the women. For daring to believe they could enter a man's world without consequence. For daring to become engineers.

They were murdered because they were women. For having opinions. And desires.

Oh yes, and breasts, and a sweet pear hidden in my body.

Whenever there's talk of demons, these come in handy.

Later, years later, Armand would read those words by Ruth Zardo, his favorite poet. And he would know the truth of it.

Death sits on my shoulder like a crow

. . . Or a judge, muttering about sluts and punishment.

And licking his lips.

Fourteen white roses. Fourteen murdered.

Thirteen wounded. Including Nathalie Provost.

It became known as the Montréal Massacre. The catchy alliteration made it easily digestible for those reading the headlines. Something awful had happened. They read the story and shook their heads in genuine sorrow. But most did not look deeper.

The Montréal Massacre.

For the families of victims and the survivors there were no words to describe what happened. It was both much bigger than the blaring headlines and more intimate. More personal. More universal. Much worse.

One of the police officers had entered the building and found his own daughter among the dead.

That had haunted Armand, and never more so than when, a few years later, he and Reine-Marie had Annie. He tried not to imagine, but couldn't help . . .

Many of the families and survivors returned to the École Polytechnique each year to attend the graduation. For more than thirty years they'd supported and applauded those who walked across the stage to accept their degrees. In some ways surrogates for their daughters, sisters, friends. Fellow students. Who never made it that far.

These graduates were testaments to the fact that the gunman had not won. Hate and ignorance had not won. Though even now, those who listened closely could hear the mutterings, the talk of demons. That never really went away.

Many of the first responders, the cops and ambulance attendants from that day, also came to each graduation. In solidarity.

Gamache's paramedic supervisor had died a few years earlier of breast cancer, after having joined the campaign for gun control. As had Armand. And he continued to press for even tougher gun control. Arguing as a now senior Sûreté officer that there was absolutely no reason a member of the public should have a handgun. And certainly not an assault-style weapon. They were only designed, and intended, to shoot humans.

A few months after the shootings, Nathalie Provost found Agent Gamache and returned his paramedic coat.

"I had it cleaned," the young woman said, holding it out to him. "But . . ."

There were stains that would never come out. Nor should they.

Yes. Armand Gamache hated guns.

Finally, after all the testimony before Parliament, it was the clear, thoughtful, powerful voices of the families of the victims and survivors that swayed lawmakers to enact stricter legislation. Though some politicians privately complained that tougher gun control was a huge overreaction. The fact only women were killed was a coincidence.

The Montréal Massacre, while tragic, held no greater lesson. It was the act of a single deranged individual. Not an indictment of society, they said.

These women, they said, were understandably upset. Emotional. But there was no need to pander to them. That would be wrong.

The shootings, the denials, the scoffing at all evidence of institutionalized misogyny, the pushback against gun control, the patronizing attitude of editors and politicians, only served to radicalize those women.

Before the shooting, they were students.

Now they were warriors.

Before I was not a witch, wrote Ruth Zardo. *But now I am one.*

Before that day, that long night, Agent Gamache had wanted to go into the Criminal Intelligence Division of the Sûreté. Had applied. Was waiting to hear.

The next day he withdrew his application. And instead applied to homicide.

CHAPTER 4

～

*P*atron?"

Both Chief Inspector Gamache and Agent Beauvoir turned to look at Inspector Chernin.

A man, a stranger, had joined her by the woman's body, still half in, half out of the lake. He was looking a little lost, very cold, and a lot unhappy.

The coroner, Gamache guessed. Called up from the nearest large town.

The Chief Inspector let go of Beauvoir's arm, and the young agent suddenly felt set free, but also adrift. For the first time he realized how close "free" and "lost" were.

Gamache brushed by him, then turned. "Coming?"

"*Oui, oui*" was all Beauvoir could manage as he stumbled along the shore, losing his footing now and then on the wet rocks.

"And no more talking, right? You've probably said enough."

"It's murder," Agent Beauvoir called after him. "She was murdered."

Gamache stopped and turned. "You don't take orders well, do you."

"You need to know. It wasn't suicide or an accident. The wound. Look at the shape. Look at what's stuck in its"—at a scowl from Gamache, he adjusted—"her skull. It, she . . . her, it . . ." He was completely confused now about what he should say. Pointing to his own head, he said, "It wasn't crushed by a rock or stone in the lake."

"Then what, in your opinion, did it?"

"It's not an opinion. I know. She was killed by a brick. Someone hit her with a brick and threw her into the lake."

Gamache stared at Beauvoir, then walked away to join Chernin and the coroner.

After introducing himself, Gamache said, "Tell me what you know."

"I know she's dead," said Dr. Mignon. "I have to get her onto my examining table before telling you more."

It was maddening, though not unexpected. Chief Inspector Gamache knew that most local doctors, designated as coroners, had only accepted the position because it came with much-needed extra money and absolutely no responsibility.

Most deaths were not at all suspicious. There were some hunting accidents. Some suicides. Car accidents. All tragic. But not homicide.

A country coroner in Québec could, and most would, go through their entire career without meeting a murder victim.

But this poor man just had. Fortunately, he was also conscientious enough not to pretend to know more than he did.

Dr. Mignon looked down at the body, then at his shoes, soaked through and caked in muck. Then, as a loon called, he gazed out at the misty lake.

"A terrible place to die," he said. "I'm guessing she's the missing woman. Heard about it on the news." His eyes returned to her body. "Her poor kids."

The woman's eyes were still open, her right arm lifting and dropping with the movement of the waves. Languid. Graceful, even. As though waving hello, or goodbye.

Like "free" and "lost," it was often difficult to tell the difference.

After doing a slightly more thorough exam, the doctor stood back up and removed his gloves.

"A catastrophic wound on the side of her head. No other obvious injuries. I'll need to look closer. See if there's water in her lungs."

If there was, she went in alive, and it might have been an accident or a suicide. If not, then she went in dead, and it was definitely murder.

While Gamache already knew the answer to that question, he would see what the coroner concluded.

"*Merci*" was all he said.

Out of the corner of his eye, he saw Agent Beauvoir practically vibrating with the effort not to shout out his opinion. To his credit, he remained silent, if not still.

Gamache nodded to Inspector Chernin. They could move the body now.

As his agents pulled her out of the cold water, Gamache walked Dr. Mignon to his mud-spattered vehicle and gave him some guidance on what to look for in the autopsy. The coroner listened, then thanked the Chief Inspector.

"Who's going to break it to the children?"

"We need to confirm her identity first, but once we do, I'll tell them."

The coroner put out his hand. "Better you than me. I'll be at the hospital, waiting for the body."

From the shore, Agent Beauvoir watched the two men talk, then turned to Inspector Chernin, who was kneeling beside the corpse and going through her pockets.

"The coroner doesn't know what he's doing."

"And you do?" she said, not looking at him.

"I know enough to recognize murder. I told Gamache, but I don't think he was listening. Here, let me show you."

He knelt opposite her and reached out, but Chernin stopped him. "Don't touch."

"Then give me gloves."

"You're getting nothing. Step back before you contaminate the scene."

"Hey, look, this was a murder," he said, taking a few steps away. "I told Gamache to look closer at the wound."

"For this?" Inspector Chernin held up a small evidence bag. In it were tiny chunks of red. Almost as red as Agent Beauvoir's face became. "We saw it right away."

"Then what was that talk about accident or suicide?"

"Just examining every possibility. But yes, before he took you aside, the Chief Inspector and I conferred about the shape of the wound, the sharp indent, and the red material embedded in her skull. Almost certainly a brick." She looked around at the lake. "Where would someone get a brick out here?"

When Beauvoir opened his mouth, she held up her hand. "It was a rhetorical question, Agent Beauvoir. Thank you for your help. I'm sure the Chief was grateful."

She watched as he seethed, his brilliance having gone unrecognized and unrewarded. With, perhaps, the dawning suspicion that in this company he might not actually be the brightest light. It was a new and unpleasant thought for Jean-Guy Beauvoir.

The Inspector smiled. She'd been this young agent once, a lifetime ago. Linda Chernin almost envied him his ignorance. He had no idea what he was in for.

"Inspector?" one of the agents called. He was walking along the shore in waders and holding an evidence bag.

In it was a sodden purse.

"Well done," said Chernin.

Opening the purse, she brought out a wallet. It was wet and worn but had been pretty once. A rose, needlepointed onto it, was now scuffed and dirty, and threads had been pulled loose.

There was no money in it, but there was ID.

Gamache returned from seeing the coroner off and joined them, motioning Beauvoir to step into the scrum.

"It's her. The missing woman." Chernin handed the plasticized driver's license to Gamache.

Clotilde Arsenault stared out at them. Her hair was blond. Straggly and stringy. It looked unwashed and uncombed. Unkempt.

Her cheeks were sunken. Her blue eyes were glassy. She stared at the lens as though trying to figure out what it was.

Her face was thin, almost emaciated, and her complexion sallow. The photograph more resembled one of the thousands of mug shots Gamache and Chernin had seen in their careers than a driver's license photo.

Gamache looked at the woman on the rocky shore. Then back to the picture.

In life Clotilde Arsenault had looked eerily as she did in death. She lived, it seemed, at the place where the river Styx narrowed. It had not been a long journey for the ferryman.

The woman in the picture was only thirty-six, but life had not been easy, or kind. And neither had death.

There was one other photograph in her wallet, in the sleeve where the money would have been. It too was plasticized. A studio portrait of a girl and boy. Sister and brother, he assumed. Clotilde's children. The boy, striking in his good looks, was smiling. The girl wore a school uniform and her hair was in pigtails. Looking closer, Gamache realized she was young, but not the little girl she appeared to be in the picture.

His brows drew together and he took a deep breath. "Have it checked for prints," he said. "When you're done, return it to me, please."

"Yessir," said the agent.

Gamache looked over at one of the Sûreté vehicles. When they'd arrived, he'd noticed a man and woman sitting in the back seat. Watching them.

"Those the two who found her?" he asked.

"*Oui*," said Chernin. "Hikers. Not from around here. They're up from Montréal."

"Hikers?" said Gamache. "Out here? Today?"

He already had that information. It was in the short report the captain had given him. But seeing this lake, these surroundings, raised all sorts of questions. Ones he would ask in time. But first—

Kneeling once more beside the body, Armand did something the coroner had not thought to do. He pushed up Clotilde Arsenault's sleeve to reveal the tracks. Then he looked down the length of her body. Her shoes were missing, having probably come off in the water, but her jeans were still on. The movement of the waves hadn't tugged them off. And her killers hadn't ripped them off. But that didn't mean there'd been no sexual assault.

He'd advised the coroner to take copious DNA samples and do a toxicology report, full spectrum. And to look for semen. To check for hairs. Tissue under nails. Foreign biological material everywhere, including her mouth.

There was bruising on her face. It was either immediately premortem, or very soon after her death.

And there were more bruises on her arms. Older ones. Previous assaults.

He pondered, staring down at her.

What had happened here? Why was Clotilde Arsenault dead? In a life clearly filled with violence, with pain, what had happened to take that next, that last, irrevocable step?

Why had someone found it necessary to kill her? Was it an accident? Had someone, addled by drugs, picked up the nearest object, a brick, and swung? Not intending to kill, but killing?

Or was it intentional? For the money? Her drugs? None were found on her, so perhaps they too were stolen.

But the big question, beyond who did this, was why had the killer brought her here? To this lake? Why not just leave her where she fell? Or, if he wanted to get rid of her body, why not leave her in the forest for the wolves and bears to find?

His eyes moved back to Madame Arsenault's face. Inspector Chernin had tried to close her eyes, but they'd been open too long. The lids would not move.

There is always a wicked secret, a private reason for this.

"Tell me your secret," he whispered again. This time there was no snort of laughter from young Agent Beauvoir. Only silence and the lapping of the waves. "Who did this to you?"

He waited, but nothing happened. He'd have been shocked if it had. Her eyes remained fixed on his, as though she were trying.

One thing seemed clear to the Chief Inspector. Clotilde Arsenault's last feeling wasn't fear or shock. It was worry. And that worried the head of homicide. It was an unusual expression for a murder victim. Surprise was what he normally saw. Sometimes anger, often terror.

But not this. Though he also suspected that Madame Arsenault had spent most of her life worried. Getting back to his feet, he turned to Chernin, who was going through the purse.

"A chocolate bar. Some wet Kleenex. What looks like house keys. No car keys. No phone."

"The report says it was left behind in her home. Her children found it, but don't know her password."

"A pair of dark glasses. Cheap. From a drugstore. Aaaaand . . . ahhhh." She called to a Scene of Crime officer. "I need this photographed."

He clicked a few shots of the inside of the cheap imitation-leather handbag while the others craned to see. When he finished, Inspector Chernin pulled the lining away.

Shoved down behind the lining was a small packet of white powder.

Chernin held it up. Gamache raised his head, looking up into the clouds. Thinking.

That answered a question that didn't actually need answering. She was an addict. But was she also a trafficker? He doubted it. She might have been once, but she appeared much too far gone now.

She was just a user. Whoever did this must've known she'd probably have drugs on her. And yet, they'd taken the money and left the not-very-well-hidden heroin. He sighed.

Very little of this made sense.

Why bring her here?

Why take the money but not the smack?

One thing Gamache did know was that people stole what they needed. What they wanted. What would be useful. In this case, the money.

But they hadn't bothered about the drugs. Because. Because.

Because drugs were not what they wanted or needed. Which meant she probably wasn't killed by her supplier. Or another addict.

So who . . . ?

Gamache looked over at the hikers. "What do they say?"

"Just that they were out for a walk and came across her body," said Chernin.

Gamache turned to Agent Beauvoir. "What do you think?"

"Me?"

"Yes. Your thoughts."

Beauvoir took a breath, and actually thought. It was, he realized, the first time he'd really stopped to consider something since he'd arrived at the detachment. It was also, he realized, the first time he'd been asked to.

He glanced over at Inspector Chernin, expecting her to be surprised or even annoyed that the Chief had consulted him. But she was just watching him too, waiting to hear what he had to say.

"Nobody comes out here for a stroll. I think they were up to something. Poaching probably. Fishing illegally. This lake is known for trout and walleye. Maybe hunting moose or deer without a license. It's the season. You haven't found a rifle or rods or other equipment?"

Chernin shook her head. "But . . ." She looked at the thick forest and the lake.

It was, for the homicide detectives tasked with investigating murders outside of Québec cities, the perpetual problem. In a city, losing a body or a weapon might be a challenge.

Out here? You could lose a tank.

A loon gave another call, and over Beauvoir's shoulder Gamache saw a formation of Canada geese heading south. Hurry, he thought. Winter's closing in.

"I'd like a chart of the currents in this lake," he said. "The local bureau de protection de l'environnement should have it. If not, try the Fish and Game Club."

"Will do," said Chernin. She waved toward the man and woman in the car. "If they were poachers, that might explain why they're here, but it doesn't make them murderers."

"Unless they were her dealers," said Beauvoir, pivoting. "Meeting out here where no one could see."

"They're from Montréal," said Chernin. "Are you saying they came all the way up here to make a five-and-dime sale? Then killed her? Two days ago. Then returned to the body, and reported it?"

"They knew their DNA would be found," said Beauvoir. The pivot had turned into a scramble. "This way they could explain it."

They all looked over to the car, where the hikers were now leaning forward, aware they were being discussed.

Gamache shook his head. "It doesn't make any sense."

"Why not?" asked Beauvoir, peeved at being doubted.

"For one, she wasn't killed here."

"How do you know?"

"You told me yourself. Think about it," said Gamache, before turning back to Chernin. "Why not just leave her in the forest where she'd never have been found."

Clotilde Arsenault would have then joined the long, and growing, list of missing women.

She was a known prostitute. A junkie. The local cops wouldn't try too hard.

Her children would spend the rest of their lives wondering. Looking into the faces of pale women with blond stringy hair. In restaurants, shops, walking toward them on the street.

Even when they themselves were elderly, they would still be looking. Wondering if that young woman sitting over there could be their mother.

Could that possibly be the reason Clotilde had been left where she might be found? To spare her children?

Was a person capable of murder also, in that same moment, capable of kindness?

Gamache took a deep breath, his exhale coming out in a stream of vapor as the temperature dropped still further.

He turned toward his car.

"I'll come with you," said Chernin, knowing what he had to do now.

"No, you stay here and coordinate the scene of crime. I'll meet you at the station after I've broken the news to the children."

Though Armand Gamache knew it would be more than news he'd be breaking. Fortunately, he supposed, Captain Dagenais would have found someone to stay with Clotilde's children for the past few days. Someone who could now comfort them.

Armand Gamache needed to get to them quickly before word

leaked out, though news of a body was probably already spreading through the community.

He looked across the lake, past the relative protection of the cove, past the whitecaps roiling farther out, until his gaze stopped at the thick old-growth forest. It had seen its share of violent death.

Most wild animals did not die of old age. They were killed but not murdered. There was premeditation, yes. One animal stalking another, with intent to kill. But no *mens rea*. No malice aforethought. No evil intent.

He was reminded again what Abbie Hoffman had said: *We must eat what we kill. That would put an end to war.* And, thought Gamache, an end to murder. Or most.

Inspector Chernin accompanied him as he walked toward his car. Their heads together, they discussed the practicalities of the investigation, including where to set up a command center and where to stay.

"What do you think of him?" Gamache asked as they neared the vehicle.

"Beauvoir? Well, *patron*, you sure know how to find the biggest piece of shit around."

"It's a gift, and"—he stopped and smiled at her—"my track record is unbroken. He should fit right in."

"You're not—"

"I haven't yet, but I'm considering it. There's something about him."

"It's called insubordination. He hasn't got a chip on his shoulder, he's got a boulder. With those anger issues, he becomes unpredictable, and that could be dangerous."

"His station chief agrees with you."

"And yet—" said Chernin.

Gamache studied the woman who'd been his second-in-command for several years. He said nothing. Just watched her. Inviting her to consider.

This habit of his of just waiting, quietly, she'd found unnerving for the first few years of her posting in homicide. But now she was used to it. Kind of. Most senior officers could not wait to impose their ideas. Gamache insisted his agents think for themselves.

"And yet," she continued, "he saw the shape of the wound and recognized the murder weapon. I saw it too. You saw it. But none of the other agents, not even the coroner, realized the significance and knew a brick had killed her. Knew it was murder."

"He not just saw that, he spoke up. To a senior officer. He's not afraid to speak his mind."

"The trick is getting him to shut up."

Gamache smiled. "True. That might take some work. But the point is, he put the truth ahead of his career."

"The truth or his ego?" she asked. Linda Chernin too was not afraid to challenge her boss.

"Good question." They looked over at Agent Beauvoir, who was pretending not to be watching them. "I guess we'll find out. When you're done here, have them taken to the station." Gamache nodded toward the two hikers. "Let them stew for a while. There's something, maybe quite a lot, they aren't telling us. Have you applied for a warrant?"

"To search their vehicle? Yes. I've also applied for one for Madame Arsenault's home. Both should come through soon. I'll let you know." She looked again at the hikers. "You think they did it?"

"I don't know."

Chernin returned to the shore and Gamache returned to his car. He could hear a vehicle approaching over the rutted road. No doubt the ambulance to take the body to the morgue and the news back to the community.

He'd have to hurry. And yet, his hand on the car door, the Chief Inspector hesitated. He stood very still and listened to the rustle and scramble of small creatures in the forest.

Then he closed his eyes, escaping into the peace of the moment. Taking a deep breath, he inhaled the cool, fresh air and with it the scent of pine needles and musky earth and rotting leaves. It was somehow comforting. Familiar. Natural.

He paused. Paused. Even as the sound of the ambulance got louder and louder, Armand Gamache held on to the peace and quietude for as long as he could. Before . . .

But it had to be done.

Opening his eyes, Gamache caught sight of a chipmunk racing up a tree trunk. Was it running or fleeing? Hunter or prey? Was another death imminent?

What must it be like to run for your life through a forest, knowing your pursuer was getting closer, closer? It was the stuff of nightmares.

He looked away and saw Agent Beauvoir still watching him.

Making up his mind, Gamache called out, "Come with me, please."

"*Moi?*" said Jean-Guy Beauvoir, touching his chest and looking around.

"*Oui. Vous.*"

The fact this superior officer had just used the formal, respectful "*vous*" surprised him.

"Well," said Gamache, as Beauvoir got into the driver's seat.

"Well, what?"

"Why is it clear Madame Arsenault wasn't killed here?"

"I don't know. Why?"

But Gamache just shook his head and looked out the window at the impenetrable forest, and Beauvoir settled into a silent huff. He was clearly being sent back to the basement.

He should have been so lucky.

CHAPTER 5

~

They'd taken their seats in the increasingly warm, increasingly stuffy auditorium.

Jean-Guy had arrived and was sitting, perspiring, on the other side of Reine-Marie. His knee bounced up and down. He might still get to the barbecue in time for a burger. Or two. If they started soon.

Though he knew his agitation had very little to do with the burgers. That was a distraction, a counterirritant, so he didn't have to think about why they were there. And who else would be.

The hubbub slowly died down, then a stir could be heard as those at the back of the room got to their feet. Like a wave at a hockey game, though far more polite and contained, the audience rose row by row as the Chancellor and President of the Université de Montréal, as the professors and board of governors and honored guests, entered in procession.

They wore flowing black robes and caps, some of which were stiff and covered in silk, some velvety soft and floppy.

What would look ludicrous out on the street was impressive here.

The procession was solemn. Reflecting the importance of this day.

After they'd taken their places on the stage, the President nodded and the next procession began. This one was far different. Friends and family members, already on their feet, began applauding, unable to contain their excitement.

Some whistled, some shouted names. No doubt embarrassing, and secretly delighting, the young woman or man. Phones were held high, recording the event. To be shown later to friends and relatives who hoped the dinner was delicious enough to warrant having to watch.

The procession became a parade, a celebration, as graduates in their caps and gowns entered the hall in alphabetical order, to cheers from relieved and a few privately surprised parents.

Watching this, Jean-Guy, despite the dark stains under his armpits and the rumble in his stomach and his slight foreboding, could not contain a smile. One that grew as more young people arrived.

Their joy was infectious.

He thought of the day he and Annie would rise up and applaud as Honoré entered just such an auditorium. Idola never would, of course. But she had other gifts. Not everyone was cut out for academia.

He looked across Reine-Marie, to Armand. He actually looked like he might cry. Was that possible? He was certainly gripped with a strong emotion, probably never having dreamed this day would come.

Armand and Reine-Marie craned their necks to find her in the crowd. Fiona Arsenault.

And then, as Jean-Guy watched, Armand's expression changed. It first froze and then the smile melted away, leaving something cold and flinty behind.

Jean-Guy followed Armand's eyes, though he knew what, who, he'd find at the other end.

And sure enough. There he was. A young man, still handsome, perhaps even more handsome than when Beauvoir had first seen him. The same day he'd first met the Chief Inspector.

The young man was looking past the stream of joyful graduates. Past the cheering and applauding parents. He paused briefly to look at Jean-Guy and smiled in recognition before moving on. Past Reine-Marie.

Sam Arsenault's stare landed on Chief Inspector Gamache, and stayed there.

"Turn right here," said Gamache.

"But the detachment's that way." Agent Beauvoir jerked his head to the left.

"We're not going to the detachment."

"Then where . . . Oh."

He drove in silence while Gamache reread the police report. Familiarizing himself with the family. With all those who'd been interviewed in an effort to find the missing woman.

It didn't take long.

There was no mention of the children's father or Clotilde's partner. No mention of relatives or even friends. Neighbors were interviewed, but that was about all.

Clotilde Arsenault and her children had moved to the community six years earlier from a town down south.

She was a known prostitute and addict. But not, it seemed, a dealer.

Then he reread the news stories, which were, shamefully, more detailed and enlightening than the official police report. But even they had scant solid information.

No one knew anything, though he sensed they were not trying very hard. No one had seen her the day she disappeared. Or admitted—Gamache automatically inserted the qualifier—to seeing her.

There was about these interviews the whiff of wishful thinking. That Clotilde Arsenault was indeed gone. Forever.

The ambivalence was slightly softened by sympathy for her children. Though even then not as much as Gamache would have thought.

The sister and brother, ages thirteen and ten, respectively, lived alone with their mother. They'd gone to the police saying she hadn't come home. She'd been away overnight before but never without telling them, and never two nights in a row.

They were worried.

The girl, Fiona, looked younger than her age. The boy, Samuel, looked older than his years.

Gamache searched the police report to see who was looking after the children in their mother's absence but couldn't find a name.

"Captain Dagenais, it's Gamache," he said into his phone. "Can you tell me who's staying with Clotilde Arsenault's children? Yes, we've positively identified her. I'm on my way over there now. I need to know—I'm sorry?"

Beauvoir glanced over at the Chief Inspector. Gamache's eyes had hardened, his face grown rigid as he struggled to contain his outrage. To not let his rage out.

"Are you telling me that two children came to you about their missing mother, and you sent them home alone?" There was silence as Gamache listened, his knuckles turning white as he gripped his phone. "I don't care that the girl is mature. She's still a child. Her mother's missing. Someone should've been found to stay with them, a friend, a state-appointed guardian, one of your agents. We'll discuss this later. Send someone now. Then put in an urgent call to Child Protection."

He hung up, cutting off the tiny, whiny voice.

"He's a real—" Beauvoir began.

"That's enough, Agent Beauvoir," snapped Gamache, and looked out at the gloom. The sun set early in November, and even earlier this far north. The light swallowed by the mountains and ancient forests.

"We're here." The car turned into a small, single-story home.

The vehicle was barely stopped when Gamache got out and walked quickly up the front path, righting a rusted and dented garbage can blocking the way.

While part of Gamache wished he could give these children a few more moments of blissful ignorance, a few more minutes when their mother might still be alive, the Chief Inspector knew that false hope was not a kindness.

If they were watching, and he suspected they were, they'd have seen the car drive up, and they'd know. They probably knew, deep down, when they'd made the missing person report.

Their mother was not coming home.

He needed to put them out of that misery, and into the next. A loss like this was a progression of miseries, like stepping-stones. Until they reached the other side. The new continent. Where the terrible reality lived, and the sun never fully came out again. But where, with time and help, they might find acceptance and, with that, peace.

He knew, from experience, that there was no avoiding this pain. In a sense, they were fortunate. Their mother had been found and, as horrific as that was, the not knowing would have been worse.

It was cold comfort at best.

Agent Beauvoir was not in as much of a hurry to get to the door. With each step forward, the realization of what was about to happen dawned. What had started as a career opportunity was mutating into a human tragedy.

The Chief Inspector had barely raised his fist to knock when the door opened.

"*Oui?*"

The girl stood there, small for her age, thin, her eyes wide and filled with a plea.

Don't say it. Don't say it.

And yet, thought Beauvoir, she'd opened the door. She could have hidden. Pretended they weren't home. She could have lived in blissful, or semi-blissful, ignorance for a little while longer.

But instead, the girl had chosen to face the truth.

He wanted to grab the Chief Inspector's arm and drag him away, muttering apologies to the girl. They had the wrong home. The wrong person.

Never mind . . .

But he didn't, of course.

"Fiona?" said Gamache, his voice gentle and steady. "My name is Armand Gamache. I'm with the Sûreté. This is my colleague Jean-Guy Beauvoir." He paused. "We have news." Pause. "May we come in?"

She didn't ask why. She didn't say anything, just nodded and backed up.

The home was barely more than a trailer. Single-story, with junk on the front yard and a rusty wreck of a car on blocks in the drive. Shingles had blown off the roof, and the siding was chipped and dirty, with green mold growing in places. Some rotted boards had pulled away, some had fallen off. It could barely be described as a structure. It was the bricks-and-mortar version of Clotilde Arsenault.

And yet, it was not, Beauvoir noted, made of brick. In fact, there wasn't a brick in sight.

His face opened in realization. That's what the Chief had meant when he said it was clear that Clotilde had been killed somewhere else and dumped. Had she been killed at the lake, it would have been with a rock. Or a knife. Or a gun. Or a scarf. Or a piece of petrified driftwood. Not a brick.

No. She was murdered where her killer could grab a brick and smash her with it.

As he followed the Chief Inspector through the door, he picked up a scent. It wasn't the odor Jean-Guy had expected. He'd braced for the reek of sweat and decay. Of cheap drugstore perfume and stale makeup.

The ghost of Clotilde Arsenault.

Instead, what met them was the familiar and soothing scent of lemon cleaner.

But the most obvious sensation was noise. There were bells and applause and people shouting. It was a game show on a television turned up full blast.

Gamache looked around, quickly taking in his surroundings. The sounds. The smells. The feel.

The walls were covered in faux-wood paneling. There were scratches and dents and holes the size and shape of fists in the walls.

To their left was an opening into the living room, where the sound was coming from.

Straight ahead, down a short, dim corridor, Gamache could see a sink and a stove. The counters uncluttered.

While dreary, the home was neat and tidy. And clean. Almost sparkling. Given how Clotilde looked after herself, he'd expected her home, her children, to be in the same state of neglect.

And Gamache was reminded, yet again, of the folly of expectation. Especially in his job. How easy it was to go down the wrong road and turn his back on the real threat escaping down another path. Or creeping up behind.

The girl's sweater and jeans were worn but washed. Her hair, no longer in pigtails, was long and blond and shiny. Not with grease but from a recent shampoo. Fiona Arsenault was about the same age as Annie, his daughter. Slightly younger, but close.

He wished he were anywhere else but here. Doing anything but this. But here he was, and there was no turning back.

Fiona paused in the hallway, uncertain.

"May we go into your living room?" Gamache asked, his deep voice kind but still firm.

Don't do it, thought Beauvoir. How can you do this to her?

To them.

A boy was in the living room watching a huge television. He turned to them but didn't stand up. He just stared.

Beauvoir almost gasped. He'd never seen such a handsome child. Like his sister, he was small for his age. His eyes were large and blue green and thoughtful, almost soulful. His hair was light brown, thick and wavy around his face. His features looked like something an artist would draw, of a perfect waif.

Given what was about to happen, Beauvoir felt himself suddenly light-headed. To destroy such innocence seemed itself a murder.

"Are you Samuel?" Gamache asked.

"Sam. *Oui*." The boy now looked suspicious.

Gamache again introduced himself. "May we sit down?"

Fiona indicated chairs.

"Not there!" Sam shouted. Beauvoir twisted away, a split second before his bottom hit the seat cushion.

While neither child said anything, it was clear that had been their mother's chair. It still had her outline in it. And that sheen where her unwashed head had rested.

"Do you mind?" Gamache nodded toward the television.

He'd had to raise his voice to be heard. This was difficult enough without having to shout the news of their mother's death, her murder, at the children.

"No!" snapped Sam when Fiona went to turn the TV off.

She stared at him, then relented, putting the remote down on a table. Sam snatched it up and held it tight to his chest. It reminded Beauvoir a little of the Chief Inspector's white-knuckle grip on the phone when talking to the captain.

He glanced out the window, hoping to see another vehicle draw up.

Someone who would stay with these children and absorb their grief and anger. So he didn't have to.

But all he saw was his own reflection in the window, and darkness outside. Where the hell were they?

Gamache waited to see if Sam would turn down the TV. But nothing happened. The game show continued, with its cheering and applause and cheerful music when a contestant got an answer right. It was macabre, but probably necessary.

The child might need, Gamache suspected, some sense of control over something, if only the television.

He let it go.

While her brother stared at the TV, Fiona continued to stare at the senior cop.

As Gamache began to speak, Sam slid a glance his way. Where there was fear in Fiona's face, there was something else in the boy's. It was unmistakable.

It was, Beauvoir could see, loathing. And why not, he thought as he watched the riveting child. He loathed himself and the Chief at that moment too.

"You're alone here?" Gamache asked, and when Fiona nodded, he went on, "Is there someone you can call? A friend of the family? One of your friend's mothers? A neighbor? Someone who can come over?"

She shook her head. "We're all right."

He held her eyes. "I'm afraid I have news of your mother."

As he spoke, the sound on the television increased. The cheering became manic, the applause an assault. The walls of the small room almost shook.

Beauvoir's ears began to buzz. He wondered if maybe they were bleeding.

"She was found a few hours ago," Gamache said, having to raise his voice, but trying, trying, to keep his tone steady. Gentle. Even as his ears also began to ring.

And still the sound increased. The game show host was shouting a question. There was a pause, while the contestant considered and the live audience fell silent. There was just the loud ticktock of the game show clock counting down.

Gamache took advantage of the near silence to say, "I'm so sorry to have to tell you that your mother is dead."

The contestant answered.

Please, please, thought Beauvoir. Let it be the wrong answer. But it was not.

The audience, the television, exploded with cheering and applause. Canned celebratory music filled the tiny living room.

It was grotesque. But worse was to come.

"I'm afraid there's more," the Chief Inspector was saying. He was leaning closer to Fiona, his focus complete. As though the noise weren't happening. While Sam stared straight ahead, at the leaping, joyous woman on the screen.

Dear God, thought Beauvoir, now glaring at Gamache. Do you have to tell them everything now?

Again, Gamache had to raise his voice, to shout this. He wished with all his heart he didn't have to tell them this next bit, but they'd hear it soon enough. Best, he knew, to get it over with.

"Your mother was murdered."

Are you a monster? thought Beauvoir, staring in disbelief at the Chief Inspector.

But the monster was yet to appear.

Gamache waited a moment, to let the children take in what he'd just said, though he was not certain that Sam had heard for the sound blaring out of the television.

Fiona's eyes had widened, her mouth opened. Not to speak but to breathe.

Gamache wanted to take her small hands in his, but did not. He said something else, but Beauvoir, just a couple feet away, would never know what. The words were drowned out by more applause, and the howl in Agent Beauvoir's head.

"I am so sorry," said Gamache, his voice steady, his gaze intense. "We'll find out who did it." He paused. "People can blame themselves when something like this happens. I want you to know"—he held her eyes—"there was nothing you could have done to prevent this."

He knew that loved ones often added guilt to the burden of grief. Making it even more crushing. Managing, against all evidence, to find things they could have, should have, done differently. That would have, could have, averted the tragedy. He wanted to spare these children that, if possible.

Fiona nodded, but he doubted she took it in.

The phone in his pocket vibrated. Probably Chernin, he thought, but didn't answer. He sat there, waiting. Giving Fiona space and time. Every now and then, he glanced over to the boy Sam, who sat stiff-backed, eyes forward. Staring at the contestant, now grabbing the host and dancing him around the stage.

These children would need help. Lots of it. But first, they'd need someone here, preferably someone they knew, who could comfort and look after them.

He looked out the window. Nothing. No one came. No one cared.

These children were well and truly alone in the world. His heart ached for them, and he wished there was something he could do to ease their pain.

What he could do was not make it worse. But he couldn't even do that. He had questions for them, things he needed to know about their mother. About her movements on her last day. But not just yet.

As Agent Beauvoir watched, Gamache got to his feet. Were they leaving? Beauvoir wondered. Could they leave now? Was it over?

The Chief said something to Fiona. Something about tea. Was that possible? Beauvoir thought he must have misheard.

Tea?

Gamache turned to him and . . . murmur. Murmur. Murmur. Not a word got past the howl in Beauvoir's head and the jubilation on the television. Then the Chief Inspector left the room.

Leaving him alone with two grieving children??? What the fuck??

Get out, his mind screamed. Leave. Take the car, drive to the detachment. Hand in your resignation. Go back to civilization and take a job disarming bombs, or trucking toxic material. Or as a tightrope walker in Cirque du Soleil.

Where I'll be safe. Where no one will look at me the way this girl is now.

The smell of lemon cleaner had become cloying. He could feel his gag reflex kicking in.

He needed to get away from the screaming contestants. Away from the look of despair on the girl's face, and the boy's rigid back. The bones of his spine visible through his thin shirt.

Away from the grief that was sucking up all the oxygen. Like a fire.

He looked outside. Still nothing, only some stranger staring back, wide-eyed, wild-eyed.

There would be no help.

CHAPTER 6

⌇

The kitchen was spotless. Or almost. There were some marks on
the otherwise gleaming stove top where the enamel had been
chipped away. There were burns on the counters and linoleum floor,
made from smoldering cigarettes and joints.

Gamache put on the kettle, then pulled out his phone and checked.
Yes, it had been Inspector Chernin.

Calling her back, he got the news that both search warrants had
come through.

"Good. There's no working vehicle here. Any sign of one by the
lake? Hidden in the forest?"

"We'll look, but no, nothing so far. She got to the lake somehow.
We'll go over the hikers' car."

Though both investigators knew few would be stupid enough to
report a murder and still be in possession of the victim's vehicle. Still,
some people were just that stupid.

"When you drop them off at the station, find out if Captain Dagenais
has arranged for a family friend to come be with the children. If not,
then send Agent Moel." She was trained in grief counseling and had
worked with children in the past. "In fact, send her anyway."

"*Oui, patron.*"

He hung up and slipped the phone back into his jacket pocket.

"I did it."

Armand turned at the sound of the voice. Fiona was standing in the doorway.

"*Pardon?*"

"Cleaned. Sam helped. We wanted it clean and tidy for when she came home."

Armand nodded. He understood, though it was actually the opposite of his reaction when at the age of nine his own parents had been killed by a drunk driver.

He'd grown hysterical whenever anyone tried to move anything. Change anything. Even cook. Or do the laundry. He refused to change out of the flannel pajamas his mother had put him in before she left. Before.

There was always, even now, a before and an after. As there would be for these children.

After days of this, Armand's grandmother had had to sit him down and explain that his mother and father were not in the objects. They were not in the dust that was accumulating. They were not even in the home.

It was more permanent, far stronger than that.

"They're here." Zora touched his head. "And here." She touched his heart. Then laid her thin hand over her own heart. "A house can change. Things can get lost or broken. But the love you keep inside you is safe, forever. They're safe, inside you."

He understood. But still, young Armand needed something more tangible. As long as everything stayed exactly as it was when they'd left for dinner that night, then maybe, maybe nothing else would change.

Maybe they'd come home. It was his job to keep it just the way it was. In case. But if something, anything, changed, then the spell would be broken. And it would be his fault.

It wasn't so much irrational as magical. And powerful. Only his trust in his grandmother allowed him to loosen his grip. But it took time.

Yes, he understood Clotilde's children and their need for some control over a situation fast spinning way out of control.

They'd had to do something to survive the long, interminable, cruel hours of waiting. To take their minds off, however briefly, what was becoming inescapable.

And so they'd scrubbed the place clean. For when their mother returned.

"I'm sorry," he said, holding her gaze. "If you want to talk about what's happened, I'm here. I'll give you my number." He took a card out of his jacket pocket. "I promise we'll find out who did this. But I'm afraid, Fiona, I'm going to need your help. We have questions that need answering."

She nodded in her solemn way.

He'd just turned back to warm up the teapot when he felt a hand on his hand. He leapt away and stared at her.

The touch had been soft, gentle. Intimate.

Armand broke the eye contact and looked toward the stage and the gathering graduates.

He was determined not to sully the day. A day, an event, he and Reine-Marie had worked toward for years. And that had, years earlier, seemed impossible.

As a sort of palate cleanser, Armand did what he always did. He looked at Reine-Marie. She too had seen him, though Sam Arsenault had less of an effect on her. In fact, she didn't really understand Armand's aversion to the pleasant young man.

She took his hand and squeezed.

Armand could not explain it to Reine-Marie or anyone else. He'd looked into the faces of some of the worst humans possible. Truly vile, truly terrifying people. But it was this boy, this young man, who had somehow found the cracks, and a way into Gamache's head. And messed around in there. Only one other person had managed to do that, and he was in prison for life.

Armand tried to remember when it had begun. When he'd first had an inkling.

* * *

"What're you doing?" he said, staring at Fiona.

"You've been so kind," she said, her voice soft. Inviting. "And you look so sad. I just wanted, just want, to comfort you."

It was grotesque. And clearly the expression on his face told Fiona she'd misjudged. But still, she came forward, even as Gamache backed up.

"Stop," he said. His voice held so much authority that she did. Staring at him, perplexed. She was not used to this reaction.

"You're safe now, Fiona," he said, keeping his distance and looking into her eyes. This girl had been raised, groomed, to replace feeling with touching. To confuse caring with caressing. And more.

"I'm not here for that. You don't need to do that anymore."

"Do what?" she asked, her schoolgirl persona now fully in place. Her head at a coquettish angle. Her voice innocent. And yet dripping with sexuality.

He tried not to show his revulsion.

He knew, of course, what this was about. Had suspected since he'd seen the studio photo in Clotilde's wallet. Of the teen made up to look like a little schoolgirl, and the boy with seductive eyes. The photo was in the space where Clotilde's money was kept.

These children were currency. Investments. As was the studio photo. Not a school picture, like most parents kept, like he and Reine-Marie had in their wallets. This was an advertisement.

He'd hoped, as he'd stood beside that lake, beside the corpse, that maybe he was wrong and his time among the worst of humanity had twisted his perceptions.

But he knew in his heart, a heart that ached now as he looked at the confused girl, that he was not wrong. What Fiona just did, an unmistakable, intentionally clumsy, practiced invitation, confirmed it. She was offering herself to him. As her mother had taught her.

Had Clotilde Arsenault walked through the door at that moment, Armand Gamache was far from sure he'd have been able to control himself.

But she was gone and had left behind a deeply damaged daughter. And a son no doubt equally, if not more, broken.

In the living room, Jean-Guy continued to stare at Sam's back.

The boy turned around once, but thankfully not to look at the uncomfortable Sûreté officer. Sam had glanced at his sister. It was fleeting. A look Jean-Guy could not decode. She got up and left. Following the Chief Inspector to the kitchen.

It was a relief.

Now he only had the boy to deal with, and Sam seemed completely absorbed in the game show. Though Jean-Guy was not quite so thick as to believe that.

Just as he was beginning to relax—to believe maybe he could handle this, at least until the Chief came back with the tea, tea? tea??—Sam moved.

Picking up the remote, he lowered the sound to a normal level. Then the boy's head dropped until his chin touched his chest and hair flopped over his eyes.

Beauvoir watched as Sam's thin shoulders rounded. Then lifted. And fell. Lifted. Fell.

"Sam?" said Jean-Guy, quietly.

The boy turned around and Jean-Guy saw a child. Not a chore.

Sam's face had crumbled. Tears were streaming down his cheeks. Had been, Jean-Guy could now see, for a while.

Sam looked at Jean-Guy. Jean-Guy looked at the boy.

Then he opened his arms and Sam rushed into them. Clinging to Beauvoir. Sobbing. His breath coming in heaves and shudders as Jean-Guy rubbed his back and whispered, "*Ça va bien aller.* It'll be all right. It'll be all right."

It wasn't.

Gamache returned to the living room with Fiona. He realized that while he needed to protect these children, he also needed to protect himself. The girl could easily accuse him of coming on to her. And worse. Even if easily disproved, the accusation alone would be enough.

He could not give her that opportunity. She was so clearly unbalanced. And who wouldn't be?

As he entered the room, he saw the boy in Beauvoir's arms and stopped dead. Could . . . ?

"Agent Beauvoir." But even as he spoke, he knew there was nothing sexual about this embrace, at least not on Beauvoir's part. It was clear he was just trying to comfort the sobbing child.

Beauvoir looked over, then released Sam, whispering again, "It'll be okay, buddy. Right?"

"*Oui*," sniffed the child.

As he pulled away, Sam looked at his sister, a questioning glance. Then at Gamache. And smiled. Just for an instant. But it was enough to freeze the head of homicide for the Sûreté in place.

Headlights appeared, and a few moments later Agent Hardye Moel came through the door.

Gamache took her aside. "We're going to need the provincial guardian. Someone needs to take charge of these children. We're trying to track down family, even close friends, but so far nothing."

"I'll put in a call," she said, and took out her phone.

"And Hardye, there're signs these children have been abused."

"Physically?"

"And sexually."

"Oh, for God's sake." She exhaled and shook her head.

"I need to question them."

She stared at him for just a moment, then nodded. "I'll be in in a minute."

And she was, saying quietly to Gamache, "Someone will be sent, but probably not until the morning. I can stay with them until then."

"*Merci*," he said.

Agent Moel introduced herself and took a seat beside Fiona, who moved a few inches away, while Sam remained stuck to Agent Beauvoir's side.

"Do you mind answering some questions now?" the Chief Inspector asked, looking from Sam to Fiona.

Sam shrugged and Fiona nodded.

He started off with some simple questions. How long had they lived there? What school did they go to? What grades were they in?

Questions with clear, definite answers. Ones without, he hoped, an emotional resonance.

Then he moved to the next level.

"Is your father part of your lives?"

The brief report on Clotilde did not list a husband or partner, or father to the children.

"No," said Fiona. "Mom never talked about him."

"And we never asked," said Sam. "We don't want to go live with him, if that's what you're getting at. You can't pawn us off on him."

"No, that wasn't what I was thinking."

In fact, the thought that had come to Armand in the kitchen was what the children's father would have done if he found out what Clotilde had done to the children.

Would he have lost his mind? Lost his head? Would he have found his hand closing around a brick? Had he lashed out, killing her?

But if that was the case, the father would have to be someone visiting from elsewhere, not a local man. Someone for whom this situation would be news. Someone the children might not have even met.

Gamache's mind went to the hikers. A man and woman. About the right ages.

"Did your mother have any visitors just before she disappeared?"

"No," said Fiona. "No one visited."

Gamache leaned forward. "That isn't true, is it? You can tell me. You need to tell me. We'll find out eventually."

"Just the usual," mumbled Fiona.

"Do you know their names?" He kept his voice neutral, matter-of-fact.

Fiona shook her head. "Just nicknames. Mr. Smells Like Shit. Mr. Fat-ass. Mr. Garbage Breath."

Gamache suspected there were other, less juvenile, names they called these men. He certainly had some himself.

Beauvoir listened to this, perplexed. It seemed the Chief Inspector knew something he did not. He looked over at Sam, whose expressive face had gone blank. Jean-Guy had never seen a face so devoid of thought or human emotion. It was like the boy had turned into a waxwork.

"Did your mother have a special friend?" Gamache asked.

"Is that supposed to be code?" Fiona demanded.

"Just a question. But an important one."

"No. No one special," said Sam, his voice as flat as his expression. "You'll never find out who did this, will you."

"Why do you say that?" Gamache asked.

"I just know. We know cops. They don't care."

"I do. Agent Beauvoir here does. Agent Moel does."

"Right." Sam turned away and stared at the blank television screen.

Gamache did too. "That's a nice television. Is it new?"

"We've had it for a while," said Fiona.

"When was the last time you saw your mother?" he asked, returning his attention to the girl.

"That morning, when we went to school. She was in bed."

He had to ask. "Alone?"

"Yes, alone."

He wasn't convinced. But there was time to get at that truth. The autopsy and DNA samples would help.

"Did she take the car when she left?" he asked.

"Well, it's not there, is it?" said Sam. "What do you think?"

Just then Inspector Chernin arrived with the warrant.

"We're going to have to search your home," Gamache told the children. "We'll be as quick as we can and return everything to the way it was."

Agent Moel said to Fiona, "Is that all right?"

Beauvoir wondered what would happen if Fiona said no. But she didn't. She just nodded.

Agent Moel looked at Gamache. "We'll be fine. I'll make more tea."

Again with the tea, thought Beauvoir. Was there something about that drink he'd missed? Unless it was brewed from marijuana, he doubted it would do what Agent Moel hoped.

Inspector Chernin coordinated the search, assigning Beauvoir to join the officers outside and leaving Agent Moel with the kids.

Gamache pulled Chernin and Pierre Gendron, the IT specialist, aside, and told them what Clotilde had been doing.

"Oh, shit," said Chernin, and shook her head. "What mother, what monster, does that?"

There was no answer to that question, so they focused on the ones they could answer. "I'll check her computer and phone," said Gendron. He headed off to find them.

"The hikers now admit they're members of the environmental group Assez," said Chernin. "They came to investigate the old-growth forest. Apparently logging rights at the lake have been sold and a protest is planned. They're the advance team."

"Why not tell us that to begin with?"

"Well, they're more than a little paranoid, given that their group isn't often welcomed with open arms by the locals. What they're planning is probably illegal. There were reports in the local paper that they'd be in the area, though they say they just arrived this morning."

"You believe them?"

"Reserving judgment, *patron*. But that's their story. By the way, their vehicle is clean, and yes, it belongs to the man."

Gamache found it interesting that it was known around town that someone from the radical environmental group would be at the lake.

Jean-Guy Beauvoir was still in the living room. He found he was reluctant now to leave the boy, who clung to his hand.

"It'll be okay, Sam." He knelt at eye level and held the boy's bony shoulders. "Do you trust me?"

Sam held his eyes. Held. Held. Then nodded and whispered through hiccups and caught breath, *"Oui."*

"Bon," said Jean-Guy. He found a Kleenex and wiped Sam's face, then got him to blow his nose, as though he were four years old and not ten. "When I get back, we'll talk. Okay?"

He looked down at the slimy tissue, then at Sam, and made an exaggerated grimace.

Sam gave a grunt of laughter.

It took less time than Chief Inspector Gamache expected.

The old desktop computer was on a crate in Clotilde's bedroom, her passwords "hidden" in one of her dresser drawers in a jumble of underwear.

The keyboard yielded no prints. Any that had been there were wiped.

Gamache stood behind his agent. It took slightly over a minute to find what Gamache had known, from the moment he'd looked at the photograph in Clotilde's wallet, would be there.

But still, it was a shock. Was always a shock when he and his agents came face-to-face with how truly abhorrent some people were.

He tasted bile and felt a burning in the stomach, and wanted to turn away. Seeing the images felt itself like a violation.

Gendron went from file to saved file. Clicking. Resting just long enough to know what was happening on the videos. Then moving on to the next, and the next. And . . .

Gamache's jaw tightened, and he took a ragged breath. He leaned forward and hit pause. He couldn't take any more.

"That's enough. Get a copy of everything. And I want names. I want to know who these . . ." He gestured to the screen, trying to find the word. But no appropriate one existed. ". . . are."

Gamache forced himself to stare at the picture frozen on the screen. Then he looked toward the living room. His heart pounded. He was overcome with the need to act. To do something, to burn off this surge of rage. He felt, for a moment, unable to breathe. As though he'd fallen into a cesspool and was drowning.

Who did this to children? To their own children?

He forced himself to stay calm. He needed to keep his eye on the long view. If he was going to help Fiona and Sam, he had to shove his own feelings, his revulsion, down. When he'd made sure the children were safe and would get the help they needed, then he'd go after each and every one of these . . . these . . . creatures.

He was about to leave when he turned to the unfortunate Agent Gendron. "Someone was here after Clotilde disappeared and before we arrived. Otherwise, we'd have found her prints on the keys. If that person wasn't here to erase that"—he gestured toward the image on the screen—"then why?"

"I'll find out," said Gendron.

"*Merci.*" He held the agent's eyes for a moment. "I'm sorry, Pierre."

He'd have to get this man counseling. And time off, after this. Of all the caves they had to enter, this one was the darkest.

He turned to another agent in the room. "Find out, please, where in the house those videos were shot."

"*Oui, patron.*"

"Still no sign of her car?" he asked Chernin when he found her.

"We're looking. If it was used to move her body, then the killer must've ditched it."

"And walked back?" said Gamache, more to himself than anyone there. This crime had all the markings of a two-person job.

"The videos could've been shot somewhere else," said Chernin.

"Maybe, but I doubt it. These things are kept close to home. Is there a basement?"

"Not that we've found. The garage is too full of junk. They weren't shot there."

Gamache needed some fresh air, needed to try to clear his mind and slow his heart before going back into the living room to face those children. Knowing what had happened to them was one thing, seeing it was something else.

The air outside was bracing. He took several deep breaths and pulled his coat tighter around him. Flashlights were bobbing as officers searched the backyard. Calling one of the lights over, he saw it was Agent Beauvoir.

"What've you found?"

"No bricks."

"Anything else?"

Beauvoir raised his brows. He'd only been looking for the murder weapon. He thought that was the purpose.

"Well"—he searched his mind—"there's a lot of junk. Old tires. Boxes. Plastic containers. It's basically a garbage dump. They just tossed the shit out the back door."

"Show me, please."

Gamache accompanied Beauvoir around the overgrown yard. It was indeed clogged with garbage. Including something interesting. Putting on gloves, Gamache yanked an unwieldy shipping box from the pile.

It was what the television had come in. Replacing it, he called over a senior agent and had a word with him before walking back to the house.

But his footsteps slowed as he approached the back door. Reluctant, he admitted, to return inside. He stood in the cold and dark and stared at the small house. It looked so plain. So much like all the other houses on the street, on so many Québec streets. Modest homes with decent men and women inside. And some who were not so decent.

How to tell them apart? It was impossible, from the outside. You had to go in, and even then, you had to look closely. And even then . . .

There is always another story, there is more than meets the eye.

That was part of the horror, and the price, of his job. Paying close attention as warped minds tried to pass as normal.

Wondering, always wondering, what was really happening on all the quiet streets. In all those homes. In all those heads. And whether, despite looking and listening closely, he was still missing something.

Through a lit window he saw his IT specialist hunched over the computer keyboard.

Then his eyes dropped to the base of the house. Turning on his flashlight, he let it play over the cinder block foundation. Then he began to walk around the building, following his light.

He hadn't gone far before he saw it. What so many of these older rural homes had. On so many roads just like this.

A root cellar. Accessed from the outside.

Calling several agents over, one of whom turned out to be Beauvoir, he instructed the Scene of Crime officer to video what was happening, and the forensics agent to swab the handle and check for prints. Then he nodded to Agent Beauvoir, who stepped forward and gave the door a mighty yank.

It opened so easily, he stumbled backward into the Chief, who held him upright in a grip far stronger than Beauvoir expected.

They stared at the opening. A black hole. This door had been opened often. And recently.

Gamache went in first. There was silence behind him as the agents followed. Alert. Watchful. Tense.

No one liked going into a dark, enclosed space, least of all cops.

Gamache instinctively held his flashlight away from him as he played it around the walls. If there was a gunman hiding there, he'd aim for the light. Best not to have it in front of his chest or face.

He saw cinder block walls, a dirt floor. The ceiling was beamed. At slightly taller than six feet, Gamache could just stand upright.

The cellar was colder than the outside. It smelled of dirt and decay. Something played against his face and he batted it away before realizing it was a string. Pulling it, a single bulb came on, revealing a cot shoved against the far wall.

There was nothing else in the open space.

No root vegetables were stored there for the winter. No mason jars of preserves. No wood stacked up for the woodstove. This was a space used for only one thing.

The lightbulb swung lazily, playing off their faces.

Beauvoir stood in the low, dark room and could feel the walls closing in. He'd never been fond of enclosed spaces, but now he could feel panic welling up. Unaware of what had been found on the computer, he still knew this was not a place he wanted to linger in.

But he also realized he would have to. He took a step forward, but Gamache stopped him and gestured to the dirt floor. When Beauvoir still didn't see it, Gamache knelt and pointed his flashlight.

There were three small holes. The indents made by a tripod, which would have been pointed toward the cot.

"You know what you have to do," he said to the officers, then turned to Beauvoir. "Come with me."

While relieved to be leaving, Beauvoir was also miffed. The Chief Inspector didn't seem to trust him to collect evidence.

And he was right.

Once back in the house, Gamache approached the head of his forensics team and instructed him to go into the root cellar. "Have the mattress wrapped and taken to the evidence locker at the detachment. Make sure it's locked inside along with everything else, and keep all copies of the key."

"Yessir," he said. "All copies? What about the station commander?"

"All copies."

Then he told Chernin what they'd found.

"I'll look for the camera," she said.

As Gamache and Beauvoir approached the living room, they could hear that the television was once again on but at a normal volume.

Agent Moel got to her feet, but Gamache waved her down. Then he looked at the children, who'd turned to him. Seeing his expression, they dropped their eyes.

They knew he knew.

Gamache sat on the footstool opposite Fiona and said to Sam, "Please, join us."

The boy looked at Jean-Guy, who nodded. Then Sam went over and sat beside his sister on the sofa.

Fiona was trembling slightly. Agent Moel saw this and, knowing what was coming, she shot a glance at the Chief Inspector.

Is this necessary? she was clearly asking.

Apparently it was.

"I need to ask you some questions."

Agent Moel took Fiona's hand. It was cold to the touch. The children seemed shell-shocked as their world exploded around them, spewing their guts, their secrets, everywhere. For all these strangers to see.

"Did anyone come to the house after your mother disappeared?" Gamache asked.

It was obviously not the question they'd been expecting. They looked at each other, then shook their heads.

"Are you sure?" he pressed, gently.

"Yes," said Fiona. "We're sure."

He waited. The show on the TV was now some crime drama. Cars were zooming through city streets. Shots were being fired.

And still, he waited.

"You can tell me," he finally said, his voice barely above a whisper. "You're safe now."

He heard Sam snort.

He did not lean closer, as he would have with an adult, as he would have with any other children. Instead, he let them have their space.

"We opened your mother's computer. And we found the basement. I know. Everything."

But he was wrong. He didn't yet know everything.

"No one came," mumbled Fiona, staring at the patch of carpet between her running shoes.

Beauvoir, watching this, was just beginning to suspect what that tripod, what that soiled mattress and cot in the root cellar were for. But his mind stopped at the entrance to that dark place. Unwilling to enter.

"*Patron? Désolé.*"

Agent Gendron was standing at the door to the living room.

"*Excusez-moi.*"

Gamache got up and took the IT agent aside. "What is it, Pierre?"

"Someone tried to wipe files from the hard drive. They got most of it, but some images, while corrupted, remained. Only a few frames. Here's a screen grab."

Armand Gamache stared at the photograph and knew he had now seen the worst.

But still he was wrong.

He was right, though, in one respect. He knew it was no longer possible to separate his feelings from his thoughts.

Seeing the look on the Chief's face, Agent Gendron asked, "Do you know this man, *patron*?"

Gamache didn't answer. His hand hung loose at his side, the photo still in it, as he searched the horizon. Putting pieces together.

The children's lying. The brick. The computer images. The big box behind the house. The hikers. The fact no one had been found to look after Clotilde's children.

This photograph.

"Get everything you can off that hard drive. I want it all emailed back to Sûreté headquarters and copied to my address. Then secure the computer."

"I'll send it to the evidence room."

"No. Keep everything here for now. Prepare to fly back to Montréal with it."

"*D'accord, patron.*" The order contradicted what they'd been told earlier. Before the screen grab.

"*Bon. Alors*, there must be records too. Either on the hard drive or a notebook. Names, addresses. Accounts. Dates and times. Look for it. Take this place apart if you have to."

Though Gamache suspected they wouldn't find it. It would be the first thing destroyed by the killer. He adjusted that. The second thing destroyed. The video was the first.

"Someone tried to erase or destroy at least one, maybe more, of the videos, but others he left untouched," said Gamache.

"Looks like he only tried to erase his own."

"Yes. I want to know if he tried to destroy any others."

"Yessir." Gendron left.

Folding up the picture, Gamache placed it in his jacket pocket. He thought for a moment, then had a word with the head of forensics, who looked at him, astonished, but nodded assent.

As he headed back down the hall toward the living room, Gamache saw Fiona staring at her feet. But her brother was staring at him.

It was a look the Chief Inspector had seen before. Rarely, but it was unmistakable. It was the look of someone who'd done something spectacularly wrong and would keep doing it until stopped.

It was the look of someone who knew they would not be stopped.

It was the look of someone unhinged.

CHAPTER 7

﹏

"Fiona Arsenault."

The name was read out, and a woman, older than most of the other graduates, walked across the stage to accept her degree.

Armand and Reine-Marie beamed and clapped, while Jean-Guy recorded the moment. The video showed a tall, slender young woman with long, loose blond hair walking with poise across the stage.

She looked like every other student graduating that day from the École Polytechnique. But anyone watching closely might notice a difference, and quite a significant one.

Behind Fiona on the stage, it was possible to see Nathalie Provost clapping, albeit barely, but none of the faculty were. They just sat there. Watching.

That could be put down to the fact that Fiona Arsenault had not actually attended classes at the École Polytechnique and was only allowed to accept her engineering degree that day because Armand Gamache had interceded on her behalf.

He'd asked the board of governors, the Chancellor, the President, and, most important, the survivors and families of the victims of the shootings years before Fiona had been born for their approval.

It was given. Though reluctantly. And the École had only approved because the families and survivors had.

Fiona Arsenault put out her hand to shake the Chancellor's, as the grads had been instructed. There was a moment, a pause. He took it, briefly, and gave her the scroll. Then moved the tassel on her hat from one side to the other. The signal that she was now a graduate.

Finally, he gave her the little box. She stared down at it, then thanked him. Inside the box was a symbol that would tell anyone familiar with the code that she was an engineer.

Before leaving the stage, Fiona looked out at the audience. Scanning. Her eyes stopped at the Gamaches. She smiled. But then moved on. And found who she was really looking for.

Her brother, Sam.

Reine-Marie squeezed Armand's hand but said nothing.

The ceremony continued, ending with Nathalie Provost approaching the podium.

The audience, as one, rose to their feet. The applause was sustained and heartfelt. When it died down, she spoke. About that terrible day, a little. But mostly about the consequences. The fight, ongoing, against misogyny. Against all hate crimes. The fight, ongoing, for gun control.

But mostly Nathalie Provost talked about hope. About perseverance. About change.

About courage. About the future.

Then, picking up the bouquet of white roses, she named the young women murdered that day in 1989. There were sobs scattered around the auditorium. As though sinkholes had opened.

And then, Nathalie Provost announced another name. A woman she described as the future. A reason for hope, for optimism. The woman engineering student who had been awarded that year's Order of the White Rose scholarship, for graduate work.

This's it, this's it, this's it. Shit.

Standing in the wings, Harriet felt her hands grow numb, her legs become weak. She felt herself leave her body and thought she might pass out. Waves of panic washed over her. Blinding her. She looked behind her, into the darkness, for the exit.

Run! Run! Get out.

She gasped for breath. Her heart pounded, her face flushed.

And then she heard her name. Heard the applause. She wanted to scream, to scream. To run. Run!

Now Madame Provost was looking offstage, at her.

Harriet took a deep breath. Then another.

Reine-Marie looked at Myrna. Her face was alert, staring at the side of the stage. Others were beginning to as well. There was a slight murmur.

Myrna started to rise, then sat back down.

Harriet closed her eyes, took a deep breath, and stepped off the cliff and onto the stage.

There was ringing in her ears that was probably applause but sounded like an assault. The lights were blinding. She focused on Madame Provost, who stared, then walked toward her.

Nathalie put her arm protectively around Harriet's waist and whispered, "*Ça va bien aller.*"

Myrna was crying. Great tears of joy.

Not because of the scholarship, but because Harriet was walking across the stage. She'd made it this far. She'd made it so far.

Myrna knew how close Harriet had come to turning down the scholarship. Because she could not face this moment.

But here she was, facing it.

Myrna rose to her feet, followed closely by Armand and Reine-Marie, Jean-Guy. Clara and Olivier and Gabri. And then the rest of the auditorium.

Ruth Zardo was not there. She'd stayed behind saying someone had to look after the village. They expected to return to cinders. Still, worth it.

Myrna wiped her sleeve across her eyes so she could better see the girl she'd helped raise. Who'd stayed with her for weeks every summer.

When Harriet had first visited, it was all Myrna could do to get her out the door. And now, here she was.

Harriet accepted the bouquet, and turned to face the standing ovation, and knew she was a fraud. The scholarship was created in honor of the young women who'd dared and who'd died. She was as far from them as it was possible to be. Barely the same species.

She thanked Madame Provost, then turned and walked stiffly off the stage, not saying another word.

Harriet Landers knew if she was the future, they were all fucked.

"She's coming back with us," said Clara, at the reception after. "Right? The party's all organized."

"For a few days, yes," said Myrna. She was holding hands with Billy Williams, who'd taken the day off from spreading compost to be there.

"Does she get to keep the robes?" asked Gabri. "Do you think she'd let me buy them off her?"

"Why in the world would you—" began his partner, Olivier, then stopped. Not wanting to know the answer.

Armand and Reine-Marie were across the room, talking with the Chancellor. Then, seeing Fiona Arsenault standing alone, they excused themselves and walked over to her.

Jean-Guy had left a few minutes earlier, but not before reassuring Armand that Sam Arsenault had left the building as soon as the ceremony was over.

"I saw him off. I suspect he wants to meet you even less than you want to meet him."

Armand knew that was not true but left it at that.

"*Merci*," he said. "Did you speak with him?"

"Briefly. He won't be back."

Gamache nodded. He didn't want, or need, to know more. The fact was, he'd kept tabs on the young man and was far more aware of his movements, his life, than Jean-Guy. He'd expected Sam to be there that day, and he was.

What Armand had not expected was to feel that frisson, that sharp spike of anxiety, when their eyes had met. Now he turned his mind from that young man to his sister.

Reine-Marie hugged Fiona, while Armand stood back and watched. Smiling.

He'd never have thought, never have guessed, on that cold November day so many years ago, in that horror of a house, that this could ever happen. Once again, he reflected on the folly of assumptions.

"*Merci*, Monsieur Gamache," said Fiona, looking down at the scroll and small box in her hands. "I know this was because of you." She turned to Reine-Marie. "You both."

"You put in the work," said Armand, looking her straight in the eye. "I'm proud of you."

And he was. Not many could turn their lives around. After what happened.

"You're coming down to Three Pines with us, right?" said Reine-Marie. "We have your room all ready."

"Can't wait." Fiona looked at the small box, then held it out to Armand. "Would you?"

His smile widened, and without a word he opened the box and brought out the thin iron ring. It was simple, unadorned except for the marks where it had been pounded into shape. Not a ring anyone would choose at a jeweler's. But it could not be bought, it had to be earned.

He slipped it onto the little finger of Fiona's right hand. She looked down at it, shaking her head slightly. "I'd never have dreamed—"

"*Bonjour.*"

Armand stiffened and his smile froze.

"Sam!" Fiona brushed between the Gamaches to embrace her brother. "Thank you for coming."

"Are you kidding? Miss this? Never. I'm so proud of you. First person in our family to go to university, never mind graduate. You definitely got the brains."

"While you got the rugged good looks," she said with a laugh.

It was a running joke between the siblings. Though, as Reine-Marie watched, she recognized it was true. She'd met this young man only once before and had liked him. She suspected most people would.

Except her husband. It went beyond not liking, into a territory she'd rarely seen with Armand. She'd asked him once about it, about Sam Arsenault, but he'd just frowned and shrugged and said he couldn't explain it.

She thought he meant that he wouldn't explain it.

Still, she didn't press. It didn't matter. The young man had no place in their lives. Unlike his sister.

Sam embraced Fiona again, holding her tight. "I've missed you. Missed this." Then he turned to the other two. "Madame Gamache. Chief Inspector."

"Sam."

There was no question of a handshake.

Armand held the young man's eyes. While he'd kept tabs on Sam Arsenault, he hadn't actually seen him in years. The boy had grown into a man. He was tall. Almost as tall as Armand. He'd filled out, grown fit.

But his eyes had not changed. They were remarkable. Clear, bright, a bluey green. They sparked with intelligence and warmth and good humor.

But, Armand knew, if he held them long enough, really looked, he'd eventually see it. The flecks on the irises. The dark spots where the real Samuel Arsenault hid.

But what Armand would always recognize was intangible, invisible. If he were blindfolded and Sam Arsenault walked into the room, Armand would know it.

"*Excusez-moi*," he said, breaking eye contact.

He and Reine-Marie began to walk away when Sam called after them. "I'll see you there."

Armand stopped, paused, then turned. "Where?"

"Didn't Fiona tell you? I'm coming down to Three Pines too. I've made a reservation at the B&B." He smiled at Gamache. "It's gonna be fun."

"You all right?" Nathalie Provost asked a few minutes later. "You look tense."

Armand's smile was tight. "I was coming over to ask how you were feeling," he said, deflecting the question. "It was a beautiful ceremony. But emotional, I know."

"*Oui*. Always is. In a good way too."

"Thank you for what you did for Fiona. I know it added an extra stress."

Nathalie didn't answer. Her eyes were locked on the young man standing with Fiona Arsenault. She wasn't the only one watching him. Almost all the female grads, and their sisters, and their mothers, and more than a few of the men had at least glanced over. Some were openly staring.

"Who's that?" Nathalie asked.

"Her brother," said Reine-Marie. "Sam."

Nathalie nodded, examining him. "Attractive."

Though she looked anything but attracted. Her brows were drawn together. And she'd taken half a step back.

She feels it too, thought Armand. He wondered if those who'd experienced death recognized the boatman.

"Auntie Myrna, who's that?"

Harriet was standing with her back against the wall, beside the bright red *Sortie* sign and the door. As close to out as in could be. She was openly staring at the most beautiful young man she'd ever seen. His gleaming brown hair, auburn really with its natural highlights, was slightly longer than fashionable, though however he chose to wear it would be de facto fashionable.

His clothing was casual, though appropriate to the occasion, and fit him well.

But a green garbage bag would have looked good on him. Though Harriet thought it was a shame to cover up that body at all. She spent a moment imagining . . .

She'd noticed that the young man had looked over at her aunt and nodded. He clearly knew her. So she must know him.

"His name's Sam Arsenault," said Myrna.

Harriet grabbed her hand and started forward. "Come on, introduce me."

But Auntie Myrna didn't move, and after a few tugs Harriet realized it was futile.

"Why not?"

"We don't have time. We need to get back to the village before Ruth sacks the place. She's already stolen half a dozen books from the store this week."

It was clear this was an excuse. That her aunt, for whatever reason, didn't want to approach the man.

Harriet would have argued, but she was sidetracked by the mention of the elderly poet. It conjured up so many images, so many feelings.

So many summer evenings sitting on the dilapidated front porch of the ramshackle house, Ruth in her rocker, her cane across her lap. In another era it would have been a shotgun, thought Harriet. And she'd have had a corncob pipe.

Rosa, the mad duck, would hop up and settle on Harriet's lap. Exhausted after a day of terrorizing the villagers.

"Fuck, fuck, fuck," one of them muttered, though it wasn't always clear which one.

Harriet loved listening to the old poet and the duck while sipping lemonade and watching life in Three Pines come to a rest. Across the village green, she'd see light through the mullioned windows of the bistro. And above the bookshop, another light in the loft where her aunt lived.

On those summer evenings, Ruth often talked about the history of the village. Some of what she said was documented, though much had been passed down verbally. Some of the stories had the mist of myth about them.

There'd been people living there long before the huge pine trees were planted. Before Champlain "discovered" the territory.

"What he discovered," said Ruth, "was that there were people already here. Of course, the Abenaki and Iroquois should have slaughtered them. An opportunity missed."

Harriet had laughed, then noticed that Ruth was not actually joking.

Mostly, though, Ruth listened as Harriet talked about her dreams, her perceptions. Her demons.

"A poem begins," Ruth had said one evening, as they watched Monsieur and Madame Gamache walk hand in hand, while their young dog Henri played on the village green, "as a lump in the throat."

Harriet understood. She woke every day with a lump in her throat. Sometimes it felt more like a bone.

Except when she was there, in the peaceful little village.

"Okay," she said now to her Auntie Myrna. "Let's go." They started for the door, but Harriet hesitated and looked back. "I need to thank Madame Provost."

She paused, clearly hoping Auntie Myrna would tell her it wasn't necessary.

"I'll wait," said Myrna and watched her niece, still clutching the bouquet of roses, go around the room, talking to strangers, despite the bone caught in her throat.

But Myrna's eyes kept being dragged back to the handsome young man. And every time they did, he was staring at her.

"Are you all right?" Billy asked, putting his hand in hers.

Myrna smiled. She could never express why, but when she looked at this grizzled man, in his ill-fitting suit and unshavable face and untamable hair, who was about as far from an intellectual as possible, she felt safe and content and at peace.

She was happy before meeting him. But she was happier now. "I am."

But that didn't last long. Armand and Reine-Marie joined them moments later.

"He's coming down to Three Pines," Armand whispered.

He didn't have to say who.

"Hardye?"

"*Oui, patron.*"

Agent Moel joined the Chief Inspector in the hallway.

"I'm going to the local detachment. Inspector Chernin's coming with me. You're in charge." He glanced toward the Arsenault children in the living room. "How are they?"

She considered. "Numb. Disconnected. I'm hoping to stop them from completely disassociating. It's a balance. I think right now they need to know they're safe. Can you imagine? The abuse is traumatic enough, but to be pimped out by your own mother? And now to be told she's dead?"

Armand shook his head. Every day he faced the unimaginable. But this was worse than most. "At least they have each other."

"*Oui.*"

He looked at Agent Moel. "What is it?"

"There's a strong, almost unnatural bond between them."

"Unnatural?"

"Not, I think, in that way. It's a sort of fusion. I've seen it before in deeply traumatized children. They lose themselves in someone else. Hiding there until they can heal."

"Is it mutual?" Gamache asked and saw her smile.

"Now that's an interesting question. Why do you ask?"

"It just seems . . ."

She nodded. "The boy."

"Yes."

"If what you think happened to them actually did—"

"It did. There's video," said Gamache.

"Christ," she muttered. "Then, being the youngest, he'd be the most damaged. His personality sealed up tight. And we both know what happens to things left too long in the dark. And yet . . ." She considered them again. "He's the one who cried. The girl still hasn't."

They both knew that was a bad sign. A warning sign.

CHAPTER 8

~

Chief Inspector Gamache slapped the photograph onto the desk. His hand hit with such force the sound reverberated beyond the four walls and out into the bullpen at the Sûreté detachment.

"Captain?" One of the agents peered into the office.

Linda Chernin used her boot to slam the door shut. The agents working in the outer room could still see through the window into the station commander's office, but they couldn't hear. Unless voices were raised, and it seemed likely they would be.

Captain Dagenais looked down at the screen grab, his face growing pale.

"Give me your gun." Gamache held out his hand. "You're under arrest."

Dagenais looked up into the Chief Inspector's eyes. Then he looked behind Gamache to the two officers standing on either side and slightly behind him.

Gamache's second-in-command, a woman, had her hand on her gun, though it was still in its holster at her hip. The other, that fucker Beauvoir, also had his jacket open, ready if need be.

And he could see by the look on Beauvoir's face that he hoped need would be.

Dagenais's mind worked fast. He looked through the window at his agents, now all on their feet. Staring in. Alert. Ready. He'd long regretted that window and the lack of privacy. Now it just might save his ass.

Dagenais did a quick calculation. Six of them. Heavily armed. Seven if he counted himself. Three of Gamache's people, including the unarmed Chief Inspector.

"On what charge?"

"Give me your weapon," demanded Gamache.

Dagenais hesitated, then pulled it out of its holster. Chernin moved, but Gamache signaled her to stand fast.

Gamache hadn't told Beauvoir what this was about. He'd been silent on the drive over to the station, though he had exchanged a few words with Chernin. Orders.

Now Beauvoir saw why they were so silent. So strained.

The picture on the captain's desk showed the station commander clearly naked. Clearly nearing the climax of a sexual act. An act performed in that dim, filthy root cellar. Performed on . . .

Jean-Guy felt like retching.

How could anyone . . . ?

His eyes traveled from the photograph to Dagenais's gun. Still in Dagenais's hand. Not actually pointed at Gamache, but close.

Beauvoir could feel his own, cold to the touch, under his hand but still in its holster.

Why wouldn't Gamache let them draw them out? Because, Beauvoir suddenly realized, Gamache didn't know the captain like he did. The man was a tyrant, running the isolated detachment as though it were his own personal army. He commanded, demanded, absolute loyalty. Which Beauvoir refused to give.

Which was why he'd been isolated in the basement, as though he were the contagion. Not because he was a rotten Sûreté officer, but because he was a good one.

Though he didn't turn to look, Jean-Guy could feel the presence of the other agents in the outer room. Waiting for a signal from Dagenais.

Beauvoir knew their loyalties. Gamache did not.

This was not, Agent Beauvoir knew, going to end well.

"Put it down," Gamache demanded, and Dagenais slowly placed the Glock on the desk.

Gamache picked it up, but instead of holding it on the captain, or even putting it in his own belt, he took out the magazine and replaced the gun on the desk.

"There's another one," said Beauvoir. "In the right-hand drawer."

Dagenais shot him a look of such loathing, had it been a gun Beauvoir would've been dead.

"Stand up, step away from the desk," said Gamache.

When Dagenais did, the Chief Inspector opened the drawer, not even locked, and found it. A Sig Sauer. Illegal, thanks to Nathalie Provost and the others. This one no doubt confiscated in a drug bust.

Once again, Gamache removed the bullets and replaced the gun.

"Hands where I can see them." Gamache walked up to Dagenais, and for a moment both Chernin and Beauvoir thought the Chief Inspector was about to beat the crap out of him. Neither would have raised a hand to stop it.

Instead, Gamache patted him down, though the act of touching the man clearly disgusted him. Then he stepped back.

"Alexandre Dagenais, you're under arrest for sexual assaults on at least one minor. For—"

"You might want to look behind you, Monsieur Gamache." Dagenais's voice was filled with amusement.

Beauvoir's heart sank. He knew what he'd see. Still, he'd dared hope . . .

He turned. Chernin turned. But Gamache did not. He continued to stare at Dagenais. Slowly, the smile was wiped off the captain's face.

"You're under arrest," Gamache repeated and brought out his handcuffs. "Turn around."

When Dagenais did not, Gamache grabbed him and in one practiced move spun him around, shoving his face into the wall and yanking Dagenais's hands behind him. As he did, Gamache snarled something into his ear.

Once Dagenais was cuffed, Gamache pushed him back into the

chair. Only then, after running his steady hand through his disheveled hair, did Chief Inspector Gamache turn and look through the large window into the outer office.

He saw exactly what he expected to see. Six Sûreté agents with guns drawn. In the attack posture.

"What the fuck?" whispered Chernin.

She turned her gun on Beauvoir, expecting, since he was also a member of this detachment, to see his weapon aimed at her. And Agent Beauvoir understood then why he hadn't been warned about any of this. Gamache did not know whose side he was on.

He did have his gun out, but it was pointed at the window and his colleagues. His now former colleagues. His loyalties, perhaps at terrible cost to himself, were clear and declared.

Beauvoir, trying not to tremble, darted his eyes to the Chief.

What do we do? What do we do???

He expected to see him now armed with Dagenais's Glock, pointing it at the agents in the outer office. But he was not.

The Chief Inspector was standing still and just staring.

We're fucked, thought Beauvoir. We're dead. The man's paralyzed. Oh shit, oh shit, oh—

Gamache stepped forward. Far from being paralyzed, his mind was working quickly. Assessing, looking at options.

Coming to a conclusion.

"Do not lower your weapons, no matter what happens," he said quietly to Chernin and Beauvoir, so Dagenais didn't hear.

"*Patron?*" she said, not taking her eyes off the agents in the outer office.

"Trust me."

"*Oui.*" She adjusted her stance, bracing for what seemed inevitable, at least to her, if not to the Chief.

Gamache turned to Agent Beauvoir and smiled. "Your first day on the job, and this happens."

For a moment Beauvoir was confused. He'd been working as a Sûreté officer in this detachment for months. But then he understood.

This detachment was not the Sûreté. His time with the Sûreté had started the moment he followed Chief Inspector Gamache out of the basement.

That was the start, and this was the finish. All in one day. Young Jean-Guy Beauvoir had little doubt what was about to happen.

"If there was ever a time to follow orders, this is it, Agent Beauvoir. Do you understand?"

Beauvoir nodded.

"Do you understand?" Gamache repeated, his voice firm, the authority complete.

"Yessir."

"Good." Again dropping his voice, he whispered to both, "Do not fire, no matter what happens, unless they shoot first. And then, give 'em everything you've got."

"And you?" Beauvoir asked.

"I think by then you'll be on your own. With my profound apologies. However . . ." Gamache looked behind him. ". . . there is something that might help."

He walked over to Dagenais and cuffed him to his chair. Then he wheeled the captain in front of Chernin and Beauvoir. In the direct line of fire.

"Oh, fuck," muttered Dagenais.

"That's better." Gamache smiled, though his eyes held no amusement.

"Wait." For the first time, there was desperation in Dagenais's voice. "I know who killed Clotilde. Let me go and I'll tell you, then I'll disappear. Everyone wins. Everyone lives."

Do it, thought Beauvoir. He could, at last, see some daylight between himself and catastrophe.

"I know who killed Clotilde," said Gamache, staring at Dagenais.

"You think it was me? If it was, I'd have made sure she was never found."

"You went to the house after she disappeared," said Gamache. "That's why you didn't send anyone to look after the children. You needed time alone, to do what you had to do. You threatened them, if they told. And you gave the kids a huge new television. Textbook abuser. Threaten, then reward. They claimed no one visited, but that was clearly a lie. Someone did. There were no fingerprints on her keyboard, files were destroyed, and though the kids said the TV was old, we found the packaging in the backyard. It arrived after Clotilde disappeared."

Beauvoir kept his eyes forward, trained on the agents. He knew Gamache had just lied. Yes, they'd found the packaging, but there was nothing on it to show when it had been delivered.

"You erased what you could of the hard drive, though not"— Gamache looked at the photo of the naked man—"quite well enough. And you found her record book. Did you destroy it?"

He stared at Dagenais, considering.

"No. You were selective in the videos you erased. Or copied? That's what you did, didn't you? You copied those incriminating videos Clotilde had made and kept her written records to blackmail the others."

"You're guessing."

"True," admitted Gamache. "But we'll find the evidence."

"You'd have to leave to do that, and there's no way you're getting out of here."

"We'll see," said Gamache.

He stepped away from Dagenais, nodded to Inspector Chernin, then said quietly to Beauvoir, "You're doing well."

Jean-Guy Beauvoir felt himself steady. He nodded to the Chief, then watched in amazement. Surely he wasn't . . .

But Gamache did.

He opened the door and stepped out. With a clatter, Dagenais's agents turned to him. Weapons pointed. Poised to fire.

While his face was composed, Gamache's heart pounded. This was, his desperate mind had told him, the only hope they had. But still, but still . . .

He opened his arms wide to show that he wasn't concealing anything.

The next few seconds were the most dangerous. All it would take was for one agent to panic. Then there would be a bloodbath. And it wouldn't be just him lying dead in a pool of blood, but Chernin and Beauvoir and Dagenais and at least some of these agents.

And those two hikers, waiting in an interview room, would have to be killed. These agents couldn't just let that man and woman go. Not after this slaughter.

They'd chosen a bad day for a stroll in an ancient forest.

The seconds ticked by. Five. Six. The agents were jumpy, staring back at him and glancing at each other. Unsure what to do.

Eight.

Of all the things they'd expected, this was not one.

Ten seconds passed before Gamache spoke. "Surrender your weapons. Put your Sûreté ID on your desks. It's over."

He spoke with authority. His voice deep and quiet and calm. As though he actually expected them to do it.

"Fuck you," shouted the most senior agent. He stepped closer to Gamache, raising his weapon.

Oh, Reine-Marie, I'm so sorry . . .

Beauvoir heard Chernin inhale and saw her tense. Preparing . . .

Oh God, oh God, oh God, Jean-Guy prayed.

Gamache didn't flinch, didn't pull away from the gun practically touching his forehead. He'd expected to be dead already, so any hesitation on the part of his killers was a bonus.

"Let Dagenais go," the agent shouted, his face so close Gamache felt a spray of spittle.

"And then what?" Gamache asked, as though they were having a reasonable conversation, a civilized disagreement. "You let us go? We all just walk away and pretend this didn't happen?"

He had to lower the temperature. To do that, he had to sound like what he was not. Perfectly calm.

Half the agents in the room were prepared to shoot. Even, he thought, wanting to. Perhaps needing to. And he suddenly understood why.

Alexandre Dagenais was not the only one from this detachment who'd visited the Arsenault home.

This was a problem. A further complication.

Gamache's mind raced. How to get out of this?

While it was true that three of the armed agents looked prepared to kill fellow Sûreté officers, the other three seemed less committed. More afraid.

Clearly this was not what they'd signed up for. Brutalizing the population. Stealing drugs and arms. Okay. Especially since it was sanctioned, rewarded, even organized by the leadership.

But this? Murdering not just other agents, but one of the most senior officers in the Sûreté? That was something different.

Still, Gamache knew he could not appeal to them. They were cowards and would always bend to whoever had the upper hand. And it was not him.

"Alexandre Dagenais is under arrest." Gamache raised his voice for all to hear. "We will not give him up. But I will give you a choice. If you put down your weapons and surrender your Sûreté ID, I will let you leave." He counted to five in his mind, letting that sink in. "Or you can shoot. And you know what will happen then. You'll kill me, but Inspector Chernin and Agent Beauvoir will return fire and kill you. In the exchange, Dagenais will also die. Some of you will too. Or at least be badly wounded. Any of you who survive will be hunted down by the rest of my department. In fact, by every Sûreté officer in the province. Every police officer in the country. And when you're found . . ."

He could see his words were having some effect. Partly what he was saying, but also how he was saying it. His voice was calm, matter-of-fact. Almost mesmerizing.

"Put down your weapons."

There seemed a hesitation. A moment when it looked like that might happen.

But the senior agent, clearly the most desperate, knew he had to do something to regain control. He grabbed Gamache, hauling the Chief Inspector in front of him and locking his arm around his throat. His gun to Gamache's temple.

"Drop your fucking weapons," he shouted at Chernin and Beauvoir. "Or he dies."

The arm tightened, cutting off his air supply, leaving Gamache gasping for breath. He didn't buck or fight. He stared at Chernin. At Beauvoir. Willing them to stay the course.

Would they follow orders not to shoot unless the others shot first? Not to surrender.

A moment passed. Two.

Chernin did not move. Did not react. Her weapon remained trained on the cop holding Gamache. Poised to fire. And while Beauvoir's eyes had grown so wide it seemed his eyeballs must fall out, he also remained perfectly still. His gun raised. Aimed. But not fired. Yet.

The seconds ticked by.

The buzz in Gamache's ears had built to a roar. He knew it was just a matter of time, perhaps moments, before he blacked out. Suffocated. He could feel the tip of the gun pressed hard against his temple and wondered what would come first. The bullet or the strangling.

His legs were growing weak. But still he didn't struggle, though every instinct was kicking in. He knew if he grabbed at the arm around his throat, the gun would probably go off. Triggering the one thing he was desperate to avoid. More killing.

He could feel his legs going out from under him, and his vision blurring as his brain began to shut down.

He heard from far, far away a shout: "Do it!"

Do what, Gamache wondered. Shoot. Or . . .

"Lower your weapons," shouted Dagenais. "He's right. No one wins if you start shooting."

The senior agent still hesitated. Clearly, while Dagenais's man, he also had his own agenda. And that was to survive. And not be arrested.

Finally, he loosened his grip. Not to save Dagenais, but to save himself.

Gamache fell to his knees, gasping. His hand to his throat. His vision swam and he slumped against a desk. He heard voices but could no longer make out the words. Then hands grabbed him and dragged him to his feet.

"You all right?" Chernin asked, staring into his eyes.

"Their weapons," he croaked. "Get their weapons."

"We have them."

"More. There'll be more. On them or in their desks."

"We have them all," said Agent Beauvoir.

Gamache fell back against the desk. He'd clearly blacked out for a minute or so, while Chernin and Beauvoir had taken control. Propping himself up, he saw Beauvoir practically festooned with firearms.

"Well done," rasped Gamache.

"*Merci*," said Jean-Guy Beauvoir. "*Patron*."

CHAPTER 9

The party for Harriet Landers was in full swing on the village green. Multicolored lanterns had been strung and a bonfire lit. There was music and dancing and a table full of food, where Henri and Fred and Gracie and all manner of other creatures, including children, lay, looking up every time one of the revelers took a brie burger or a honey-lime chicken kabob. Or a butter tart. There was a table for alcoholic and nonalcoholic punches, and a long metal feed trough of ice with beer and wine and soft drinks in impossible shades of purple and orange.

Many of the younger children were dozing off in sleeping bags, gummy bears stuck to their hands, and faces, and hair.

"Relatives?" Gabri asked Clara, who had mustard and chocolate down her sweater.

"Apprentices."

Those not sleeping were chasing each other around and around the outer ring of the village green, ignored by parents who tried to pretend their progeny weren't one jelly bean away from *Lord of the Flies*.

Three Pines smelled of charred hot dogs and sugar from the marshmallows that had melted off sticks and plunged, sizzling, into the bonfire.

While the younger people danced to keep themselves warm in the cool late-spring evening, the older ones sat in lawn chairs drawn up to the blaze.

"I remember my own graduation party," said Robert Mongeau, the minister at St. Thomas's.

"From divinity school?" asked Reine-Marie.

"No, I didn't graduate from that until just a few years ago," he said, with a laugh. "Late to the cloth. It was from Harvard Business School."

"Really?" said Armand.

They'd been away in Paris when this new minister had been hired, and they hadn't had much chance to talk with him. Though Armand and Reine-Marie had heard some of the broad strokes of this new-comer, who seemed both more worldly than the previous pious min-ister, and more caring. Here was a man battered to his knees, not by failure but by too much success.

Robert Mongeau was of medium height, and while not rotund, he was heading that way. His hair was thick and still flecked with brown. His beard was trim and white, and his eyes a sort of hazel. He was in his late sixties, Armand guessed. There was an ease about him, and his good humor was obvious to anyone who spent more than a minute with the man.

Though Armand knew it concealed a private anguish. That much was also obvious to anyone who looked at the Reverend and Madame Mongeau.

"Really," said Mongeau, replying to Armand with amusement. Then he turned to his wife. "Shall we?"

"Always." Sylvie Mongeau lifted her arms. He pulled her out of the chair, took her in his arms, and they swung away, joining the young people on the green.

The others watched, smiling. It was clear, and becoming clearer by the day, that Sylvie Mongeau was dying. Myrna and Clara and even Ruth had approached her within a month of their arrival in Three Pines with offers of friendship. And to talk. Sylvie had accepted the friendship but declined the implied offers to discuss her health.

Myrna and Billy Williams finished their dance and joined the oth-ers, having first stopped at the food table.

"I've never seen her look happier," said Myrna after eating an asparagus roll. It tasted of every childhood picnic.

At first the others thought Myrna meant Sylvie Mongeau, but they quickly realized she was watching her niece. Harriet was dancing with abandon, her arms waving over her head, her face turned to the stars. There was a sort of wild ecstasy about her. It was joy, gilded by extreme relief. And awash in booze.

The worst was over. She'd done it.

The adults were quiet, each watching the young people. Each remembering their own dances. And that first kiss.

Armand put his hand on Reine-Marie's and remembered his last first kiss.

Then, one by one, they turned to the Mongeaus. Swaying slowly. Even though it was a fast song. He held her, his cheek against hers. Their eyes closed.

Armand took a sharp breath against the sudden pain. He looked away. Had to. Toward the bright, the luminous, the joyful young people. Their lives ahead of them.

When the song ended, the Mongeaus returned to their lawn chairs. Sylvie with a fresh glass of rosé, Robert with a beer.

"Armand," he said, his voice low and soft. "Who's that? I haven't seen him before."

Mongeau had tipped his beer bottle toward a young man standing on the other side of the bonfire.

"That's Fiona's brother, Sam. He's staying at the B&B."

"Ah. Fiona is the young woman who stays with you from time to time?"

"*Oui.*"

"But he doesn't?"

"*Non.*"

Mongeau examined Gamache and seemed about to say something, but the man's face in profile, lit by the dancing flames as he watched Sam Arsenault, did not invite conversation.

The minister decided to change the subject. Slightly.

"How did you come to meet her? A friend of your daughter's?"

"*Non*" came the answer, perhaps a bit too quickly. Then Armand turned to him and smiled. "We met a few years ago. Reine-Marie has become a sort of mother figure for her."

"Lucky her." Mongeau waited, but that seemed to be that.

"Harriet isn't the only one celebrating," said Olivier, who'd overheard their conversation. "Fiona also graduated today from the École Polytechnique. Armand and Reine-Marie helped get her in."

It wasn't the whole story, thought Armand. Olivier was being discreet. Though he suspected the minister would find out soon enough. It wasn't exactly a secret.

What no one there knew, not even Reine-Marie, was why Armand felt as he did about Fiona's brother. Sam Arsenault.

Only one other person knew that.

When Jean-Guy had heard that Sam was now in Three Pines, he'd offered to come down. But Armand had declined.

"I appreciate it, but it'll be okay. *Merci quand même*," Armand had said on the phone that afternoon. Thanks anyway.

Through his study window he could see Billy Williams assembling the wood into a sort of teepee for the bonfire that night.

"It might even be a good thing."

"How so?" asked Jean-Guy.

"Running away only makes things worse. I suspect the more I see him, the more I'll realize he's just a regular young man. Nothing—" What to say? *Nothing sinister? Nothing disturbing? Nothing monstrous?* "—more."

Jean-Guy had long suspected the Chief Inspector had it backward. Beauvoir quite liked Sam. It was Fiona . . .

Jean-Guy never could get his head around Armand's reaction to the boy. It was as though he was afraid of him. Beauvoir tried to set that thought aside as ludicrous but could not quite shake it. And his father-in-law's reaction, immediate and visceral, that afternoon at the graduation only underscored that there was more there than met the eye.

While his offer to go down to Three Pines was sincere, the truth was it was the last thing Jean-Guy wanted to do. He was exhausted.

He'd arrived at the neighbors' barbecue just as the last overcooked burger was dropped onto the grass by some kid and eaten by some dog.

Then he'd spent eternity chasing Honoré, who was fueled by devil's food cake, around the yard while Annie held Idola and smiled. Jean-Guy's need to corral chaos almost always amused her, especially now there were two young children in the house. And with Honoré, they'd given birth to mayhem.

That boy loved being dirty and hated baths. Idola, on the other hand, loved baths. Loved being clean. Loved being dirty. Loved being held up, loved lying down.

She was still very floppy. The specialist said she would be for a while but would eventually, with training, be able to sit up by herself.

As he spoke to his father-in-law, Jean-Guy carefully supported Idola's head while she slept in his arms, secure in the knowledge that she was safe and loved.

Jean-Guy Beauvoir thought about the Arsenault siblings and all the other children who never felt that. In fact, were raised knowing the opposite was true.

"Now that's interesting," said Ruth, breaking into Armand's thoughts, just as Billy put another log on the bonfire, sending sparks into the night sky.

Across the village green, they saw Harriet laugh and place her hand on Sam Arsenault's forearm. She said something, and he laughed. Just touching her arm before removing his hand.

Armand and Myrna exchanged glances.

"Well," said the Reverend Mongeau, getting to his feet, "time to get to bed, I think."

Again, he helped Sylvie up, and everyone rose to say goodbye. It seemed a good time for the adults to leave the party to the kids. Best not to see what happened next, they thought, remembering their own dances.

"Wait!" Harriet was walking quickly, if a little unsteadily, over. "You can't leave yet, Auntie Myrna. I have something for you."

She bent down and picked up a package wrapped in a towel that was under her chair.

"When I first came here, I was afraid of everything and everyone. It was all you could do to get me out of the bookstore."

"Spiders!" said Clara. "Remember the spider incident? You got out fast enough then."

"Peppermint toothpaste," said Monsieur Béliveau, who ran the general store. "I had to hide it behind cans of mushroom soup. Actually, you were afraid of mushroom soup too."

"Mushrooms could be poison," said Harriet, as though that was reasonable.

"Heights."

"Holes."

"Okay, I give," laughed Harriet. "Was I really afraid of peppermint toothpaste?"

Monsieur Béliveau nodded. "And Ivory soap. You thought it was made from elephants."

"You thought guacamole was made from lawyers," said Myrna.

"Well, that's just sensible," said Harriet. "Avocado. *Avocats.* I'm still not convinced . . ."

"And yet, you still order it," said Olivier.

"Meh," she said. "It's tasty. What can I tell you."

"I also have eaten my share of—" began Gabri before Olivier snapped. "Stop it!"

"I felt safe here, for the first time in my life. Not physically. I knew that bad things can happen, do happen, anywhere." She looked at the bouquet of white roses on the banquet table. Then she looked around at the homes and shops. At the three huge pines. "Bad things can happen even here."

"She got that right," said Ruth, and Rosa nodded. Though ducks often did.

"But I knew if something did happen, I'd be okay. Because I wasn't alone."

She approached her aunt and handed her the towel. Myrna unwrapped it, then stared at the object in her hands.

"Is it a sculpture?" asked Clara. "A work of art?"

"Is it a cake?" asked Gabri. It was hard to see in the demi-light.

"A book?" asked Sylvie Mongeau.

"Is it a joke?" asked Ruth. "For fuck's sake, the woman paid for four years of university, and you give her that?"

Everyone was so focused on the gift, no one noticed the expression on Armand's face.

Well, that was not totally true. Two people did. The brother and sister standing across the festive village green were watching him.

While he stared at the brick in Myrna's hands.

It wasn't over yet, Gamache knew.

They had the weapons. The cell phones. They had Dagenais. They'd regained control of the building. But it was temporary. There were off-duty agents, Dagenais's officers, out there. Once they got wind of what was happening, things might change. And not for the better.

The Chief Inspector knew the only reason Dagenais had called off his people was to buy time. To regroup and give them another chance to attack.

It wasn't a surrender, it was a tactical retreat.

He could, of course, go back on his promise to let the agents go. That seemed a pledge it would be insane to keep.

But. But.

Gamache knew there were holes in their case. A clever lawyer might get these agents off, claiming they were just defending their captain. Their detachment. That it was reasonable for them to assume they were under attack from Gamache and his people.

There were two pieces of crucial evidence they had to find if they were going to build a solid case.

Clotilde's records and the weapon Dagenais or one of his agents had used to kill her. The brick.

There was work to be done and done quickly. He took Chernin aside. "Get a search warrant for Dagenais's house. Fast."

"*Oui, patron.*"

To Beauvoir he said, "Lock him in a cell."

"*Oui.* What about them?" Beauvoir looked at the agents glaring back through the window in Dagenais's office.

Gamache considered. "Lock them in, and bring the hikers to me."

Then he got on the phone to Agent Moel.

"Hardye, get the children and all the evidence and go to the airport. Fly back to Montréal. Send the rest of the team here to the detachment. Let me know when you're in the air. Hurry."

"The forensics team isn't—"

"Just do it."

"Yessir."

He had to get the children out before another attack was mounted. And, if possible, get the rest of them out too. But they could not leave until all the evidence was collected.

While he waited for word that Moel and the children were on the plane and in the air, the forensics team had arrived at the detachment and been brought up to speed. They started the investigation into wrongdoing at the detachment, while Gamache and Chernin interviewed the man and woman.

Turned out they were who they said they were. At least as far as it went.

Longtime activists with the environmental group Assez, they'd volunteered to drive up to begin organizing the protest to protect the old-growth forest.

No, they'd never been there before. They'd arrived that morning. What was happening?

Well, yes, they smoked weed, but nothing more. No, they didn't deal. What was happening?

Did they know the dead woman? No. And, by the way, what was happening?

"Can we leave? We're not under arrest, are we?" the man asked.

"No," said Gamache. "But for your own safety, you need to stay here with us."

It was possible that the off-duty agents were already outside the station. Waiting for someone to leave. Waiting to take someone hostage, or worse.

"Safety?" asked the woman. "What's happening?"

"Some officers have been found to be involved in criminal activity." Gamache figured they had a right to know something, if not everything. "We need to get the situation under control. Then you can leave."

They stared at him, barely believing what they were hearing.

Taking Chernin aside, he said, "Check their records. I want to know more about them."

"You're not convinced?"

Gamache told her his thoughts about the children's father. And what he might do if he found out what his ex had done to their children.

"You think he's"—Chernin glanced behind her at the male hiker— "the father?" She considered. "He's the right age. I'll see what I can find out. I'm also looking into Clotilde's history. Where she lived before coming here. Where the children were born."

"*Bon.*"

Gamache looked at his watch. Still no word from Agent Moel.

He occupied himself by studying photos of the house. The children's rooms seemed unexpectedly typical. Not unlike his son Daniel's and daughter Annie's rooms at home.

That, not surprisingly, made this worse.

Fiona had put up wallpaper with butterflies, as well as posters of boy bands. Sam seemed interested in puzzles and model planes and cars. He'd taken a crayon and drawn on the walls.

Daniel had done the same thing. No doubt testing his parents. But it was his room, and they had decided as long as it wasn't offensive, Daniel could do what he wanted.

Clotilde had either come to the same conclusion or, more likely, simply didn't care. Or notice. Gamache looked more closely at the drawings on Sam's walls, but it was difficult to make out the images.

"They're in the air, Chief," said Chernin.

"Excellent. The warrant?"

"I'll check."

Gamache could wait no longer. He walked over to Agent Beauvoir, who was guarding the door to Dagenais's office. "Unlock it, please."

When Beauvoir did, the Chief Inspector stepped inside and, without preamble, said, "You three are staying here. You three"—he pointed to the most aggressive, including the one who'd almost killed him—"can leave."

Beauvoir looked at the agents, then at Gamache. Had the man lost his mind? Was his brain oxygen-starved?

"Chief—" he began.

"You have their Sûreté ID?" Gamache said. Beauvoir nodded. "You've searched their vehicles?"

"*Oui*. We found assault rifles." Illegal, Gamache knew, for ordinary Sûreté agents.

"We're sure they're now unarmed?"

"Absolutely, but in their homes there might—"

"Good." Gamache waved at the agents. "Leave. Now. Just you three. Before I change my mind."

Beauvoir looked around for Chernin. Surely the Inspector could stop this madness. But she was busy on the phone.

The three agents looked at each other in disbelief, then hurried out the door and into the darkness.

CHAPTER 10

~

A re you insane?" Beauvoir seethed. "You'll get us all killed." He turned to Chernin, who was now off the phone. "He let them go."

Chernin looked at the Chief Inspector with surprise but didn't challenge him. Instead, she said, "The warrant for Dagenais's property has come through."

"Did you hear what I said?" Beauvoir demanded, looking from one to the other.

"Good," said Gamache, ignoring him and replying to Chernin. "You're in charge. Good luck, Linda."

"And you, *patron*." She watched as Gamache picked up one of the Glocks and loaded it.

"Agent Beauvoir," said Gamache, fixing the gun to his belt, "do you know where Dagenais lives?"

"I don't know the address, but I know how to get there."

"Well, I know the address, but not how to get there. Come with me."

At the door, Beauvoir looked back at Chernin. He needed reassurance that he wasn't about to get into a car with a crazy man. An armed crazy man. But Inspector Chernin had already turned away.

As he drove, Jean-Guy was tempted to pepper the Chief Inspector with questions, but did not. He was afraid of the answers.

As they turned off the main road, Gamache asked, "Does Dagenais live alone?"

"Yes."

"Let me know when we're almost there."

A few minutes later, Beauvoir said, "It's down here a couple hundred meters."

"Shut off your lights, please, and turn the car around in that cul-de-sac."

The light rain of the early evening had turned to sleet. Once parked, Beauvoir reached for the door handle, but for the second time that endless day, Chief Inspector Gamache stopped him.

"Wait."

Dear God, thought Jean-Guy. Not more poetry. Shoot me now.

But the Chief Inspector just sat, and stared out the window at the dark house, barely visible through the trees. One dim light shone in a downstairs window.

"Do you see any vehicles in the drive?"

Beauvoir squinted. "No. Dagenais's car is at the station."

Gamache would know that, thought Beauvoir. So why ask? And what were they waiting for? They had the warrant. None of this made sense.

A couple of minutes later a pickup truck drove by and turned into Dagenais's driveway.

"Do you recognize it?"

Beauvoir did. His face, unseen in the dark, had gone pale.

"It's the second-in-command. Dagenais's man. The one who almost got us all killed. The one you released."

Beauvoir expected some reaction from Gamache. An acknowledgment that he'd fucked up. The guy must be there for the same reason they were. To find the evidence. And Gamache was letting him do it.

"*Oui*," said Gamache. "This's why I released him."

"You expected him to come here?"

"I hoped."

It took Agent Beauvoir a few moments to adjust, and see the man beside him as not an incompetent lunatic.

"Holy shit, you expected him to come here." The words were the same, but the tone and emphasis had changed. "You released him so he could do our work for us."

"So he could find what we almost certainly never would," said

Gamache. "Dagenais would've hidden the evidence too well. But his second-in-command, also implicated, would know where."

He reached for the door handle, as did Beauvoir. "*Non*. Stay here."

"But—"

"I need you here. If he gets by me, if he tries to leave, stop him. Block the road. Assume he's armed. Arrest him."

"*D'accord*. And you?"

"When you have him secured, come find me. Got it? Whatever you hear, do not leave your post. Do you understand?"

Beauvoir knew what that meant. "Are you sure—"

"You're the last line of defense, Agent Beauvoir. You have to stop him. We have to get that evidence. They'll find other children. Might even be grooming some right now. You have to stop him. I'm counting on you, Jean-Guy."

"Yessir."

Beauvoir watched as the Chief Inspector disappeared into the swirling rain and snow.

The sleet hit Gamache's face and made it difficult to see. But it also meant it would be difficult to be seen.

Crouching low, he approached the house slowly. Slowly.

Beauvoir was right, of course. In waiting, he'd allowed this man to get a head start on finding evidence. And maybe destroying it. This might've been a huge misjudgment.

He'd soon find out.

Going from window to window, he looked in. There was one light on, in the living room. But no one was there. Then Gamache noticed a dim glow in the woods.

He crept over, careful, careful not to step on any twigs. Not to lose his footing on the dead leaves, made slick by the sleet. Getting to a nearby tree, Gamache watched as the man knelt and brushed away a pile of leaves, revealing a large log half buried in the wet ground. Reaching into the rotten tree trunk, he withdrew first one package, then another. Gamache couldn't see what they were. The objects were wrapped in something. The man shoved them into a knapsack and got up.

Then he stopped. And looked around.

Had he heard something? Sensed something? The man reached into his coat and brought out a gun.

The moment stretched on. The sleet kept falling, dribbling through Gamache's hair and down his face. It tickled and he almost wiped it away. It was instinctive, but he stopped himself. Staying absolutely still. Barely breathing. Finally, the man lowered his weapon and started forward. He was approaching Gamache, who considered taking his own gun out now but decided against it. There was no way to do it without making a sound. Besides, he needed both hands free.

Wait. Wait.

The man was within a foot of him. One more step and Gamache would make his move. But now there was a hesitation, a change in the man's body.

He was turning toward the tree. Toward Gamache. Lifting his weapon.

Gamache leapt. His hand, slick from the sleet, grabbed the man's wrist. Groping for the hand, the gun.

It went off.

Beauvoir heard the shot and scrambled out of the car. Taking his gun from its holster, he started forward.

Then slid to a stop on the muddy road.

Breathing heavily, he stared into the snow and rain and darkness.

There were no more shots. Had that been the Chief? Or . . .

His heart pounding, Beauvoir stood frozen in place. Every instinct told him to run forward. To do something. Something.

Anything. But he knew the Chief was right.

If Dagenais's man had shot, maybe killed Gamache, then he was the last line of defense. He had to use the car to block the road. The agent would assume Gamache was on his own, and not be expecting it.

Keeping his eyes on the forest, Beauvoir got back into the car and prepared himself.

Will this day never end?

It was over in a matter of moments.

"Fuck you," the man shouted, spitting rotten leaves out of his mouth as Gamache turned him over. "I should've killed you when I had the chance."

"Probably. You're under arrest."

"On what charge. I haven't done anything wrong. You've assaulted me, you fuck-head."

Gamache scooped up the gun and put it in his pocket, then he grabbed the knapsack and looked inside.

There they were. The video camera and an exercise book, with butterflies on the cover. And monstrosities inside.

"Looks like stealing to me." Gamache took off his coat and wrapped it around the items for extra protection against the sleet, now pouring down. "Unless these belong to you."

The agent was silent.

"I thought not." He hauled the man to his feet and pushed him forward. "Walk."

When he saw the two figures appear out of the swirling sleet, Beauvoir leapt out of the car and ran forward, meeting them halfway. "You got him. I thought . . . I wondered . . ."

Gamache handed the man over. "Secure him in the back seat."

"Yessir. With pleasure."

The man who'd been his supervisor until a few hours ago was letting rip with a string of abuse and threats. That gave Beauvoir even more pleasure, as did the rotting maple leaf plastered to the side of the man's face. Which Beauvoir left there.

"I heard a shot. You okay?" he asked when he got back into the driver's seat.

"I am. You heard the shot, but stayed here? You didn't leave your post?"

"You sound surprised. The truth is, I was getting caught up on emails. I'd have gone eventually."

Gamache gave a small grunt of amusement. He'd seen Beauvoir's dark hair, dripping wet. He'd obviously heard the shot, gotten out of the car, and stood there for a while. Tempted.

But he'd followed orders.

"You got them." Beauvoir nodded toward the items the Chief Inspector was placing in evidence bags. A video camera and an exercise book.

"He got them."

Gamache was soaked through and shivering. He leaned back in the seat and closed his eyes. Not to sleep, not to rest. Time for that later. He was trying to see the next step.

It wasn't over yet. But almost. Almost.

Beauvoir, cold and wet himself, turned the heat up full blast, pointing the vents toward Gamache, and drove back to the station in silence. His questions answered. Or most of them.

An hour later all three of the agents Gamache had released, and two of the off-duty officers, had been arrested. Their names found in the careful records in the exercise book. Forensics had taken prints and DNA off the video camera and the tape still inside, as well as the ledger, then handed it back to Gamache and Chernin for closer study.

Clotilde had been, among other things, a businesswoman. She'd kept detailed records. There were names and dates and addresses. And amounts paid. As well as stickers beside certain names. Unicorns for some. Roses. Fairies. Puppies.

"Code?" Chernin asked.

"Seems so." It was far from clear what those cheerful appliqués meant. Gamache wasn't sure he wanted to know.

No, he was sure. He didn't want to know. And wished he didn't have to think about it. But he did.

Between these records and the videos, there was more than enough evidence to charge everyone involved.

"I want photographs taken of every page and emailed to Serious Crimes," said Gamache as he closed the book. Squeezing it shut as though it would trap the rot in. "And copies made of the videos."

If anything happened to them, if somehow this evidence was destroyed, there would be a record of it.

Once he'd issued assignments, Gamache went to the bathroom to splash warm water on his face and disinfect his hands. He changed into the clean and dry clothes he'd packed, knowing they'd probably have to stay at least a few days.

He gripped the side of the sink and closed his eyes. Then, opening them, he stared at himself in the mirror. There was a middle-aged man, with graying hair, gray stubble, and deep lines down his face. How quickly this happened.

He longed to call Reine-Marie. To speak to Daniel and Annie. To hear about their day at school. About Reine-Marie's day. She worked at Québec's National Library and Archives, but her hobby was tracking down lost documents from Montréal in the 1600s.

There was one book in particular she was desperate to find.

"It's called a grimoire," she'd told him one night, when the kids were asleep and they were relaxing on the back balcony of their apartment in the Outremont *quartier* of Montréal. "Most of my colleagues think it's a myth, but I'm not so sure. I found a reference to it in Mother Catherine's writings."

"The mystic?" asked Armand, who was an avid, though amateur, student of Québec history.

"Well, mystic or lunatic," said Reine-Marie. "She was an Augustinian. Helped found one of the first orders in Québec, back in the mid-1600s."

"What's a grimoire?"

"It's a book to summon demons."

Armand turned in his seat to look at her. "Demons?"

Reine-Marie nodded. "It was an age of demons and witchcraft. Mother Catherine was obsessed with them. A woman in Montréal, accused of being a witch, was said to have a grimoire. But if she did, it was lost."

"And you think you can find it?" he asked.

"I think we might have it somewhere in the archives."

"Wouldn't the clerics have destroyed it?" asked Armand.

"Not necessarily. Mother Catherine was a powerful figure. My theory is, she'd have asked to keep it. To study it."

"Know your enemy."

"Yes. We have her papers and books in the archives."

"Then wouldn't this grimoire have already been found among them?"

Reine-Marie gave him a pitying look. "And what do the Sûreté archives look like?"

"Archives? You mean the piles of old papers going back a hundred years, dumped into containers in the basement?"

"That's pretty much what the basement of the Bibliothèque et Archives nationale du Québec looks like."

He envied her her job. Had he not been a cop, he'd have loved to be a historian or archivist. Going over old papers, finding curiosities buried in obscure libraries.

Now, as he stared at himself in the mirror, Armand wondered if he hadn't just found a grimoire. Not the same as Reine-Marie described. Not an ancient book to summon demons. This one simply named the ones already here.

It was late, well past midnight, and he could not wake her up to tell her about his own grim discovery. Instead, he dried his face with a rough paper towel and willed himself to go back out.

As he returned to the open office, he half expected to see four horsemen. But instead, he saw his officers hard at work and, among them, Agent Jean-Guy Beauvoir.

The young man in the basement. Who'd refused to be corrupted. Who'd stood his ground.

And Armand knew there was hope.

Jean-Guy Beauvoir looked up from booking one of his former colleagues and watched Chief Inspector Gamache surrounded by his officers. He looked tired and rubbed his forehead as he listened closely to each report. Each person vying for his attention.

Under the look of fatigue, thought Jean-Guy, *the attack of migraine and the sigh / There is always another story, there is more than meets the eye.*

CHAPTER 11

The forensics team flew back to Montréal early the next morning
with their prisoners.

The hikers had been released, though Gamache had assigned an
agent to look more closely into their identities. He also wanted to
know more about Clotilde's history and her family. There must be
someone. Parents, siblings, the father of her children.

He and Inspector Chernin stayed behind to fill in some details,
leaving Agent Beauvoir to run the detachment.

"You mean I'm in command?" He looked around the empty space
as though he'd been given the keys to the kingdom.

Less than a day earlier he'd been in the basement, and now he was
in charge.

"Yes," said Gamache. "It's all yours. Don't burn it down."

As they left, they heard a phone ring. "Sûreté. Agent Beauvoir.
How can I help?"

Gamache and Chernin met first with the coroner, who confirmed
that death was due to a blow to Clotilde's head. Almost certainly a
brick.

There was no semen. It appeared she had not been sexually assaulted. Most of the bruises were either older or postmortem.

"Toxicology?" Chernin asked.

"Well, she was loaded. Cocaine, heroin. Amphetamines. Looks like
she'd have snorted the living room sofa, given a chance. It's possible

she'd have died of an overdose anyway, had the murderer waited or known. The good thing, I suppose, is that given her state she probably didn't see it coming, or feel anything."

"But death was the catastrophic blow to her head?" Chernin asked. "Yes."

That at least was definite, though it seemed her life was also catastrophic.

"She was dead when she went into the water?" Chernin confirmed, reviewing the report while Gamache looked down at Clotilde's body. At her face. At her worried expression.

He thought maybe Dr. Mignon was wrong and that, at the last moment of life, she had seen death coming.

"Yes, but this is where it gets interesting," said the coroner. "As you know, I'm no specialist, so I didn't put it into the report. I could never swear to this, but I don't think she was ever completely submerged."

Gamache turned around. "What do you mean?"

"I think, by the texture and mottling of her skin, and by the damage done by fish and birds, that she spent at least two days only partly submerged."

He showed them the marks.

"We need her body sent to the coroner in Montréal," said the Chief Inspector.

Dr. Mignon stripped off his gloves. "I'll share my report with your coroner. The children?"

"They're being cared for" was all Gamache could say.

Mignon shook his head and glanced back at the body. "I hope she was a better mother than she appears. Poor one. I can't imagine she wanted her life to turn out as it did."

Gamache and Chernin took the report, thanked him, then returned to the Arsenault home for a closer look around in daylight.

After the sleet of the day before, this one had dawned bright and fresh and clear. The ground was wet, of course, but the air smelled fresh, with a bite of cold. Such was the month of November. Unpredictable. Changeable. It could not be trusted.

The sunshine didn't make the bungalow look more cheerful. In fact, if possible, it looked even worse. Though it didn't help that they now knew what had gone on inside.

The scent of lemon cleaner still hung in the air. What had seemed fresh now smelled stale, cloying, chemical. Gamache and Chernin walked from room to room. Sometimes picking up items with gloved hands and placing them in evidence bags. Gamache noticed the exercise books with homework done by both Fiona and Sam. He bagged them, along with other small items.

He also picked up a stuffed dog from Fiona's bed and a model plane Sam had made. Not as evidence. These would, he hoped, offer some small comfort in their new and unfamiliar surroundings.

He paused to look at what Sam had drawn on the walls. It was just meandering lines in crayon. Without, it seemed, purpose or destination. Like ley lines on a map, leading nowhere.

He took a photo.

They did not yet have the murder weapon. There was a pretty good chance it had been tossed into the lake. If so, it had sunk into the mud, to be lost forever.

Still, Gamache had ordered a diving team to look.

It could also have been thrown out a car window to be swallowed up by the thick forest. Leaving the house, and the smell of disinfectant, he walked into the backyard and looked at the mess.

He knew his people had been thorough. If the murder weapon, or any other evidence, was there, they'd have found it. Still, he spent half an hour lifting bedsprings, and tires, and broken garden furniture.

He did not return to the root cellar. He'd seen all he needed, and anything of value to their investigation had been taken away.

Going back to the house, he found Chernin once again in Clotilde's room.

"Find anything?"

Linda Chernin held up an evidence bag. "I found this in her bedside drawer. And another just like it in Fiona's room." She shook her head. "She couldn't even let her daughter have these without soiling them."

"These" were sheets of stickers. Unicorns. Angels. Fairies. Mythical, magical creatures. The same ones used as code beside the names of abusers.

"You?" she asked.

He shook his head and took another tour of the house. Finally, when there was nothing else to see, he returned to the living room.

"What's bothering you?" asked Chernin, joining him.

"Pains were taken to lose the brick, but not the body. Why? I think whoever killed her wanted Clotilde to be found. The coroner says she was put in shallow water. That cove—the one place any visitor to the lake was likely to find her. If the killer had taken her that far, he could've carried her along the shore and dumped the body where it wouldn't be found."

"True. Maybe he thought the lake itself was far enough. No one would find her there."

"But there'd been reports in the media that environmental activists would be scouting out the lake."

"Yes. I've pulled copies of the articles and the interviews on local radio."

"Do they say when?"

"This week."

"And when did the reports appear in the news?"

"The first story was two days before Clotilde was killed."

Gamache nodded. "So whoever put her body there probably knew that those environmentalists would be at the lake. And there's only one road in. They were bound to find her. But not too soon."

Chernin nodded, knowing where this was going. "Dagenais said if he'd killed her, he'd have made sure she was never found."

"*Oui.* I think that's true. Once the body was found, he had no option but to call us, and that was a disaster for him. No, if he killed her, he'd make sure she was listed as just one more missing woman. An addict and prostitute. A cursory search would be made, and the file closed."

"Shit. You think he didn't kill her?" When Gamache didn't answer, she continued. "Then who did? The hiker? Could he be the kids' father? You thought maybe . . . But they just arrived yesterday morning, and their car shows no signs of blood. We'll have the DNA report later today. Still . . ."

Still. It seemed unlikely. They were the ones who reported the body.

"Suppose Clotilde was blackmailing one of her clients. That's a pretty good motive for murder."

"Yes," said Gamache. "But he'd also have to find and destroy her records. No use killing Clotilde, then have us arrive and find the videos and the ledger. Dagenais was the only one who searched and found them."

"Well, he might have been the only one who found them but not the only one who searched."

Gamache's brows rose. "That's true."

"Those kids lied to us about Dagenais, they might be lying about someone else. Someone who also threatened them if they told. It seems they're so used to hiding the truth, it's become second nature."

"Agent Moel thinks they've been so damaged for so long they might not be able to tell the difference between lying and the truth," said Gamache. "And maybe not between right and wrong."

He leaned forward, placing his elbows on his knees, his fingers knitted together as though praying. But what he was thinking, what had just entered his mind, was as far from divine as it was possible to be.

Two days later, and back in Montréal, Gamache listened to the handwriting expert who'd studied the record book. It seemed the ledger contained the handwriting of not one but three people.

Clotilde had partners.

He reread the interviews with the men arrested in the pedophilia sweep and reviewed, yet again, the evidence found in the house. Spending extra time with the stickers beside the names.

Finally, dropping his head and closing his eyes, he brought one hand up to his forehead. And massaged. Then, no longer able to avoid it, he gave the rest of the evidence to the handwriting expert.

Clotilde's car had been found in the possession of one of those men. The one with the unicorn beside his name. The DNA evidence found in the vehicle proved it was how Clotilde's body got to the lake.

The man had already been arrested, but now Gamache had another talk with him. And with Dagenais.

Only then was he ready to speak to Clotilde's children.

First, though, since it was going to be delicate and emotional, he called the provincial guardian and the counselor who'd been sent to help the children. He also spoke to the doctor who'd examined them. Her report was both predictable and devastating.

Finally, he called Agent Moel, advising her that he and Chernin would be going over to talk to Fiona and Sam.

"May I make a suggestion, *patron*?" Hardye Moel had spent the days and nights since the discovery of their mother's body with the children. She knew them well.

"Of course."

"Any talk of her killer needs to be handled with care. I know you're aware of that, Chief, but there is something you can do that might help."

"What's that?"

"Get Agent Beauvoir down so he can be there when you speak to them."

Gamache knew that Beauvoir and Sam had, with his permission, kept in touch. With the understanding that if the boy said anything important to the case, Beauvoir would pass it along.

"Agent Beauvoir seems to have made a connection with Sam, which for that boy is pretty remarkable," Moel explained. "I think Sam sees Beauvoir as a sort of big brother, maybe even a father figure. He trusts him. I think, if you'll forgive me, he sees you as an authority figure. Someone likely to judge and punish him. He doesn't like or trust you."

Gamache heard this without surprise. He'd seen the expression on Sam's face, had felt the hostility radiating off the boy. He suspected Agent Moel was understating Sam Arsenault's feelings toward him.

"Having Agent Beauvoir here," Moel continued, "might make it less traumatic."

Gamache wasn't so sure about that, given what was about to happen, but anything that might help the children was worth doing.

He'd handed the stuffed toy and model plane to Agent Moel to give to them. And he'd bought another model for Sam to make and a packet of stickers for Fiona. He wondered if putting fairies and unicorns on things acted as a kind of charm? The way others use incense and a crucifix? Was it a way to ward off evil?

How much worse would the girl's life have been without the help of angels and fairies and unicorns? And yet, the cheery stickers had ended up in that terrible tally of abuse.

He sent for Agent Beauvoir and put off the meeting with Fiona and Sam until Beauvoir could arrive the next day.

It turned out to be a disastrous decision. One that would have consequences for years to come.

That night the children got by the Sûreté officer guarding them, mostly because she was looking for external trouble, not runaways. It took the combined efforts of the Montréal police and the Sûreté, as well as emergency and social services, to find them. And even then, they only found Sam.

He'd been badly beaten and left for dead in a back alley in the inner city. When he'd come to in the hospital, Gamache was there. Agent Beauvoir was holding the boy's hand.

It seemed the boy's injuries, while bad, were not as life-threatening as they appeared. It was mostly cuts and bruising around his head where he'd been hit, repeatedly, with a brick.

Sam Arsenault, tiny and vulnerable in the big hospital bed, roused. Jean-Guy Beauvoir bent over him and whispered that he was safe. That it would be okay.

Armand listened, and was glad he'd made one good decision, and that was not to tell Agent Beauvoir what they knew.

That it would not be okay.

Sam's bruised and bloodshot eyes shifted from Jean-Guy to Gamache. And remained there. And Armand knew then with certainty that Sam was not safe. Never was. Probably never would be.

When questioned, the boy refused to say who'd done that to him.

Gamache found it interesting, even telling, that he didn't say he didn't know. He just wouldn't say.

He also refused to tell them where Fiona was. While others were afraid she was dead, Gamache himself, though worried, never actually believed that.

They found her a day later, hustling on boulevard de Maisonneuve. Her first question was "Is Sam okay?"

"He's recovering in hospital," Gamache said, watching her closely.

"From what? What's happened to him?" Her voice rose. Her panic sounded genuine. But Gamache knew that her entire life had been an act. A magic trick, meant to misdirect, to deceive. To hide what was really happening inside that home. Inside their lives. Desperate for people to see the happy stickers and not the horrors.

Fiona was an accomplished liar. What she did not do well, if at all, was tell the truth. Though not for the first time Gamache wondered if she and Sam could even tell the difference.

When Sam was well enough, he rejoined his sister at the home in Montréal where they were staying. Gamache, Beauvoir, and the counselor sat in the kitchen with the children, mugs of hot chocolate and tea in front of them. Inspector Chernin and Agent Moel sat in the next room, where they could follow what was happening but not overwhelm Fiona and Sam.

"How are you feeling?" Gamache started. His voice soft. Calm and calming.

"Okay," they said, as one.

Gamache looked at Sam. The boy's face was swollen and bruised from the beating in the alley. There was a bandage on the side of his head.

"Are you sure?"

Sam just nodded, not meeting the Chief Inspector's gaze.

"I know you've been asked this before, but I want to ask again. Is there anyone we should be calling? Any family?"

Sam shook his head, and Fiona said, "It's just us."

Gamache caught the eye of the counselor. They both knew this was a hallmark of abuse. Isolation.

Armand had planned to tell them something he rarely talked about. His own childhood. That he'd lost both parents suddenly when he was about Sam's age.

He wanted to open up to them in hopes they'd relax and open up to him. It was, he admitted, slightly manipulative. But more than anything, Armand wanted Fiona and Sam to know that while shocking and devastating, it was possible to survive. And even, with help, be happy one day.

Behind the children, he could see into the neat living room of the cheerful house. There, on the coffee table, was the new model plane he'd given Sam. Already built.

Armand was glad. Daniel, his son, had also loved making models. They'd done quite a few together. The model he'd chosen for Sam had looked like a good one.

But now he hesitated to tell them about his parents, for a number of reasons, not least of which was that this was about their loss, their pain. Not his. Though there was another reason, one that was instinctive and indistinct.

Instead, he asked, "Why did you run away?"

They looked at each other, each waiting for the other to speak. Finally Fiona said, "We were bored."

It was not the answer any of them expected, but upon reflection Gamache realized their lives had been, from the moment of waking to going to sleep, chaotic. Filled with violence, anxiety, danger, pain. Uncertainty. Drama. Activity. People.

It's not that they liked it. It was all they knew.

A nice, comfortable, safe, and calm home was completely foreign. Perhaps even frightening. It allowed thoughts and feelings to surface.

They wanted to get back to the distractions, to the devil they knew. So they'd headed to the inner city.

Though Gamache was not convinced. He thought there was another reason. Leaning forward, he repeated, "Why did you run away?"

"I told you," said Fiona, clearly annoyed at being doubted.

"You didn't take any clothes with you. You didn't pack." His voice

117

remained calm, kindly even. But his eyes were steady. "You didn't leave. You ran away. Why?"

Fiona looked at Sam.

"Tell us." Beauvoir spoke gently, looking at the boy. "It's okay. We won't be mad."

"We heard that you were coming over." Sam's eyes shifted now, landing on Gamache. "We didn't want to see you."

"Why not?" he asked, though he could have provided the answer.

He'd have been partly right, but mostly wrong. The answer, when it came, stunned him.

"Because we don't like you, okay?" snapped Sam. That much Gamache expected. The rest he did not. "We've seen men like you. We know what you really want."

Then the thin, bruised child made an obscene gesture.

Gamache was prepared for some sort of verbal abuse, but he had not expected this. Even though he knew that Sam did not believe what he said. Even though he knew no one at that table believed it. Even though he knew it was a calculated, perhaps even rehearsed, attack designed to inflict maximum damage, still it left him shaken.

He stared into Sam's eyes. And there he saw not fear, not pain, but triumph. The boy knew he'd scored a direct hit. Somehow this child had recognized the very worst thing this grown man could be accused of. And then accused him.

But along with the triumph, there was something else lurking in those eyes. It was relief. Like an addict getting a hit. Or a starving creature that fed on someone else's pain, enjoying a meal.

This was a child whose only feelings involved agony.

The slap, the punch, the kick, the burn, the penetration. The betrayal. And sometimes it was the spoken word. It was all he knew. So why wouldn't he inflict all that on others?

Armand looked at Sam and his heart broke. And out of that wound came the words from the Zardo poem.

Who hurt you once, so far beyond repair / That you would greet each overture with curling lip.

But he knew the answer. They had the names. And addresses. They had them in custody. They had the body in the morgue.

The question now was, were Fiona and Sam beyond repair?

He turned to Fiona. She seemed surprised by what Sam had said, had implied. Though he couldn't really tell. Was she? Maybe not. Maybe it was part of the act.

Maybe that was their game, their unnatural connection.

Armand realized with a jolt that while the accusation was patently false, it had, against all odds, succeeded. Sam Arsenault had done something the very worst, the most brutal criminals had failed to do, though God knew they'd tried.

The boy had found a way into Gamache's head and left the Chief Inspector foundering. Unsure. Questioning his judgment, his perceptions.

The way in had not been the insult. Armand Gamache's extreme empathy for them had left him vulnerable. The way in was through his heart.

And that was why, he now realized, he hadn't told them about his own loss. It was too personal. He'd sensed even then the danger of opening up too much.

Fortunately, Gamache didn't have to rely on judgment when he had facts.

"We've arrested the men who visited your home—"

The counselor had advised Gamache and the other agents not to ask Fiona and Sam about the abuse. They'd need a lot of therapy, a lot of help, before they could talk about it. And for now there was no need. There was more than enough evidence to charge the men.

"One of them was found to have your mother's car."

"Did he do it?" Fiona asked.

Gamache hated every moment of this. Only Chernin and the counselor knew what was coming next, and he could sense their discomfort. But he pressed forward. Deeper into the cave.

"No. He didn't kill your mother."

"How do you know?" demanded Sam.

"Because we know how he got her car. He told us."

"He could be lying," said Fiona. "Don't murderers lie?"

"All the time," said Gamache, his voice soft. "We also found the record book and video camera." Now he paused, looking at them. "We know."

"You know what they did to us," said Sam, his chin dimpling, his lower lip quivering. "I don't want to talk about it."

"I'm not asking you about what you both went through. I wouldn't make you talk about it. But there is something I do need to talk to you about."

His voice was neutral. As though the subject, the next words, were not going to explode their lives. It was vital not to feed any hysteria. To remain, and invite, calm.

"The writing in the record book started off as your mother's, but then, about six months ago, it changed. Two more people took over. You two."

"That's a lie," Sam shouted. His small face crumpled and his eyes filled with tears. He looked at Beauvoir. "It's a lie." His voice was high now, barely more than a squeak.

Agent Beauvoir was so surprised by what Chief Inspector Gamache had just said, had just implied, that he sat there, openmouthed.

"It isn't," said Gamache. "We gave your exercise books with your homework to our expert. There's no doubt."

They were staring, eyes wide. But he pressed on.

"We found your mother's blood in the trunk of her car. The man who bought it said you"—he turned to Fiona—"threatened to expose him if he told anyone who sold it to him. He tried to burn it, but we still found enough DNA."

"No!" Fiona looked terrified. "It never happened. He's lying. He killed her and stole it."

Gamache's heart ached, but still he had to do this.

"I think you killed your mother, Fiona. I think you did it in self-defense, after years of abuse. I'm not sure you meant to, or that you even really knew what you were doing. And I think Sam helped you."

There it was.

Armand stood in the darkest cavern in the deepest cave with these two children, surrounded by dripping nightmarish stalactites. Sharp, slimy spikes of undeniable facts that had snagged and caught these children.

At that moment Armand Gamache hated his job.

Sam had thrown himself into Jean-Guy's arms, burying his head in his chest. Clinging to the young Sûreté agent and sobbing that he didn't do it. That it was a lie.

Then he looked up and whispered something.

Jean-Guy bent down, and Sam, slobbering and shuddering, repeated it.

No one else heard, but when Beauvoir looked over at Fiona, they could guess what Sam had just confided. And Beauvoir confirmed it.

Sam had told him that it had been his sister's idea. She'd killed their mother, then forced him to help. He was afraid of her. She'd tried to kill him too. In the alley.

Fiona's eyes widened. But she did not deny it.

Jean-Guy missed the look in Sam's eyes as he turned to the Chief Inspector. But Gamache did not.

He saw satisfaction. Almost amusement. He saw a challenge.

CHAPTER 12

⌒

The Reverend Robert Mongeau stared at Armand.

"Are you saying that that young woman is a murderer? She killed her mother?"

"She was found guilty, yes."

They were sitting in one of the pews in the tiny St. Thomas's church in Three Pines. It was early on Sunday afternoon, the day after the graduation and the party.

While the Gamaches rarely attended services, they had asked the minister and his wife to their home afterward for Sunday lunch. Then Armand had walked back up to the church with Robert, leaving Sylvie and Reine-Marie to have a lemonade in the sun-trap of their back garden.

Fiona had joined them for the meal, then helped clean up the dishes before going across to the bistro to see her brother.

As they'd arrived at the church, Armand noticed the new caretaker touching up the white paint that had chipped off in the winter.

"He's quite a find," said Armand. "Obviously cares for the place."

"Claude never misses a repair or a weed or a spot of dirt. Or a service, for that matter," said Robert, watching the older man carefully scraping off the chipping paint. "I often find him sitting in the church alone."

"I thought Gabri looked after the church and grounds."

"Yes, as head of the Anglican Church Women. But Gabri hinted he was done with that. Claude was recommended by a guest at the B&B actually. He needed a job and I needed a caretaker."

Claude was slender, wiry really. For a man who spent a lot of time outside, his skin was surprisingly sallow. He wore dark glasses and a baseball cap low over his face.

At the top of the stairs leading to the chapel, Armand paused. From there he had a good view of the village. Patrons were sitting on the terrasse outside the bistro enjoying lunch or a drink this early June afternoon.

Any mess from the party the night before had been cleared away. The only evidence was the trampled grass on the village green. But it would soon spring back.

Armand had suggested a stroll to walk off the large meal, but the minister had needed to return to the church to do some work and clean up after the service.

"Clean up?" asked Armand. "What exactly do you do in your services?"

"The usual. Sacrifice a chicken. Dance naked. Sure you don't want to come?"

Armand laughed. He could see why Robert and Sylvie had fit in so quickly and so well.

He had an ulterior motive in inviting Mongeau for a walk. It was to see if the minister wanted to talk privately. About anything, but specifically Sylvie's health. Not her condition. That wasn't his business. He wanted to hear about Mongeau's condition. How he was doing. How he was feeling.

Armand knew that severe illness could be very isolating.

But he didn't get a chance. As they'd entered the peaceful little chapel, Robert had asked him about Fiona and Sam.

"I noticed the way that young man was looking at you," said the minister. "And how you were looking at him. Do you want to talk about that?"

Armand, while a little surprised by the question, found no reason not to answer. There'd been the public court case, the reports in the media. Granted, it was more than ten years ago now, but it was a case not easily forgotten. Everyone in Three Pines was aware of it.

So he found himself in the quiet little church telling the minister about the murder of Clotilde Arsenault. When he'd finished, Robert seemed at a loss for words.

"Then," he managed, "how . . ." He moved his hands, trying to form the thought into words.

"How, if she's a murderer, did she come to stay with us?" Armand helped him out.

The minister nodded.

"After a few years, Fiona came up for parole, one day a month. I'd been visiting her in prison, making sure she was all right. Reine-Marie and I agreed to supervise her. The parole board eventually extended that to one weekend a month."

Fiona spent those weekends in Three Pines with the Gamaches.

"But why . . . ?" Again the poor minister struggled. "How—?"

Armand took pity on him again. "—could I trust her? I was the arresting officer."

At that, Mongeau's eyes widened. "Really? But you don't do that for everyone you arrest."

Gamache smiled. "God, no. This was a special case. It's all in the public record, so I'm not telling you anything you can't find by looking it up."

What the public record didn't show were his doubts. He suspected Fiona might've been the one to administer the blow. To actually kill her mother. But he was far from sure it had been her idea.

In his heart, Armand believed Fiona was not responsible, could not be held responsible. She'd been abused by every adult in her life, and then abused again by the court.

He'd wanted to do something to try to make it up, and Reine-Marie had agreed.

Armand and Robert sat in the light through the stained-glass window. It had been commissioned and created at the end of the Great

War by a mother who'd lost all three of her children. The window in the chapel showed the three brothers, two of whom were in profile, marching forward into battle. Afraid but determined.

One, the youngest, was staring straight out at the congregation. At generations of congregations. Not in blame or anger, not in fear or even sadness. But in forgiveness. He forgave them. As though, thought Armand, such a thing were possible.

But now the boys had been turned into light. And warmth.

Below the window was a plaque listing all the young men and women from the region who'd been killed in wars. And the simple words below the names.

They Were Our Children.

Armand sat in the cheery blue and green and yellow light spilling through their bodies, and described the abuse Clotilde's children had suffered in that house. Years of it, according to the ledger their mother had carefully kept, and then the children kept up when she'd become too drug-addled to do it.

That had been one of the many elements that had muddied the waters at Fiona's trial.

Instead of running away. Instead of turning away the men when their mother could no longer function, Fiona and Sam had continued the business.

A psychiatrist who specialized in this field had testified that by then they were so programmed, so damaged, they no longer knew different. They'd known "wrong" so long they no longer recognized "right." Or felt they had a choice.

On top of that, it brought in the money the children needed to survive.

They were trapped.

"I arrested Fiona on charges of manslaughter, but with extenuating circumstances. I argued that the charges should be dropped, and she and Sam should be given counseling. The prosecution disagreed. Even though she was a minor, they chose to try her as an adult."

"Why?" asked Mongeau.

"She was almost fourteen by then. The prosecution argued in keeping those records and running the household, she was essentially acting as an adult—"

"But the abuse started—"

"Based on the records, when she was ten."

"Oh, dear God," sighed the minister.

"Between the written records, the fact it seemed she'd taken over from her mother and was prostituting her brother, and that she'd sold the car to that man, the car used to take their mother's body to the lake, well, it looked like she was less a victim and more an instigator. But there was one more damning piece of evidence. One I contributed to. Her brother said she'd tried to kill him too. In the alley. She was the one who'd beaten him almost to death."

"How did you contribute? How could you have?" Robert asked.

"I delayed arresting them by a day. By then they knew that I was coming over, and they suspected why. It spooked them. My decision to delay gave them the time they needed to run away."

"But that wasn't your fault."

"If I'd gone over right away, Sam wouldn't have suffered those injuries, and the prosecution and ultimately the judge wouldn't have decided Fiona was a willful murderer who'd succeeded once with her mother, and attempted again with her own brother. She was a danger."

Robert Mongeau looked down at his hands, then lifted his eyes to Armand's. "Were they wrong? If she did those things . . ."

"She was a child herself. Even if she did those things, was she likely to be able to make rational decisions? I don't think so."

"But still . . ." Mongeau struggled. He looked around and settled on the brittle boys before turning back to Gamache. "If she did those things, if she couldn't tell right from wrong then, are you sure she can now? I know you believe in second chances. So do I. God knows, I've been given one. But there is a limit, isn't there? Could she still . . . be a danger?"

Armand lifted his hands in resignation. "I don't think she ever was."

He'd fought the prosecutor's decision. He'd been appalled, infuriated, that they'd tried Fiona Arsenault as an adult. That they'd tried her at all. He'd argued that even if what Sam said was true, Fiona was clearly not responsible for her actions. She'd been hurt, abused, raised in a twisted environment without a moral compass or a role model. She needed help, not punishment.

He'd argued, even shouted at the prosecutor. To the point where he'd been threatened with expulsion from his office.

Not only was it patently unfair to try Fiona as an adult, there was another reason the head of homicide fought so hard to have the charges reduced or dropped completely.

He didn't believe Fiona had acted alone. In fact, he came to believe that Fiona hadn't even conceived the plan. Sam had. And he suspected Sam had hurt himself in that alley, banging his head against a wall to create injuries that looked much worse than they were. Head wounds bled, and there was a lot of blood. But they were, finally, superficial.

It was not a murder attempt. It was an attempt to shift blame.

He did not tell Robert Mongeau this. Only Beauvoir knew his suspicions. Ones that could never be proved.

And so the case had gone to trial. Sam had, at the very least, been an accomplice in the murder of his mother. That was not denied. But he was deemed too young, too fragile, too damaged to know what he was doing. The prosecution argued that he'd been controlled, abused, assaulted by his older sister.

Sam Arsenault was sent to what was apparently a happy and calm foster home, where he was followed closely and received psychiatric help.

Fiona was convicted and sentenced to fifteen years in prison.

"But if Sam was cleared of all charges," Mongeau asked, "why that look between you last night? He looked . . ." The minister searched for the word. "I honestly don't know how he looked. But it wasn't pleasant. And you." He stared at Gamache, bathed in the light through the stained-glass boys. "Forgive me, Armand, and I might be very wrong, but just for a moment there you looked frightened."

Armand was about to deny it, then stopped himself. Robert Mongeau was right. He was afraid of Sam Arsenault. Yesterday had confirmed what Armand had suspected. The boy, now the man, could still get into his head. Could still mess around in there.

Only one other person had been able to do that. A serial killer, a psychopath named John Fleming. A genuine lunatic who was now in prison for life. Not the person you want wandering around in your thoughts. And since thoughts can drive feelings, he'd invaded those as well.

Armand checked once a year to be sure Fleming was still in the Special Handling Unit, reserved for the most dangerous criminals. Though no one would ever release such a maniac.

And now, Sam Arsenault was not just in his head, he was in the village where Armand lived. Where his family and friends lived.

Yes, Armand was frightened. It was a free-floating fear. As though an arrow had been shot but hadn't yet found its target.

"You might be right" was all he said to the minister, and made a note that not much got by this man. "I seem to have dominated the conversation. I meant to ask how you are."

Mongeau took a deep breath and exhaled. "Honestly? I'm frightened too. What a pair we make." He gave a small laugh, then looked around. "As long as I'm here, in this space, I feel at peace. I know what's happening to Sylvie is God's will." He could not bring himself to say exactly what was happening. "And that thought comforts me, while I'm here. But as soon as I leave, go through that door, I'm lost and terrified."

"Of what?"

"Of losing her, of course."

"But there's more," said Armand, quietly.

The minister looked at his companion and seemed to come to a decision. "I'm afraid of not being enough. Not being able to do it. I'm afraid it'll get so bad I'll run away. Not physically but emotionally. I'm afraid I already am, when I come here. To hide." He appealed to Armand. "You know?"

Armand nodded. He knew that feeling. The fear of not being strong enough. Not being able to do what was needed.

"This isn't hiding, this is comfort. This is respite. It gives you the strength you need to go back and be there with Sylvie. For her. It's natural to feel as you do. It would be strange if you didn't. Believe me, you won't run away." He remembered the dance from the night before. The intimacy. "If you ever feel you want to, come to me. We'll talk. Sylvie knows she's loved. What more do any of us want?"

"Time?" Robert looked around again as though surprised to find himself there. Then, placing his hands on his knees, he pushed himself up. "*Merci, mon ami.* I might take you up on that. But only if you promise to come to me when you're afraid."

"Deal."

"Shall we go back and join our wives?"

Now you will feel no rain / For each of you will be shelter for the other, Armand thought as he too got to his feet. It was the First Nations blessing he and Reine-Marie had had read at their wedding.

Now there is no more loneliness.

Go now to your dwelling place / To enter into the days of your togetherness.

He and Robert emerged into the sunshine of the early June day. In this village that seemed to defy time. If only, thought Armand, that were true.

And may your days be good and long upon this earth.

Clara, Ruth, Myrna, and Billy Williams sat on the terrasse with a pitcher of iced tea, and waved as Armand and the minister walked across the green. Armand waved back, then noticed Harriet sitting at another table. Wearing dark glasses. He was about to go over and find out how her head was when Fiona and Sam emerged from the bistro with three lemonades and joined her.

Sam looked at him, and in an instant Armand was back in the courtroom.

Chief Inspector Gamache remembered one thing above all else from that day. It wasn't the verdict. It wasn't even Fiona being led away.

No, what lived in the longhouse of Armand's memory was Sam Arsenault when the verdict was read.

The boy had turned to him and winked.

And he did it again now.

CHAPTER 13

~

"So," said Clara, turning to Myrna. "I have to ask. What's with the brick?"

"Yes," said Ruth. "Exactly. I was going to ask but thought it might be rude."

They stared at her.

"Don't you mean not rude enough?" asked Gabri.

He'd brought over another pitcher of iced tea and what looked like a scotch for Ruth but was actually also tea and had pulled up a chair to join them.

"I think the brick was a kindness," said Ruth.

Now their eyes widened. Shocked she even knew the word, never mind claimed to recognize an act of kindness.

"Harriet must know you're one brick short of a—"

"There it is," said Clara.

"Either that, or that you're as thick as a—"

"So," Clara asked Myrna. "What's the story?"

"Starving student?" said Gabri. "Couldn't afford anything, so she gave you—"

"A brick?" said Clara.

"Armand once gave Reine-Marie's mother a toilet plunger as a gift," said Gabri.

"But that makes sense," said Ruth.

No one followed up.

"People give strange presents," said Gabri. "I once gave Olivier a—"

"Not the doorknob story again, I'm begging you," said Myrna. "Actually, Harriet collects bricks."

This did not advance the conversation. In fact, she'd finally, after years in Three Pines, managed to silence them. And then reduce them to monosyllables.

What? Why? How?

It was possible she'd broken them.

"But why that particular brick?" asked Billy, who was not so easily broken. "She seemed to think you'd recognize it."

"I don't know. I was going to ask her last night, but she got in after we'd gone to bed and was still asleep on the sofa bed in the living room when we got up."

"We can ask now," said Ruth, turning in her seat and shouting, "Hey, you. Jackie O. What's with the brick?"

Harriet turned to look at Ruth, guessing that was directed at her, though the reference to someone named Jackie O was lost on her.

She pushed the oversized sunglasses up the bridge of her nose and tried to rise.

"It's okay," said Auntie Myrna, in a more soothing voice. "You can explain later."

But Harriet was already on her feet, lurching unsteadily from chair back to chair back, to get herself across the terrasse. Billy rose to give her his seat, but she waved him down.

She recognized the courtesy, but did not want to encourage the view that women were the weaker sex and needed to be protected and coddled. By men.

Though as she swayed slightly, fighting the hangover that was eating her will to live, she wished she'd accepted the offer. If ever there was a time for situational ethics, this was it.

"I collect bricks," she said, her voice almost a whisper.

"Right," said Gabri, as though everyone collected bricks. "But why that one?"

"It's special."

"Ahh," said Ruth. "Her lucky brick. Seems she takes after her aunt in the load department."

Rosa nodded, as ducks often did.

"No," Harriet began, then, waving Billy to his feet with a weak smile, she all but collapsed into his chair. It was a lifeboat situation. "Though I was lucky to find it. Took me months."

"I'm bored," said Ruth. "If there's a point, please get there."

"It's from the same factory that made these buildings." Harriet waved at the shops behind her. "If you look on it, there's the factory's name and a date stamp. Those are the best. The most collectible. They don't identify factories and dates anymore."

"You collect bricks?" said Clara.

"We've moved past that, keep up," said Ruth, then turned back to Harriet. "Still bored."

"You've talked about how much this place, these people, mean to you," Harriet said to her aunt. "How you found not just home here, but belonging. I wanted to give you a piece of it, to always remind you."

Myrna leaned over and hugged her niece, gripping her tightly. "Thank you," she whispered. "For knowing. It's a perfect gift."

"And it's even more important now," said Harriet, when released. "Since you're leaving."

"What?" said Clara. "What?"

"You're leaving?" said Gabri. "What?"

"Fuck, fuck, fuck," said Rosa.

"I heard you and Billy talking this morning," said Harriet. "I'm sorry. I thought the others knew."

"We haven't decided yet," said Myrna, looking at Clara's stricken face.

Clara just stared, unable to form words. Ruth was so shocked she'd dropped the bored act along with the invisibility cloak that hid her true feelings.

It was up to Gabri to ask why.

"I love the loft, but with the two of us pretty much living together, it's just too small. And then, if we ever want people, want Harriet, to stay, they have to sleep in the living room."

"They can stay at the B&B," said Gabri. "For free. You can't leave Three Pines."

"Thank you, *mon ami*, but we'd still need more room," said Myrna. "I've thought about this a lot, but only mentioned it to Billy this morning. I'll keep the bookshop, of course."

"What bookshop?" asked Ruth. "It's a library. Says it right on the sign."

"Oh, you old hag," said Gabri. "Give it up. You know perfectly well '*librairie*' is French for bookshop."

"Come on now. That's just ridiculous," said the poet. "Why call a bookstore a library?"

"There must be a place in the village you could move to," said Clara. She could feel panic welling up. "Or we could switch. You can live at my place and I can take over the loft. An artist. A loft. It's perfect."

Myrna looked at her best friend, at the desperation in her face and the potato chips in her hair. And wondered how she would ever leave.

Harriet was right. This was not just bricks and mortar. This was her beating heart. It was the first time in fifty years Myrna felt like she really belonged. As though Three Pines had set a place at the table and had been waiting for her.

And now she was considering leaving.

"You love your house—" Myrna began before Clara interrupted.

"I love you more."

"There's no rush," said Billy, placing his large, worn hands on Myrna's shoulders.

"Why don't you break into the attic space?" asked Fiona, who'd gone over to join them.

"The loft is the attic," said Gabri.

"Yes, but there's more. You can see by the roofline. I'm not an engineer for nothing. If you look over the roof at the back of the bookshop, toward the river, there's a whole other space. Not huge, but maybe big enough to convert into another bedroom or study."

"That's not right," said Gabri. "If there was more space up there to rent, Olivier would know."

Olivier owned the row of shops, and rented space out.

"Believe me," said Fiona. "There's a room up there. You should check it out."

"What's to lose?" said Clara, her face filled with glee.

"Before you get out your sledgehammer," said Myrna, "let's talk to Olivier. He must have plans of the buildings."

A quizzical look passed between Billy and Ruth. He leaned down and whispered, "Can I come by your place later?"

"Yes. You have the key."

The key was a bottle of scotch.

That afternoon Myrna, Clara, Harriet, and Fiona joined Olivier in the back room of the bistro. Where Harriet was a civil engineer, Fiona was mechanical. Between them, they figured they should be able to work it out.

"Found these when we bought the place years ago," Olivier said as he unrolled a yellowed and damp-stained scroll. "They're the original plans. As you can see, there's no hidden room up there. Besides, who'd want to build a room, then hide it?"

Harriet and Fiona were leaning over the old drawings.

"I'm sure it's there," said Fiona, shaking her head in puzzlement.

"We need to get onto the roof," said Harriet. "Then I could see for sure."

"Not now we're not," said Olivier. "It's getting late and we're almost at the dinner service. Tomorrow, if the weather holds."

"Before we climb all over the roof," said Fiona, "why don't we go up to the church."

"To pray?" asked Clara. "Who's the patron saint of wasting time?"

"No," said Fiona. "Haven't you ever noticed that from St. Thomas's you can see the roofline of the shops?"

"You can?" said Olivier. Sometimes it took a relative stranger to see things others missed.

"I wouldn't have, but the caretaker pointed it out. Said the roofs would need replacing soon and if they expected him to do it, they could go fuck themselves. When I looked, I saw another room, right here."

She placed her finger on the plans, which showed just air. "At least, I think it's there, though I agree, why would anyone hide a room?"

They decided to meet back at the bistro the next morning and head up to the church.

Word spread quickly, if not accurately, through the village.

Myrna Landers was leaving. Myrna Landers had left.

The library was being turned into a bookstore. That was from Ruth, who wanted them all to sign a petition against it.

"So," said Reine-Marie later that day as they sat in Clara's back garden enjoying a predinner drink. "I hear you're pregnant."

"Twins," said Myrna, with a laugh. "Actually, I started that rumor myself, to show how ridiculous the other ones are."

"Should warn Gabri," said Clara. "He's already planning the shower."

"Then you and Billy aren't leaving?" There was no hiding the hope in Reine-Marie's voice.

"Well, not right away. But we are looking for a bigger place, if you hear of one."

"For the babies," said Clara, and Armand laughed. Though like everyone else, he found the idea of Myrna leaving Three Pines, even if she kept the bookshop, upsetting.

Robert and Sylvie Mongeau arrived just as they were moving inside. It was getting chilly.

"We only stopped by for a quick drink," said Sylvie.

She was looking tired as they walked through the kitchen, which smelled of garlic and basil from the linguine primavera. They settled in the living room.

"Is the rumor true?" Robert asked.

"Which one?" Myrna asked.

"That you and Billy are moving to Australia to start a kangaroo rescue," said Sylvie.

"Because you're running an illegal bookstore and tattoo parlor out of the back of the library and got caught," said Robert. "Ruth told us."

"Well, that is true," said Myrna, laughing. "But there might be another option besides the kangaroo plan, brilliant as that is. Fiona says there's an attic room we might be able to break into. That might solve the problem."

"Fiona says that?" asked Armand. "How would she know?"

"Your caretaker told her," Myrna said to Robert.

"Claude? But how in the world would he know?" asked the minister. Myrna explained.

"What does Olivier say?" asked Reine-Marie.

"He knows nothing about it," said Clara. "We saw the plans of the building, and they don't show the space, but we're going up to the church tomorrow to see."

"Huh," said Sylvie. "Now why would someone hide a room?"

It seemed the question of the moment.

Billy placed the letter on the preformed plastic table in Ruth's kitchen and moved his chair a few inches away from Rosa, who was in her bed beside the stove, snoring or snorting.

He tried to remember if ducks got rabies.

Ruth opened the envelope, withdrew the letter, and read it again. He'd brought it to her a few weeks earlier, since Ruth collected stories about the history of Three Pines.

The letter was so vague, she'd shown little interest then. She showed much more now.

"What do you think?" she said, laying her hand on top of it.

"I think he might be talking about the room above the bookstore, the one Fiona said is there."

"But the room isn't on Olivier's plans?" When Billy shook his head, Ruth stared down at the yellowed paper. "I don't believe it. He doesn't even say which place in Three Pines he was working on. Could be any of our homes, and with all the renovations in the past hundred years, if it ever did exist, it must've been uncovered by now. Besides, why would someone brick up a room?"

"I don't know, but he obviously didn't like doing it." That was an understatement. There was a sense of dread in the letter. It reeked of it. "I knew he was a stonemason, most of my family were back then, but obviously at some point he turned to bricks."

Better, thought Ruth, than turning to stone. But for once she left something unsaid.

"The letter is dated 1862. That's more than a hundred and fifty years ago."

"It's also the same as the date on the brick Harriet gave Myrna."

"Come on," said Sam. "They'll never know."

"I've heard that before," said Fiona. "Monsieur Gamache specifically told me you're not allowed in their house."

"Jesus fucking Christ. What's wrong with the guy? What did I ever do to him?"

Fiona had no answer to that.

"Well, fuck him," said Sam. "Come on. A quick look around."

She looked at his lopsided grin. The puppy dog eyes. Not for the first time, she wondered how, after all he'd done, she could still love him. But she did.

How she could forgive him. But she had. As he'd forgiven her. At least, she thought so.

He was all the family she had. And while Reine-Marie and Armand had become a sort of family substitute, it wasn't the same thing. She and Sam were not just connected, they were bound in ways that went beyond blood.

"Look, let's just get some food and hang out here." She glanced around the B&B.

He shifted in his seat. "I'm bored."

Fiona said nothing. She knew what could happen when Sam got bored.

"Look," he said. "You owe him nothing. He arrested us. We were just kids and he arrested us. He fucked up our lives."

"We fucked them up. He just found out. And he never arrested you."

Sam stared at her, that penetrating gaze she knew so well.

He knew what she was really like.

And she knew what he was really like.

"Okay," she said. "Come on."

CHAPTER 14

———

"C ome on," said Fiona. "Enough, Sam. They'll be home soon. We have to get out."

But Sam was wandering around the Gamaches' living room as though he owned it, picking up objects and putting them back slightly askew. Moving furniture just a few inches this way or that, Fiona following behind, putting everything back the way it was.

The dogs, used to Fiona, hadn't protested when she'd let herself and Sam in.

He was filming as he went along, opening drawers and cupboards. Examining books and mementos and family photographs. Picking one up, he recognized Jean-Guy Beauvoir. Older now, with two children. But unmistakable. He'd seen him at the graduation, of course, the first time they'd met in years.

Sam took a photo of that photo, then replaced it. But not quite as he'd found it.

He scanned the books on the shelves, then went into the study and sat at the computer. Tapping the keyboard, he woke it up. It was locked, of course, but he stared at the screen saver photo of the four grandchildren.

"Sam, enough." Fiona stood at the threshold to the study.

But it was not enough.

He went upstairs while she returned to the kitchen, where she had a good view of Clara's home. All was quiet. But if they returned and discovered what she'd done, the whole thing could be blown. She could probably explain and Madame Gamache might believe it, but she was far from sure Monsieur Gamache would.

A few minutes later she found Sam lying on Armand and Reine-Marie's bed.

"Oh, shit. Get off. They'll know someone's been here."

But he continued to lie there. "Which side is his, do you think? I think this one. He's reading something called *What Might Have Been*. It's alternative history. Looks interesting."

He put the book down, then picked it up again and moved the bookmark. Then he went into the bathroom and sprayed some cologne onto himself.

"Mmmm," he said. "Sandalwood. Nice."

"Oh, God," she moaned, and opened the window to air out the scent. With Sam she always felt like the character in the circus cartoon, cleaning up the shit.

Before leaving, he found the door into the basement.

"*Merde*," said Fiona, her voice rising. "They're coming."

"Is that where it is?" he asked, pointing down into the darkness. "The room you told me about?"

She hustled him to the French doors from the living room onto the back patio. "You've got to go."

A minute later the front door opened.

"We're home," called Reine-Marie, in a singsong voice.

"I'll take the dogs out," said Armand.

"No, let me," said Fiona.

"It's all right. I can."

"Please. I'd like the air."

He stepped aside, though he stood at the open door and watched, wondering why she'd been so insistent.

Fiona tossed the ratty old tennis ball on the village green and watched Henri race and Fred lumber after it. Out of the corner of her eye, she saw Sam come around the B&B. From the side garden. A direct line from the Gamache home.

"May I join you?"

Fiona started and realized Monsieur Gamache was walking across the road toward her.

"Of course."

Did he notice? Does he know? She couldn't help but look toward the B&B, but there was no sign of Sam.

"I heard about the hidden room in Myrna's loft," he said, and noticed her relax, though he didn't know why she'd been stressed. "You might've solved a problem."

"Might not be there," she said, throwing the ball again. "But I thought I should mention it, in case."

They strolled along through the dusk. The sun set late as they approached the summer solstice, but when it did, a chill set in.

"Do you know what you'll do with your degree?" he asked.

"Well, it's a little difficult, but I'm sure I'll find something. I have some nibbles. Can I run them by you?"

"Absolutely."

It was Monsieur Gamache who'd encouraged her to consider engineering. She'd never heard of the profession and thought, understandably, it had something to do with trains.

But when he explained and took books to her in prison on the subject, she got very excited. It was as though her world suddenly made sense. Those intricate models in Sam's room, which Chief Inspector Gamache thought the boy had made, had actually been put together by Fiona and given to her brother.

Once Monsieur Gamache realized his mistake, he began to take the girl models and puzzles of increasing difficulty and intricacy.

Finally, during one of his visits to the prison, Fiona had asked him about the École Polytechnique and if she could take university courses remotely. He'd used his connections with the Chancellor to advocate for her. And now, many years later, here she was. A graduate mechanical engineer.

While the road ahead for Fiona was far from clear, at least there was one. And he was fairly confident the young woman could pull it together.

Her brother was a different story. Still, he'd be gone in a few days,

Fiona would move into the monitored halfway house in Montréal, and life in Three Pines would return to normal.

But once again, he was wrong.

Later that night while brushing his teeth, Armand picked up the very slight scent of his cologne, though he hadn't put any on that day.

When he went to get into bed, he noticed the slight indent of a head on his pillow. It was odd, but sometimes Henri snuck onto their bed when they were out.

Opening his book, Armand froze, all his senses tingling.

The bookmark had been moved.

Had it been just that, he'd have thought it must've dropped on the floor and the bookmark fallen out. And someone, probably Reine-Marie, had slipped it back in the wrong place.

But it was not just that. There was also the cologne and the pillow.

He got out of bed, careful not to disturb Reine-Marie, who was already asleep.

"Stay here," he whispered to Henri and Gracie, who'd lifted their heads. Fred was mostly deaf now and would sleep through anything except the slight rustle of the kibble bag.

Putting on his dressing gown, Armand first searched the upstairs rooms for an intruder. He paused at Fiona's room, then moved on. He was pretty sure he knew who had been there. And might still be.

Moving downstairs, he double-checked that the front door was locked, then picked up the baseball bat that was leaning against the doorjamb as he searched the rest of the main floor.

Methodical, stealthy, hyperalert. His trained senses took in everything.

In the study he noticed other subtle signs. The desk chair had been turned around and some items had been moved. Slightly.

He touched the keyboard and the computer sprang to life, showing the screen saver.

Returning to the living room, he stood quietly. Something was different. Something was wrong. And then he saw it.

One of the photographs had been turned around so that it faced away from the room. He picked it up.

The framed picture was of the family at Christmas. He, Reine-Marie, and Stephen were holding the children. Daniel, Annie, and their spouses were standing behind them. Somehow Ruth had managed to photobomb them, peeking in from the side of the picture.

Everyone was smiling. Laughing. The Christmas tree, festooned with strings of tinsel and Christmas lights and baubles, was in the background.

He stared at the photograph and fought to keep his head above this outrage, even as it threatened to overwhelm him.

He had no doubt that it was a deliberate message. And he knew who'd sent it.

Armand took three deep breaths, and when he felt his heart return to normal, he turned to the one place he hadn't yet searched.

Gripping the baseball bat, he opened the door to the basement and turned on the lights. There were two rooms down there, the largest of which had a dirt floor and was used for storage. Shelves of preserves lined one wall. A large chest sat on a pallet. He opened it and saw the winter blankets and smelled the cedar. There was a small pile of bricks on the dirt floor. He'd meant to get rid of them. Maybe, he thought, he should offer them to Harriet.

Luggage and boxes with Christmas ornaments sat on wooden pallets against the far wall. Firewood was carefully stacked up for the winter.

Finally, he stood in front of the second room. Its closed door was different from any other in the house. This was of solid metal and not just locked but bolted.

He punched in the code and stepped inside.

Turning on the overhead lights, he looked at the bank of special fireproof file cabinets, essentially vaults. Near impossible for anyone, even a skilled safecracker, to break into.

The floor of this room was concrete. Armand had had it poured just before the special cabinets had been installed.

Against one wall there was a desk, a reading lamp. A chair. It was the sort of room a cloistered monk from the Middle Ages would have found sparse.

These were Armand's archives. The notes, interviews, papers, photographs, testimony. Evidence from cases, solved and unsolved.

These were his own files, containing evidence gathered but unused. All the secrets people had told him in the course of his investigations. All the notes from his subsequent private investigations, done on his own time.

He kept them here, safe under lock and key.

Armand stood in the middle of the room and looked around. He knew that no one had been in there. Still, he paused a moment. To be sure.

As he left, relocking the door behind him, something on the ground caught his eye. Thinking it was the tab of a soft drink can, he stooped to pick it up.

Brushing off the dirt, he saw that it was a ring. Thin, iron, with worn facets where the edge had been pounded.

It was an engineer's ring.

He stood there very quietly, then heard a sound behind him. Turning quickly and raising the bat, he saw it was Fred. The old dog had followed him down. He was standing in front of the shelf with the large bag of dog food, his tail slowly swishing from side to side.

Armand placed the ring in his dressing gown pocket, leaned the bat against the cinder block wall, and picked Fred up in both arms. He knew that while Fred could make it down the stairs, he could not make it back up.

After rechecking the windows and doors, he went back to bed. Picking up his book, he read for a while, then turned off the light and fell asleep, wondering what if . . .

CHAPTER 15

"Well," said Olivier. "I'll be damned."

A small delegation stood on the landing just outside the church and stared across the village to the rooflines of the interconnected shops below. Monsieur Béliveau's General Store, Sarah's Boulangerie, the bistro, and finally the bookstore.

A very light rain had started falling, more like a fine mist. Low clouds shrouded the hills, surrounding and enclosing the village.

"You were right," said Myrna, looking at Fiona.

A roof, just visible, was jutting out at right angles from Myrna's loft.

"How could we not have seen it before?" asked Clara.

"We weren't looking," said Myrna.

"Well, we would have found it eventually," said Gabri. "As soon as we fixed the roof."

"In about twenty years," said Billy.

"Can I get my sledgehammer now?" Clara asked Olivier.

"You might want to wait." But it wasn't Olivier who'd spoken. It was Billy.

"What's wrong?" asked Myrna.

"What's wrong, Armand?" asked Reine-Marie.

They were sitting in their kitchen. He'd waited for Fiona to leave before bringing out the ring and placing it on the table. And then he told Reine-Marie what had happened the night before.

When he'd finished, she picked the ring up, turning it over and around. "An engineer's ring, for sure. It's pretty worn. Old. Looks to me like it might've been there for a while."

She replaced it on the table.

"True. Fiona still has her ring, I checked. And I'll check out Harriet, just to be sure. The ring aside, someone was here last night."

"You think it was Sam, don't you."

"Who else could it have been?"

"Fiona." She raised her hand slightly, to indicate she had more to say, but needed a moment. Which he gave her. "It's possible none of this is threatening. She might've just been curious and bored. Wandering around the house, picking things up. Snooping more than spying."

She studied him, holding his eyes.

"It's possible," he admitted.

Reine-Marie admired Fiona's spirit, but, if she was honest, she was never completely comfortable with the young woman. Never totally trusted her.

In fact, neither Reine-Marie nor Jean-Guy could understand Armand's support for Fiona and his enmity bordering on hostility toward Sam.

Jean-Guy had even, albeit at Armand's suggestion, kept in touch with Sam for a few years after the trial, eventually losing track of him in his late teens.

But Armand had not lost track. He'd kept a close eye on Sam, as he'd grown from a child, to a teen, to a young man. Sam had not committed another crime. Not that Armand could see. Though crimes had been committed around him.

Assaults. B&Es. There was a murder in Saskatoon, in the building where Sam worked as a janitor. Sam had not been implicated.

Armand had flown out and gone over the evidence. Making sure.

Two other murders happened in other parts of Canada where Sam lived. It was, Armand knew, rare for anyone to have one murder in their life, never mind a series of them.

A serial.

But he never could connect Sam Arsenault to any of them.

As for Fiona, Reine-Marie had agreed to join him in sponsoring her parole. But there was always a membrane, a very thin barrier Reine-Marie had put up between herself and the young woman. The one thing she'd said to Armand when he'd first broached the idea of Fiona's parole was that she was not to be around the grandchildren.

Armand had no trouble agreeing to that.

"Why would Sam want to snoop around our house?" Reine-Marie now asked.

"I don't know," Armand admitted. "But someone did. And they didn't just snoop. They turned the family photo around. They moved items. They sprayed cologne. They lay on our bed."

If it sounded to Reine-Marie like the Three Bears, she did not say anything. But for the first time, after reading that story to their children and now the grandchildren countless times, she stopped to think how frightened the three bears must have been.

"There was no effort to hide it," Armand was saying. "In fact, whoever was here wanted us to see. To know. There was an intimacy about what they did. Can you see Fiona lying on our bed? Picking up my book and moving the bookmark?"

"No, but I can't see Sam doing it either. You think there's more to it, don't you? You think it was a deliberate message."

He nodded.

"To say what?" she asked.

"I don't know. I suspect it's just a mind game. Nothing sinister."

He looked down at the ring on the old pine table, then picked it up. "But I am just going to make a call."

Going into his study, he called Nathalie Provost. After brief pleasantries she asked what he wanted.

"I've found an engineer's ring in our basement. It looks old. Can you tell me something about them?"

"Well, I think you know that they were originally made from the metal remains of the first Québec Bridge. It collapsed in 1907, killing eighty-six workers. It was a catastrophic failure of engineering. The rings were made to remind engineers of that disaster, and the consequences of what they, what we, do."

"I don't see a name inside," he said, holding it up to the light. "Is there any way of knowing whose it is, or was?"

"I don't really know. I'll have to check. The rings are supposed to be returned to the Société when the person retires or dies, so no name would be engraved. They're given out over and over again. A sort of thread that connects us to each other."

She looked down at her own. Few were so hard-won.

"If you can make some inquiries, I'd appreciate it."

"Consider it done."

"*Merci*," he said and hung up just as there was a shout from the living room.

"*Bonjour?*" It was Clara. "You two home?"

"I'm in here," Reine-Marie called from the kitchen.

Clara appeared at the door and Armand arrived right behind her.

"Can you come to the bistro?" Clara asked. "Billy wants to show us something. Something to do with the hidden room."

"It's there?" asked Reine-Marie.

"Looks like it. Billy's gone to get Ruth to bring her along too."

"Why Ruth?"

"Oh, how often have we asked that question," said Clara.

"So, Billy," said Olivier when they'd all assembled in the bistro. "What's this all about?"

They were sitting around the huge fieldstone hearth. The fire had been lit, as much for comfort on the gray morning as warmth, and Gabri had brought over rich cafés au lait and lemon loaf.

Armand glanced at Harriet's hand, where a freshly polished engineer's ring sat snug on the little finger of her right hand. A tiny memento of a huge tragedy.

He shifted his focus to Fiona. He'd suggested to Reine-Marie that they say nothing about the night before. Better to pretend they hadn't noticed anything and see what happened next. If anything.

It was possible, probable, that it was done to provoke, and when there was no reaction, Sam, or whoever, would tire of the game.

Billy put a letter on the coffee table. "I got this in the mail a couple of months ago."

"Jesus," said Gabri. "Look at the date. It took Canada Post a hundred and fifty years to deliver it?"

"No," said Billy, with a small laugh. "Someone must've found it. It was sent to my old family home, and the woman who lives there now forwarded it to me."

They passed it around. When it came to Armand, he put on his glasses and read it through. Twice. Then passed it along.

Only when it returned to Billy did Armand ask, "Who's Pierre Stone?"

"My great-great-grandfather. Might even be another 'great' in there," said Billy.

"I wouldn't count on it," said Ruth.

The fact that "*pierre*" was French for stone, making the letter writer's name essentially Stone Stone, or Pierre Pierre, surprised no one coming from a family with a Billy Williams.

Besides, centuries ago, people were often identified by their trade. In this case, a stonemason.

"The date on the letter is 1862," said Myrna. "The same as the brick you gave me."

"Yes," said Harriet. "Do you think he was talking about this place? That room?"

Monsieur Stone was writing to a woman, perhaps his wife or fiancée, maybe a sister. He described having to learn bricklaying in order to get a job. Fewer and fewer places were made with stone, now that bricks were being manufactured.

It was a glimpse into a changing world, and the sadness a skilled craftsman felt having to give up that craft. For a man named Pierre Stone, switching to bricklaying was clearly painful.

But the emotion in the letter went far beyond that.

The stonemason had, for the sake of his livelihood, accepted a job in a village he'd never heard of, though he'd lived in the area all his life. It was called Three Pines.

The job was small, but he was desperate. He'd accepted it, but with growing unease.

He did not meet his employer. They only communicated through written instructions, and part of the payment was left at a public house in the nearby village of Sweetsburg.

He was to build a wall. Just that. It would seal off an attic room in a newly made building. The materials and tools were already on-site in the attic. He was to arrive after dark and finish the job in one night, leaving before dawn. He was not, under any circumstances, to go into the room.

Just seal it off and leave.

Talk to no one. Take his own food and drink. Leave no evidence behind.

Pierre Stone wrote that he'd been told never to visit the village again. To forget it even existed. He regretted taking the commission but couldn't see any way out now. Besides, he needed the money. He ended the letter wondering what else he'd do for money. For family.

"'The Cask of Amontillado,'" said Myrna, quietly. Saying what they were all thinking. Well, almost all.

"What?" said Harriet and Gabri at the same time.

"An Edgar Allan Poe story," said Ruth.

Seeing Gabri's eyes widen in dread, Olivier said, "It's about happy puppies."

"Yeah," said Myrna. "Like 'The Raven' is about happy birds."

"What do you think?" Billy asked.

Armand's eyes narrowed as he recalled "The Cask of Amontillado." He stared into the fire for a few moments, then looked over his left shoulder toward the door that connected the bistro to the bookstore.

All eyes followed.

"You say you think the room is there?" he finally said.

"Yes," said Harriet. "We could see it from up at the church. The roofline."

"How do you feel about breaking through that wall?" Armand asked Olivier.

"Sure. I'm as curious as anyone else."

Olivier kept his tone light, but Gabri heard the strain. While he didn't know what the "Amontillado" thing meant, Gabri was pretty sure whatever was up there wasn't happy puppies.

While Billy got his tools, Olivier took the plans over to the long wooden bar of the bistro and unrolled them, using the candy jars to hold down the corners.

"Looks like the room would be here," said Harriet, placing her finger on one of the walls in her aunt's loft. "You agree?"

Fiona leaned in and nodded.

Olivier had taken photographs when they were at the church, and he brought one up on his phone. They gathered around. Now that they could see it, it seemed so obvious. And yet, for a hundred and sixty years, that room had remained hidden.

"The caretaker said we would've found it eventually," said Myrna. "Once you replace the roof."

"What? There's no—" began Olivier.

"Breathe, honey," said Gabri. "You don't have to do it tomorrow."

"Roof's fine," he muttered as they climbed up to Myrna's loft.

Once there, they lined up, staring at where the room would be, should be. Probably was.

"Still a bit of a risk," said Myrna. "We might knock a hole right through into thin air."

"Not much of a risk," said Billy. "I can chisel out one brick, and look."

"What's the fun in that?" asked Ruth. Though it seemed this cavalier attitude was a pretense. She was, in fact, pretty tense.

At a signal from Olivier, Billy began to chip away mortar that his great-great-great-grandfather had put in place one very long night, a hundred and sixty years earlier.

Reine-Marie, at Armand's quiet request, had brought out her phone and was videoing it.

Once the brick was loose, Billy wiggled it out of the wall and handed it to Fiona, who gave it to Harriet. Who examined it.

"Exactly the same as your brick, Auntie Myrna."

"May I?" asked Armand, and Billy stepped aside.

He shone the flashlight on his phone through the small opening. By instinct he also sniffed the air. Not that he expected to smell anything. If it had really been sealed up for more than a century and a half, anything organic would have fallen to dust. Anything, or anyone.

As a homicide investigator, his mind naturally went there. Though it seemed unlikely.

He squinted and peered, but his light only illuminated motes of dust hanging in the air. Undisturbed for more than a century. But that was about to change.

As he went to step back, his light caught something. It looked like a face. And then it was gone. It so surprised him, he leaned away with a start.

"What is it?" Myrna's voice became unnaturally high.

"I think there's something in there, but I can't see clearly." He did not say "someone."

"Oh shit, oh shit, oh shit," said Gabri, his eyes wide.

He'd looked up "The Cask of Amontillado." It was the story of some guy who'd walled up a rival and left him there to die. Not a puppy in sight.

Armand looked at Olivier, who nodded to Billy, who swung his sledgehammer.

CHAPTER 16

⁓

The wall came down. Though it took more swings from Billy's sledgehammer than expected.

"Your ancestor did a good job," said Olivier, as Billy wiped the sweat from his face.

"Looks like he wanted to make sure whatever was in there stayed in there," said Ruth.

Armand had gone home briefly, with instructions to those gathered not to go into the room until he returned.

"I think we can promise that," said Clara.

He returned a few minutes later, holding a worn satchel. His scene-of-crime kit, Reine-Marie knew, though she suspected the others did not. At least, she hoped they didn't.

"Can you do the rest by hand?" Armand asked when the opening was almost big enough to climb through.

Billy put down the sledgehammer and pulled at the loosened bricks.

They crowded around the opening, craning and jostling for position, trying to see in. But it was still too dark to make anything out.

"I think it might be better if you stepped back." Armand's voice was calm, his tone pleasant, as though suggesting they might want to wait for the next bus.

They stepped back.

"This enough?" asked Billy, dragging his sleeve across his forehead again and leaving a streak of dirt.

"*Parfait.*"

Armand had put on latex gloves and slung the satchel over his shoulder. Where some might carry a briefcase to work, Chief Inspector Gamache carried the tools of his trade. Gloves. Evidence bags. Fingerprint kits. Swabs. Tweezers.

"Stay here." Though it really didn't need to be said.

Holding his phone in front of him, he pressed record and stepped over the low brick threshold and into the room.

Then stopped. There in front of him were bright eyes staring back.

He was prepared, having seen this a few minutes earlier, but still he felt his heart leap in his chest.

"What is it?" Reine-Marie asked from the other side. "What do you see?"

There was silence. It lasted just a second, but seemed to go on forever before he spoke.

"It's a painting. Huge."

He shone the light over it, taking in the detail, though there was so much of it, the only impression he was left with was one of a certain chaos. As though someone had thrown all their possessions at a canvas and they stuck. Including two children.

He stared at them for a moment. One, the little girl, looked familiar, and he wondered if he'd seen this painting, or a reproduction of it in a book, before.

"Can we come in now?" Olivier asked.

"In a moment."

After staring at the extraordinary work for a few moments, he moved on, deeper into the hidden room.

"You okay?" Reine-Marie asked, leaning toward the hole.

"Just fine," said Armand, and he heard Ruth chuckle and say something he couldn't hear but could imagine.

"What do you see?" Myrna asked.

Armand was walking the perimeter of the room, ducking his head so as not to hit the eaves and shining the light over the walls, the floor, the ceiling. Into the corners. The room was small, about twelve feet by twelve feet, with wide plank wooden floors, and exposed beams in the ceiling.

There was no sign of life. Or death.

"Nothing alarming."

His eyes fell on an assortment of items behind the painting. It looked like a small pile of junk, like most attics had. He moved on. His only interest was making sure the evidence kit could stay on his shoulder.

Finally he said, "It's okay. You can come in."

They stepped through, flashlights bobbing. And then the lights coalesced.

"Holy shit," whispered Olivier.

The attic room seemed packed, jam-packed with conch shells and sculptures, clocks and chairs and musical instruments. And faces, people.

The friends stared, slack-jawed.

"Holy shit," said Myrna.

It took a moment, but a long one, to realize what they were staring at.

The dots of their phone flashlights played over the painting, picking up details but not the entirety.

Billy had brought up construction lights, and now, with a flick of a switch, the place was bathed in blinding light.

And then the whole painting burst out at them.

There was a little girl and an adolescent boy dressed in a fashion from hundreds of years earlier. They sat at a table that was piled full of items. All jumbled together. It looked not so much like a painting as a portal into another time. Another world.

Leaving them to marvel, Armand walked around the other side of the painting to examine the things back there. An old leather-bound book. A bronze sculpture of an elephant. A jigsaw puzzle. A teddy bear.

"The sorts of things people throw into attics, when they don't know what else to do with them," said Reine-Marie, joining her husband. "I see it all the time."

Now retired as Chief Archivist at the National Library and Archives of Québec, Reine-Marie had decided to use her skills to help people sort through their own, often inherited collections.

"Except," she said, "most are not walled up."

Armand nodded.

Reine-Marie was about to pick up the book when she and Armand heard Clara's voice from the other side of the painting.

"Holy shit. It's A World of Curiosities."

"It is that," agreed Ruth.

"No, it's what the painting's called."

Armand came around from the back of it. "You recognize it?"

"It's *The Paston Treasure*."

"Now," said Olivier. "Did you say 'treasure'?"

They'd gone back to Myrna's living room, though every now and then one of them would get up and wander over to the gaping hole in her wall and stare in, muttering, "Holy shit."

"*The Paston Treasure*," agreed Clara. "Yes."

"And is it worth anything?" asked Gabri, casually.

"It's priceless," said Clara. "Except that it's in a museum in Norfolk. In the UK."

"Well, what's that then?" asked Ruth, slopping scotch out of her glass as she gestured toward the hole. This time it really was scotch.

"A reproduction," said Clara. "Maybe a study the artist made before working on the final painting."

"Here?" said Harriet. "Why's it here? Was he a Québec artist? I don't understand."

"Got it," said Myrna, and brought over her laptop.

She'd looked up *The Paston Treasure*. They crowded around, pushing and shoving each other for a better view. Harriet and Fiona had brought it up on their phones. The image was too small to get a sense of the detail, but they could read the text.

"Says here it was painted in about 1670," said Fiona. "Commissioned by one of the Pastons."

"Big surprise," muttered Ruth. "It's called *The Paston Treasure*."

"They lived in Norfolk, in England," said Fiona, continuing to read the internet page. "No one knows who the artist was."

Ruth walked over to the hole. "Ours isn't signed either."

"Clara's right," said Myrna. "It was nicknamed A World of Curiosities."

"Looks like a world of junk to me," said Ruth.

And it did. To the modern eye. It was a pile of stuff most people wouldn't buy in a garage sale nowadays.

Reine-Marie joined the old poet. "Ahhh, but in the mid-1600s? This would've been amazing. Most people rarely got more than a couple of miles from their homes. They'd see the same things every day. Cows, pigs, sheep. Imagine coming face-to-face with a parrot? A monkey? Look, there's a lobster. Almost no one in England had ever seen those things. These would be exotic, amazing. Maybe even frightening. Evidence that there were mysteries beyond the known world. Yes, this collection would be remarkable. Treasures."

"There's a young Black man," said Myrna, joining them. The revulsion apparent in her voice. "Barely more than a boy. Just part of a collection."

She looked at her niece. The young man in the painting could be their ancestor.

"Yes." Reine-Marie sighed, shaking her head.

"Says here that there were at least two hundred items in the Paston collection," said Fiona, continuing to read the page. "Brought back from around the world by explorers."

"And slave traders," said Myrna.

She wanted to look away in disgust, but found herself drawn back to the painting. There was something about it. The young man, yes. But something else.

"It's incredible," said Clara. "I'd heard about the painting, but have never seen it."

"Even if it is a copy or an early study," said Harriet, "what's it doing here in your loft, Auntie Myrna?"

"More to the point," said Ruth, "why was it walled up?"

"May I see that letter again?" Armand asked. When Billy handed it over, Armand reread it, examining it more closely. "There's Monsieur Stone's return address on the envelope—"

"It's my family home, though we no longer live there," said Billy.

"—but we can't see who he sent it to. Someplace in Québec City, but the address itself is smudged. All we have is the salutation. *My dear Clémence*. But no last name."

"Does it matter?" Olivier asked.

"It would be interesting to know if Monsieur Stone wrote any more letters to this Clémence," said Reine-Marie, the archivist kicking in. "Maybe with more explanation."

"But he never spoke to his employer or looked into the room," said Gabri. "So there's not much more he could say."

"We don't know that," said Armand. "We know the instructions Pierre was given, but not what he actually did."

"He might've peeked," said Clara. "Wouldn't most people?"

"I always do," agreed Gabri.

"But all he'd see is what we see," said Olivier. "So any letter wouldn't really tell us anything we don't already know."

"Not true," said Armand. "It might tell us why those things had to be walled up and hidden. You say you received this a few weeks ago," he said to Billy. "How?"

"Through the mail."

"Yes, but how did it find you? Monsieur Stone's return address is on his letter, not yours."

"The new owners of the family home found it and forwarded it to me."

He'd said "new" owners, but Myrna knew they'd lived there now for more than ten years. But they would always, in Billy's mind, be new.

It was the home Pierre Stone himself built. It had been in the family for generations. Billy's parents had sold the place when it got beyond them.

Times change. You had to roll with it. But it was impossible to roll without getting bruised.

Armand, now standing by the hole in the wall, looked up from the letter and at the painting. It seemed stuck in time. But it actually was a testament to a changing world. A larger, more wonderous, in many ways more wicked world. One where lobsters existed. And so did the slave trade.

"I guess someone found the letter and decided to send it back," said Billy. "All they had was the old address."

"It's curious. I wonder why," said Armand.

"Why what?" asked Myrna.

"Why send it back to an address obviously more than a century and a half old?"

"Why not?" said Clara. "Old documents pop up all the time, right?"

"True," said Reine-Marie. "The descendants of this Clémence must've been clearing out an old home and came across it."

"It's strange," said Gabri. "Wouldn't you just toss it out? Why go through the trouble of mailing back some letter between two long-dead people you'd never heard of? To an address that's more than a hundred years old?"

"I agree with Monsieur Gamache," said Fiona. "It doesn't make sense."

"I didn't say it didn't make sense," said Armand, looking at her.

He'd tried not to make eye contact with Fiona all day. He was used to hiding things from suspects. But what she'd done wasn't criminal, it was personal. In letting Sam into their home, Fiona had betrayed his trust.

He didn't want her to see that he knew. And he didn't want her to see his hurt.

But as he looked at her now, all he saw was the young woman who'd worked so hard to put her life back together.

"I just said I was curious." Armand held her eyes for a moment before turning to Billy. "When your family sold the house, were there old letters and things you had to go through?"

"I don't know," said Billy. "My sisters and I offered to help our parents sort through things, but they preferred to do it themselves. I think they threw a lot away, and anything else went to charity jumble sales."

"What's bothering you, Armand?" Reine-Marie asked.

He shook his head. "It just seems"—he looked at Fiona and smiled—"curious."

She smiled back.

Harriet had wandered away from the dissection of an old letter, by old people, and was looking at the painting.

"Have you noticed that this isn't exactly *The Paston Treasure*? At least, not the one we see online."

"Well, we already know that," said Ruth. "The real one's someplace in England. This's just a copy."

"That's not what I mean," said Harriet. "Come see. It's made to look like the other one, but it's different. Look."

Reine-Marie leaned closer, then pulled back as though given an electric jolt. "Is the girl in the painting wearing—"

"A digital watch," said Harriet.

"You're kidding," said Olivier. He and the others crowded around.

Now that they examined it more closely, they could see other anomalies. Oddities.

The boy held a small model airplane. A straight-back chair was upholstered in a William Morris print.

What had looked like a rolled-up scroll was actually a tourist poster. They could just make out the lettering. It featured the *Manneken Pis* and the Atomium, in Brussels. Armand knew that because he'd been there.

Something stirred in him. Something deep and dark and disconcerting.

This painting was strange, there was no denying that. How did it get here? Why reimagine *The Paston Treasure*? And if the room had been bricked up more than a century ago, how did these modern elements get into the painting?

And why?

Why?

Why?

And who?

Yes, it was definitely strange, but not necessarily alarming.

So why was he alarmed?

"Oh, my God." Reine-Marie's voice came from the other side of the painting.

"What?" said Armand, hurrying around. "What's wrong?"

She was holding, grasping, the dust-covered book and looking down at it. Then she raised her eyes to his.

"Look." She held it out.

"What is it?"

"It's a grimoire."

And now his alarm spiked.

CHAPTER 17

S o what's a grim . . . ," Clara began. "A grimmmm—" she continued
in the hopes it would come to her.

"Grimoire." Reine-Marie turned to Myrna. "Do you know it?"

"Never heard of it."

While Olivier had had to go back down to the bistro for the lunch
service, and Fiona had left to meet Sam, the rest had returned to
Myrna's living room.

No one really wanted to move far from the newly discovered room
and its collection of increasingly odd oddities.

Reine-Marie clasped the book on her lap, reluctant to give up this
long-searched-for treasure.

Ruth hadn't taken her eyes off the book since it was found. It was
difficult to tell if the elderly woman was looking at it or watching it.

"You know what it is," said Reine-Marie.

Ruth nodded, but remained uncharacteristically quiet, her eyes
fixed on the leather cover. It was plain, simple, without design or writing, though it was scorched.

There was no title. Nothing to identify it. And for good reason.

The book dated from the 1600s, and anyone found to be in possession of a grimoire then would almost certainly have been burned
at the stake. In fact, it looked like an effort had been made to do just
that.

"It's a book of spells," explained Reine-Marie. "Incantations. Recipes for elixirs. Instructions on how to call up spirits."

"Demons?" asked Harriet.

Gabri made a hissing sound, to shut her up. In case the very word would summon them.

Reine-Marie was about to answer when Ruth cut in: "No. Well, not necessarily." She lifted her eyes from the book to Reine-Marie. "Have you looked inside?"

"Just to make sure it's the real thing."

"And?"

"It is."

Ruth exhaled and shook her head. "So, it's true then."

As much as Armand wanted to stay and listen, there were other questions he had.

He took Billy aside and said, "Can we talk?"

"*Oui*. Where?"

A few minutes later they were in the Gamaches' kitchen. Armand had cut slices from a fresh miche from Sarah's Boulangerie, and made egg salad and tomato sandwiches, while Billy poured them each a glass of lemonade.

"Pink?" he asked, raising it.

It was a shade unknown in nature.

"The girls," said Armand.

"Your granddaughters haven't been down for a while," said Billy, accepting the sandwich and sitting at the old pine table.

"Okay," said Armand. "I can't lie. Reine-Marie likes it."

It was so clear that it was actually Armand who liked the pink lemonade that Billy laughed.

He took a large bite of the sandwich, the bread soft and chewy and the crust crisp. The egg salad had an unexpected hint of curry.

"What do you know about that room?" Armand asked.

Billy raised his brows. "Nothing. Why do you think I would?"

"Because of the letter."

"Pierre Stone knew about the room," said Billy. "But I didn't. You think if I did I wouldn't have broken through years ago? And certainly when Myrna and I started living together?"

Armand believed him. He saw no reason for Billy Williams to lie.

Though the room had been bricked up for a hundred and sixty years, the items hadn't been there for that long. That was obvious.

Someone had gone through a great deal of trouble to place those items there. And that same someone, Armand was sure, wanted them to be found.

"How long ago did you say you got that letter?"

"Must be five weeks. I have the envelope at home. I can show you."

"Yes, I'd like to see it."

"What're you thinking, Armand?"

"I'm more feeling than thinking."

Billy smiled. "And what are you feeling?"

"That this isn't just a joke. Someone who goes through this much trouble has been planning it for a while. That painting must've taken a long time to do. That book, the grimoire? Reine-Marie has been looking for it for years, but it shows up here?"

Was it placed there specifically for her? He hoped not. He thought not.

"I want to know why."

"And who," said Billy.

"And how. If the room was bricked up, how could those things have gotten up there?"

Billy heaved a sigh and put down his sandwich. "I don't know. I do know those bricks sealing up the opening haven't been moved since they were laid."

"So there must be another way in. Through the roof, or the floor."

"*Oui.*" Billy got up.

"Where're you going?"

"To look."

"That'll wait. I want to talk to you about the letter." Billy sat down again. "What do you really think of it?"

"I can't see that the letter is the strangest thing about today."

Armand smiled. "Agreed, but it is where all this started. With Pierre Stone." He looked down at the paper, now sitting on the table. "I wonder if whoever sent it to you, or to your old house, wanted you to go looking for the hidden room."

"But we didn't. I showed it to Ruth, but we just dismissed it. It wasn't until Fiona mentioned the room yesterday that we thought to look. But there is something strange about the letter."

"What?"

"I don't think Pierre Stone wrote it."

"Go on."

"Pierre was a skilled craftsman, but I doubt he got beyond third grade, if that. He'd have been literate enough to be able to read plans, but this—" Billy tapped the old paper and shook his head. "This was written by an educated person."

Billy had hit on something that had niggled at Armand since reading the letter, but he hadn't quite put it together. It didn't seem like the sort of letter a stonemason a century and a half ago, living in the countryside, would write.

"He might've had someone else write it," said Armand, wanting to explore all the corners. "Though it seems unlikely. This is a very personal letter, describing something clearly meant to be private, even secret. Why did you show it to Ruth?"

"She knows the history of Three Pines better than anyone. I thought if there was a hidden room, she might know about it. Might know the story. The room might've already been found and it was all in the past. Behind us."

But it was not. Something was in front of them. Approaching. Or already there.

"I can't believe we found a grimoire," said Reine-Marie, still clutching it. "The only one I've heard of belonged to a woman in Montréal three hundred years ago. But it was lost, probably destroyed by the church."

"Anne Lamarque," said Ruth.

"You know her?" Very little about Ruth surprised Reine-Marie, but this did.

"We never met," said Ruth.

Harriet laughed. Then, seeing the serious look on Ruth's face, she stopped. And looked at Gabri, who did not seem surprised.

"She'd be very old," he whispered to Harriet. "Pickled."

"Who's this Anne Lamarque?" asked Myrna.

"A witch," said Ruth.

"Oh, God," moaned Gabri. "Of course she is."

"You think it belonged to her?" asked Myrna. "Is that possible? What's it doing here?"

Reine-Marie opened the grimoire and carefully, carefully turned the first few pages. There were notations in the margins. Drawings of plants. What looked like recipes.

"No name," she said. "But that can't be a surprise. A grimoire would be proof of witchcraft. The Catholic Church in New France frowned on that."

It was an intentional and monumental understatement. Bishop Laval, a Jesuit and head of the church in the New World, had hunted down and punished anyone even suspected of witchery.

No. No one would be foolish enough to put their name on a grimoire.

"Can you get me a knife?" Reine-Marie asked.

When Myrna did, Reine-Marie used it to carefully pry up the lining of the inside cover. And there it was, as clear as the day it was written three hundred and fifty years earlier, unfaded by light and time. Unseen. Until now.

Anne Lamarque, 1672.

About the same time *The Paston Treasure*, the real one, had been painted.

Fiona popped her head back up into the loft and invited Harriet to have lunch with them.

"Sam really wants you to come. I haven't told him about what we found. I'm waiting for you. We're in the bistro. Come on, it'll be fun."

Harriet was torn, though in truth it was not much of a tear. While she wanted to find out more about a book that had belonged to a witch, of all things, the fact was, that was history. And Harriet was looking to the future. Her future. If the immediate days ahead included Sam, well, history could wait. It wasn't going anywhere. But she was.

"Sounds good."

The rain was coming down heavier now and had brought with it a chill. It was only early June, and it was possible, rare but possible, to still get snow. The day had the sort of damp chill that settled even into young bones.

After ordering cheeseburgers with melted brie and fries, Harriet and Fiona told Sam about the discovery.

"Are you kidding?"

"No, it's true."

"So someone put that painting up there and made it look like the old painting? Then bricked it up with other stuff, including a book on witchcraft? Well, that's just weird. This's all your fault," he said to Harriet.

"Mine?"

"You started it, with the talk of the hidden room." He was clearly teasing her, and she responded. Laughing. Teasing back.

Sam playfully nudged her, then grabbed a spicy fry off her plate.

"Oh," said Sam. "Sorry. Better be careful or the big tough cop'll throw me in jail for stealing. Wouldn't put it past him. Though that asshole seems to prefer picking on children."

"Monsieur Gamache?" asked Harriet, surprised.

"You don't know him like we do," said Sam, looking at his sister.

"But you're staying with him, them, aren't you?" Harriet said to Fiona. She knew in broad strokes, as did everyone else, about Fiona's past. But she also knew that the Gamaches had all but adopted her. "They're friends of yours."

"Of hers, yes," said Sam. "But not me. He thinks I killed my mother and framed my own sister for it."

"Sam!" said Fiona.

"Well, he does. He's obsessed with me. He even told Fiona I wasn't allowed in their house. How crazy is that? That scar he has? I think he walked into a tree and it's made him soft in the head."

He made a circular motion with his finger around his temple.

There was the scraping of a chair behind them and the clearing of a throat.

"I'm sorry." The minister, Robert Mongeau, was standing by their table. "But what you're saying is not only unkind, it's untrue."

His voice was soft, but his eyes were shrewd as he looked at Sam.

"Armand Gamache is a good man," Mongeau continued. "A decent man. You could do worse than learn from him."

"Oh, I've learned from him," said Sam. "You want to know what? I learned not to trust anyone. I learned that cops are cruel. I learned to swallow my feelings, to hide my thoughts. To not tell the truth because it'll bite you in the ass. I learned that the world is filled with terrible people, and the worst, the very worst, are the ones who should protect us. Who we turn to for help. That's what I learned from Armand fucking Gamache."

Sam took a few deep breaths to steady himself.

"He saved you from terrible abuse," said Mongeau, gently.

"Saved us? We'd already saved ourselves. He ruined our lives." Sam softened his voice. "We were children, and he made us the guilty ones, for trying to survive. Do you know what that does to a kid? To be made to feel all the abuse was our fault?"

"I can't imagine what you've been through," said Mongeau. "But I do know that holding on to resentments only binds you to the person you hate. You need to let go of it. For your own sake, not Monsieur Gamache's. Not anyone else's. For yourself."

He paused and studied Sam for so long it was just on the verge of awkward when the minister finally spoke again.

"There's goodness in you. I see it." Then Mongeau turned to Fiona. As he looked at her, his brows dropped very slightly, then he looked away.

"You have no idea what we've been through." Sam's voice was small, shaky, and he seemed unable to look up from the table.

"Robert?" said Sylvie, from the next table.

He stepped away then paused. "I'm sorry to have interfered. It's none of my business. But please, I'm at the church most days if you want to talk. No lecturing. No judgment. I promise. Though I do want to just say that the scar you mentioned"—Robert brought his finger up to trace where the scar was, deep and jagged, by Gamache's temple—"was made by a bullet. Armand was shot while trying to save a young man, about your age."

"Did he?" asked Sam.

"Save him?" said Robert. "No."

Sam snorted. "Of course not."

"At least he tried," said Robert. He looked at his wife, then spoke softly, softly to the immortal young people. *"Now here's a good one: You're lying on your deathbed. You have one hour to live. Who is it, exactly, you have needed all these years to forgive?"*

The minister stared at Sam for a beat. Two. Then turned and returned to his wife.

"Well," said Sam. "That was weird."

"That was from one of Ruth's poems," said Harriet.

"That crazy old woman? She's a poet?" said Sam.

"Won the Governor General's Award."

Fiona was watching Mongeau, then turned to her brother. It was a good question.

Who is it, exactly, you have needed all these years to forgive?

"After lunch I'd like to go over to your old house," said Armand. "Is that all right with you?"

"Yes, but why?" asked Billy. "I don't know what they can tell us. This's all strange, but it's not criminal."

"I think it's a little more than strange."

"Okay, I agree. But no crime has been committed. Nothing's been stolen. In fact, we have more than we started with. I know you said you don't think it's a joke, Armand, but what else could it be?"

"What happened to her?" asked Gabri, waving at the grimoire as though it was the woman.

"Anne Lamarque?" said Ruth. "She was accused of witchcraft."

"Why? Did they find the book?" asked Clara.

"They heard about it," said Ruth. "But never found it. If they had, it wouldn't be sitting here now. They didn't need the grimoire. They didn't need proof. All a woman had to be was alive. Just being a woman was, in the church's eyes, evil."

"But there must've been a reason," said Gabri.

"Is there a reason gay, lesbian, and transgender people are attacked?" asked Ruth. "Is there a reason Black men are shot? Is there a reason women are raped, abused, refused abortions, groomed and sold as sex slaves?"

"Murdered," said Myrna, looking at the bouquet of white roses on the kitchen island.

"*I was hanged for living alone*," said Ruth. It was rare, almost unheard of, that she quoted her own poem, but they heard it now. "*For having a weedy farm in my own name / And a surefire cure for warts.*"

The old woman looked at the book on Reine-Marie's lap, in which, they were certain, was a surefire cure for warts.

"*Oh yes*," she continued, "*and breasts / And a sweet pear hidden in my body. / Whenever there's talk of demons, those come in handy.*"

It was the poem Ruth had written for the women murdered in the Polytechnique.

They were silent for a moment, before Reine-Marie spoke.

"Anne Lamarque was one of the Filles du roi. One of the women recruited by the King to help colonize New France. But rather than be subservient, as expected, she stood out."

"How?" asked Clara.

"Well, among other things, she wore glasses and could read," said Reine-Marie.

"You'd have been screwed," Ruth said to Reine-Marie. "All of you. All of us. We'd be witches."

Myrna laughed. Then grew serious, realizing Ruth was right. They'd have been screwed. They'd have been witches.

"It went beyond the fact she could read," said Reine-Marie.

"True," said Ruth. "She pissed off the authorities by owning and running a business. A successful inn in the seedier part of town, back when Montréal was little more than a puddle of shit and broken promises."

"The church wanted to exert control, so they imposed a curfew," said Reine-Marie. "And banned alcohol."

"When the priests showed up to close her down, Anne told them to fuck off," said Ruth, as though she'd been there. "Then chased them down the street shouting abuse. That pretty much sealed her fate. Bishop Laval and the Jesuits hated her for defying them."

"For proving it was possible to defy them," said Clara.

"*Oui*," said Reine-Marie, nodding. "She was a brave woman. By all accounts a robust, generous, and brilliant woman who loved to sing and dance and laugh. A bit undisciplined, perhaps. She might not have seriously considered the consequences. But she meant no harm. New France was a pretty joyless place. She and her inn were bright spots."

All four women in the room knew they too would have been targeted. For dancing and reading and having breasts and wombs and minds of their own. For laughing.

And God only knew what would have happened to Gabri, to all the Gabris.

They were quiet for a moment, imagining Anne. Her inn. The dirt floor, the homemade booze. The dancing. The singing. The laughter. The respite from the wilderness. From fear and despair.

And then they saw the black-robed figures, the joyless Jesuits arriving.

Myrna, Clara, Ruth, Reine-Marie, and Gabri watched as Anne kicked the clerics out, into the filth that was Montréal in the 1670s. They could hear the riotous, the dangerous, the lethal laughter that followed the humiliated men as they ran away.

And then . . . And then . . .

Reine-Marie looked down at the book. And then what? How did it get here? In Three Pines.

Sam looked out the window, then said, "Let's get some fresh air."

"It's raining," said Fiona. "I'm staying here."

"Fine." Sam got up and looked at Harriet. "How about you? You won't melt in the rain, will you?"

Harriet smiled. "Like the Wicked Witch? I don't think so."

Fiona watched Sam. She hadn't seen much of him, not since she was put in prison and he wasn't. She hadn't seen him grow up. Into a man. And yet, she still thought of him as a child.

Were they ever children?

The talk of forgiveness had shaken her. Could everything really be forgiven? Even what she'd done? Even what she was about to do?

She remembered what the minister had said to Sam. About goodness. And what he had not said to her.

After standing on the front porch and putting their coats on, Armand and Billy ran through the rain just as Sam and Harriet emerged from the bistro. Gamache made it to the car, then looked over at the two young people standing in the pouring rain.

Sam was staring directly at him.

As he watched, Sam slowly put his arm around Harriet's waist. It was an act not so much of affection as possession.

Then he raised his other hand to his face and lifted his index finger up and down. It was the movement of someone taking a photograph. Sam was all but admitting he'd been in their home and had not just moved items but had taken pictures. Of his home. His family.

"Coming?" Billy called from inside the car.

Armand had never, as an adult, raised his middle finger to anyone, but it was all he could do not to do it now, then stride over and have it out. To demand to know why Sam was there. Why he'd been in their home.

Handling family photos. Taking photos.

But he knew that was exactly what Sam Arsenault wanted him to do. He was trying to provoke so that Harriet and anyone else watching would see him, a senior Sûreté officer, pick a fight for no apparent reason. So that Sam would appear the maligned innocent, facing police harassment.

It was close. So close. Too close. Armand felt that spike of fear. Not of Sam, but of himself and what he might actually do. Might be manipulated into doing.

Instead, Armand smiled at Sam, shook his head, then got in the car.

Grasping the steering wheel tight, he drove out of Three Pines.

CHAPTER 18

⁓

They stopped at Billy's on the way and picked up the envelope and Post-it note that had come with the letter: *I think this might interest you. Patricia Godin.*

From there Armand drove to Billy's ancestral home. The heavens had opened, and by the time they got to the porch, they were soaked.

Billy knocked on the door and looked around while they waited.

The house was, perhaps not surprisingly, made of stones yanked from the ground as it was turned from forest into fields for farming. The floors and beams and even the front door were milled from trees that had grown up and been cut down within sight of where they were standing.

As a child, Billy had held his grandfather's calloused hand, and together they'd walked through the forest, the old man touching the trees and describing their character. From him, young Billy learned that trees had feelings and personalities of their own.

With his grandmother, little Billy had walked through those fields picking wildflowers, and herbs, and sweetgrass. From her he learned how to make teas and poultices and a surefire cure for warts.

He tried to be happy for the new owners, but still, as he stood on the porch and knocked on what still felt like his own front door, Billy Williams ached.

There was a rattle, and then a man in his late sixties or early seventies stood there, looking surprised.

"*Oui?*"

"Monsieur Godin?"

"*Oui.*" He was staring at them, trying to figure out if he knew them. His eyes shifted from Billy to the man with him. Tall, solid in build. Wavy gray hair, and that scar . . .

"My name is Billy Williams, I—"

"Ah, *oui*. Of course." Godin stepped back. "Your family owned this home. Come in."

Billy stepped inside and looked around. Not much, physically, had changed. The walls, the floors, the beams were where he'd left them. Only the furniture was different.

He introduced Gamache, though by then Monsieur Godin had clearly recognized him. The Chief Inspector was a familiar presence in Québec media and was known to live in the area.

Monsieur Godin turned to Gamache. "Finally. Is this about Patricia?"

Billy raised his brows, but Armand was more adept at hiding surprise, though that didn't mean he didn't feel it.

Billy began to say, "Is she he—" when Armand interrupted.

"Patricia Godin is your wife?"

Billy looked at his companion. There was a change in Armand's voice, in his whole demeanor. It was subtle but there.

Monsieur Godin nodded. "Yes. My late wife. I spoke to the local Sûreté detachment when it happened. That is why you're here, isn't it?"

"May we sit down, please?" asked Gamache, and Monsieur Godin guided them into the comfortable living room, where a small fire was muttering in the hearth.

"Can I get you anything? You're wet. You must be cold. A hot tea or coffee?"

"Not for me, thank you," said Gamache, and Billy also shook his head, though both men sat close to the fire.

Billy was aware that Armand had been replaced by Chief Inspector Gamache.

"I need to be honest with you," said Gamache. "We came here

174

to discuss the letter your wife forwarded to Monsieur Williams. I'm sorry, but I'm not familiar with what happened to her."

"Letter? What letter?"

"Perhaps you can tell us about your wife first."

"So, the local Sûreté didn't contact you?"

"*Non.*"

"They said they would, but . . ." He raised, then dropped his hands. "I contacted them a few times, but then stopped . . . And then when so much time passed . . . But when I saw you at the door . . ." He stared into the fire. Unable, it seemed, to form a complete thought or sentence.

"What happened?" Gamache leaned forward, not a lot but enough to show Monsieur Godin that he had Gamache's full attention.

"They say she killed herself. Hanged herself, out back. I know it's not true. Pat would never do that."

"I'm sorry," said Gamache and paused a beat before asking, "When was this?"

"April twenty-first. I found her . . ."

"Five weeks ago," Billy whispered, and Gamache nodded. He was thinking the same thing. It was exactly the time she'd forwarded the letter to Billy.

"Did she leave a note? Any message explaining?" Gamache asked.

Monsieur Godin shook his head. "She'd had a hysterectomy and the coroner said that had upset her hormones. Made her depressed. That's bullshit. She had trouble sleeping, but she wasn't depressed. There's no way Pat killed herself. And . . ."

"Yes?"

Godin heaved a sigh. "Even if she had, she wouldn't have hung herself. That must be a terrible way to go. Wouldn't she have tried pills?" He was beseeching them. "Wouldn't you?"

Billy had to agree. If it came to that, he'd try many things before hanging. And there was something else.

"You say it happened out back? A tree?" When Monsieur Godin nodded, Billy asked, "Which one?"

Monsieur Godin stared at him with something akin to disgust. "Does it matter?"

"It might."

"I can show you, if you want." This was said to Gamache.

"Please." Though he was also unsure why Billy would want to know. But he knew Billy Williams, and knew it was not prurient interest.

"I wanted to cut it down," said Godin as he took them through the kitchen and out onto the back porch. "But the children stopped me. Said it wasn't the tree's fault." He pointed. "That's the one."

In the middle of the yard, about twenty meters from the house, there stood a huge maple. Old, gnarled, its limbs thick and solid.

"Mable," said Billy, as rain pounded the roof overhead and cascaded down, creating a wall of water between them and the tree.

"Mable?" said Gamache and Godin together.

"Mable the maple," said Billy. "It's what my grandmother called her. We used to climb all over her. Fell out of her more than once. She was old in my day." He shook his head and smiled. Then he remembered what had happened, and his smile fell from his face.

"So do our grandchildren," said Monsieur Godin. "That's why our son and daughter didn't want it cut down. But they didn't see . . ."

No, thought Armand. They didn't.

Armand understood now why Billy had asked the question.

He turned to Monsieur Godin. "If she did want to hang herself, would your wife have chosen this tree?"

Godin, still staring at it, shook his head. "No. Never. She wouldn't do that to the kids. To me. To the tree."

The three men stared at Mable. Gamache believed him. Which meant, if Madame Godin did not take her own life, someone else did.

And it almost certainly had something to do with the letter. The one in his breast pocket.

"We need to talk, but first I need to make a call."

Jean-Guy Beauvoir was sitting at his desk at Sûreté headquarters in Montréal when the call came through. It was mid-afternoon, and he was going over reports on the various investigations under way.

"Chief? Everything okay?"

"I think I've discovered a homicide," said Gamache.

"Where?" said Jean-Guy, sitting forward and grabbing a pen.

"Just outside Cowansville. I need you to look up the file on a Patricia Godin. She died on April twenty-first of this year." He gave the address. "It was ruled a suicide."

"But you think it was murder?"

"I'm almost sure it was. She was cremated, so we can't exhume her body, but I want the autopsy report and anything you can find from the local Sûreté."

"They missed it?"

"Yes. They put it down to depression caused by a hysterectomy."

"Oh, Jesus."

"Oh, Jesus" was right, thought Gamache. He'd hoped they were well beyond the days when women went to a doctor with pain and it was dismissed as hysteria. When "that time of the month" became a euphemism for derangement, and menopause became an illness.

He would have words with the station commander, but first things first.

"How did you discover it?" Beauvoir asked.

When Gamache told him about the letter and the hidden room, Beauvoir was silent for a moment, then asked, "So you think someone killed her to stop her from reading the letter?"

"Maybe," said Gamache. "But it was too late. The letter had already arrived, and she'd forwarded it."

"So why kill her? Because she'd read it? Then why not kill Billy? Why not try to get the letter back? Presumably the murderer would have found out from Madame Godin where she sent it."

"True. Before we go too far, we need to make sure it was murder."

"I'll get you the information and come down."

Rejoining Monsieur Godin and Billy in front of the fire, he brought out the Stone letter.

"Did you ever see this?"

Monsieur Godin looked at it, then shook his head. "It's strange, old. And that stuff about bricking up the room. But why are you showing it to me? Does it have anything to do with Pat?"

"We don't know. We do know the letter came here first, then your wife forwarded it to Monsieur Williams here."

"So? An old letter came here by mistake and she sent it on. People do."

"Did your wife mention this letter?"

"*Non*. How could this have anything to do with her death?" He held Gamache's eyes. "That is what you're thinking."

Gamache now showed him the Post-it note. "Is this your wife's handwriting?"

"No." It was so unequivocal, Gamache raised his brows. Seeing this, Godin got up. "Pat had terrible handwriting. I can show you."

Godin returned with a shopping list his wife had made and stuck to the fridge with a magnet. He clearly wasn't yet ready to throw out anything she'd touched.

Godin was right. Her handwriting was almost unintelligible.

"*Merci*," said Armand, taking the list. "Do you mind if I keep this?"

Godin shook his head and watched as the Chief Inspector placed it in a baggie, along with the Post-it.

Gamache had one more question. "Do you have Billy Williams's address?"

"His?" Monsieur Godin pointed to Billy. "If you need it, why not just ask him?"

"*Non*," said Gamache, almost smiling. "I mean, would your wife be able to forward mail to him?"

"I doubt it." He turned to Billy. "We had your parents' address in the seniors' home, but that was years ago and I know they've since passed away. We never had yours. Besides, nothing's arrived for your family in years."

"*Merci*." Gamache got to his feet. He now had a pretty good idea why Madame Godin was killed. Like most murders, it had started long ago, and in the most banal of ways.

When she and her husband had bought a home. This home.

He picked up the envelope and looked at the crossed-out address and the new one, Billy's, added. In the hand of her killer.

Patricia Godin was murdered not to stop the letter, but to make sure it was sent on. To the people who needed to see it.

Then he looked at the Post-it note, also written, he was sure, by her killer.

I think this might interest you.

It was almost, Gamache thought, as though the words were meant for him.

"You weren't kidding."

As soon as Jean-Guy Beauvoir arrived in Three Pines, Gamache had taken him up to Myrna's loft to see the no-longer-hidden room.

The two men stood in front of the painting and were joined by Myrna, who now felt a certain ownership over it.

"Quite something, isn't it?" she said, with a mixture of pride and uncertainty.

Jean-Guy was shaking his head, trying to get his mind around it. Then he leaned closer and pointed.

"Why put a poster in the painting?" asked Jean-Guy.

"Why put anything?" asked Myrna. "Why remake a masterpiece?"

"They remade *Total Recall*," said Jean-Guy.

"Let it go," said Armand gently. "You can still watch the original."

The three of them stared at this remake and wondered. Why. Though the two Sûreté officers also wondered if, and how, this could have anything to do with the death of Patricia Godin.

"How did they get it up here?" asked Beauvoir, looking around.

"Billy and Olivier are going over the plans for the building and trying to work out the how," said Gamache. The why would take longer.

"They're down in the bookstore now," said Myrna. "Looking at the ceiling. If it didn't come through this wall, and obviously it didn't, then it was either the roof or the ceiling."

"But how could they have gotten it in here without you seeing?" asked Jean-Guy. "I mean, it would take a damned big hole to get that"—he gestured toward the painting—"in."

"And it would take time," said Gamache. "Were you away recently? I don't remember you going anywhere."

"Not recently, no. I went to Charlevoix with Clara, whale watching, for a week. When you were in Paris."

"Did anyone stay here?" Gamache asked.

"No. Ruth offered to look after the store, but that didn't seem like a good idea, so I just closed it."

"And no work was done on the place while you were away? Renovations?"

"Olivier? Do improvements? Have you met the man?"

"Can you give us the dates?" Beauvoir asked.

She went to look up the days she and Clara were away, while Jean-Guy walked around the rest of the newly discovered room. "I'll get the Scene of Crime team to fingerprint and swab the items."

"Good. And we need everything moved to someplace secure."

"I'm having the Old Train Station set up as an Incident Room." Jean-Guy looked around. "But honestly, *patron*, I'm not sure how this relates to the death of Patricia Godin."

"Neither am I. The only link is the letter." And it was, they both knew, a flimsy link.

Myrna was coming back with the information, so they said no more about murder, preferring to keep that to themselves for now. Besides, they still needed proof it was murder.

Armand gave Jean-Guy the Stone letter along with the envelopes and Post-it. "I'll make copies," said Beauvoir, "and send the originals to the lab."

When he left, Myrna said, "Something's changed."

"What makes you say that?"

"Come on, Armand. Jean-Guy's here. You're whispering. There's activity at the Old Train Station. What's happened? Is it something to do with—?" She jerked her head toward the hole in the wall.

"I can't say yet. I'm sorry."

Which was, they both knew, an answer in itself. As they made their way downstairs, she said, "I hear there was a dustup in the bistro today at lunch."

He stopped and turned. "What do you mean?"

"Harriet told me that Sam Arsenault and the minister had words."

"Robert Mongeau?" He couldn't imagine the minister getting into an argument with anyone. "What about?"

"You."

"*Moi?*"

"Yes. Sam was bad-mouthing you, and Robert defended you. Though it all ended amicably enough." She paused. "I think Harriet's got a crush on Sam. Should I be worried?"

Armand remembered the young man putting his arm around Harriet's waist in a way that spoke less of affection and more of ownership. Or even hostage taking.

"Honestly?" he said. "If it was my daughter, I would be."

Myrna had known that would be the answer. Ever since she'd interviewed Sam Arsenault on the eve of his sister's parole hearing, she'd felt something was wrong.

That hadn't been part of the formal parole hearings, but Armand had wanted her professional opinion before committing Reine-Marie and himself to be Fiona's sponsors.

So, Dr. Landers had gone to the women's prison. She'd met Fiona before in Three Pines, when the young woman had stayed with the Gamaches on weekend parole. But that was social. Now she was a psychologist specializing in criminal behavior, interviewing a known murderer.

Fiona readily admitted she'd killed her mother. She also admitted attacking her brother. Dr. Landers found Fiona Arsenault to be open, well-balanced, truthful. Remorseful. And she said as much to Armand and Reine-Marie.

Sam was another matter. It wasn't anything Myrna could put her finger on, which was strange given her experience with so many different, and often aberrant, personalities. And that was what disconcerted her to the point of ending the interview early. It was like talking to a blank spot.

"I want to say something to Harriet, but I don't know what, and I have no proof that Sam is . . . ," said Myrna. What?

Sick.

"There is something else, Armand. Harriet told me Robert said he could see goodness in Sam."

"Really? He said that?"

"Yes. And according to Harriet, he turned to Fiona, clearly wanting to say the same thing about her."

Armand waited.

"But he didn't. He just stared at her, then looked a little confused and looked away." Myrna paused. "You don't think . . ."

Armand knew what she was thinking.

That they were wrong, and Reine-Marie and Jean-Guy, and now it seemed Robert Mongeau, were right. As was the court. That the dangerous one wasn't Sam. He was manipulative, angry, vengeful. But not murderous.

Maybe the really dangerous one was the one who looked, acted, seemed okay.

Evil is unspectacular and always human, Auden had written. *And shares our bed and eats at our own table.*

Armand had no proof that Sam was dangerous. Was unwell. But there was a great deal of proof that the sibling who ate at their table had been. And maybe still was.

When Gamache walked into the Old Train Station, familiar from past investigations, he expected to see chaos. The sort of turmoil that accompanies the setting up of an Incident Room.

Instead, he found a young plainclothes officer directing the operation. Though to say she was in plain clothes would be unfair to her clothes. They were anything but plain. They were, however, plaid. And frayed and ripped. A white T-shirt was visible under a sweater that looked eaten not just by moths, but ravens.

Tattoos covered her arms and crawled up her neck.

She stood in the middle of the room, and when not issuing orders, she was clicking her tongue post against her teeth.

It was grating. She was grating. But she was also getting results. Neither senior officer had ever seen an Incident Room come together

so quickly. Mostly because the technicians just wanted to get out and away from Agent Amelia Choquet.

"I thought you didn't like her," Gamache said, going up to his second-in-command, who seemed to be cowering in a corner.

"I don't. Who does? I brought her in right after you called me. We needed someone, but with Isabelle on vacation, and this not being officially a homicide yet, I thought it best to bring in someone who at least knows Three Pines and the people."

It was, Armand thought, a very good idea. They were playing catch-up with this murder. Five weeks old, dismissed as suicide, body cremated.

The quicker they could get a handle on what was important and what was not, the better.

A conference table had been set up, and Jean-Guy pointed toward it. "Can we go over the timeline? I just need to be clear, *patron*."

Gamache nodded. He too wanted to be clear.

"In," Beauvoir started, already consulting his notes, "1862, Pierre Stone is approached to build a wall."

Beauvoir could barely believe he was saying those words. In a murder investigation they always looked to the past, but never that far past.

"*C'est correct*," said Gamache.

"He writes a letter to a woman named Clémence, describing the commission."

Gamache nodded and looked at the copy of the letter, sitting between them on the table. The original, along with the other documents, had been sent to Montréal for analysis.

"He builds the wall and seals up the room next to what is now Myrna's loft."

"The row of buildings was originally put up as workers' cottages by the owner of the mill," said Gamache. "The date on the bricks corresponds to the date on Pierre Stone's letter."

"So that fits," said Beauvoir. "But the letter doesn't. You don't think Stone wrote it."

"What letter?" said Agent Choquet. "Is this it?"

They looked up and realized all the technicians had gone and the Incident Room had been set up, complete with coffee machine, mini-fridge, blackboard, desks, computers. And fiber-optic cable, something Inspector Beauvoir rarely managed to get technicians to connect.

She must've scared them silly, thought Gamache.

She must've scared them shitless, thought Beauvoir.

Both were correct.

Gamache was about to suggest Amelia join them, but she'd already taken a seat and was reading the letter.

"He was a stonemason in the mid-1800s?" she asked. "There's no way he wrote this." She shoved it away from her.

"Thank you," said the Chief Inspector, before turning back to Beauvoir, who was glaring at Agent Choquet. "Continue, Inspector. And you"—Gamache turned to Amelia—"listen."

Beauvoir actually smiled. It was almost exactly what the Chief had said to him that day years ago, by the shores of that lake.

"Fast-forward to five weeks ago, when the Stone letter arrives at the former home of Pierre Stone, mailed by some unknown person. Patricia Godin reads it, then either she forwards it to Billy Williams or someone else does. Shortly after that, she dies—"

"But don't you—" Amelia began.

"Listening," said Gamache. "Listening."

"The local police put her death down as suicide," Beauvoir continued.

There was a clicking sound from Agent Choquet. But no actual words.

Beauvoir stared at her, then noticed that Gamache was looking at the table and fighting unsuccessfully to suppress a grin.

"What?" said Beauvoir.

The clicking was Morse code.

Bullshit. Bullshit.

Gamache gave Amelia a stern warning glance and the clicking stopped. "Nothing. Go on."

"Billy Williams reads the letter and shows it to Ruth. Both think

it's strange, but nothing more. Just some incident from the past, until Fiona mentions the hidden room."

Gamache sat forward, as did Amelia, who was clearly tempted to talk but managed to remain silent.

"They broke through the wall this morning," Beauvoir continued. "And found the painting and other items."

This was too much for Amelia. "Painting? What?"

"*Oui.*"

"Sealed in a hidden room?"

Amelia Choquet, tattooed and pierced, a former heroin addict and prostitute, was surprised by very little in life except, perhaps, kindness. But this surprised her.

"The painting was made to look old," said Beauvoir, "but isn't. Made to look like a copy of a masterpiece, but isn't."

Cloaked in cynicism and armored by indifference, Amelia rarely showed interest, but she could not hide it now. "And sealed up a hundred and sixty years ago?"

"We should show her," said Jean-Guy.

"You do that, I'm going over to Clara's. I'll meet you in Myrna's loft when I'm done."

Myrna, downstairs in the bookstore, greeted Amelia like another niece. Since Myrna was a purveyor of books, and the young agent was addicted to them, this made the bookseller her pusher, though actually more like her priestess.

"Find anything?" Beauvoir asked Olivier and Billy, who'd just finished examining the ceiling.

"We think there's a section that's been repainted," said Olivier, "but hard to tell."

Once in the loft, they stood at the jagged hole in the wall.

"Holy shit," whispered Amelia. She stared at the painting, her concentration so complete she forgot to click her tongue post. But if she had, it would have been three short. Three long. Three short.

CHAPTER 19

*B*onjour?" Armand called. "You home?"

"In the studio," came Clara's singsong reply.

"Can I come in?"

"Of course." The words were slurred by the brush between her teeth like a bit, but he understood the gist.

Armand stood on the threshold of her studio and watched her work. The large, vaulted room smelled of oil paints and old banana peels, turpentine and an undercurrent of lemon. Not the chemical, headache-inducing scent of lemon cleaner. This smelled of lemonade in summer, and lemon meringue pie at celebrations. It smelled of gin and tonics with a twist on the terrasse on hot afternoons, and honey and lemon tea to soothe a sore throat when sick.

As he watched, Clara applied thick swirls to the canvas. Not with a brush—that remained forgotten in her mouth—but with a palette knife. Great globs went on, apparently at random, with abandon.

Clara Morrow was the real thing. A genuine artist. Not because she was a success—that came and went—but because she was bold and creative. And brave. Audacious. She tried new things, took chances, and evolved.

What was on her easel now was like nothing Gamache had seen her do before. It was abstract, almost aggressive.

She put on one more slash of paint, considered it, then turned to face him.

She was smiling. Her face dabbed with paint, and her expression filled with delight.

"Why so happy?" he asked.

"I was just thinking about Anne Lamarque." She took the brush from between her teeth, smearing more paint in her hair and on her cheek, and used it to motion at the canvas. "She was punished for many things, including being happy. So I wanted to capture that. The power of it. Happiness as an act of defiance. A revolutionary act."

He looked at the canvas and saw bold swirls of reds and greens and yellows. And bright blues. All intermingled. They formed no image. And he got no feeling.

He closed his eyes. Paused. When he opened them, he let the painting come to him. To enter through his heart, not his head. With Clara's painting, like all great works of creation, there was more than met the eye.

And then he saw it. Or, rather, felt it. Without realizing it, he began to smile. The image itself would become clear later, when she'd finished. Or not. Maybe it already was clear. In her smile, and his.

"What can I do for you?" She got up from her stool and waved the brush at the old sofa against the wall of her studio, indicating they should sit. He looked at it, his smile fading.

The sofa always reminded him of the Monty Python sketch when a man, about to be tortured in the Inquisition, was threatened with the "comfy chair."

Dear God, he thought, not the sofa.

It was an unexpected, certainly unintended, torture, though Clara didn't seem to see it. The springs had long since let go, so that you either hit the concrete floor or, worse, a spring.

He hovered over it for a moment, then, like a cliff diver, he committed. He felt his bottom hit the floor. It was, he admitted, the better option.

"The painting we found in the attic," he began. "I have questions."

She laughed. "So do I. You first."

"Mine are technical, I think. It's not framed, but it is on a frame. And it's huge. How could it get up there?"

"That's easy. The frame must've been assembled in the attic and the canvas tacked to it there. Look."

She struggled to her feet, then grabbed one of her unused canvases. Turning it around, she showed him what he'd seen many times before. The canvas was folded over the wooden frame, then stapled there.

"That's how they did it," she said, with complete confidence. "I didn't look at the back. Too consumed by the front, so I don't know what they used. Staples are relatively new. Old canvases are nailed. The one in the attic, well . . ."

"Good, easy enough to check. The nails or staples, and the paint itself, can be dated."

"As can the canvas. The Musée des beaux-arts in Montréal or Sherbrooke can do that for you."

"How long would it take to paint?"

Clara smiled. "I've been trying to figure that out too. A canvas that size, with so much in it? So many objects and such detail? The original, the real *Paston Treasure*, must've taken many months."

"But this isn't the original, so whoever did it wouldn't need to struggle with composition or details. At least, not much. Could ours be done in less time?"

"For sure. But how much less, I can't say. Depends on the skill of the artist. From what I saw, there was considerable skill. There is another way it could've been done that would be even faster."

"Go on."

"If it's a paint-by-number."

Armand stared at her as though she'd gone mad. "Like what the grandchildren do?"

"Not exactly. I think if you have it examined, you'll find a reproduction of the original *Paston Treasure* underneath. It's not uncommon these days for artists to have high-resolution, digital copies made of their works. They're called giclées."

"Yes, I've seen them. They look like originals. But this is different, isn't it?"

"In that it isn't exactly the original, yes. I think it's possible someone had a copy of the original printed onto an old canvas. Then they painted over it, adding new stuff, like the watch and poster. It would still take time and skill, but far less than if it was painted from scratch."

"We think the items were put up there in the week that you and Myrna were in Charlevoix."

Clara made a guttural sound. "I hate that thought. Must freak Myrna out too."

Myrna was not easily freaked, but it was clearly unsettling.

Armand began rocking himself out of the sofa, but she stopped him. "Wait a minute. My turn. Why were the painting and that book Reine-Marie found and the other things put there, then sealed up? Were we meant to find that room? If you're right, the stuff's been there for more than a year, but the room was sealed up a hundred and sixty years ago. There must've been a reason back then to seal the room, and there must be a reason someone was there recently."

Armand leaned back, lifted his legs, then in one mighty swing hoisted himself to his feet.

"I honestly don't know why those things are there."

"Were we meant to find them, Armand? It seems so. But if the caretaker hadn't pointed out the roofline, we'd never have found it."

It was true. It seemed like a coincidence, but in Gamache's experience, almost everything that happened was the end result of a series of apparently unconnected events. Often set in motion years earlier. Remove one, and the thing did not happen.

Like the book he was reading. What if . . .

But Armand suspected there was more than a series of chance events at work here. Someone was not leaving it up to chance. Whoever was behind this had planned well, thoroughly, and for a long time. There was no way they were not going to find that room, and probably exactly when they did.

And that led him to another question. Not just why, but why now?

"Oh, come on."

As he entered the bookstore, Armand heard the words floating down from above.

"Guess who's up there," said Myrna.

"Our mini-Ruth?" asked Armand.

"If Ruth and a trash compactor had a child, yes."

On entering the loft, Armand saw Amelia glaring at Beauvoir.

"He wants me to take the painting over to the Old Train Station," she complained.

"What? Too hard for you?" asked Beauvoir.

"Too hard for the laws of physics," she said. "You've heard of them, haven't you? That painting's massive. How'm I supposed to get it through—" She waved toward the opening.

"Well, it got in, didn't it?"

"Here," said Gamache, walking around to the back of the painting. "Clara told me how."

Olivier and Billy were behind the painting, kneeling on the floor and examining the boards.

"Anything?" he asked them.

"We might've found how they got the stuff up here," said Olivier. "I can show you."

"In a moment." Armand put on his glasses, turned on the flashlight app, and looked at the back of the painting. "Nails. They look old, handmade. And the wood frame also looks old."

Taking off his glasses, he told them what Clara had said. "Take out the nails, save them, then roll up the canvas and get it to the evidence locker."

"None of this makes sense," said Beauvoir. "Why would someone go through the effort to make the painting look old, right down to the nails. And then paint in stuff that's modern. Why?"

"Distraction," said Amelia. "Or just a good, old-fashioned mind-fuck."

"Like Grandma used to do?" said Beauvoir.

"Jean-Guy, call the Musée des beaux-arts in Montréal and get a senior conservator to come down."

Beauvoir got on the phone while Amelia went to work on the nails.

Gamache walked over to Olivier and Billy. "What've you found?"

"We think the stuff came in through the floor," said Olivier. "Looks like the ceiling in the bookshop has been repaired and repainted, and we can see where a couple of boards up here have cracked."

"We think they used a knife to remove a section of the bookstore ceiling," said Billy. "Then a rubber mallet to push up these boards, creating an opening just large enough for a person to get through. But in doing that, they cracked a few when the wood pulled away from the nails."

Gamache had to get on his knees and lean close to see the cracks. Getting up, he brushed off his slacks. "They knew what they were doing."

"True," said Billy. "It takes some skill to repair the drywall downstairs."

"Huh," said Olivier, who'd wandered away and was looking at the pile of other things in the attic. He reached out, but Beauvoir, still on the phone, stopped him.

"What is it?" Gamache asked.

"The elephant."

Sure enough, there was a largish brass elephant among the items behind the painting. It was about eight inches tall and ten inches long.

"What about it?" asked Gamache, joining him.

"Well, we're missing one exactly like this."

"You're missing an elephant?" asked Amelia, peering around the painting, where she was dusting for prints.

"We had a guest at the B&B, and when she checked out, the elephant was gone too. It was in her room."

"Sounds like an old Marx Brothers routine," said Amelia.

They looked at her. How someone her age, and with her background, knew so many things was mystifying. Even Beauvoir had no idea who the Marx Brothers were, except that one of them had something to do with Communism.

"Was it wearing pajamas?" she asked, baffling Beauvoir even more.

"Is it your elephant?" Gamache asked. It was, he had to admit, a question he'd never asked in a murder investigation before. Actually, had never asked, period.

Olivier bent down but didn't touch. "It sure looks like it, but this one has engraving on it, ours didn't. But man, it sure looks like it. Gabri would know."

"Can you get me the guest's name and when they were here?" Gamache asked.

"Easily."

From the other side of the painting they heard very soft singing. *"Hooray for Captain Spaulding, the African explorer . . ."*

"But how can it be ours?" asked Olivier.

"How can any of this be?" Billy asked.

"Hooray, hooray, hooray," sang Amelia.

CHAPTER 20

The investigators were gathered in the Old Train Station. The photograph of Ruth, taken when she'd won the Governor General's Award for poetry, glared down at them.

Jean-Guy had contacted a conservator at the Musée des beaux-arts in Montréal, who'd be arriving first thing in the morning. The painting was now safely locked away in the Incident Room along with the other items from the attic. Except the grimoire. Reine-Marie still had that.

Crime scene tape had been placed across the hole in Myrna's wall. When asked why, since no crime had actually been committed, neither Gamache nor Beauvoir explained fully, preferring to say it was a precaution.

The autopsy report on Patricia Godin hadn't yet arrived, but the investigators were assured it would before morning, and analysis of the Stone letter was under way at the Sûreté labs.

That too would arrive the next day.

"Come over to our place for dinner," Gamache said to Amelia. "But first, check into the B&B. There's a young man staying there, Sam Arsenault. I want you to get to know him. You have any marijuana on you?"

"Me? Marijuana?"

It was now legal in Canada. Gamache understood the hypocrisy of him enjoying a scotch after work but discouraging his agents from relaxing with a joint. Which he did.

"Yes, you."

He'd consider himself lucky if all she had was a joint, though in joining homicide she'd pledged to be clean.

"Why? You want some?" she asked.

He smiled thinly. "If you do, offer it to him. Imply that you're breaking my rules."

"I would be," she said. "No need to imply."

"It's not a rule," he said. "Just a strong suggestion."

She smiled at the all-but-nonexistent distinction. "For what it's worth, I'm clean, but I know where I can get some."

"Good. But don't you use."

Chief Inspector Gamache knew Agent Choquet well. Very well. Knew her better than she realized.

He was the one who'd reviewed her application to the Sûreté Academy. He'd seen her all-too-obvious flaws. Her frailties. Her drug use, her petty crimes. She'd dropped out of high school and ended up on the street, at times resorting to prostitution.

He'd seen the tattoos, many obviously self-administered. Not as body art but as a form of self-mutilation. The piercings and studs, the tears and scars.

But he'd also seen that she'd read every school textbook she could get her hands on, either borrowed or stolen. She'd devoured books on philosophy, math, literature. Art. Poetry. She'd taught herself ancient Greek and read Socrates, and Italian and read Italo Calvino in the original. Her favorite, and his, was, *If on a winter's night a traveler*.

She spoke Russian and learned Mandarin.

She'd passed her high school equivalency with such high marks the education board had given her, just out of curiosity, the test to get into McGill University. She wrote her answers upside down and backward. Once her examiners figured it out, they saw that she had scored higher than anyone else that year. McGill offered her a scholarship.

She'd accepted, then didn't show up. Amelia Choquet had disappeared back into the sewer of inner-city Montréal.

But then she'd bobbed up again, one last time, and applied to, of all things, the Sûreté Academy.

At first, Gamache thought it was a joke. A dare perhaps. Then he'd looked deeper and seen it wasn't a joke, it was a lifeboat. He saw the totality of her application. Of her life. It was immediately apparent that Amelia Choquet was an omnivore, the greatest autodidact Armand Gamache had ever come across.

She was clearly a genius. Or perhaps she was mad. Gamache couldn't decide.

In the end, he'd rejected her application. As the new head of the Sûreté Academy at the time, he was responsible for all the cadets. He could not risk letting Amelia Choquet into an Academy already riven with deceit and corruption. Armand Gamache was very aware of the effect of one bad apple. And there was the smell of rot about Amelia Choquet.

He had a duty to protect the other students. Had to protect a fragile institution from an unstable, disruptive, even dangerous influence.

The truth, though, was far more complex, and far less noble.

He'd ultimately changed his mind and admitted her. Not everyone thought it was the wisest of decisions. And even he took a long time making peace with it. With her.

Now they sat in armchairs Agent Choquet had wrangled from Olivier. At least, they assumed Olivier was aware she'd taken them. The chairs now formed a sitting area in the Incident Room, along with a rug, side tables, and lamps. Also from the bistro.

Beauvoir brought over drinks from the well-stocked mini-fridge, and had to admit it was not only the most efficient Incident Room he'd ever worked in, it was about the most comfortable.

Though that was not saying much. Over the years, he and the Chief Inspector had worked out of pigsties, spider-infested toolsheds, hotels they were pretty sure were haunted. At least, Beauvoir was.

They'd once dug a quinzhee out of snow when caught in a blizzard while investigating a murder in Nunavut. It was so comfortable they ended up using the snow hut as their Incident Room. Far better than the two-hole outhouse they'd been forced to use in the Gaspé.

Annie refused to believe that was true, but it was.

"I want you to bad-mouth me to Sam Arsenault," said Gamache, taking a fistful of nuts Amelia had put out in bowls, along with chips. "Subtly."

"Do you do subtle?" asked Beauvoir.

Amelia spread her arms and smirked. Her tongue stud clicked against her teeth.

She was tapping out, *Subtle, c'est moi.* Gamache wondered if she realized he too knew Morse code.

"I want Sam Arsenault to think you're unhappy," said Gamache. "That you're only in the Sûreté to steal drugs. Evidence. Whatever. You can figure that out. But be careful. He's smart. He has a rare ability to see into people. To find their triggers. To manipulate."

Jean-Guy shifted and inhaled. They both looked at him.

"What? I didn't say anything."

"Who's this Sam guy?" asked Amelia.

Gamache nodded to Beauvoir, who told her about the investigation into the death of Clotilde Arsenault and the fallout.

Amelia listened. It was a just-the-facts account, and when he'd finished, she said to Gamache, "But you don't believe it? You don't think the sister did it."

"I believe they killed their mother. As to who delivered the actual blow, I don't know. I'm willing to believe it was Fiona, but I don't think that part matters. Those children were tortured, abused, broken. They were acting in self-defense. I believe the justice system failed them both, but especially Fiona."

"Then what's with this Sam Arsenault stuff?" she asked. "You want me to get close to him. Sounds like you suspect him of something. You think Sam Arsenault was the one who should've been in prison?"

"*Non.*" Gamache's voice was curt and clear. "Absolutely not. He was ten at the time, sexually abused, prostituted out by his own mother. No. Here was a child deeply traumatized. There's no way he could be considered guilty. They were both victims. But I think he needed far more intensive counseling and oversight than he got."

"*Désolé, patron*," said Beauvoir, "but it's more than that. You think he was beyond help."

"By then, by the time we first met him . . ." Gamache considered. "Yes." He nodded his head slowly. There were very few people he felt were beyond redemption. Even at ten, Sam, he sensed, was one of those people. Born bad and made worse.

Beauvoir looked at Amelia and weighed what to say next. He decided on the truth.

"The Chief Inspector and I differ on this. I think Fiona Arsenault got what she deserved. I think she was the planner. I think she controlled her mother's business when Clotilde was too far gone. The ledger we found in the house has her handwriting and the little stickers she collected. I think she murdered her mother so that she could take over prostituting her brother and was probably grooming other kids."

"What we do agree on," said Gamache, "is that we're pretty sure the only reason Clotilde's body was put where it would be found is so the children could collect the insurance."

"You think she set up one of the molesters for the murder," said Choquet. "The one she sold the car to. Not a very good attempt."

"She wasn't exactly a criminal mastermind," said Beauvoir, grabbing some corn chips. "She probably didn't think anyone would suspect children. It was a shitty mess."

"It was a tragedy," said Gamache.

"But you arrested her," Amelia said.

"I did. I had to. To be honest, I never dreamed the prosecutor would go so hard on her."

"And if you had known," said Amelia, "what would you have done?"

Gamache smiled and shook his head at her. It was a question he would not answer. Could not answer. He didn't really know the answer.

"The whole thing makes me sick," he said. "Despite my arguments, the prosecution tried Fiona as an adult."

"You really don't think she was guilty?" said Amelia.

"I think, I believe, Sam instigated it, battered his own head against the brick wall in the alley, then blamed his sister. His injuries, while dramatic, were not all that serious."

"Why did she accept the blame? Why not fight back? Why not tell them that Sam was responsible?"

"Because she loved him," said Gamache. "Because she felt she needed to protect him. Maybe felt guilty about not being able to protect him against their mother. Against what happened. And maybe because she knew in her heart what he really was and was afraid of him."

"And what is he?" asked Amelia.

A monster, he almost said, but did not. Instead, he said, "I'm not a good judge."

"No, but you've obviously judged that the sister is safe. You've taken her under your wing."

"Not just that," said Beauvoir. "He watched over her, visited her in prison, helped her get parole and graduate with an engineering degree from the École Polytechnique."

"Jesus," said Amelia. "We should all be arrested by you."

"And be wrongly convicted," Gamache reminded her. "Which in your case is unlikely."

She laughed. Then grew serious. "Why do you believe that Sam was behind the murder of their mother?"

It was, Gamache knew, a fair question. Could he possibly say it was because the boy had winked at him that day long ago, when his sister had been found guilty?

That he could feel Sam's presence inside his head. Messing about. Moving objects around in there so that the Chief Inspector was stumbling about. Struggling to see clearly.

But despite all the mind games, Gamache had seen, could still see, clearly enough to know that Sam Arsenault was unbalanced. Unwell. Malevolent. And time had only made him worse.

"I have no evidence," he admitted. "Just a feeling. I didn't encourage the prosecutor to arrest Sam. I never mentioned my suspicions. I did not arrest him. In fact, I tried to get him help. But I knew it was useless. He was beyond our reach in every way."

Amelia didn't pursue it further. How do you pursue a feeling, after all? She knew this man well enough by now to know he saw hope where others saw only malevolence.

But he could also see evil where others saw a ten-year-old boy.

"You"—Armand turned to Beauvoir—"were the one who came closest to reaching him."

Jean-Guy took another handful of chips and nodded. "I liked the kid. Felt for him."

He remembered that moment when the child had clung to him, clutched at him, and sobbed.

Was Sam a model citizen? Probably not. Who could be after that?

Was he taking this opportunity to mind-fuck the man who'd seen what they'd done and arrested his sister? Maybe. That wasn't okay, but neither, from what Beauvoir could see, was it dangerous.

Was he a psychopath? No. Was his sister? That, for Jean-Guy, was an open question.

It worried him a lot that his father-in-law could not see it.

"But how's this connected to that." Agent Choquet waved toward the locker, with its assortment of curiosities. "And the murder of Madame Godin?"

"Probably isn't." The Chief Inspector checked his watch. "Dinner's in an hour."

"Great." She dumped the remaining nuts into her pocket. "I might get the munchies."

They crossed the bridge over the Rivière Bella Bella and walked toward the light in the night that was the Gamache home. Then Amelia left them and headed to the B&B.

When she was out of earshot, Jean-Guy whispered, "What have you done?"

It was clearly said in jest, unleashing Amelia on an unsuspecting public.

"You're the one who assigned her here," Gamache pointed out.

But as he walked through the June evening, Armand wondered, What have I done?

CHAPTER 21

W hen he got home, Armand put the grimoire in an evidence bag while Reine-Marie watched. Though she understood, he still felt he'd come between his wife and a long-lost friend.

Now the diners helped themselves to grilled salmon, fresh-cut asparagus, and baby potatoes, while Jean-Guy sliced the baguette. A green salad with vinaigrette was already on the table.

Amelia had joined them just as dinner was being served in the Gamaches' kitchen.

Ruth was also there, though uninvited. The final guest was Anne Lamarque, very much present, if only in spirit.

Ruth and Reine-Marie had described for the newcomer what the grimoire was. Amelia, always fascinated with books, was wide-eyed.

"What happened to her?" Amelia asked.

"Anne Lamarque?" said Ruth. "She died."

"At the stake?" asked Amelia.

"Steak? Is there steak?" Ruth looked around, hopefully.

"The stake," said Amelia. "The stake," she repeated, as though the word sounded strange in her mouth. "Staaaay-kuh."

Giggles burbled up, like indigestion. Out they came, in short hiccups of laughter.

Everyone stopped what they were doing to look at the young woman.

She grabbed a piece of baguette and stuffed it in her mouth, but it only seemed to make it worse.

"Is she . . . ?" Reine-Marie whispered to Armand.

"You're high," said Ruth, glaring at Amelia.

"Hi!" she replied, then made a sputtering sound, clearly cracking herself up.

"From your stash?" Ruth asked Armand.

"If I had one, I'm sure you'd have taken it by now." He passed her the salad, which she ignored. "My only stash these days is eclairs."

"Yeah," said Reine-Marie. "Those should be made illegal."

"I'm going to have to take the grimoire over to the evidence locker after dinner," Armand said.

"Bye-bye," said Amelia.

Reine-Marie sighed but nodded. "At least I got to hold it."

Armand wished she hadn't. It was his fault, but at the time there was no way they could have known the items in the hidden room had anything to do with a murder. And, to be fair, they still didn't know. Not for sure. The only connective tissue was the Stone letter.

"So how did she die?" asked Reine-Marie. "We never got that far in the story."

"She was arrested and put on trial," said Ruth, pouring hollandaise sauce over the salmon and asparagus.

"For witchcraft?" asked Jean-Guy.

"Not at first. It was for promiscuity, running a brothel, adultery. Then the Jesuits heard about the grimoire and added witchcraft. Her husband testified against her, of course. Interestingly, his name was Folleville."

"Crazy town," declared Amelia, popping up straight in her chair, her voice loud and happy. She placed an asparagus spear between her nose and upper lip and turned it into a drooping mustache.

Reine-Marie pressed her lips together to stop from laughing.

"Exactly," said Ruth, who didn't seem to find anything at all odd in the behavior of the young agent. But then, the old poet had a duck on her lap.

"Her customers, all men, also testified against her—"

"Testified. Testified. No testes," said Amelia, then bit the tip off the asparagus spear. Jean-Guy grimaced.

"Said her spells had lured them to her tavern against their will."

"Did they believe it?" asked Jean-Guy. "The priests? Or were they just using fear to control the population?"

"Well, if they didn't believe it at first, they eventually convinced themselves," said Ruth. "People do begin to believe their own lies. Besides, these were men who supposedly believed in God. The Devil came as part of that package."

That left them quiet. Most of those around that pine table believed in God. And, yes, the Devil came along for the ride.

Unlike for most people, for Armand Gamache neither God nor the Devil was abstract. He didn't just believe in them. He knew them. Had met both. Had shaken hands with them. He had the scars to prove it.

Evil is unspectacular, and always human,
And shares our bed and eats at our own table,
And we are introduced to Goodness every day.
Even in drawing rooms, among a crowd of faults.

He looked around the table and smiled. If ever there was a crowd of faults . . .

"Any random calamity was blamed on witches," said Reine-Marie. "Accidents, illnesses, drought, torrential rain, blizzards. If a pig ran away, or a child got sick, or an early frost killed the crops, it was the work of witches."

"I read where a mosquito bite was thought to be a teat for the Devil to suckle," said Ruth. "You can imagine the hysteria."

"So what happened to Anne Lamarque?" Armand asked, picking Amelia's napkin off the floor and handing it to her. "Was she burned?"

Amelia looked at her napkin, then let it drop again, watching as though gravity were magic.

"Burned?" said Ruth. "No."

"Well, that's good," said Jean-Guy.

"What they did to her was worse."

"Worse?" he said. "What could be worse?"

"Back in the 1600s, in New France? What's worse is being banished. She was sent out of Montréal, rowed across the river, and left on the far shore for the demons to claim. Burning would be too quick."

"She had to be damned before she died," said Reine-Marie. "All the so-called witches were expelled, sent into the forests to die. Slowly."

They tried to imagine what that would be like. Standing on the banks, Anne would have watched the boatman return to Montréal, the cesspool that passed for civilization. But however harsh, it was home.

Turning around, she'd face her future. The forest. Infested with terrifying creatures.

If the bears didn't kill her, the demons certainly would.

It would be slow, and it would be agonizing, and when it was finally over, she'd be in Hell. For eternity.

"She wasn't the only one," said Ruth. "Most were never heard from again. They were swallowed up by the forest."

"Most but not all?" Armand said, handing Amelia the napkin. Again. And looking into her eyes.

"Anne apparently survived into ripe old age," said Ruth.

"How?" asked Jean-Guy.

"She traveled south until she came to a valley with a meadow and a river of spring water. There she stopped. Two other women, also banished as witches, found their way to her. They built homes. Planted crops. With the help of the medicinal recipes in the grimoire, they survived. Formed a small community. Eventually they each planted a tree in a clearing, as a sign for others. There was a safe place." She looked at Reine-Marie and smiled. "For witches."

"Here?" said Jean-Guy. "Are you saying Anne Lamarque founded Three Pines?"

"Who knows?" said Ruth. "Believe whatever you want."

After the dessert of ice cream with salted caramel sauce, Armand went into his study and picked up the grimoire, now encased in plastic, noting again the charred leather cover.

He was sorely tempted to take the book into the living room, sit by the hearth, and read it. But he had to get it into the locker. As he left with the book under his arm, he looked back and saw Reine-Marie and Ruth watching.

He wondered if Anne was standing with them, the third woman. Watching over them. He then turned and watched Amelia make her way back to the B&B.

"Is she okay?" Jean-Guy asked.

As a recovering addict himself, he knew the dangers of even one drink, one toke. One snort. The problem was never the second or third, it was that first.

"Yes, she's okay."

They paused on the village green, looking up at the three huge pines. Was this the spot where an exhausted, emaciated, frightened woman, condemned for being strong and wise and independent, had stopped running?

Where she made a home. For herself and generations of others who were also lost. Who also needed a safe place. Including the two men standing shoulder to shoulder in the darkness.

Once back at the Incident Room, Gamache himself dusted and swabbed the book.

Some prints appeared, emerging from the pages, as though surfacing. Or expelled.

Jean-Guy watched him work, then asked, "Do you think Ruth was right? That Three Pines was founded by witches?"

"Not witches, Jean-Guy." Armand handed the samples to him to bag and placed the book in the locker. "Just women. Like Reine-Marie. Like Annie."

"Like Ruth."

"No one's like Ruth," said Armand, peeling off the gloves.

Jean-Guy laughed. "What I don't get is how Ruth knows all that about Anne Lamarque."

"I sometimes think it's best not to ask."

"Maybe she was one of the women. I wonder how old she is."

"I wonder how old the duck is," said Armand.

Jean-Guy laughed. "Maybe Rosa's one of them. Transformed into a duck."

That might explain a few things, thought Armand.

It was a good point. Not the age, or duck, thing, but how Ruth knew. If Anne Lamarque and two other women really had founded Three Pines, how would anyone know that? They presumably died here. Would their stories not be buried with them? Lost and forgotten?

But was anything in Three Pines ever lost? Or forgotten?

There was a ding and Jean-Guy walked over to his desk. "The autopsy report on Patricia Godin has come through."

Before Armand could get to his own desk to look, he heard the door open.

"*Bonsoir*," said Olivier. "We were closing up the bistro and saw the light on. Thought we'd check."

"Everything okay?" asked Gabri.

"Everything's good," said Gamache. "We're just tidying up a few things."

"Has something happened, Armand?" Olivier asked. "The crime scene tape in the loft. Is it a crime scene?"

"The truth is, we don't think a crime itself was committed there, but there is a small possibility some of the things found in that room are connected to a crime."

"A murder?" asked Gabri.

Gamache lifted his hands, to show he either could not or would not answer.

Olivier took a few steps into the Old Train Station and Gabri followed. The men were very familiar with the large open space. It was home to their volunteer fire department. Both were members, and Ruth was the chief. Self-appointed, admittedly. But being essentially a dumpster fire herself, she was familiar with flames.

"Is there something else?" Armand asked.

"Well, yes. I was telling Gabri about the elephant, and thought, since you're here . . ."

"You want to see it?"

"Do you mind?"

"No, as long as you don't touch it."

A minute later they were standing in the evidence room. A single bright bulb hanging from the ceiling lit the odd assortment of items.

Armand put on gloves and picked up the bronze statue.

Gabri, by instinct, reached out, then drew his hands back and leaned in, moving his head this way and that. Then he stepped away.

"That's it. That's ours. My great-grandfather brought it back from India. I dusted it every day, I should know."

"Every day?"

"Well, whenever we had guests staying in the room. It has the dented ear and crooked tusk from when someone dropped it."

"Someone?"

"Focus, Olivier, that isn't the lede here."

"But ours didn't have all that engraving, did it?"

"No," Gabri admitted, looking closer. "But it's still ours."

Armand lifted the piece to the light and took a closer look at what was etched into the animal's bronze skin. It didn't form a pattern and it wasn't writing of any sort. But there was something.

"All right, let's say it is your elephant," said Gamache. "Tell me again what happened. How and when this went missing from the B&B."

"A guest was staying in that room," said Olivier. "And when she left, the elephant was gone too. You asked for her name. I have it. And her address." He brought a slip of paper out from his pocket.

"Lillian Virginia Mountweazel," Armand read.

"Yes!" said Gabri. "That's her. Can't forget that name. I tried to get in touch with her, but she never answered the messages."

"When was this?" asked Gamache.

"Eighteen months ago," said Olivier. "I can give you the exact dates of her stay."

"How long was she here?" As Armand spoke, he noticed Jean-Guy trying to catch his eye.

"She was booked in for a week, but left after five days," said Olivier.

"Why would she want to take my great-grandfather's elephant?" said Gabri. "Never mind put it in the attic room. It's just bizarre."

"It is that," said Armand.

Replacing the statue, he ushered the men out of the room and to the door.

"Well, good night." He gently closed the door in their baffled faces. Then he quickly crossed to Beauvoir's desk.

"What've you got?"

"Look."

Jean-Guy had highlighted a passage. It described Patricia Godin's injuries and concluded they were compatible with a death by hanging. Suicide.

"But they're not," said Jean-Guy. "With hanging, the bruising would be up here." He drew a line on his throat under his chin. "But see here. Her cartilage is crushed flat and the bruising is a perfect ring around her neck. These injuries were caused by ligature strangulation. Not hanging."

Gamache reread the passage, then scrolled up and began reading the entire report. Jean-Guy gave up his chair so that the Chief could sit.

Ten minutes later, he took off his reading glasses, rubbed his eyes, and nodded. "You're right. Patricia Godin was already dead when hung from the tree."

"She was murdered."

"*Oui.* The coroner missed it. He'd assumed suicide, then saw what he expected to see. To be fair, it's an easy mistake to make." Armand got up. "We change the cause of death and institute a full murder investigation. First thing in the morning, I want a team down here and a warrant to search the old Stone house."

"*D'accord, patron.*"

As they walked back across the bridge over the Bella Bella, Jean-Guy said, quietly, to Armand, "She wasn't stoned, was she."

"Amelia? *Non.* She was practicing. A dry run. I think she figured if Ruth believed it, Sam will too. Smart woman."

"I saw the look on your face when we were telling Amelia about the Arsenault case. Are you having second thoughts about Fiona?"

"Did I hear my name?" A voice came out of the darkness.

Fiona was sitting on the swing on the Gamaches' front porch. Voices carried in the stillness of night, and she'd heard part, or all, of what they'd said.

"Yes," said the Chief, thinking quickly. "We were talking about you. Jean-Guy here wanted to know if I was having second thoughts about you."

There was nothing for it but to admit it. Lying about it would only heighten her suspicions.

"About my guilt, or my innocence?" She stood up.

Before Armand could answer, Jean-Guy jumped in.

"It's the first time we've seen you and your brother together since the trial. I guess it brings back memories. Doubts even. Your case was far from clear."

She gave a small unamused laugh. "'Case'? You call it that? It's my life. And yes, it was far from clear. What's gained by reexamining it? I've done my time. I'm trying to rebuild my life. Are you trying to rebuild your case?"

They could only see half her face in the light spilling onto the porch from the kitchen. But even half a face was enough to show her anger. Though her tone more than made that clear.

"You want to get the whole family? Is that it? The box set of Arsenault kids?"

"I didn't have a chance to answer Jean-Guy's question. The answer," Gamache said, looking her in the eyes as she turned to him, "is no. I am not doubting you."

It was, of course, a lie.

Armand sat in the dark living room waiting for the footsteps in the bedrooms overhead to stop.

When there was finally silence, he crept upstairs and saw there was no light under Fiona's door. Fortunately, her room faced the forest at the back of the home. She would not be able to look out her window and see what he did next.

He sent off a quick text: *Meet me in Clara's garden.*

Not waiting for a reply, he put on his field coat and left the house. Glancing behind him to make sure he wasn't followed, he walked quickly across the village green, skirting around the far side of the three huge pines. Using them as cover.

He let himself through Clara's gate, leaving it open, and into the familiar backyard. There were no lights at the windows. Clara and the village were asleep.

He'd chosen this place because her garden could not be seen from anywhere in the village. They could not be overlooked or overheard.

Though the rain had stopped, clouds were still overhead, blotting out the moon and stars. Putting the village into near complete darkness. But there was no sensory deprivation. He could smell the lilac and wet earth. He could hear the rainwater still dripping off the leaves. But most of all, he could hear the riotous crickets and the spring peepers, tiny frogs and their high-pitched chirps.

They must be, he thought, all around him. While he knew what they were, he wondered what Anne Lamarque would have made of this racket.

He was just about to send off another text, and, if there was no answer, to go over there himself, when he heard a bump and a hissed "*Tabarnak*. Fucking hell."

"Shhhh," he said, and grabbing Amelia's arm, he pulled her toward the river at the bottom of the garden.

"What is it?" she whispered.

"You need to leave. It's possible Fiona overheard me telling Beauvoir that you were not really high."

"You knew?"

"Of course I knew."

"How?"

He looked at her and smiled. "Thirty years as an investigator has taught me one or two things. Besides, you promised you'd stay straight and sober, and I believed you."

From anyone else, what he said would have sounded ludicrous, naïve. But she believed him.

"And," he said, "I know how much you like mind games."

She smiled. Mind games. Not mind-fucks. She realized she'd never actually heard him swear.

"You're not sure Fiona heard what you said?" Amelia asked.

"No. But if she did, she'll tell Sam, and there's no telling what he'd do to you."

"You really do think he's sick."

"*Oui.*"

"Then I should stay. I should help."

"I'm not arguing, this isn't a discussion, Agent Choquet. You'll pack up and leave. Now. Tonight. If all seems clear, I'll call you back."

"For what it's worth, I hope you're wrong about him."

"You like him?"

"God, no. I think the guy's a whack-job. But you think he's here to do something. Something bad, right?"

Gamache was silent.

"That's where I hope you're wrong. 'Cause I think if he wanted to, he would. And almost nothing would stop him. I also think you might be wrong about his sister. When I got back to the B&B, they were together. Not doing anything at all suspicious, but when they saw me, they sure looked guilty. It was not a . . . normal look."

"And you know normal?" He said it with a smile.

She looked at him, surprised by the small tease. "I have observed normal, from a distance. Like in a zoo."

"And which side of the bars were you on?"

Now she gave a small, stifled laugh. How well he knew her.

"What happened at the B&B?" he asked, serious again.

"Well, for one thing, it was Fiona who was pumping me for information, not Sam."

"About?"

She paused. "About you. And what I knew about your family. She said she'd never met your grandchildren, but was hoping to. Sam said he was also hoping to meet them. Soon."

Into the night she heard him whisper: "Fucking hell."

CHAPTER 22

The team from homicide met at the Incident Room the next morning, where Chief Inspector Gamache and Inspector Beauvoir went over the case so far.

The formal investigation into the murder of Patricia Godin had begun.

Everyone listened respectfully, though there were a few raised brows when they were told about the Stone letter and the hidden room.

The search warrant had come through, and they headed to the old Stone house, arriving just after seven a.m.

Disheveled, unshaven, and tying up his dressing gown, Monsieur Godin glanced past the Chief Inspector to the men and women ranged behind him. Then his eyes returned to Gamache.

"You believed me."

"*Oui.*" Gamache introduced Inspector Jean-Guy Beauvoir and the team from the Sûreté homicide unit. "May we come in?"

Godin stepped back, and they followed him into the living room, where Gamache explained, in a voice that was gentle and clear, that Monsieur Godin was right. His wife had been murdered.

The man sank into a chair and stared ahead of him. It was one thing to believe something, it was another to know it. And now he knew.

"Why?"

Gamache had taken the seat across from him. "We don't know.

That's what we hope to find out, but that means searching your home. We have a warrant."

Beauvoir brought it out of his pocket, but Monsieur Godin waved it away.

"Just do what you have to. The house is yours. Tear it apart if you need to."

While Inspector Beauvoir coordinated the search, Gamache took Monsieur Godin into the kitchen. There he made a pot of coffee for the stunned man, then joined him at the table.

"Did you have any visitors in the days before your wife died?"

"Only the family."

"Had your wife been in contact with anyone? Anyone new?"

He shook his head.

They'd take her computer and go over her emails and texts. In case. It was the worst part of any investigation. This invasion of privacy. All those even remotely associated with the crime would have their private lives exposed. Events, messages, decisions, actions that had seemed reasonable, or perhaps a little shady, would suddenly look contemptible. Shameful. Even suspect, when examined closely and taken out of context by strangers.

Sometimes they discovered crimes not related to the investigation. If not outright evidence, then strong suggestions of wrongdoing.

Those were the things Armand kept in the locked room in their basement.

Everyone, he knew, had one. A locked room. Either in their home, or their head, or their heart. Where things that should never see the light of day lived, and waited. For their chance to escape.

"Was she worried about anything? Anything at all?"

Monsieur Godin considered, then shook his head. *Non.*

"Were you and your wife on good terms?"

"Yes, of course."

"Arguments? It's natural to have some."

"Sometimes over money. And travel. Pat wanted to go places now that I'm retired. But I like it here." He paused. "I'm afraid to fly."

He stared down at the table, where they'd had so many meals.

Many in silence. After thirty years of marriage, there didn't seem to be a great deal to say to each other. It wasn't an angry or regretful silence. More a peaceful quietude.

And now there was just silence.

"She wanted to see England. I should've gone."

Armand let the moment rest before he continued. "What was your job?"

Monsieur Godin looked up and smiled. "I was a plumber. Like my father."

Armand met his smile with one of his own. "I wish my son or daughter had married a plumber. I think my wife wishes she had too. We live in an old house, and in the winter, on particularly cold days and nights, we need to leave a few of the taps dripping so the water doesn't freeze and burst the pipes. Happened our first winter there. Flooded the basement. What a mess."

Godin nodded. "I bet. Was your home built before there was much indoor plumbing?"

"Must've been. It's fieldstone. Looks like it was built in the early 1800s, but we don't really know."

"When plumbing was finally put in, it was often installed next to the outer walls, so there'd be something to support the metal pipes. But that means they freeze when it's really cold. And drafts get in between the stones when the mortar gets old and loose."

"What can be done about it?" Armand asked.

"Well, you have to move the pipes. Expensive job. They'd all have to be replaced. We use PVC now. Easier to manipulate and they don't crack and burst."

"But that would mean breaking into the walls, right? And then repairing and repainting them."

"For sure. Like I said, big job. Expensive."

"Did you do the repairs too, or someone else?"

"You'd need to get someone in to put in new drywall, then a plasterer, but I used to do that too if it was a small job. Not hard. I could recommend someone."

"*Merci.*"

It was what Billy had said when showing him how the items got into the attic. Someone with skills had repaired and repainted the ceiling. Someone like Monsieur Godin.

The Gamaches had replaced all the wiring and plumbing before they'd moved into the home. He did not need it fixed, nor did he need to know how it was done.

But he did need to know if Patricia Godin's husband could remove a section of the bookstore ceiling and then repair it.

"You know, someone did come by," said Monsieur Godin, "but it was a month before Patricia died. He was interested in old documents. Asked if we had any. Said it was the latest thing. All the antiques in old barns and homes had been picked over, and now people were interested in paper stuff. He was looking for old books and maps and deeds and photographs."

And letters? thought Gamache, though he remained quiet.

"Asked us to get in touch, if we found any."

"Did you meet him?" asked Gamache.

"Yes. He seemed nice. Though I can't see there'd be much of a market in old deeds."

"Can you remember his name?" It seemed a long shot and, indeed, it was. Godin shook his head.

"Can you describe him?" Gamache almost made the mistake he always warned his agents against. Leading the witness, guiding them to an answer.

He was tempted to describe Sam Arsenault, young, auburn hair, slender, and ask if that fit the man who visited. Instead, he remained quiet while Godin thought.

"I'm sorry, I'm not good at that sort of thing."

"But it was a man?"

"Yes."

"Young? Old?"

Gamache waited.

"Oh, older. About my age. But I can't really remember anything else."

"Was he a big man? Or slender?"

Godin shook his head. "*Désolé.*"

"Did he return?"

"Not that I know of. I think Pat would've told me." Now he stared at Gamache. "You don't think . . ."

"He said to get in touch. Did he leave a card or anything?"

Godin's brow dropped in thought. "Well, he must've, don't you think? But I can't remember seeing one. Now that I'm thinking about it, he called himself a detective."

"He was a police officer? A member of the Sûreté?"

Surely not, in his late sixties or early seventies. But age was hard to guess. He suspected some younger agents thought he himself was ancient. Maybe the man was a retired detective, and this was his hobby.

"I think he was a sort of private detective," said Godin.

"That old letter, from Pierre Stone, was sent here by someone," said Gamache. "Do you have any idea who?"

"Not a clue. I didn't even know it came here."

"And you say you didn't have a forwarding address for Monsieur Williams?"

"No. I have no idea how Pat got it to him. I mean, how would she even know that he was related to this Stone fellow? Different last names."

Yes, thought Armand as he got up. Good questions.

He left his card for Monsieur Godin, had a word with Beauvoir, then drove back to Three Pines to meet the conservator from the Musée in Montréal. Well aware that he was leaving with more questions than when he'd arrived.

CHAPTER 23

◡

"*A lors*," Dr. Mirlande Louissaint said, cocking her head slightly. It tipped further and further over until she was actually leaning to one side. Then the other. Like a very large, very slow pendulum.

She and her assistant had watched as Gamache unrolled the giant painting on the floor of the Incident Room, using books to weigh down the corners. As more and more of the work was revealed, Dr. Louissaint had made a series of sounds. Increasing in their astonishment but decreasing in volume.

Until finally the entire thing could be seen, and she whispered, "*Alors*."

Then repeated it. "*Alors*." Well. Well, well.

At least, thought Gamache as he straightened up and stretched, the Chief Conservator from the Musée had graduated from guttural sounds to an actual word.

"A World of Curiosities," she whispered.

"*Pardon?*"

"*The Paston Treasure*." She motioned toward the painting. "It's the nickname given to it. *Alors*." She leaned over the canvas before straightening up. "But this isn't the real thing."

"No."

"What exactly do you want from me?"

"Anything you can tell me about it. How long ago it was painted. If the technique reminds you of any artist. Is there a painting underneath?" He brought out a baggie with the nails. "And I'd like you to look at these. Are they genuine or reproductions?"

She took the bag, glanced at it, then handed it back. "They're real."

"You're sure?"

There was a slight snort from her assistant, amused anyone would question her *patron*.

Dr. Louissaint stared at Gamache, but he just waited. A glare was not a reply. He needed the words.

"Yes, the nails are hand-forged and date from the era of the original *Paston Treasure*, the mid-1600s." She widened her eyes, as if to say, *Heard enough?*

"*Merci.*"

"Is this"—Dr. Louissaint tilted her head toward the canvas on the floor—"part of an investigation, Chief Inspector?"

"To be honest, I'm not sure."

This admission of doubt seemed to impress her.

"Your colleague, Inspector Beauvoir, was it?" When Gamache agreed, she continued, "Told me a little. Enough for me to bring some equipment and—" She pointed to the young woman now setting up what looked like a scanner. "Maryse."

"*Bonjour*," said Gamache.

"*Bonjour, monsieur*," said Maryse, then went back to work.

Dr. Louissaint turned to Gamache. "I've seen copies of *The Paston Treasure*. And photographs. Read books on it. I even visited it in the UK." She spoke of the painting as though it were a person. "It's a masterpiece, one of the most studied works of art, and yet"—she leaned closer to the copy—"it remains a mystery."

"How so?"

"It was painted in the great age of exploration, when ships and merchants were pushing the boundaries of the known world and bringing back their finds. The Pastons gathered a huge collection and then commissioned someone to paint at least part of it. But how did they decide which of the two hundred pieces would be in the painting? Why so much emphasis on music? On time? The hourglass, the timepiece, the clock. Does it say six o'clock or half past eleven? Is the time signif-icant?"

"We studied the painting in art college," said Maryse, piping in. "Partly as a work of art."

"But also art history?" suggested Gamache.

"Not just that, but history itself. And natural sciences, and geogra-phy. It's described as a portal into the past."

He could hear the young woman's excitement as she talked about the original.

"And yet, it left so much of itself unknown," said Dr. Louissaint. "Including who even painted it. Must've taken months and months, and then not to sign it? Why? I see yours isn't signed either."

"No, that would be too easy."

She smiled, then bent closer to the painting. "Do you mind if I take some samples?"

Gamache gave them both gloves and watched as the conservator, on hands and knees, scraped a corner. Then she put on headgear, like jewelers wore, and moved farther along. Examining closely. Closely. Maryse turned on the scanner and moved it back and forth across the work.

After a few minutes, Dr. Louissaint rose, shoved the magnifying glasses up onto her head, and went over to the monitor.

"This isn't a copy."

"If it's not a copy," asked Gamache, "what is it?"

He joined them by the screen, where a ghostly image of the origi-nal *Paston Treasure* appeared.

"A paint-by-number."

Gamache gave a small grunt of amusement. "A local artist, Clara Morrow, said the same thing. Thought it must be that. Not a real paint-by-number, of course, but the same idea."

"Clara Morrow lives here?" said the Chief Conservator and her assistant, as one. Both sounded like teenage girls being told their fa-vorite actor was next door.

"She does."

"I'd love to meet her." Again the women spoke in unison.

"I did my thesis on her," said Maryse.

"I went to her first solo show at the Musée d'art contemporain," said Dr. Louissaint, as though trying to one-up Maryse.

"Perhaps . . . ," suggested Gamache, and tilted his head toward the painting on the floor.

"Right, *désolée*. Whoever did this just painted over the copy and added their own bits." She pulled the loupe over her eyes again and turned to Gamache as though examining him closely. "Now why would anyone do this?"

He shook his head and hoped those glasses didn't help her see his complete and utter bafflement. Though it was hardly hidden.

Dr. Louissaint knelt down again and minutely examined the canvas before struggling back up.

Gamache helped her to her feet, and she thanked him. "Too many years kneeling on cold floors or standing on scaffolding trying to save murals."

"I know the feeling." He did not say what he'd spent years kneeling beside. And that they were beyond saving.

Dr. Louissaint took off her headgear and stared down at the painting. Then she stepped back, taking in the full effect of the overpainted image.

"There's something about it, isn't there? And not just because of the deliberately modern touches, which are bizarre, and yet seem to fit in. It's both compelling and"—Dr. Louissaint searched for the word—"offensive. I'm not sure that's the right word. But close. It's not just because of the young Black man as part of the Paston collection, or the fact they've ruined a masterpiece. It's something else."

Gamache felt it too. "Offensive" was, he thought, the right word. Offensive in all its meaning. It not only offended, but there was something aggressive about it. It seemed an attack, even as it just lay there on the cold concrete floor.

Dr. Louissaint wandered the room, walking off stiff joints. She stopped at the open door to the evidence locker, stared. And turned.

"What's that?"

Gamache joined her. "The book?" He assumed she'd seen the grimoire.

"No, the elephant. Can I see it?"

Gamache put on gloves and brought the statue out. She took his elbow in an imperious way and walked him and the elephant over to a window. Re-donning her loupe, she bent close to the bronze sculpture. Getting Gamache to turn it this way and that.

"Nice, nice," she mumbled. "Late eighteenth century. Maybe early nineteenth. Indian, of course. Solid?"

She peered at Gamache, who nodded. It was getting heavy in his hands.

"But these markings don't make sense," she continued. "Any work like this I've seen has had almost no etching. Besides"—she leaned closer, then lifted her headgear—"it's recent. Someone's put them on in the last couple of years, I'd say."

He looked at the lines more closely. Then at Dr. Louissaint. "Do they look at all familiar?"

"No. They look like Sanskrit or . . ." She looked closer. "No, not hieroglyphics. But they do appear to be writing of some sort." She turned to look back at the huge canvas. "There are similar marks on the painting."

He stared at her for a moment, then both of them almost ran back to the canvas and knelt beside it.

He couldn't see them, but when she handed him her special glasses, they popped out. There they were, passing as wood grain. As texture in the heavy curtains. Etched into the trumpet.

What had looked like random lines to the naked eye now came into focus. They were shapes. He looked up and down, left and right. Scanning the immense canvas. They were everywhere.

It was as though the painting were screaming at him. Trying to tell him something.

CHAPTER 24

⁓

While Dr. Louissaint continued her examination, Armand placed a call to a former colleague, now retired and living in Vancouver.

Thérèse Brunel had been a senior officer in the Sûreté. She worked well past retirement, partly because she was so valuable to the force and partly because no one had the guts to have "that" conversation with her.

She'd come into policing later in life after a career as a senior curator with the Musée des beaux-arts. An investigation into art theft brought her into contact with the Sûreté, and she discovered a fascination with, and aptitude for, crime. Solving.

Over the years she and her husband had become good friends of the Gamaches.

"Thérèse? Armand."

"Armand, it's just after seven in the morning here."

"Did I wake you?"

"Do you care?"

He smiled at her reply.

"Something's happened," she said. "What is it? The family?"

"Is fine. It's a case. At least, I think it's a case."

"Could you be more vague?"

He laughed. "I need your help and probably Jérôme's. It's about *The Paston Treasure*."

"Really? One of my favorite paintings. Now why would it be involved in a homicide case in Québec? That is what we're talking about, isn't it?"

"So you know the painting?"

"I do. A real curiosity."

He explained what they'd found, and where. At first, there were sounds as people make when they're absorbing information. But after a while, she fell silent.

"I'm glad you called in Mirlande," said Thérèse when he'd finished. "She'll be able to help. But I suspect the one you really want to talk to is Jérôme."

"Eventually, yes, but I'd like to hear what you can tell me about *The Paston Treasure*."

"Let me think." There was silence down the line while she gathered her thoughts. "It was painted in the 1670s, or thereabouts, and shows many of the curios collected by the Paston family in Norfolk. That in itself would make the painting worth noticing, just as a historic record of the times. But there are a number of mysteries surrounding it, not least of which, why didn't the artist, who clearly put a huge amount of time and effort into the thing, sign it?"

"Theories?"

"He died before he could. Or he didn't want to be associated with it."

"Why—"

"—wouldn't he? I don't know, Armand. Wish I did. It was a strange and dangerous time in England. Political unrest. Religious unrest. Talk of witches."

"Witches?"

"Yes. One of the stranger details in the painting is almost hidden. Look closer at the roses around the neck of the cello."

"Okay." Armand was bending over the painting. "I don't see anything."

"Look closer. Though it might not be there in the version you found."

"May I borrow your glasses?" he asked Dr. Louissaint, who, while surprised, handed them over. He looked again, then pulled back sharply. It was as though he'd been plunged into the folds of the plump white rose.

And then he saw it. Lifting off the loupe and handing it back to the conservator, he said into the phone, "It's a ladybug."

"Right. An exquisitely rendered one, at least in the original." She paused, then said, almost to herself, "Interesting that your artist chose to copy such a tiny detail." Then her voice returned to lecture mode. "In England, the bug was, at the time, known as a symbol of the Virgin Mary. But in Norfolk, where it was painted, that bug is called something else. A bishop-that-burneth."

"Why?"

"Well, what were bishops burning at the time?"

"Witches."

"Right. It's possible there's something in the painting—maybe the ladybug, maybe something else—that made it dangerous for the artist to be associated with it. It might be something lost to our modern eyes. There're other oddities about the original, like why it was painted. Is it meant as a statement of wealth and prestige? Or perhaps a *memento mori*."

"A remembrance after death?"

"Yes. Something that would immortalize the Pastons. But that's another mystery. We don't know if it was the father, William, who commissioned the work, or the son, Robert. This might interest you, Armand. Robert was an alchemist."

Thérèse was rattling off other secrets, other mysteries, contained in the painting and, so far, unreleased. Like who the figures were. The humans but also those carved into the chair and the head of the cello.

"It seems the painting, or painter, was trying to say something. I wonder if those lines and symbols are in the original, but we just never noticed. I'll have a look."

And that brought Armand back to the main purpose of his call. "Is Jérôme there?"

"I'll get him. Jérôme? *Où es-tu?*"

Thérèse's husband had been an emergency room physician, but his hobby and passion were codes. He'd solved at least one for Gamache in the past and was on the team of volunteers trying to crack Dickens's Tavistock letter and other literary works written, for reasons that might never be known, in coded markings.

While waiting, Gamache sent them pictures of the painting and the elephant. Overviews, but mostly close-ups of the markings and other details, including the bug. The bishop-that-burneth.

When Jérôme Brunel got on the phone, Armand explained.

"*Oui*, Armand, I'm looking at what you sent. Fascinating. Let me get back to you. Can I consult my group?"

"Other decoders? Not yet. Thérèse knows, of course, but otherwise, please keep this to yourself."

"Tell Armand there are no markings on the original," Thérèse shouted in the background.

"I heard," he said.

Jérôme laughed. "So did all of Vancouver."

After he'd hung up, Armand put on a pot of coffee. As the room filled with the welcome aroma of the rich, strong drink, he stood at the window, one hand clasping the other behind his back.

It was a beautiful, bright morning, sun gleaming off the moisture from the rain the day before. It would soon evaporate, but for now, it gave an otherworldly look to a village that already appeared out of time and place.

He saw Harriet leave the B&B and wondered if she'd been home last night. And wondered what Myrna would say to her niece.

Then he saw Fiona leave their home. As he watched, he realized that over the years of visiting her in prison, of trying to soften the judicial blow he'd helped land, he'd come to think of her as a sort of niece. Not, of course, with the depth of love he felt for his real nieces, but a member of the extended family nevertheless.

And now, after Amelia's report the night before and other evidence, he was forced to confront something else.

Matthew 10:36.

It was something his first mentor, his first chief in homicide, had told him.

"Oh, one other thing, Armand." He'd stopped the young agent as he was leaving a meeting with the other officers. This was shortly after he'd joined homicide. Shortly after the shootings at the Polytechnique that were to haunt him for the rest of his life.

"Matthew 10:36."

Agent Gamache had stood at the door waiting for more. But that was it. He was dismissed. A week or so passed before Armand, in a quiet moment, remembered and looked up the reference in the family Bible.

A man's foes shall be they of his own household.

Agent Gamache hadn't believed it. Had dismissed it as the sad perception of a highly effective officer who'd grown cynical with age.

But Matthew 10:36 had proven true. If the definition of "household" included the wider extended family of colleagues within the force. That was what his first boss had been trying to tell him. To warn him.

Almost too late, Gamache, by then the head of homicide himself, had seen it.

Armand watched as Fiona began walking. *The bistro*, he sent out the plea. *Go there. Or the bookstore. Or the bakery.*

Anywhere but—

She walked straight to the B&B. To join her brother.

—there.

Now he had to face the possibility that Jean-Guy was right, and his foes were literally within his own household.

And yet, his mind said, why shouldn't she spend time with her brother? Was it so wrong?

Was he doing to Sam Arsenault what had been done to Anne Lamarque and so many others? Judging and condemning without evidence. He believed the boy, the young man, was mentally ill. And yet, there was no proof beyond two winks and the subtle movement of one finger. And a lingering chill in his core. Was that enough to condemn? Surely not.

Could he have been wrong about him? About her? Did he, as Jean-Guy believed, have it backward? That yes, there was a psychopath in that family, but it wasn't the boy.

Once again, he remembered the conversation Amelia had described. It had been Fiona who'd asked about the grandchildren. Not Sam.

A cold resolve settled into his core.

Earlier that morning, in the car over to the Stone house with the search warrant, he'd told Jean-Guy about sending Amelia away, and what she'd said to him in Clara's garden. What Sam and Fiona had asked her the night before. About the family. About the grandchildren.

Beauvoir was silent, then finally said, "They could just be interested."

"For God's sake, Jean-Guy, you know it's more than that. Sam Arsenault's clever. He's doing this to get back at me, and God knows how far he'll go."

"What I know, *patron*, is that you're obsessed with him. You've had it in for him from the first moment you met. I don't know what that's about, but it's blinding you to the real threat."

"You mean Fiona. I arrested her. Hardly the act of a blind man."

"And you vouched for her, got her parole. Invited her into your home." Beauvoir took a deep breath, trying to calm himself. "I'm sorry. I'm just worried if there really is trouble, we'll be looking in the wrong direction. You remember that day when we first met them? When you told them their mother was dead?"

"Of course."

"One of them cried. One of them did not. Which one is most likely to be a psychopath?"

That gave Armand pause. Though he also knew one of the great skills of a psychopath was the ability to feign appropriate emotions.

"Let me talk to Sam," said Beauvoir. "See what I can find out."

"The children, Jean-Guy. Whether it's Sam or Fiona or both, they've brought in the children. You'd better be sure."

Now back in the Incident Room, while Beauvoir led the search of the Stone house, and the conservators examined the painting, Gamache went over reports.

When they'd finished, Dr. Louissaint approached him.

"We've taken samples of the paint and the canvas. I can tell you that, judging by the brushstrokes, more than one person worked on it."

"More than one? Two? Three?"

"I don't know. The painting's so big it's hard to tell on a short exam. The scans might tell us more." She turned back to the painting. "What I don't get is how someone managed to print a life-sized copy of *The Paston Treasure* onto this canvas."

"Would it be difficult?" asked Gamache.

"I can't think of any machine that could do it."

"I've heard of one," said the young apprentice. "Or at least there was a proposal for one a few years ago. They came to my art college for advice, since we also have a big printer, but not this size."

"Who was asking?" asked Gamache.

"Corrections Canada."

"The prison system?" said Gamache.

"As part of art therapy, I guess. They wanted inmates to copy some masterpieces. Kenojuak Ashevak. Group of Seven. A few Morrows. Clara, not Peter, of course."

Of course, thought Gamache, and felt a pang of pain for the man. No *memento mori* for Peter Morrow.

"Why would they need advice from your college?" he asked. "Surely that's easily done with existing technology."

"For those smaller works, yes, but they were interested in larger canvases too, so that the inmates would have to work in teams. Learn to work together," said Maryse.

Gamache looked at Dr. Louissaint. Two or three artists . . .

He knew that choirs had been formed in penitentiaries for that same purpose. To literally create harmony. Teams of inmates had also been trained to work with puppies to become guide dogs.

Was it possible this was painted by inmates, as part of art therapy? But that raised a whole lot of other questions. Not just how it got into the attic, but how it got out of a prison.

And why didn't the inmates just copy the original, which would have been the assignment, but put their own spin on the masterpiece? Why these particular modern touches?

"*Alors*, it is puzzling," said Dr. Louissaint. "A joke perhaps?"

"Perhaps."

"Will you let me know what the markings say, if anything? Maybe they're just random."

"Could be."

But he doubted it. And he knew she did too.

After seeing them off, he pulled a chair over in front of the painting. And stared. Trying to enter it. Trying to enter the mind of the person who'd conceived it.

Was there, perhaps like the original, something dangerous here?

Ten minutes later Armand's phone rang. It was Jean-Guy.

"You found something?"

"A ticket to an art show. For *The Paston Treasure*. In the UK."

"When?"

"Three years ago. Monsieur Godin swears he's never seen it before and that his wife wasn't at the show."

True, thought Armand, remembering Godin saying they never traveled.

"Send me a picture of the ticket."

Armand heard a sound behind him and turned to see Robert Mongeau, the minister, at the door. He had his hands pulsing in front of him as if to say he did not want to interrupt.

Gamache waved him in.

There was a ding as Jean-Guy's photograph arrived.

"There's something else," said Beauvoir. "It was used as a bookmark. Get this. It was in one of Ruth's poetry books."

Gamache felt the hair on the nape of his neck go up.

"Godin doesn't recognize the book either and seemed surprised. They never read poetry. I've had forensics go over the book. No prints."

"Which book is it?"

"*I'm F.I.N.E.*"

They both knew Ruth's code. The letters stood for "Fucked up, Insecure, Neurotic, and Egotistical." Which Ruth was. Which most people were.

"And the poem where the card was?"

"Just a moment, I'll find it." There was rustling as the book was taken out of the evidence bag. Gamache knew that slim volume of poetry well. He and Reine-Marie had a dog-eared copy in their own bookcase. Ruth had even signed it, if a scribbled *Fuck Off* could be considered a signature.

Robert Mongeau, with his back to Gamache, was studying *The Paston Treasure*. It was almost certainly the reason for his visit. While his calling might be from God, that did not stop the minister from answering more human callings. Like curiosity.

"Oh, by the way, I've arranged lunch with Sam at the bistro," said Jean-Guy. "Fucking gloves," he mumbled.

Armand noticed that Mongeau was peering closely at the painting and was just about to ask him to step back when the minister did just that. And started softly humming.

"Got it," said Jean-Guy. "The poem is called 'Waiting.'"

"I know it."

And the tune the minister was humming? Did he know that too? It seemed familiar.

Mongeau's voice grew more assured, so that Armand could now hear the song clearly.

"*We sat down and wept*," Mongeau sang in a soft but a clear tenor. "*And wept.*"

Armand turned to face the minister, and as he did, the phone and Beauvoir slipped from his hand.

"*Patron?*" came the tiny voice from below. "Armand? Is something wrong? What's happened?"

Words from Ruth's poem "Waiting" sprang to Armand's mind. Dredged up by the music.

And now it is now, and the dark thing is here.

The waiting, it seemed, was over.

CHAPTER 25

⁓

Gamache picked up the phone.

"Come back," he said to Beauvoir. "And bring that book with you."

"On my way."

Gamache then walked over to Robert Mongeau. "Why were you singing that song?"

"'By the Waters of Babylon'?" said the minister, surprised by Armand's tone. "It's a hymn." He waved toward the painting. "There. The sheet music by the girl. That's what it is. Why? What's wrong?"

There was obviously something very wrong. His hazel eyes searched Armand's, but found no answer there. Just more questions.

"Can you help me roll up the painting? It needs to go back into the evidence room."

"Yes, but, Armand, what's wrong? Was it the song? I'm sorry, I didn't mean to upset you." Mongeau himself seemed upset now.

"It's all right," said Gamache, even as he tried to steady the slight tremble in his right hand. The one that shook, since the shooting, since the grievous head wound, whenever he was especially tired or stressed. It, along with a small limp when exhausted, was his "tell."

"What a strange painting," said Mongeau. "Is that the Québec Bridge?"

The minister pointed to a jug, almost obscured by the other items on the table. It was painted in relief, and so the image was doubly difficult to make out.

Armand stared, then looked more closely.

It was the bridge. Painted at the very moment it collapsed. Tiny flailing figures were dropping into the cold waters of the St. Lawrence River below.

He reached into his pocket and felt the old ring. This could not, he knew, be a coincidence.

"Armand?" said Mongeau. "Everything okay? Is it the Québec Bridge?"

Gamache nodded, only partly hearing the minister. His mind occupied with an old hymn, and an old bridge. And an old ring.

He locked the door to the evidence room, and double-checked. More afraid that whatever was in there would get out than that anyone could get in. He knew it was insane, but he also, now, had some inkling who was behind all this. And yes, "insane" was the word that sprang to mind.

Gamache and Mongeau stepped into the shiny midday, as though emerging from a cave. Armand took a deep breath of the fresh air, turned his face to the sun, and felt his hand steady. Then the two men walked over the stone bridge across the Rivière Bella Bella and back into the village.

"What is it, Armand?" said Mongeau.

Gamache was sorely tempted to tell him about the last time he'd heard that song. The last person who'd hummed it. But he could not. Mostly because it might be a vital piece of the puzzle, but also because, well . . .

Armand Gamache knew how powerful words could be, and he did not, yet, want to utter them. That name.

"It's nothing."

"Something to do with the song?"

"It's nothing, Robert," Gamache repeated, his voice firm. The message now clear. *No further. You will go no further.*

And it was clear by his expression that Mongeau got the message.

To soften it a little, Armand said, "I heard that you defended me to Sam Arsenault. Thank you for that."

"Troubled young man."

"*Oui.* I also heard that you said you could see goodness in him. Is that true?"

Mongeau smiled. "I see goodness in most people. I think you do too."

"Most, but not all. Do you see it in his sister, Fiona?"

Mongeau took a few steps in silence. It was a lovely spring day. The air was soft with the scent of sweet woodruff, and the lilac that flourished in Three Pines. Plants that appeared to die each fall but came alive again each spring. It always seemed a miracle.

But Gamache knew that resurrection was not always a blessing. Not everything dead should come back.

"*My sight is imperfect. I see through the glass darkly,*" Mongeau quoted in answer to Armand's question about Fiona. "Sorry. Easier to take someone else's words. Makes me sound smart." He smiled. "What St. Paul said happens to be true. I only see part, not the whole."

"And what do you see when you look at Fiona Arsenault?" Gamache pressed, knowing his own sight was almost completely obscured when it came to those two young people.

Mongeau stopped. "This is where I leave you. If you ever do want to talk, about yourself, let me know."

Gamache watched the man head to the church. To his sanctuary. Where his wife was healthy and would outlive him.

Armand longed to spend a moment, just a moment, sitting on the bench on the village green. To close his eyes and tilt his face to the sun. A quiet moment of peace next to the three huge pines. These particular trees were planted more than a century ago by three brothers just before they headed off to war. They were still saplings when all three returned, as stained-glass figures.

Armand didn't stop. There was no time to rest. No peace yet.

"*Excusez-moi?*" Reine-Marie said.

"I need you to go to England."

"Why?"

Armand put out his hand to stop her slicing the bread. "Let's sit."

He told her about the ticket to the exhibition that Jean-Guy had found, tucked into the copy of Ruth's poetry book.

"I think the person who was asking Patricia Godin about the Stone letter left it there."

"When? Why?"

They were legitimate questions, and she deserved the answers. If he was asking her to go all the way to England, she needed to know why.

"I think he left the ticket in the book when he killed her. I think it was put there for us to find."

"That's a lot of thinking, Armand. Are you sure it isn't guessing?"

He smiled. "Yes, maybe. But if the ticket was left on purpose, we need to follow up. *The Paston Treasure*, the real one, is at the Norwich Castle Museum. I need you to go there and see what the curators can tell us. And"—he paused—"can you use your maiden name?"

"But if what you're saying about the ticket is true, wouldn't we just be doing what the murderer wants?"

She'd hit on his big worry. "Yes. But we can't ignore it."

"You can, though, just call the Norwich Castle Museum. Or ask one of your colleagues in the UK to check it out. Why does Reine-Marie Cloutier, not Gamache, have to go?" Then she studied him more closely. "What aren't you telling me?"

He stared at her for so long, she began to color. Then he picked up her hands and held them, twisting her simple, thin wedding ring. They'd both had to have them resized as their fingers had grown thicker, along with the rest of them.

He smiled, thinking again of the First Nations blessing at their wedding. The priest had been less than happy doing it but had finally agreed to have someone else read it.

And so Stephen Horowitz, Armand's godfather, had gotten up and recited,

Now you will feel no rain,
for each of you will be shelter for the other.
Now you will feel no cold,

for each of you will be warmth for the other.
Now there is no more loneliness.

There was a cold rain falling. Armand could feel it. And yes, he wanted to shelter Reine-Marie Gamache, née Cloutier, from it.

Armand told her. Almost everything. He didn't yet tell her about "By the Waters of Babylon," and the abomination he thought was behind this. Not until he confirmed it.

Reine-Marie listened, taking it in.

"You want me to go away in case someone wants to harm us?"

As usual, she went straight to the heart of the matter.

"Well, yes. Partly. But I really do need information about *The Paston Treasure*, and I need the visit to be discreet. Unofficial. And in person. You have credentials as a senior archivist and historian."

"You really expect me to run away?" She was glaring at him now. Rarely in their marriage had they had arguments, and most of those were over family. Their children. But this was different. It was about them as a couple.

"It's not—" he began before being cut off.

"I'm not finished. I'm a grown woman, Armand, not a child. This's my home. You're my husband. I won't run away, and I sure as hell won't leave you behind to face whatever this is."

She pulled her hands from his.

"I'm sorry," he stammered. "I didn't mean to treat you like a child. And you're right. I'm your husband, but I'm also a senior Sûreté officer with responsibilities far beyond my own family. I need to focus completely on what's happening, and the reality is, I can't do that and worry about you. I know you say I shouldn't, but I can't help myself. I'm begging you. Please. Go to England. Find out what you can. We both know there's no substitute for standing in front of a work of art. Being there in person. *The Paston Treasure* is obviously central to what's happening. We need to find out why." He held her eyes. "Please, Reine-Marie."

"The ticket was left by the killer?" she repeated.

"Yes, I think so."

"And Monsieur Godin didn't notice?"

"No."

"Does that strike you as odd? His wife died five weeks ago and he never noticed the poetry book lying around?"

"He didn't strike me as the noticing kind." Though even to his ears that sounded off. She had a good point. "Do you think it was left there more recently?"

"I don't know," she said. "Where in Ruth's book was the ticket to the exhibition left?"

"At the poem 'Waiting.'"

She got up and found their worn copy of *I'm F.I.N.E.* Turning to the poem, she read, "*And after all it is nothing new / It is only a memory, after all / a memory of a fear.*" She closed the book. "That was meant for you, wasn't it? Jean-Guy might know the book, but he'd never recognize that exact poem. Whoever killed that poor woman put it there as a message. For you." She held his eyes. "I'll go."

He sighed. "*Merci.*"

"Come with me."

Oh, how he wanted to, but he shook his head. "I'm needed here. I have Jean-Guy and others. I'll be fine."

She tried not to, but still her eyes drifted up to the deep scar at his temple.

"But I will send someone with you," he said. "Someone discreet. To help."

To protect, he knew, she knew, but didn't say.

"Who? Isabelle?"

"*Non.* Lacoste is away with her family." He pulled out his phone and made a call. "Agent Choquet? Do you have a passport?"

"Amelia?" Reine-Marie mouthed.

He nodded, then said into the phone, "Good. You and Madame Gamache are going to England. I'll email you the details."

He hung up and Reine-Marie began to laugh. "Who was that really? Isabelle?" When she saw his expression, her amusement stopped.

"You're serious? She's the discreet investigator? You might as well send me with a marching band."

"Well, no one will ever suspect she's a cop."

Reine-Marie nodded. That was certainly true.

They made the travel arrangements. Reine-Marie and Amelia Choquet would catch the seven p.m. Air Canada overnight flight to London.

When Jean-Guy arrived, the Gamaches were just finishing a quick lunch.

"Join us," said Reine-Marie, getting up. "There's plenty."

He was sorely tempted. "Can't. I already have a lunch date."

Still, he stared at the chilled mint pea soup and the grilled gruyère and caramelized sweet onion sandwiches, and swallowed hard.

"What've you got?" asked Armand, getting up and guiding Beauvoir out of the room.

"The book and the ticket, *patron*." He handed both to Gamache. "Forensics is finished with them."

They were in the living room when Beauvoir stopped, turned, and lowered his voice. "What happened in the Incident Room? You sounded shaken."

"In the painting, the girl is holding a book of music open to one song. Robert Mongeau began humming it."

Now Gamache, in his deep baritone, also hummed. Then stopped when it was clear Jean-Guy recognized it.

"'Babylon,'" he whispered. "You don't think . . ."

"I don't know. We need to check it out. I'm sending Reine-Marie to Norfolk, to see *The Paston Treasure* and speak to the curator. Agent Choquet's going with her."

"Grounds for divorce, *patron*."

"Your lunch date. Sam?"

"Yes. If what you're thinking is true, then he can't be behind the stuff in the attic. Besides, the kid isn't that clever. More a club-to-the-head sort of person."

Or a brick, thought Gamache. Though he knew Beauvoir was right. Sam was cunning, but he didn't have the patience for a plan that was meticulously thought-out and executed. Besides, the man who visited the Godins looking for the Stone letter was older.

Yes, the Arsenault kids were out of the picture.

Though maybe there was more than one "picture." Or a much larger picture. Like *The Paston Treasure*. With far more elements than he knew.

When Jean-Guy left, Armand stood in the living room and opened the thin volume of poetry. To the ticket. To the poem. "Waiting."

And after all it is nothing new / It is only a memory, after all / a memory of a fear. And then the line, the last one, that Reine-Marie had not read. Perhaps on purpose.

A memory of a fear / that has now come true.

"Is something wrong, Auntie Myrna?"

"Come with me."

Up the stairs to the loft they went.

"Sit."

Harriet sat.

Myrna took a few steps this way, then that. And finally ended up where she started. In front of her niece. She sat down and took a couple of deep breaths before speaking.

Harriet had her arguments all lined up, had rehearsed them. Prepared for the onslaught. What she wasn't prepared for was what Auntie Myrna said.

"You know what I did before I retired?"

"I'm sorry for not coming . . ." She stopped. Huh? "Pardon?"

"My job. You know what it was, right?"

"You were a therapist, weren't you?" Harriet's mind raced. Yes, therapist, but what sort? Physical? Art therapy? Massage maybe?

"I was a psychologist. Had a private practice, but I also worked in the prison system with the worst offenders."

"Really?" Harriet had been a child when Auntie Myrna had moved to this village. She'd known, somehow, that her aunt had been a therapist in Montréal, but to Harriet, she'd only ever been Auntie Myrna who ran the bookstore. "That must've been interesting."

She was trying to figure out where this was going. Surely her aunt wasn't suggesting that having consensual sex qualified as an offense, never mind a "worst" one.

Harriet wasn't just physically attracted to Sam, she liked him. He paid attention to her, listened to her. He saw her. He was even interested in her peculiar hobby of collecting bricks, offering to show her one he had that might interest her.

"Had it since I was a kid," he had said. "But don't tell anyone. Gamache already thinks I'm weird."

"You know about the Arsenaults?" said Myrna.

Ahhh, thought Harriet, here it comes.

"Yes. Their mother was murdered. Fiona was arrested by Monsieur Gamache and spent years in prison."

"Yes. But there's more."

Myrna wasn't completely sure how far to go. Sam, after all, was never arrested. His possible involvement was never made public. It was just something Armand suspected. Though he suspected more than just "possible." And more than just "involvement."

Was it fair to say this to Harriet? To smear a young man, without proof.

Rumor was loose in the air, hunting for some neck to land on.

Ruth had written those lines about witch hunts, but really the poem was about those young women killed in the Polytechnique. For being smart, independent women.

Yes. Rumor did that. Like an alchemist, it turned vague discontent into concrete action. And gave suggestive minds a target for their insecurities. Their free-floating fear and resentments were just waiting for some neck . . .

Myrna did not want to do the same thing to anyone. Turn a feeling, a fear, into a fact. But she had to say something.

"Before Fiona could be released on parole, she and her brother needed psychological evaluations. I was asked by Monsieur Gamache to speak to them, to find out if it was safe for him to vouch for Fiona. Which I did."

Harriet waited.

"I stopped the interview with Sam after ten minutes. It was clear to me that he is deeply disturbed. Unwell." Myrna searched her niece's face. "Be careful."

"Thank you."

Never very open, Harriet now did exactly what Myrna had feared. She shut down. Shut her out. She was a past master at hiding her feelings, hiding from anything that even remotely resembled confrontation.

"How are you feeling about what I just said?" she asked her niece.

"Oh, I'm okay. Thank you."

Harriet got up.

"Please," said Myrna, following her to the stairs. "Can we talk?"

Harriet turned. "No need." She smiled. "I'm just fine. Thank you."

Jesus, thought Myrna. It's like I shot her into outer space. She reached out for Harriet, but the young woman drew away.

"It's all right. I think I might stay at the B&B for a while. You're right. There's no room for me here."

"I never said that. There's always room for you. You know that."

"Thank you." Harriet looked around for her knapsack. Picking it up, she walked by her aunt and down the stairs. The bell over the bookshop door merrily jingled.

Myrna went over to the huge window and watched Harriet walk across the village green. Armand stopped to say hello, but she walked right by him and disappeared into the B&B.

Armand stared after her, then looked up at the window. At her.

Myrna dropped softly onto the window seat and looked out at the three huge trees, the message Anne Lamarque and the other women had sent out four centuries earlier.

Three Pines was a safe place, they'd declared. Not safe from hurt or pain. Not from illness and accident and death. What the village in the valley offered was a place to heal. It offered company and companionship, in life and at the end of life. It offered a surefire cure for loneliness.

Like the women who were fleeing for their lives, almost everyone in the village now had come there to find a safe haven. Once again,

Myrna questioned herself. Was she denying Sam the very thing they all sought? A safe place?

But there was a difference between Sam Arsenault and the rest of them. He was the one they were running from.

CHAPTER 26

~

"Monsieur Beauvoir." Sam got to his feet. "Is this table okay? I asked for the best one."

"It's fine. It's perfect."

Jean-Guy tried, he really did, to keep up that professional wall between them. To be courteous but cool to this young man. But as soon as he'd spotted Sam sitting alone at the far end of the bistro by the bathrooms, at the worst table, his resolve began to crumble.

By the time he greeted the young man, the wall was rubble. He once again felt the child in his arms, clutching his new Sûreté-issue coat. The small face buried in it to stifle the sobs.

Those tears, of a ten-year-old whose mother had just been murdered, had stained the coat so that each day, for years, when Agent Beauvoir put it on to go with the Chief Inspector to investigate other murders, he saw the marks.

Every day Agent Jean-Guy Beauvoir was reminded that, as Gamache had said, this was not a puzzle. It wasn't an exercise. It wasn't even a job. This was a sacred duty. To the dead, and those who wept.

"What would you like?" Sam asked. "And please, you're my guest."

"No, of course not. The Sûreté will pay."

"Are you sure—" Sam stopped suddenly.

"What?"

"No, never mind."

"Say it."

Sam shifted uneasily, then leaned forward and said, "I just don't think Monsieur Gamache would approve."

Beauvoir didn't know where to begin with that. The idea that he needed the Chief Inspector's approval to put a lunch on a tab. Sam's comment made him wonder if that was everyone's perception. That he was that much of an underling.

"It'll be fine," he said, picking up the menu. "Don't worry about it."

"But I do. I don't want you to get into trouble because of me."

"I won't," snapped Beauvoir.

They both ordered steak frites. The most expensive thing on the menu. But what the hell. He was allowed.

Snapping the menu shut, he said to Sam, "Did you go into the Gamache home the other night?"

"No, of course not. Is that what this's about?"

"I need the truth."

"Why would I go into the home of someone who doesn't want me?"

Exactly, thought Jean-Guy, studying the man, the man-child, across from him. Why would he?

"Did Monsieur Gamache say I did? Why would he even think that?"

"Some objects were moved. It seems someone was there. And you made some sort of gesture to him the next morning. Like the clicking of a camera."

Sam looked puzzled. Then Jean-Guy showed him, lifting his hand and moving his index finger up and down.

"That's not a camera," said Sam. "This's a camera." He mimicked hitting the red photo "button" on a smartphone. "I don't know what this"—he did what Jean-Guy did—"is. And I can't think when I would've even done it."

"Yesterday morning, when you and Harriet were standing outside here, and the Chief Inspector was getting into his car."

Sam thought for a moment, then his brow cleared and he laughed. "Oh, you mean this."

He made another gesture, close but not exactly what Gamache had shown Beauvoir.

"I was pointing to Harriet and smiling. I think I even winked, so he'd know I was happy, am happy. Being with her makes me happy and I guess I wanted to show him." Sam heaved a sigh and looked bashful. "I think I want his approval. Pathetic, isn't it?" He looked up at Jean-Guy. "You know?"

It was a rhetorical question. But yes, Jean-Guy Beauvoir knew.

And Sam had explained it all. Of course that gesture, for a kid his age, would not be a camera. He'd probably never held a real camera in his life. When lunch was over, he'd have to tell Armand that he could relax, at least about that. Sam had not been in their home.

If anyone had violated the Gamaches' privacy, it was Fiona, though Sam had not thrown his sister under the bus.

The meals arrived. Their steaks were charbroiled and covered in chimichurri sauce. The frites were thin and seasoned. Jean-Guy's mouth was actually watering.

As Sam moved aside to let the server put down his plate, his phone fell to the floor. He bent to get it, but Jean-Guy beat him to it.

The phone, on recognizing Sam's face, had popped open revealing a photo. Of Armand and Reine-Marie's bedroom.

"What the hell is this?" Jean-Guy gripped the phone, practically shoving it in Sam's face.

When Armand arrived in the loft, he found Myrna at the window seat, head in her hands. Crying.

We sat down and wept. And wept . . .

He sat down beside her and waited. And waited. Then he got up and did the only thing he knew might comfort Myrna. He went into the kitchen at the far end of the open loft, passing by the huge hole in the wall, and put on the kettle.

"You spoke to her?" he said when she joined him.

"Yes." She watched him swirl the hot water around in the pot to warm it. "I fucked up."

He turned to her. "I doubt that."

"I shouldn't have said anything."

"Given your suspicions, you had to warn her. Your heart was in the right place."

"The road to hell, remember?"

"That's not true. You know the difference between a lost young man and a deeply disturbed one. Harriet is young and does not. Do you think Sam Arsenault is safe?"

Myrna considered and shook her head.

"Do you think he's sane?"

Again, she shook her head.

"Then how could you not say something? You knew what might happen and you did it anyway. You put her safety ahead of your relationship. That's love."

Taking their seats again, he leaned toward her. Over Myrna's shoulder he could see the gaping hole in the wall and the yellow bands of police tape.

"Tell me about psychopaths."

CHAPTER 27

Fiona Arsenault guided Harriet out the back door of the B&B and into the garden.

"Come. Sit. What's wrong?"

They were alone.

"Where's Sam?" Harriet looked around, hoping, but not hoping, to see him there. Hoping he'd take her in his arms and wipe away her tears. And reassure her. She'd made the right choice.

"He's having lunch with one of the cops."

"Gamache?"

"No, the other one. The younger one. Beauvoir."

Harriet took a few shuddering breaths and calmed herself.

The garden was private and peaceful. The old lilac bushes were thick with blooms, the crab apples were full of bright pink flowers. Some petals had already fallen, creating what looked like pink snow on the grass.

It felt a world away from the turmoil in Harriet's head.

"I'm thinking of staying here."

"Of course, but why?"

"My aunt says Sam's sick. Mentally."

Fiona smiled. "Well, he's my brother, so of course I'm going to agree with that."

Harriet looked at her, then gave one unexpected laugh.

"Brothers," said Fiona, "are a pain in the ass. And Sam more than most. He's taking his sweet time growing up. I grew up too quickly. Had to. I can see how people like your aunt, like Monsieur Gamache, might misinterpret Sam's immaturity. But believe me, he's okay. He cares a lot about you. You're the first woman he's felt that way about."

"So you don't think Sam is . . . unwell?"

"Do you? 'Cause if you do, you really shouldn't be with him. For your sake, but also for his."

"No, no, I like him, a lot. I think Auntie Myrna put things in my head."

"She loves you. She just got the wrong end of the stick. She has a lot of respect for Monsieur Gamache, and for good reason, so she listens to him. And I think there's a chance she's overprotective of you. I'm sure she doesn't mean to keep you away from other relationships. She just enjoys having you to herself."

That had not occurred to Harriet, but it made sense. Auntie Myrna was clearly, now that she could see it, trying to come between her and Sam. Was she jealous?

"It's a generational thing," Fiona continued. "They get scared of anyone who's a little different. I'm sure they don't want to hurt you, or Sam. We just have to stick together, and they'll come around."

Harriet gripped Fiona's hand. She hadn't had that many women friends, that many friends period. Now she saw what she'd been missing.

"Tell me about psychopaths."

"You know as much as I do, Armand."

"I doubt that's true. I've met a few but never spent much time with them. You have. You had to try to treat them."

"That's just it, there is no treating them." Myrna put down her mug of tea. "The best I could manage was not letting them fuck with me. It was exhausting. They're smart, often charming. 'Beguiling' is the word that comes to mind."

"Nice word."

"For lovers, maybe. Not for a psychopath. Then it's horrifying. You can feel yourself slipping under their spell, even as you try to resist. They get in your head." She stared at him. "I think you know what I'm talking about."

When he remained silent, she continued.

"They're incredibly manipulative. They know what you want to hear, and they say it. They know what you're missing in your life, even if you don't. And they pretend to give it to you. They see things you don't. They know things you don't. They're terrifying."

"You talk about them as though they're a different species."

"Just about. If emotions are what makes us human, then yes, they're a different species. They feign emotions but don't actually feel them."

"What motivates them?"

"Getting what they want. That's it. They are purely focused on that."

"And if someone refuses or gets in their way?"

"They'll be moved aside, one way or another. Often, they're brought on side, only because it's easier, less messy, more fun. They're adept at making something untrue appear reasonable. They could make someone believe red curtains are bright blue. Then swear to it."

"What if the person refuses to see the bright blue curtains?"

"That's where you come in."

For a moment, her answer puzzled him. And then he, the head of homicide for the Sûreté, understood.

"They're smart, often brilliant," said Myrna. "Cunning, certainly. Their thoughts and actions are uncluttered by any question of morality. Uncluttered by the existence of others. They're not only the most important person in the universe, they're the only one. Everyone else only exists in relation to themselves."

"Like a black hole."

Myrna considered and nodded. "In a way, yes."

"And what happens if they're ignored?"

Myrna was silent before saying, "They'd go crazy."

What fresh horror would that be, Gamache wondered. A lunatic going crazy.

"What would that look like?" he asked.

"I think you've seen what it looks like. If they're denied, they're like an angry child. An upset, frustrated child will throw toys and dishes, breaking everything they can get their hands on. A psychopath, ignored and frustrated, breaks people."

Sam stared at the image of the Gamaches' bedroom on the phone, then at Beauvoir.

He'd never seen the cop angry. Frustrated at times, annoyed, perhaps. It was hard for Sam to distinguish the difference.

But anger he recognized by the lines down faces that looked so much like cracks. He saw crevices deepening on the cop's face. Yes, Beauvoir was very angry.

Sam shook his head and dropped his eyes. "I didn't take those."

"Look at me." When Sam did not, Beauvoir repeated, raising his voice. "Look. At. Me."

Sam raised his eyes.

"What's this picture doing on your phone?"

"When someone sends a photo, it's automatically saved to my phone. That's what happened."

Beauvoir put the device on the table with such force, other patrons in the bistro looked over. "What's it doing up?"

"Okay. While I waited for you, I was looking at the pictures."

"Pictures? There're more?"

Sam picked up his phone and offered it to Jean-Guy. "I have nothing to hide. Scroll along."

Jean-Guy did. Sure enough, there were other shots of the house. Then he stopped at the picture of the picture. The one from Christmas the year before.

He and Annie had the same framed photo, a gift from Armand and Reine-Marie. It showed the whole family, and Ruth, in front of the tree.

His hand clasped the phone, tight. Overcome with anger over this violation.

"I didn't take it, I swear, Monsieur Beauvoir. Fiona sent it to me."

"Why would she do that?" Jean-Guy's voice was almost a snarl. "And not just this one, but the others, of the whole house."

"I don't know. I think she's angry at me, angry that she spent all those years in prison. And I didn't. She wanted to hurt me."

"But how could these pictures hurt you?"

Sam looked Beauvoir straight in the face. "You've always had a family, haven't you? You've always belonged. I never have. She sent me those pictures as a message. She's welcome in their home, in their lives, and I'm not. I'm out here. You don't know her. She can be wonderful, but she can also be cruel." He examined Beauvoir. "But maybe you do know that."

He took a deep breath and stared again at the family photo. Like a starving child looking into a pastry shop, or a sinner glimpsing Paradise.

"Don't laugh, but part of me even wishes that Monsieur Gamache had arrested me. At least in prison I'd have people around. I'd have, I don't know, predictability. Stability. I'm tired of moving from place to place. I just want to stop, you know? I want someplace to go. I just want someone to care if I was home safe, even if that home is a cell. And that someone is a cop. And then, maybe, when I got out, Monsieur Gamache would take me in too."

Jean-Guy did not laugh. He'd heard it before. Prisoners who didn't want to be released. Men and women who reoffended so they could go back. Home. They weren't free, but they were safe.

"I came here hoping maybe, maybe, the Gamaches would finally see me. Really see me. As I am now. Not as a screwed-up child but as a man, trying to do his best. Maybe, I thought, maybe Fiona and I could reconnect. Become a family again." He mumbled something and Beauvoir had to ask him to repeat it.

"I thought maybe the Gamaches would invite me over for dinner." He dropped his head and spoke to the table. "I stare at the pictures Fiona sent and pretend it's my home. My family. I sit at the dinner table and listen as they talk about their day. And they ask me about mine. I even said to Fiona the other night that I hoped one day to meet the grandchildren. I know I won't, but in my dreams the kids and I toss Frisbees on the village green while the Sunday roast is cooking. I'm sorry. This's pathetic. I'm pathetic. Oh, shit."

He dropped his head.

Jean-Guy understood. He'd been raised in a large family, but Sam was wrong about belonging. Just because there were people around didn't mean you felt a part of it. For as long as Jean-Guy could remember, he'd always felt like a stranger. An outsider. Until he'd been invited one evening back to the Chief Inspector's home for Sunday dinner.

He'd never really left. Not in his heart. At night, in his little apartment, Agent Beauvoir would close his eyes and smell the roast and relive that dinner. And know such a place existed. Such a thing existed. And that maybe, one day, he would not have to leave.

Yes. He understood.

Beauvoir pushed the phone across to Sam. "Erase those pictures, now. While I watch."

"Yessir." And Sam did.

Jean-Guy nodded and smiled and said, "Don't worry. You'll have a family of your own one day. It'll be all right."

Ça va bien aller.

It was, he remembered, exactly what he'd said to the ten-year-old Sam as the boy slobbered on his brand-new jacket.

Jean-Guy had rubbed the child's back and repeated those words until the crying stopped.

It'll be all right. It'll be all right.

But it wasn't.

"You came up here for a reason, Armand," said Myrna. "Not just for Earl Grey."

It took Armand a moment to remember. "Did the Special Handling Unit in the penitentiary try art therapy?"

She raised her brows. "What brought on that question?" Then she glanced toward the hole in the wall and had her answer. "Forget I asked. We tried everything. Forming choirs. Teaching them dog training. You don't want to know how that went. Sports. Like lunatics ourselves, we kept trying and failing. And yes, including art therapy." Myrna examined him. "You've been to the SHU. It's a madhouse. Literally. All anyone wants is to prevent a catastrophe. A riot. Bedlam."

"A breakout."

"That, thankfully, has never happened, nor could it."

"Did it work?"

"Art therapy with psychopaths? Jesus, that sounds like a really bad reality show. Though"—she paused—"I might actually watch that."

They both spent a moment imagining . . .

"Did it work? Not even close. Two of them stabbed each other. One died."

"So it was discontinued?"

"I left, so I don't know. I hope so, but there comes a point where the guards and workers are as deranged as the prisoners. Rational decisions are few and far between. It's brutal."

Gamache got up. "I'm asking a few people over to the Old Train Station—"

"Your Incident Room."

"*Oui.* I need some help with the painting."

"To move it?"

"No. To decode it."

CHAPTER 28

⁓

I t looked farcical.

The villagers stood in front of *The Paston Treasure*, each of them holding a magnifying device to their face.

After inviting them over, Armand had gone into Monsieur Béliveau's shop. It was a true "general store," selling everything from fish and oranges to rubber boots and . . . magnifying glasses.

Clara held her grandmother's blue enamel opera glasses. Myrna and Billy had their own glasses. Ruth peered through binoculars. No one had the courage, or the will, to ask what she used them for.

Olivier, Gabri, Robert and Sylvie Mongeau, and Reine-Marie each accepted magnifying glasses from Armand.

They were examining something none had noticed before. The small markings that the art conservator had found.

Reine-Marie was the first to lower her magnifier. "They're everywhere."

"It's so strange," said Gabri. "What do they mean?"

"Don't you think if he knew," snapped Ruth, shoving Rosa toward Gamache, "he wouldn't need us?"

The duck nodded.

Now that they could see them, it seemed, like the roofline and the hidden room, so obvious. These weren't marks to simulate texture, these were symbols.

"Lots of paintings have hidden messages," said Clara. "Even the

Sistine Chapel. Michelangelo painted an angel essentially giving the pope the finger."

"And writers do it all the time," agreed Reine-Marie. "They're only just now decoding Dickens's Tavistock letter."

It was the letter Jérôme Brunel was working on as part of his hobby. Armand still hadn't heard back from the retired doctor and made a mental note to follow up.

"You know the Voynich manuscript?" Myrna asked Reine-Marie.

"Is that the Jesuit one?" she asked. She had a vague memory of reading about it.

"Right. Voynich was an antiquarian bookseller. In 1912 he bought a collection of books from some Jesuit college, and among them was a manuscript from the 1400s. It's more than two hundred pages all written in this unknown language, with illustrations and graphs. No one knows who did it, or why. Or what it means."

"It's strange that the marks would be put on the elephant," said Olivier.

"Elephant?" asked Sylvie. "There's no elephant in the painting, is there?"

"No, I mean the bronze statue. A guest took it from the B&B," said Gabri. "It was in the attic too, with the same markings etched in. I tried to track down Madame Mountweazel but couldn't find her."

"Mountweazel?" said Reine-Marie. "Lillian Virginia Mountweazel?"

They turned to her, amazed.

"*Oui*," said Gabri. "You know her? You weren't even here when she was."

"Who is she?" asked Armand.

Reine-Marie looked torn between amusement and concern. "She doesn't exist."

"Then how do you know her name?" asked Jean-Guy.

"And she does exist," said Gabri. "We met her."

"No, I mean the name, Mountweazel. It's a code too."

"What do you mean?" asked Sylvie. "Code for what?"

Reine-Marie was quiet for a moment, gathering her thoughts. "Years ago, before the internet and electronic ways to investigate intellectual property thefts, publishers would put traps into books. Fictitious entries in reference books, to catch copyright thieves. Lillian Virginia Mountweazel is the most famous."

"Well," said Gabri, "famous?"

"Among archivists, yes. She's almost a folk hero. Lillian Virginia Mountweazel is a fake biographical entry in *The New Columbia Encyclopedia*. She was described as a fountain designer who died in an explosion while on assignment for *Combustibles* magazine."

The minister, Robert Mongeau, was the first to break the silence, with a laugh. Soon the others were chuckling too.

"If something's called a mountweazel, it means it's a fraud," said Reine-Marie.

"Shit," said Gabri. "I wish you'd been around when she was here."

"Maybe that's why she came when she did," said Sylvie. "So you wouldn't be here."

Armand was nodding. It was a thought. And a disturbing one. It meant that someone really was feeding information about his family, their travels, their habits and interests. Someone close.

He was happier than ever that Reine-Marie was going away. Though they had to make sure that person did not know where.

"It's not that funny," Gabri said to Ruth, who was still chuckling.

Ruth was staring at the painting through her binoculars.

"It's not that," she said, lowering them. "It's that." She gestured toward the painting.

"What?" asked Armand.

"Isn't it obvious?"

"For fuck's sake, you old drunk," said Gabri. "If it was obvious, we wouldn't be here."

"I just said that to you."

"I know. Do you never listen to yourself?"

He turned to Armand. "She doesn't see anything in the painting. The duck has a better chance of decoding those marks."

Rosa nodded. But then, ducks often did. Though they almost never broke codes.

"I see a DVD," said Ruth.

"So do we." Olivier waved toward the painting.

"But do you see its title?"

They all leaned forward and brought their magnifiers back up to their faces.

"'Tire'?" suggested Olivier.

"A movie about a tire?" asked Billy. "Or maybe it means tired? Exhausted?"

"No, '*tire*,'" said Olivier. "French. It means shoot." He turned to Armand. "Shoot? A gun? Is that the message?"

"My God," said Ruth. "You're all idiots. How is it I can see what it says and you can't?"

"It's because you're looking through a telescope," said Gabri. "You could see the markings on Jupiter with that thing, you old witch."

"Bitch," she said to him.

"Children," said Armand. Though he knew they were not really fighting. This was their own code, baffling, sometimes offensive to others, but their way of showing affection. The more Ruth insulted a person, the more she cared about them.

"'Tiro,'" said Sylvie Mongeau, then repeated it. "'Tiro.' That's what it says."

"There," said Ruth. "She got it."

"'Tiro'?" said Myrna. "What does it mean?"

"Those markings?" Ruth pointed Rosa at the painting. "They're not code. They're shorthand. Almost no one uses it anymore. Technology has killed it."

"Video killed the radio star," Clara said to Gabri.

"The Buggles," he agreed.

"So what's Tiro?" asked Robert.

"Tironian notes?" Ruth looked from face to face, skipping by Gabri. "He was Cicero's secretary?" Again, she looked at them. "Anything? Nothing?"

"Cicero?" said Jean-Guy. "My mother bakes with that."

"That's Crisco, numbnuts."

"Got it," said Reine-Marie, who'd looked up Tiro on her phone. "He was Cicero's secretary."

"I just said that," said Ruth.

"Part of his job was to write down all of Cicero's speeches when he spoke in the Roman senate or elsewhere," Reine-Marie said. "And to take notes at meetings. But Tiro had trouble keeping up, so he invented—"

"Shorthand," declared Ruth. "It's all over the damned painting—"

"And the elephant," said Gabri.

"Holy shit. Sorry," Jean-Guy said to Robert.

"No need. I'm beginning to agree with you."

"Do you read shorthand, Ruth?" Armand asked.

"A bit. I worked as a personal assistant for a while."

"To Cicero," mumbled Gabri, while the rest of them spent a beat imagining Ruth assisting anyone in anything. Though that could explain the fall of the Roman republic.

"I was trained in Gregg shorthand, this looks like Pitman. Or a combination of the two."

Armand stepped away and placed a call to Jérôme Brunel.

The code breaker was deeply embarrassed. "I can't believe I missed that. One of the dangers in what we do. We're looking for the obscure, expecting it. But if something is simple, we can miss it. We see the forest, but not the trees."

"Do you know shorthand? Can you translate it?"

"Actually"—Jérôme gave a short laugh—"I don't, but I can look it up. I'm sure I can work it out."

"You know," said Olivier after Armand had hung up, "it's strange that each of us recognizes something in that room. Gabri and I recognized the elephant. Clara the painting."

"I recognized the music," said Robert.

"And Ruth knew Tiro," said Myrna.

"The hidden room's in your loft," Clara said to Myrna.

"I knew the grimoire," said Reine-Marie. "It's as though each of the elements is meant for specific people."

"Except you," said Ruth, looking at Armand.

Though Gamache was far from sure that was true. There was the sheet music. Had that been put there for him? But it was far from specific. It might have been meant for the minister.

No, if there was something in that painting just for him, he hadn't yet found it. Like Jérôme, he could see the forest, but not the one specific tree.

Armand picked up Agent Choquet and drove her and Reine-Marie to Trudeau International Airport in Montréal for their overnight flight to London.

Once there he took Amelia aside. "You know why you're going?"

"*Oui, patron.* To protect Madame Gamache. I won't let anything happen to her. I promise." He turned away, but she stopped him. "I know what happened."

"*Pardon?*"

"To your parents." She held his eyes. "I will not let anything happen to your wife."

He stared at her for a moment. "*Merci*, Amelia. And look after yourself."

After embracing Reine-Marie and whispering, "*Je t'aime,*" he watched them through the sliding doors, then drove back to Three Pines. Thinking. Thinking, all the way.

Before Gamache had left for the airport, Beauvoir had taken him aside to tell him the good news.

"God knows what this hot mess is about," he said, gesturing toward the giant painting, "and how it might relate to the murder of Madame Godin, but it looks like we can at least stop worrying about Sam."

He told Armand about his conversation. About the grandchildren reference. About the meaning of the photographs. And the gestures.

"And you believed him?" asked Armand. It wasn't an accusation. He was genuinely curious. And he realized he really, deeply, profoundly wanted to believe it too.

He glanced at the painting. If his suspicions were right, they had more than enough trouble on their hands without fighting on a second front.

"I do." It was clear the Chief was just asking, it wasn't a criticism, and yet Jean-Guy felt a sharp thrust. Sam's comment about him needing Gamache's approval for something as trivial as a meal had niggled. "But I'm not so sure about Fiona."

There. A small thrust back. The insinuation that while Beauvoir had been right about Sam, Gamache was wrong about his sister.

But Armand just nodded. "*Merci.*" He heaved a sigh, and Jean-Guy, seeing this, felt ashamed of himself.

"What can I do, *patron*, while you're at the airport?"

"Can you learn shorthand, please? Both types, Gregg and Pitman?"

"Can do. Now, what's shorthand again?"

Jean-Guy was relieved to see Armand smile.

"Actually, can you call the SHU?"

Beauvoir's smile disappeared. "I will."

By the time Armand returned to Three Pines, it was dark, though there was light in the Old Train Station. Jean-Guy met him at the door to the Incident Room.

"I spoke to the warden of the SHU. All's well. Everyone accounted for. I also asked about art therapy. He said they stopped it last year when two more inmates were stabbed by sharpened brushes."

Art Therapy with Psychopaths. Canceled. And none too soon, thought Armand.

"You hungry?"

"You have to ask?" said Jean-Guy. "I'll call Olivier and order something."

"Don't bother. I'll go over. I need some fresh air."

He found Fiona, Harriet, and Sam having dinner. He said hello to the women and mentioned to Fiona that Reine-Marie had gone to the Gaspé, to visit a sister.

"If you feel uncomfortable staying in the house without her, I'm sure Gabri can put you up in the B&B."

"You're not trying to get rid of her, are you?" said Sam, with a smile.

Armand ignored him. After an awkward silence, Fiona answered.

"No. I trust you and Inspector Beauvoir."

"Would you like to join us, Chief Inspector?" Sam asked.

Once again, Gamache didn't even look in his direction. It was as though the chair was empty.

He wanted to believe Jean-Guy, but he also wanted to hedge his bets. If Myrna was right and he ignored Sam, the young psychopath would turn all his attention on him. And leave the others alone.

He walked away, ordered dinner, then took it back to the Old Train Station, feeling Sam's rage following him every step of the way.

Back in the Incident Room, Armand pulled up a chair and sat beside Jean-Guy. Together they ate their wild mushroom ravioli with sage brown butter, drank iced tea, and stared at the painting.

But nothing new appeared.

Armand woke up in the middle of the night to make sure Reine-Marie's flight had landed. Then he struggled to get back to sleep. Finally giving up, he dressed, left a note for Jean-Guy, and walked back to the Old Train Station. Henri, Fred, and Gracie plodded sleepily along with him.

Putting the coffee on to perk, he once again pulled up a chair. By now he felt he'd memorized the painting, though he knew that wasn't close to the truth. It was so detailed. With so many elements hidden in plain sight. It was indeed, as art historians had dubbed it, "A World of Curiosities."

But this one, theirs, was also, as Dr. Louissaint had said, offensive. There was something aggressive, threatening, about it. He wondered if the real one felt the same way. Reine-Marie would soon find out.

She'd written as soon as they landed, and now there was another message. They were on their way to Norwich. He replied, then settled back with a mug of strong coffee and a chewy oatmeal cookie. And stared at the painting while the dogs, and Gracie, stared at the cookie.

The only light in the room was shining on *The Paston Treasure*. While the disturbing work was illuminated, Armand himself sat in darkness. In stillness and quiet. The only sounds were the breathing of the dogs at his feet and the slight cries of a dreaming Fred as the puppy chased squirrels.

Armand felt his shoulders drop and his breathing steady as he let the painting come to him. As Clara had taught him.

And then, one by one, he saw them. The people staring out of the painting. At him.

"Armand?"

Gamache jolted, almost falling out of his chair. The now cool coffee spilled on his shirt. The dogs lifted their heads at the disturbance.

"*Désolé*," said Jean-Guy. "I didn't mean to startle you. I saw the light and found your note." He stopped in his tracks. "What's wrong? What's happened?"

There was no doubt about it. The Chief looked more than startled. He looked frightened.

"It is him."

"It can't be." Beauvoir walked swiftly over.

Gamache got up and went to the painting, pointing. "Look. Here. Here. There."

He kept pointing. And Jean-Guy kept counting. With each number he felt the vomit rising, burning, until finally at the seventh he could taste wild mushrooms and sage brown butter in his mouth.

He swallowed hard and saw Armand turn pale. His deep brown eyes wide in near panic.

"It's not possible." Jean-Guy's voice was hoarse from the acid burning his throat. He'd turned from the painting, no longer daring to look, not daring to catch the accusing eyes of the seven figures who stared out at them.

"I called," he said, feeling his own panic threatening to overwhelm him. "I spoke to the warden. He assured me . . ."

But he knew the Chief was right.

Armand covered his mouth with his hand and turned back to the canvas. Forcing himself to meet those eyes. To let those faces, those people, come to him. And with them came some rough beast slouching toward him.

"Come on, come on." Reine-Marie's voice was soft, coaxing. It was the tone she used for Fred when she needed the old dog to try to climb back up the basement stairs.

Amelia moaned. "Can't we sleep? Just for a little while. I promise. Not long."

She'd gotten on the plane excited. She got off exhausted. Who knew transatlantic flights were so long? And boring. And now it was nine in the morning in London but—she checked her watch—four a.m. back home.

She hadn't slept. Tried. Failed. Had shifted this way. That. And then the person in front had put their seat back. All the way.

Fuck. Fuckity, fuck, fuck.

Beside her, Madame Gamache had read for a while, then closed her eyes. What made it worse was knowing that, in the front of the plane, people had beds. Beds. Beds!

"Puh-leeez," she begged.

Reine-Marie had arranged for a driver, David Norman, to meet them. The same man she and Armand used every visit.

"You can sleep in the car," she said as she spotted David waiting just beyond the barrier at Heathrow. "And by the way, you did sleep on the flight."

"Did not."

Reine-Marie didn't argue. She knew that tone from when Annie was a child. She knew it from overtired grandchildren. She also knew Amelia had slept. And had dropped her head onto Reine-Marie's shoulder. She had the drool marks to prove it.

She waved to David, who came over to greet them and take their carry-ons.

He said hello to Amelia, who just grunted.

"Your daughter?" he asked, trying to make it sound like that would be a good thing.

"A friend." She didn't dare tell him the truth.

They got in the car for the almost three-hour drive from Heathrow to the Norwich Castle Museum.

Armand stood in front of the locked and bolted metal door in the basement that housed and guarded and imprisoned his files.

Putting in the code, he unlocked it, first glancing behind him to make sure he was alone.

Once inside, he locked the door behind him and opened the drawer where the Beast of Babylon lived. Buried there. Buried alive.

Armand placed the iron ring on the desk. The engineer's ring he'd found half buried in the dirt. Then he brought out the file and reread it. Forcing himself to relive the details. To go through the photographs again. Every now and then he got up and stepped away, turning his back on the desk.

Then he walked back, sat down, and went through it all again.

CHAPTER 29

Armand placed the call.

"Special Handling Unit," said the bored voice.

"This is Chief Inspector Gamache of the Sûreté."

"Yessir."

Gamache had the call on speakerphone in the car. He could almost see the fellow sit up straight.

"I need to speak to the head guard."

"I'm sorry, sir, but it's five thirty-five in the morning. He doesn't come on until nine."

"Get him on the phone."

"He's at home."

"Then transfer me to his home. Now." He pulled to the side of the road.

"I'm not allowed—"

"Do it!"

"Yessir." The rattled guard rattled off the number, then transferred the call.

"What is it?" said the sleepy voice on the line a few rings later.

"This's Chief Inspector Gamache, of the Sûreté."

There was a groan and some rustling. "Fucking hell. It's"—there was a pause as he checked the time—"five forty. Who gave you my number?"

"I need to know about one of your prisoners."

"Call me at the office after nine. *Au revoir.*"

"John Fleming."

The line sounded dead, but Gamache could hear breathing. Sure enough, a moment later the head guard said, "Why?"

"Is he still in the SHU?"

"Of course he is."

"You don't have to look him up?"

"You don't forget or lose track of a prisoner like John Fleming."

"I'm on my way. Meet me at the SHU in half an hour."

"It's five—"

"I know what time it is," barked Gamache. "Be there."

A soft light had appeared in the morning sky.

Jean-Guy poured himself a mug of coffee and left the Old Train Station to sit on the bench on the village green. The air was fresh, bracing, and he needed both after their discovery. Most of all, he needed to get away from the damned painting.

Beauvoir had offered to go with the Chief Inspector to the prison, but Gamache had declined, asking him to try to find out who the ring belonged to.

Jean-Guy dug into his jacket pocket and brought it out again, tilting it this way and that, hoping the early-morning sun just might catch some initials or a number that had almost completely worn away over time.

But he could not see anything.

The day was fresh, new. Unsullied. And then he spoiled it by thinking of John Fleming. Was this his? Had he worn the ring while he . . .

The records said Fleming's degree was in mathematics, not engineering. But he might have falsified them. Lots of people did.

They'd visited the man once in the SHU, to get information only Fleming had.

Beauvoir had heard of Fleming, of course. Everyone had. The case was infamous. But since he didn't believe in malevolence, Jean-Guy was not at all worried about meeting the man. Just curious. And all the more curious because of Gamache's obvious unease.

Dew gleamed on the grass and leaves and flowers as Jean-Guy sat on the bench and thought about that visit. The one and only time he'd come face-to-face with the serial killer.

Gamache had warned him not to use their names. Not to answer any questions Fleming might ask, no matter how innocuous. Give the man absolutely no information, Gamache had warned him. No way into their lives. Just listen.

"And for God's sake, do not make eye contact."

Beauvoir had thought it was an almost ludicrous overreaction. Especially when a thin little man was led into the interview room, in chains. He looked, Beauvoir thought, like a bone china figurine. Small. Fragile. Delicate even.

Until Fleming met his eyes. And held them.

Up until that moment, Jean-Guy Beauvoir had thought in terms of good and bad. Guilty or not guilty. Was there enough evidence to arrest and convict or not? He believed in rational thought. Not in spirits or ghosts and certainly not in anything as cartoonish as evil.

But in that moment, in those eyes, a world opened. A world where the evidence was unseen and overwhelming. Incontrovertible and invisible. More real than the shiny metal table his sweaty hands rested on.

Beauvoir had no doubt that sitting across from him was the exception that proved the rule. The horror without hope of redemption.

"Go," Armand Gamache had whispered. Urgently. "Get away. Stand by the door."

And Jean-Guy had. He'd left the table and left Gamache. He stood with his back pressed to the wall, the hairs on his forearms raised. He could no longer see John Fleming's face. Just the back of his head. The thinning wispy gray hair. The hunched shoulders.

But he could see Gamache. Staring at the man. Holding John Fleming's eyes until Beauvoir was safe. Only then did Gamache blink. And breathe.

Gamache struggled to give nothing away even as he knew there was no hope of that.

Beauvoir had watched, helpless, as Fleming got into Gamache's head and made a home there. But, recognizing that and knowing it was too late, Gamache did the only thing open to him. He closed that part of his mind. Trapping John Fleming there. The madman could not escape. But it also meant Gamache was trapped with him. Forever.

But Fleming also had a plan. Once inside, he'd make his way, over time, to Armand's heart. Which he would then attack.

Jean-Guy Beauvoir had watched the rest of the interview from the sidelines as Gamache had faced the horror, had jousted and parried, deflected and blocked. As he walked into that dark cavern. Alone. And emerged with the information they needed. But at a terrible cost.

Jean-Guy had never forgotten those elongated minutes. Distorted by terror. And ripe with shame. He'd seen the epic battle, fought to a draw.

And now Gamache was returning, alone.

And now it is now, and the dark thing is here.

Beauvoir knew the idea of confronting Fleming again terrified Gamache. And yet, he was on his way to do just that. Jean-Guy sat on the bench, listening to the early-morning birdsong, and worried that Armand was about to roll away the wrong boulder. Walk into the wrong cave. His only protection was the belief that goodness was at least as powerful as evil. It was a muddled belief, a dangerous one, Jean-Guy feared.

But now, as the sun rose higher and the scent of lilac filled the air, Jean-Guy looked around at the peaceful village and began to see that maybe the belief in goodness wasn't a blind spot. It was a bright spot.

He put his mug on the bench, got up, and walked to his car.

On his way to his destination, he stopped at a jeweler. With the help of her high-powered lens, the woman made out the numbers.

"Almost worn away," she said, expertly dropping the eyepiece into her hand. She gave him the line of numbers.

Before getting back into the car, he sent what he'd found to both Nathalie Provost and Gamache. Then Jean-Guy Beauvoir headed to where he should have been all along. The SHU. To take his place beside the Chief.

* * *

Armand sat at the metal table. It reminded him of the autopsy tables he'd stood beside so often.

He looked down and saw his reflection, distorted, grotesque. Gamache raised his head at the small sound of the door handle moving. He inhaled.

The heavy metal door was pushed open.

Through it came a clinking. Clanging. Closer, closer. As a man in chains approached.

Gamache got to his feet, turned to the door, and braced himself. The head guard stepped into the room, followed by a man in prison garb, his hands and feet chained.

His eyes were downcast, but then he raised them and met the Chief Inspector's.

"This," said Gamache, "is not John Fleming."

CHAPTER 30

O f course it's him," said the warden as they sat in his office. "Look."

He skidded the file across his desk. Gamache stopped it from sliding right over the edge. He was also trying to keep himself from falling over an edge. He realized that his rage was not helpful. It was also, he knew, rooted in fear. In terror, in fact, that John Fleming was no longer in the SHU. He was out. Somewhere.

And Gamache could guess where.

After confronting the imposter, who refused to speak, Gamache had left the interview room.

"I need to search the prison for Fleming," he told the head guard. "You need to come with me."

"But there're hundreds of inmates."

Gamache turned on him. "Do you have any idea who John Fleming is? What he's capable of? What it means if he's not here?"

"But he is." The guard gestured toward the closed door of the interview room, where the false Fleming was still chained to the metal table.

"I've met Fleming," snapped Gamache. "I helped put him here. He's unmistakable. I don't know who that is"—he gestured angrily toward the door—"but it's not Fleming."

"Fine. We'll look. But it's a massive waste of time."

Before starting the search, Gamache called Beauvoir. "You spoke to the warden of the SHU yesterday."

"Yes," said Beauvoir. He didn't tell the Chief he was in the car on his way to the prison, for fear Gamache would order him back to Three Pines.

"Call him again. Tell him to come right away and meet me in his office."

"Why? What's happened?"

Gamache told him.

"Fucking—" was as far as Beauvoir got before the line went dead. "—hell."

"Let's go," said Gamache, stuffing the phone back into his jacket pocket.

Through the locked barriers they went. One, two, three doors. They were searched and scanned. Gamache's phone was taken away. Finally, there was a screech of an alarm as the last barrier between them and bedlam closed. They were locked in.

Gamache had been in any number of prisons, but no other was even remotely like the SHU. It was fairly new but felt ancient and derelict. A ruin.

The very air was heavier here. Denser. As though guilt and gravity had partnered, pressing the weight of the accumulated crimes down on them.

Along the concrete corridor the two of them strode, Gamache looking into the cells, looking into the eyes of every madman in the prison. Many he'd put there. Word spread through the population that Chief Inspector Gamache was there, and an uproar ensued. Men, barely more than beasts, screamed his name. Screamed abuse.

They shook and rattled the bars, dragging anything they could find across them.

The head guard began to breathe heavily, his eyes moving this way and that. Trying to keep himself from panicking.

Prisoners spat as Gamache walked past. They tried to piss on him. But Gamache walked through it all, laser-focused on finding, or not finding, John Fleming.

Halfway through, Jean-Guy arrived.

"What're you doing here?" Gamache asked, though Jean-Guy detected a note of relief.

"What? You'd be lost without me."

Around them the air was putrid with threats and sweat and the smell of piss. And worse.

Beauvoir took it all in, then said, "Feels like dinner with Ruth."

Gamache smiled and held Jean-Guy's arm, in gratitude for that small respite. Then he said, "Go to the warden's office. Tell him you need the file on Fleming, but don't open it. I'll join you when I've finished."

But instead of moving, Beauvoir just stood there. "*Non.* I'm staying with you."

"Inspector Beauvoir—"

"*Non.* You can fire me, but I'm not leaving. Not this time."

Jean-Guy Beauvoir, lashed to the mast, would sink or swim with this man. Their fates were bound together, as the winds howled, and the storm descended, and they traveled deeper into Hell.

They looked into each of the cells. Into the faces of any number of lunatics. But not the one they were searching for.

John Fleming was no longer there.

Outside the warden's office, Gamache turned to the head guard. "How long have you been at the SHU?"

"Two and a half years."

"That long." Gamache sighed.

"Do you think Fleming's been gone since then?" asked Beauvoir.

Gamache nodded. "What happened to the former head guard?"

"He retired."

"I'm guessing suddenly."

"Yes."

"And he moved away?"

"To Florida."

"Can you get us his address?" asked Beauvoir.

It was clear that the head guard was about to object, to say he'd need the warden's approval. Then he changed his mind. He'd watched these men be verbally abused. Spat on, almost pissed and shit on. And they kept going.

If they could do that, he could do this. Besides, he was beginning to believe them.

He knew John Fleming. At least, he knew his crimes. He'd familiarized himself with the details of each prisoner when he got the job. And no prisoner was more famous than Fleming.

Like everyone else, the head guard knew the broad strokes of his crimes.

Over the course of seven years, John Fleming had kidnapped and murdered seven people, men and women, young and old. One a year. His victims were completely random, from a clerk at the Hudson's Bay Company, to a bridge builder, to a fisherman, and more. Each in a different decade of their life.

That he knew. That everyone knew.

What wasn't said was what this madman had done with the bodies.

On arriving at the SHU, the head guard had read the file. Seen the photos. And then spent every hour of every day wishing he had not.

His job now was to make sure these men stayed behind these iron doors. And none more than Fleming.

It became clear to him that this was not just a job, it was a sacred duty. The Special Handling Unit was filled with murderers, mass murderers, child murderers. Serial killers.

The deranged, the criminally insane, lived out their lives within those walls, waiting for their own deaths. No family, no friends ever came. Not even the Grim Reaper wanted to visit. Many of the inmates lived to a ripe old age. Some were over one hundred years old. Unable to live. Unable to die.

Of all these criminals, John Fleming was the worst. The head guard knew that. And now, standing outside the warden's office, staring into the deep brown eyes of the head of homicide for the Sûreté du Québec, he'd begun to suspect that the worst had happened.

"I'll get it for you," he said.

"*Merci.*"

With that, the Sûreté officers walked into the warden's office.

* * *

The warden was furious. He'd been dragged out of bed, forced back to the office, and was now being accused of allowing the most dangerous prisoner in the SHU to escape.

Gamache put on his reading glasses and scanned the file, though he knew what he'd find. Lies. A deliberate counterfeit.

Sure enough, the file showed a photo and description of the man Gamache had just met. It was close, the resemblance almost uncanny. But it was not John Fleming.

The litany of Fleming's crimes was there, along with psychiatrist reports. There was an all-too-brief description of Fleming's background, including his education.

It said the same thing as Gamache's private records. John Fleming was a mathematician. Not an engineer.

Gamache snapped the file shut, then handed it to Beauvoir, but not before removing the photographs of what Fleming had done and putting them into his pocket. Leaning forward, he spoke with blistering courtesy to the warden.

"The man introduced to me just now as John Fleming is not John Fleming. I know it, and you know it, sir. And you know that, despite what the record says, I can prove it."

Though Gamache also knew that could be problematic. If as much trouble had been taken over this escape as it seemed, the DNA and prints of the false Fleming would now be in the official file.

John Fleming would have dissolved and re-formed into someone else.

But the real file, along with evidence of other crimes he might have committed, were intact. The real John Fleming was in the locked room in Gamache's basement.

But he'd have to prove that his files were legitimate, and the now official records were fakes. That would take more time than they had.

"There's nothing to prove," said the warden. "Listen closely, Chief Inspector. I'll say this once. You're a breath away from a lawsuit that will ruin you. It's one thing to come in here with both boots and insist a prisoner has escaped, when there's no proof. In fact, there's a whole lotta proof that he's safely locked up." He gestured toward the file now in Beauvoir's hands. "But you refuse to believe the evidence of your own eyes." He stared into Gamache's steady gaze and seemed to get stuck there for a moment, before plowing on. "It's a whole other thing to accuse me, accuse him"—the warden pointed to the head guard—"in front of witnesses, of a cover-up. That's actionable. Let me just be clear. Are you actually saying we've knowingly allowed a criminally insane prisoner to escape?"

"*Non.*"

"No?" The warden looked confused.

"Not him—" Gamache tilted his face toward the head guard. "Only you."

The warden colored. But Gamache went on, his voice deep and calm. It was a calm Beauvoir knew well. Had first heard on the shores of that pewter lake, a lifetime ago. When he'd first met Gamache. When he'd first learned that what met the eye and what was the real story could be two very different things.

"Now, let me be clear," said the Chief Inspector. "The lede here isn't what this means for me, or you. It's that a lunatic has been allowed out in the community. That's what matters. Finding him is what matters. Whose life is ruined, yours or mine, can be sorted later. You need to tell us everything you know. Now!"

The last word was snapped out with such force the head guard jumped.

Jean-Guy could see the tremble in Gamache's right hand. It was getting more and more pronounced. He was barely containing his rage.

"Get him out of my office," the warden ordered, but the guard didn't move.

Gamache had had enough. He stood up so quickly his chair squealed against the linoleum floor.

The warden, seeing this and sensing the danger too late, scrambled to his feet and reeled back, trying to get out of the Chief Inspector's grasp as Gamache moved forward.

He did not make it.

Gamache was upon him, stopping just inches from the man. He

didn't touch the warden, but the force of his wrath pressed the man hard against the wall.

"Do you know what you've done?" Gamache shouted, finally letting all his pent-up anger out. Aiming it at this stupid, stupid man. "You've released a monster." Gamache reached into his pocket and brought out one of the photographs.

"Look," he roared, shoving the picture into the man's face. "Look!"

The warden dropped his eyes to the picture.

And blanched.

Beauvoir, tense, ready to act, knew then that the warden had never really read Fleming's file, and if he had, he hadn't bothered, or dared, look at the pictures. Of the seven-headed creature John Fleming had created. The Beast of Babylon.

He himself had never seen it, and now Jean-Guy realized Gamache had removed the photos from the files so he would not. But the look of sheer horror on the warden's face told the story.

"You let this madman out," Gamache shouted. "How much did it cost? What were you paid? What's the going price these days for monsters, you stupid piece of shit?"

He was practically screaming. Shaking with fury and on the verge of tears.

It went beyond anger, beyond rage, into a territory Beauvoir had never seen in the Chief Inspector. Gamache was losing it.

"Where is he? Where?"

When the warden didn't answer, Gamache lifted his hand toward the man's throat. Jean-Guy stepped forward just before it got there and pulled Gamache back.

The Chief shook him off and moved toward the warden again. Beauvoir gripped more tightly and this time dragged Gamache back.

"Get away," he hissed into Armand's ear. "Go. Step away."

It was, he realized, almost exactly what Gamache had said when saving him from Fleming years ago.

Gamache stumbled back, his eyes drilling into the now pale and trembling man. He yanked his arm free, straightened his clothes, took a deep ragged breath, then turned to Beauvoir.

"Charge him. He's an accomplice in the murder of Patricia Godin. More charges will follow." Gamache, trembling with rage and adrenaline, glared at the warden, then said in a whisper, far more frightening than the shouting, "Do you know what you've done?"

"You can't arrest me. I did nothing wrong," the warden shouted as Gamache reached the door. "You have no proof."

"Be quiet, you goddamned fucker," shouted Beauvoir.

Gamache turned back. "You'd better pray we find some."

He slammed the door behind him.

"What did he mean by that?" demanded the warden.

Beauvoir turned him around and shoved him against the wall.

"Imagine what will happen if you're released," Beauvoir snarled before snapping the cuffs in place and turning him back around.

It took the man a moment to see what Beauvoir meant. To imagine what Fleming would do to him now that he was no longer useful.

While Beauvoir drove the pale and panicky warden to the Sûreté in Montréal to be booked, Gamache returned to Three Pines, needing to pull over a couple of times to regain something close to composure.

What he'd almost done, and might have had Jean-Guy not been there, shocked the Chief Inspector. If he was going to find Fleming, he could not afford to lose his mind.

He needed help.

"Captain Moel? Hardye?"

"Armand? What can I do for you?"

"I'm sorry for the early-morning call, but I need to see you."

"Of course, let me just check my agenda—"

"Now. Can you come down to Three Pines?"

The head of counseling at the Sûreté paused for just a moment, looking at her packed schedule. "Of course. I'll leave right away."

Once off the phone, and still sitting on the side of the road, he called Reine-Marie.

There was no answer. He called Agent Choquet. No answer.

Trying to keep his anxiety in check, he told himself they were safe. They were far away and well out of it. They were just busy.

But he also knew that John Fleming could be anyone, anywhere. Including at the Norwich Castle Museum.

Armand tried again. No answer. He shot off a text. *You okay? Call me.*

Then he placed a call to Florida to speak to the former head guard of the SHU.

The number on file had been disconnected.

He then called the local sheriff. After checking, the sheriff said that the man Chief Inspector Gamache was looking for was dead. Murdered. Two years ago.

No one had been arrested for the crime.

Armand placed another call to Reine-Marie and felt his heart pound with each unanswered ring.

CHAPTER 31

Reine-Marie saw the man looking around, and waved.

The docent at the Norwich Castle Museum waved back and walked across the flagstone floor to greet them.

The castle was a huge cube dropped, nine hundred years earlier, onto the highest point in the city of Norwich. It was now a public space that included an art gallery and museum.

Reine-Marie and a revived Amelia had turned off their cell phones, as per the request on the noticeboard.

"Madame Cloutier?" the smiling guide said.

"Yes, that's right. And this is my assistant, Amelia Choquet."

He looked at Amelia as though trying to decide where in the gallery she should be placed.

"My name is Cecil Clarke, I'm the head docent here. I understand you're interested in *The Paston Treasure*?"

He gestured for them to follow him.

He was in his late sixties or early seventies, Reine-Marie guessed. Of average height. Slender. His head was shaved close, as many balding men do. He had a trim white beard and cheerful blue eyes.

He sounded mid-Atlantic. Neither British nor North American.

They strolled by glass cases displaying a wide and wild variety of animals, including a polar bear.

Amelia paused to stare at the great auk, then ran to catch up to Madame Gamache and the docent.

"So many mysteries," Clarke said as they walked through the museum. "It's captivated people for years."

"A World of Curiosities," said Reine-Marie.

"Exactly that. So many secrets. What's your interest in the painting?"

"I'm writing a paper on it," Reine-Marie explained. "I'm retired now but spent my life as a historian in Québec. I want to branch out into art history."

"Well, you couldn't find a more fascinating place to start than"—they turned a corner—"here."

And there before them was an immense canvas. *The Paston Treasure.*

Reine-Marie stood in awe and Amelia actually gasped.

The painting was overwhelming, almost shocking in its display of opulence. And yet it was also deeply human, almost innocent. As though it surprised itself.

"Captivating, isn't it?" Cecil said, clearly enjoying the reaction. "I've studied it for years and am still enthralled."

"It feels as though we can walk right into it," said Amelia.

He turned and looked at her with interest. "Yes. I often feel I have. In fact, I play a game with myself. I try to imagine which objects I'd bring with me, to add to those already there. What treasures. Trophies."

"And what would you?" Reine-Marie asked, keeping her voice light.

"Oh, it changes every day."

"Today?" she asked.

"Probably a favorite piece of music. Maybe a film, definitely a book. If I could get the great auk in, I would."

Reine-Marie smiled and returned her gaze to the canvas and said, casually, "It does lend itself to that thought. Do you know of anyone who's actually done it?"

"Walked into the painting?"

She laughed. "No. I mean made a copy but added some modern touches."

He considered. "There probably are some, but none I'm aware of."

She brought out her phone and showed him a photo of the one in the attic. "What do you make of this?"

He stared at it, enlarging the image and moving it about on the screen.

"Now this is a curiosity. How fun." He looked from her phone to the original, and back. "An interesting choice of modern objects. Did you do this?"

She closed her phone and laughed again. "No. I just found this copy. I actually became interested in *The Paston Treasure* when a friend invited me to an exhibition here a few years ago. I couldn't make it, but I looked up the work. Were you here for that show?"

"The one three years ago or so? I'd just arrived. I'm Canadian too, from New Brunswick. Retired."

"Art history?"

"No. Engineering, actually."

Captain Moel met the Chief Inspector outside the Old Train Station and was glad she'd come down.

"This is where you live?" she asked as she got out of the car. "It looks like something out of a Disney animation. I half expect the butterflies to burst into song." She had her back to him. "Peaceful."

"You'd think."

She turned and saw his face. Grim. Worried.

"Are you okay?"

"Been better."

The normally well-dressed man was a mess. Hair disheveled, his clothing rumpled and dirty. He hadn't had time to shower and change after the visit to the SHU.

Hardye Moel was now head of the Sûreté du Québec counseling division, having earned her Ph.D. She'd built up her department from practically nothing.

Chief Inspector Gamache was an early advocate for, and adopter of, the service. He'd sent many of his agents for counseling. And gone himself.

Dr. Moel was his colleague and therapist. Hardye Moel was his friend.

"How can I help?"

He told her what had happened at the SHU. The fact that he'd lost it, and it was only the presence of Jean-Guy Beauvoir that prevented him from hurting, maybe even killing, the warden.

"I don't think it would have gone that far, Armand." She studied him. "But you're not sure? What did the warden do to bring this on?"

Gamache stared at her for a moment, knowing he'd have to tell her everything. But he hesitated.

Hardye waited. Giving him space and time. She saw his eyes drift from her over to the village. To the neighbors walking dogs. Sitting outside on the terrasse of the bistro. Working in gardens. She heard the birds, the lawn mowers, the shouted greetings.

And then his eyes came to rest. She turned to see that he was looking at the three huge spires of pine trees on the village green.

Of course, she thought. Three Pines.

When she turned back, his gaze was once more on her.

And then he told her. Everything.

As he spoke, he saw Captain Moel's eyes widen, then narrow. As though she was squinting at something horrible approaching.

"Dear God," she whispered. "John Fleming? He let Fleming go? He's out?"

"Let's go inside," said Armand.

Once in the Incident Room, she stared at the huge canvas.

Dr. Moel had studied the Fleming case in her courses on aberrant behavior. She remembered reading that John Fleming had been a churchgoing man. Obsessed with it. A God-fearing man, he eventually feared God so much he ran straight into the arms of the other.

The Angel of the Morning. The Fallen Angel. God's favorite. Until . . .

But Armand was pointing at the painting and saying something else.

"*Pardon?*"

"The faces, the heads. They're of his victims. Jesus," Armand said, wiping his hand over his face. "I should've seen it sooner."

Captain Moel turned away, repulsed. "How could you? No sane

person would see it, would believe an inmate at the SHU could be responsible. I read about his case, his trial. There was no mention of you."

"No. I was there as an observer, assigned by the Crown."

"Did Fleming recognize you? Is that why he's doing this?"

It didn't make sense, this obsession Fleming seemed to have with the Chief Inspector. Why not the arresting cop? The prosecutor? The judge. Why Gamache?

"A few years ago I needed his help in a case. He agreed, but in exchange I had to promise to let him go."

Moel stared at him, incredulous. "You were willing to do that?"

"I had no choice."

By then Fleming had been in the SHU for more than a decade. If he wasn't mad before, he was by then. Though Gamache knew John Fleming had almost certainly come out of the womb a lunatic.

"At the last minute, the last second, I reneged. He'd taken a few steps outside, had a taste of freedom, before I had him taken back in."

It was close, and Armand almost, almost, had to follow through with that terrible calculation. Release a madman into society to murder again. And again. Or allow plans for a weapon of mass destruction to be sold to the highest bidder.

Even at his most prolific, Fleming could not match that death toll. And Armand was confident he could recapture the lunatic, eventually. Eventually.

But finally, he didn't have to.

He could still hear the screams, unholy shrieks, like some wraith being burned alive, as Fleming was dragged back into the hellhole.

Hardye Moel nodded. She understood. That event had focused his mania, his rage, on the Chief Inspector.

Armand checked his phone again. Still nothing from Reine-Marie or Amelia.

"I'd like to get in touch with some of the people who came to the exhibition," said Reine-Marie. "To see why they're so taken with *The Paston Treasure*. Especially people who came from a distance. North America, for instance. Any idea how I might do that?"

Amelia looked at Reine-Marie with new respect. This might work.

"Not a clue," said Cecil.

"Was it possible to book a private tour of the exhibition?" Amelia asked. "I imagine a real enthusiast would want that."

"Now that's true," said the docent. "I think I can find that list if you're interested, since it would involve bookings and payment."

"Please," said Reine-Marie, and looked at Amelia with new respect.

He returned a few minutes later, waving sheets of paper.

"Here it is. The people who reserved private talks on *The Paston Treasure* during that exhibition."

He handed Reine-Marie the list. It was two pages long, mostly academics who wanted exclusive access to the painting. But there, on the second page, was one Lillian Virginia Mountweazel.

Hardye took a seat in one of the comfortable armchairs, her back to the canvas. Armand had poured them each a coffee, which she gratefully took.

As he joined her, she leaned toward him. "Do you think Fleming's here?"

"I don't know. I don't see how he could be. I'd recognize him, I'm sure. Fairly sure. I think." He heaved a sigh. "I need a clear head to find him, and I'm worried . . ."

She gave him space and time.

". . . that I'm coming unhinged."

"Because of what happened in the SHU this morning, with the warden."

Gamache nodded.

"What're you afraid of, Armand?"

"Besides going completely mad and committing murder myself?"

"Besides that."

He'd actually been afraid of this question, suspecting she'd ask. But it was no use lying. Why invite her here to help him, then hide the truth?

"I'm afraid I'll fail. I'm afraid that whatever happens, it will be my fault. Since I found out he'd escaped, it feels like only part of my brain is working. The rest is screaming at me." He lowered his voice. "He's screaming at me."

"That's only natural. Jesus, since you told me about Fleming, my head is screaming."

"But you don't have to find him," said Armand. "I do."

"True. The fear, the howl, will settle down. It's just the shock."

He shook his head. "It's more than that, deeper than that. I almost assaulted the warden."

"If it's deeper than that, then you have to look deeper." She held his eyes. "There's something you aren't admitting, isn't there."

He looked down at his hands and saw a tear, like a drop of rain, splash onto a finger. He looked up and met Hardye's eyes.

"I'm afraid Fleming will kill my family. I'm afraid I won't be able to save them."

She nodded slowly. "Did you do this on purpose?"

"Of course not. Does it matter?"

"*Mens rea*. Yes, it matters. This isn't your fault, Armand. This is Fleming's fault, the warden's fault. You and your team are the solution. You need to separate it out. You're catastrophizing, allowing fear into the driver's seat. You're reacting to things that haven't happened and behaving as though they have, or are inevitable. Focus on what is actually happening, here and now."

"Surrender to reality," he said with a small grin and, grabbing a tissue, he rubbed his eyes.

It was one of Hardye Moel's favorite sayings.

"Yes. Stop fighting battles that don't exist. Focus on what does. And don't take it all on yourself. You have a smart, effective team around you."

He took three deep breaths, closed his eyes. Then, opening them, he smiled at her.

"*Merci*. That helps."

She looked at her watch. "I need to be getting back."

"Ummm, actually, there's another reason I wanted to see you. Sam Arsenault is here."

"Ahhh," she said, sitting back down. "I see."

"You obviously remember him."

"I do. The case is hard to forget. Those children."

"You stayed with them in those early days. You observed them. What did you think of them?"

"Them or him?"

"Both, I suppose, but mostly him. My impression is that he was far more culpable in the death of their mother than we could prove. And when Fiona accepted guilt, there wasn't much more we could do. But I want to know, need to know . . ."

"How sick he was? Is?"

He nodded.

"Before I answer, I need to know if I'm speaking to you as a colleague or a friend."

Armand stared at her for a moment. "Which one will get me into less trouble?"

She laughed. "Well, let me start as your colleague. I haven't seen him in years, and when I did, I wasn't trained in criminal and aberrant behavior. So I couldn't answer your question."

"As my friend?"

"I'd say stay the fuck away from him. The kid's a nutjob."

"Well, that's clear."

She leaned forward again. "I'm serious. He hated you then, and that sort of hate only festers and grows in a personality like his."

"Is he a psychopath?"

"I'd say yes."

"And the sister, Fiona?"

"Well, that's another question. She was clearly bright, but so damaged. When there's not just a failure to protect and nurture, but pain of the most intimate type inflicted by your own mother, well, not many get out of that unscathed."

"She's here too. Jean-Guy pointed out that Sam cried when told about his mother. Fiona didn't."

"True. But what's the most natural reaction? The fact is, Clotilde made them cry before she died. Sam's tears were meant for you, not his mother. Fiona was much more honest in her reaction."

"Is she dangerous too?"

"I don't know, Armand. I wish I could tell you. It's possible that on their own they're under control. It's only when they get together that something happens. They bring out the worst in each other."

And both Hardye and Armand knew the "worst" was pretty bad.

"I need to get back to the city, but there's one other thing. You said you didn't think John Fleming was here now. That you'd recognize him. Honestly, if what you're saying is true, then he'd almost certainly be here. He'd want to see you squirm. He'd want to see his plan unfold and be here in case anything goes wrong. He might not be right in the village, he might be camping nearby, or hiding in some home. You look relieved. I'd have thought having a raving lunatic in your backyard wouldn't be the best news."

"I sent Reine-Marie to the UK, to investigate the original." He nodded toward the painting. "I wanted to get her away, but now I can't reach her." He looked again at his phone. Still no message. "If Fleming is here and not with her, that's a relief. You really think he is here?"

"Probably."

He walked Captain Moel to her car, then went home for a quick shower and to change.

Probably, thought Armand, was not a yes.

"Yes, I remember her," said Cecil. "Quite a character. Exactly what you'd expect a Mountweazel to be."

"This was years ago," said Amelia. "She must've been memorable."

"Oh, she was, but I don't remember her from back then."

"Then how do you know her?" Reine-Marie asked.

"She was here a couple of months ago. All wrapped in furs this time, and scarves, and wearing a sort of turban thing."

He indicated his head, as though a turban could be worn anywhere else.

"What is it?" he asked, seeing their surprise.

"Nothing," said Reine-Marie. "Virginia—"

"Lillian," muttered Amelia.

"Lily didn't mention she'd been back. Any idea why she came?"

"Not really. I do remember she called to say she'd lost something and wondered if we'd found it and could mail it back to her."

"What had she lost?" asked Amelia.

"An old letter she said she'd found in a flea market. Something that belonged to her family."

"Ahh, yes," said Reine-Marie. "She did mention that. And you sent it back, right? To her old address or the new one?"

"I have no idea. We had the letter in our lost and found and mailed it, but we wouldn't have kept a record of where. Why so interested?"

"We're not really. Do you mind?" Reine-Marie held up her phone. "I'd love a photo with the three of us. To show her."

"Of course."

They took a selfie.

"I'll just send it."

"No phones allowed in here, but you can go out onto the terrace."

Reine-Marie did. As soon as she connected up, her phone came alive with messages, all from Armand.

"You're all right?" he said, picking up her call before the first ring had ended. He'd showered and had just changed into clean clothes.

"Yes, why?"

"I couldn't reach you."

"I'm sorry. What's happened?"

He told her, succinctly, what he'd just told Captain Moel.

That John Fleming was out. That the former head guard had been murdered. That everything that was happening, including and especially the items in the bricked-up room and the altered painting of *The Paston Treasure*, was almost certainly done by Fleming.

Reine-Marie sat on a stone bench and stared, dazed, across the pretty city.

She remembered the trial in the closed courtroom in Montréal. They were still living in the city at the time. Armand would come home every evening more and more drained, as though his essence were seeping out as he listened to the testimony. As he looked at the photographs. Heard the recordings.

He'd become convinced that Fleming's crimes were not limited to those seven murders. To that spree in New Brunswick. There were others, he was sure. Even after Fleming was convicted and put away, he spent years tracking down possible evidence. Still did.

But now it seemed he had to find the man himself.

"He'd be in his seventies now, wouldn't he?" she said. "What does he look like?"

"He's seventy-one. Five seven. Slight build, gray hair thinning. Bright blue eyes. Remarkable eyes."

He did not sound very formidable. But Reine-Marie knew the power of madness. The strength it gave people. Not just physical strength, but strength of purpose. A person who was simply bad, nasty, would always try to justify their cruelty. A madman did not waste time and energy on that.

John Fleming at seventy-one would be as dangerous as he would have been at twenty-one. Perhaps even more so. He now had experience on his side.

"Can you send a photograph?" she asked.

"There are no recent ones. Why?"

"Because we're talking to someone, the local expert on *The Paston Treasure*, who fits your description. I have a picture. I'll send it."

"You need to come home," said Armand. "Now. Get David to drive you straight to Heathrow and get on the first flight out. Anywhere. Then make your way home."

"Oh, he's coming over," she said, then dropped her voice to a whisper. "His name's Cecil Clarke. With an *e*. Armand, he's Canadian, from New Brunswick. *Au revoir. Je t'aime.* I'll call you from the car."

With that, she hung up and put the phone away.

She forgot to send the photo. She also forgot, or didn't realize it might be important, to tell him that Cecil Clarke was a retired engineer.

Reine-Marie texted to say they were in the car with David. He could relax.

Armand called his team in Montréal and had them do a search for a Cecil Clarke, about seventy years old, from New Brunswick, now living in Norwich, UK.

When he returned to the Incident Room, cleaned up and feeling more under control, he called Captain Moel.

"Hardye, I have one more question, though I think I know the answer."

"Go on."

"Why would Fleming leave that ticket to the exhibition? He must know we'd find it."

"Why do you think?"

"Because he wanted us to go there. To waste time."

"It's not just that, it's more insidious. He's toying with you. He wants you to know that he's in control. He can make you do anything he wants."

It confirmed what Armand sensed. He was being manipulated. Every step preordained.

Fleming had had years to plan. He'd had just hours to try to catch up.

"There is one other possibility," said Hardye. "Something that came to me in the car. It's possible Fleming is working through some-one else."

"Someone who arrived in the village just before the hidden room was discovered," Armand said. "You're thinking of Sam?"

"And Fiona, yes. In fact, honestly, most likely Fiona. She has far more access to you. But that would mean there was some connection between Fleming and the Arsenaults."

It wasn't the news he wanted, but he did need to face reality.

He called Beauvoir for an update.

"The warden's terrified. Refuses to admit anything. Should I send out an alert for Fleming?"

Gamache was prepared for the question.

"*Non*. We have no proof. And we don't want him to be warned and go to ground. We need to get Annie and Daniel and the kids away. Someplace safe. I have a friend with a cabin on Lac Manitou in the Laurentians. I'll call him then send you the address."

"Yes, yes, good." Jean-Guy was feeling more and more stressed. "I'll get them there."

"Jean-Guy?"

"*Oui?*"

"About what happened in the SHU—"

"Nothing happened."

"*Merci quand même*," said Armand. Thank you anyway.

If a man's foes were of his own household, Gamache knew that his friends were too.

When he hung up, Armand noticed Robert Mongeau's car descending into the village and parking by the church.

The minister got out, slowly, as though walking through hardening concrete. Every movement forced. His head bowed. His eyes to the ground.

Armand's brows drew together as he watched the slow, labored progress. He could guess what had happened. But he didn't have time . . .

He called his friend with the lake house and got permission and a promise to tell no one. After sending Jean-Guy the address, he looked at a photo that had just arrived from Reine-Marie. It was a selfie of her, Amelia, and Cecil Clarke. The man looked nothing like John Fleming.

Armand was about to exhale when he read her message. Clarke was an engineer.

"Damn." He put in a call to Nathalie Provost.

"I was about to call you, Armand. I sent the serial number on the ring to the Société des Ingénieurs. I just got the list of people who wore it."

"Is there a John Fleming on it?"

There was a pause that felt longer than it was. "*Non.*"

"Are you sure?"

"It's not a long list, Armand. Yes, I'm sure."

"How about a Cecil Clarke?"

"*Non*, not him either."

"*Merci.*"

This was the first bit of good news. It meant Fleming hadn't dropped the ring. Hadn't been down in their basement. It meant Reine-Marie hadn't had a madman's hand on her shoulder.

He sat back in his chair and stared out the window for a moment. Then, taking a last look at the peaceful village, he turned away and tilted his head back, staring at the tongue-and-groove ceiling. If Fleming was inside his head, that might mean he could get inside Fleming's. If he tried.

Armand closed his eyes. And waited. And waited.

Out of the darkness, eyes appeared. Startling blue.

His own eyes flew open, and his chair tilted forward, almost throwing him out of it.

Unlike the elderly and embittered Ruth as the Virgin Mary in Clara's portrait, where Clara had put a dot of light in her angry eyes, creating hope in the midst of despair, Fleming's eyes gleamed bright. But in them there was a black spot. A blight. A cave.

Armand saw the invitation to enter. Into despair. And knew he had no choice.

He sat up straight, planted his feet firmly on the floor, placed a hand on each knee, closed his eyes again, and took several deep breaths.

I'm coming for you.

In the distance he heard a sound. So deep was his reverie, so complete his focus, it took him a moment to realize it was his phone.

"Gamache."

"Armand, I've figured out the code," said Jérôme Brunel. "It's written in a mix of shorthands, including Tironian. It's actually the same phrase in French, English, Latin, German, Hebrew, all mixed together. A chaos of languages, like speaking in tongues."

"What does it say?"

"*I'm coming for you.*"

Armand felt his blood rush to his core.

And after all it is nothing new / It is only a memory, after all.

A memory of a fear / that has now come true.

CHAPTER 32

⌒

Harriet and Sam went for a hike through the forest, along the trail that led up to François's Seat, the highest point of the mountains that surrounded and protected and hid Three Pines from the outside world.

The trail was steep enough to leave her winded.

"Why's it called François's Seat?" Sam asked, catching his own breath.

They sat down on sun-warmed boulders and admired the view, which fanned out 360 degrees. From there they felt they could reach out and touch the Green Mountains of Vermont.

"I asked Auntie Myrna once, but she didn't know."

The mention of her aunt gave Harriet a pang. Of sadness. Perhaps guilt. She'd turned her back on the woman who'd been an important part of her life all her life in favor of a man she'd just met.

How could that happen, she wondered, that Sam could get so deep into her heart so quickly? And eclipse loved ones?

He seemed to understand her. She wasn't afraid with him. He'd even shown interest in her odd hobby of collecting bricks, saying he had one himself.

"A hobby?" she'd asked.

"No, a brick. One I've had since I was a kid. I'll show it to you sometime."

He brought egg salad and peanut butter sandwiches wrapped in a damp dish towel out of his knapsack, and she pulled a large thermos of ice-cold water out of hers. They ate in silence, enjoying the view.

The warmth of the day was hitting the pines and balsams, bringing out the sweet fragrance of their new needles.

Harriet looked over the endless canopy of forest and saw unimaginable beauty. It was enchanting, bewitching. And if you weren't careful, it would kill you.

A few steps off the path, perhaps to pick up pinecones or look at a wildflower, and you were lost. You'd turn around. And around. And the path would have disappeared.

At first there'd be disbelief, even perhaps mild amusement. And then, as the minutes turned to hours, there'd be a quickly mounting awareness. This was trouble. Then, as the sun went down, anxiety turned to fear turned to panic.

This can't be happening.

Was that how Anne Lamarque felt when the priest turned her in, as the witnesses against her piled up? As her husband testified about the grimoire? Did her amusement turn to disbelief, turn to panic, turn to terror?

She'd strayed too far from the prescribed path, and this was her punishment.

Harriet looked over the forest and imagined a woman in long, torn skirts and a rough blouse, clutching a shawl to her breast with one hand and a burlap sack with the other.

Anne Lamarque's face and hands were torn and bloody. Her clothing encrusted with muck and stinking of sweat and piss and shit. Her wild hair was thick with leaves and twigs, as though she were turning into the forest itself.

She finally looked like what she'd been accused of.

Before I was not a witch / But now I am one . . .

The witch woman was on the run, chased through the wilderness by beasts hungry for her body and demons hungry for her soul.

Every sound became a threat. The howls of the wolves, the scrambling and shrieking of strange creatures, the bright eyes staring at her in the moonlight. Flesh-eating flies buzzed around her head, tormenting her, biting her, driving her mad. Sending her running through the forest, over the edge of the known world and into insanity.

Until she'd finally fallen to her knees. Her head in her hands. Bent over small, like a child who'd seen the closet door drift open in the night. And knew the nightmare was real.

Anne Lamarque surrendered to her fate.

What then? Harriet wondered.

Had Anne heard the soft babble of the river and raised her head? Had she lifted her face from her filthy hands and seen soft light in the sky? Had she seen a clearing just ahead? A meadow with herbs and sweetgrass?

Had she, like so many after her, recognized in this hidden place a home?

Anne Lamarque had defied her tormentors. Instead of being damned, instead of dying, she'd made a home. Here. Found a home here. Built a home here, from stones pulled from the earth, and from trees that once seemed so fearsome, but now offered themselves as shelter.

According to Ruth, two other women eventually found their way to Anne. But Harriet suspected there were more. Many more.

A bouquet of them, perhaps. Young and old. Their common crimes were breasts and a womb. And a mind.

With the help of the grimoire, they survived, built a community where all were welcome. That was the real magic.

"What're you thinking?" Sam asked, his voice soft, gentle.

"I was thinking that maybe it's not so bad being a witch." She glanced down at his knapsack. "What else have you got in there?"

It wasn't quite empty, and she hoped maybe he'd brought a cake. It was the right shape for a lemon loaf, though it looked too heavy for that.

She reached for it.

"I'm sending the family up to the lake with four agents," said Jean-Guy. He named them and Armand nodded approval. They were good, they could be trusted. "I'm on my way back to Three Pines, but I had a thought."

"Go on."

"Suppose it's Godin."

"Fleming?" Gamache was about to point out that Monsieur and Madame Godin had been married for forty years and living in that house for fifteen. Godin could not be Fleming. But then he realized . . .

"Do we know for sure that is Monsieur Godin?" Beauvoir asked, just as Gamache got to that thought. "His ID checks out, but those could be faked. Fleming could have killed them both, then pretended to be Godin, knowing we'd show up."

It could be, thought Armand. Godin was roughly the right age. He was taller, and heftier, but those could be changed with lifts in shoes and an intentional weight gain. Even eye color could be changed with contacts.

"There was her funeral," said Gamache. "People would have seen that it wasn't the real Godin. Their children would have seen it right away."

"True," said Beauvoir. "Maybe Fleming killed Madame Godin five weeks ago, but only killed Monsieur Godin a few days ago. Just before we arrived. Knowing we were coming."

"But how could he know? We didn't even know. At the time there'd been no crime, just the loft room and those items. It was strange, but not illegal. Billy and I were curious to speak to the Godins, that's all. It wasn't until we realized Madame Godin had been murdered that things changed."

But then he thought about what Captain Moel had said. That Fleming was in control, manipulating them. It was possible hints were dropped that they didn't even pick up on.

Yes, it was possible that Godin was Fleming. Just.

"Do we have a DNA sample of Monsieur Godin?" he asked.

"We do. And prints. I can check them against Fleming's records."

"That won't work. The official records have been replaced."

"Shit, of course. Fucking warden. We might be able to find one in the prosecutor's office."

"That'll take time and probably a warrant. Still, worth trying. While you do that, I'll go over to the Godin place."

"Wait. Don't go alone, *patron*. I can meet you there in forty minutes, maybe less."

Armand paused and looked up the hill to the small chapel.

"All right. Park where he can't see us. We need this to be a surprise."

Though Gamache had the uneasy feeling that nothing they did would surprise John Fleming.

"One other thing. The warden told me that a woman passed messages to Fleming in the SHU, through the head guard. He said it was Fleming's wife."

"His wife? There's nothing about that in the files, and nothing was said about a wife or family at his trial."

Though there was definitely a woman in this somewhere, wife or not. The Mountweazel fiction.

"The last we see of her," said Gamache, "was several months ago, when she 'lost' the Stone letter at the Norwich Castle Museum. Maybe her job's done."

They both knew what happened to people in Fleming's orbit once that happened. What would he do with an old chair that was no longer needed?

"Why go through all that palaver with the letter?" Jean-Guy asked.

"'Palaver'? Have you been talking to Ruth again?"

"Worse, I've been listening to her. Why didn't this Mountweazel just send the letter to Billy herself, why get the museum to send it to the Godins?"

"One more degree of separation. Fleming wants us to know he's pulling the strings, but he doesn't want us too close."

As Armand walked across the village green to his car, Ruth and Clara waved him over.

"There's news," said Ruth. "Did Robert tell you?"

"I haven't spoken to him." He could guess, though, remembering the minister's slow gait, his lowered head, as though his thoughts were far too heavy to support.

"Sylvie died last night," said Clara. "In her sleep. When Robert woke up, he found her."

"He's in shock," said Ruth.

"So am I," said Clara. "She was with us last night. She was weak but seemed okay."

Myrna came out of her bookstore, looked around, saw them, and headed over.

"Have you seen Harriet?"

"No. Why?" asked Clara.

"I haven't seen her since we had the fight."

"Let me guess. About that young man?" said Ruth.

"Yes." She seemed to notice their moods. "What's wrong? What's happened?"

"Sylvie Mongeau died last night," said Clara.

"That can't be. I was on my way over. She invited me last night when they left. She said she'd like to talk to me."

"You?" said Ruth. "Why?"

"Besides the fact I'm good company?" said Myrna. "I actually don't know. But I'm pretty sure she didn't think it might be her last conversation."

"Maybe as a therapist," said Clara. "She was obviously getting close . . ."

"But not that close," said Myrna.

"Taking the book with you?" Armand motioned to the thick volume in Myrna's hand.

Myrna looked at it, almost surprised to see it there. "Yes."

"Did she ask for it specifically?" he asked.

Myrna was a little surprised by Armand's interest in a book when clearly the headline was the death of the woman who'd asked for it.

"Yes. She saw it on your shelf, Clara, and asked if I could bring a copy with me. Said she'd always wanted to read it."

"She could've borrowed mine," said Clara.

Armand left them then and walked slowly up the hill to the small church. His thoughts going to Robert. And to Sylvie. And to her request to read *The Mists of Avalon*.

A great book, he knew. A retelling of the Arthur legend from the point of view of the women. In the traditional story, told by a man, they're witches. In the retelling, told by a woman, they're sages.

But it wasn't the plot of the book that struck him so much as the fact that a very sick woman would ask for a very long book. One she expected to have time to read.

Sylvie Mongeau had absolutely no inkling that she would be dead within hours. But then, he wondered, would he? Would anyone?

As he got closer to St. Thomas's, Armand heard a nails-on-blackboard sort of sound.

He looked up and saw the caretaker at the top of the steps scraping white paint off the clapboard.

"*Bonjour*," called Armand as he mounted the stairs.

The man ignored him.

At the top, he paused and looked over the village. To the roofline of the shops below.

"You were the one who noticed that there's an attic room attached to the bookstore," he said to the caretaker.

Still the man continued to work, his knobbly backbone visible under the worn work shirt.

Armand realized he'd never actually spoken to him, and had only really seen him at a distance. Now he looked more closely. At the thinning gray hair. The almost fragile frame.

His age indeterminant, but well north of middle age.

The only reply was the screeching of the scraper, as though the man was torturing the building.

Gamache stepped between the caretaker and the wall. The man had to stop, unless he wanted to scrape the Chief Inspector's legs.

The caretaker slowly straightened up. He was at least four inches shorter than the six-foot-one Gamache.

He glanced down at the village and shrugged. "I said the roof would soon need replacing. I never mentioned a hidden room."

"But it doesn't," said Gamache. "Look."

The man did not. "I made a mistake. I'm not a roofer."

Gamache stared at him, but the man kept dropping his eyes.

"Your name is Claude, is that right?"

"*Oui.*"

"And your last name?"

The man hesitated. It was clear to Gamache that there was enmity there. This man did not like him. At all. And yet Gamache could not imagine why that would be.

"Boisfranc."

"Monsieur Boisfranc, where were you before you came here?"

Now he did raise his eyes and met Gamache's. "Piss off."

Gamache raised his brows. "*Pardon?*"

"You heard me. Piss off. Fuck off. I don't have to answer any questions. Get out of my way. I have a job to do." He brandished the scraper as though it were a shiv.

Gamache looked deep into Claude Boisfranc's eyes and saw . . . nothing. Well, he didn't see a monster, a lunatic. He did see anger, but that was not uncommon for a cop.

This aggression was a puzzle but not, Gamache felt, a worry.

"I'm sorry for disturbing you." Stepping aside, he opened the door to the church.

It was dark and cool inside and smelled of old books and wax polish. It smelled of calm and, best of all, stability.

Robert Mongeau sat in a pew, surrounded by cheery light through the immortal boys.

Armand joined him. The two sat in silence for a few moments before Armand whispered, "*Désolé.*"

At Heathrow Airport, awaiting their return flight, Reine-Marie got a call from the museum.

"*Oui, allô,*" she said.

"Madame Cloutier? It's Cecil Clarke. I just was looking at *The Paston Treasure* and I noticed something."

"Oh?"

"I'm not sure how long they've been there, but there are markings on the clockface."

"Words?"

"No, just lines, not even pictures. Squiggles. You didn't . . ."

"Put them there? Of course not. We were never alone with it, even if we'd wanted to. Can you take a photo of them, please?"

"Why?"

"Please, just do it." As soon as it arrived, she forwarded it, with shaking fingers, to Armand, Jean-Guy, and Amelia. Then she studied it herself. The doodles of a madman.

CHAPTER 33

The two men sat quietly. One silenced by grief, the other by knowing there were no words.

Armand could not even offer companionship. The man beside him was alone. Standing on an island in some vast ocean, no mainland in sight.

And so Armand sat quietly, also bathed in the brilliant boys. He'd have to leave soon to meet Jean-Guy, but for another few minutes Armand could sit with his friend. And hope and pray that a bridge, or a boat, might one day appear that would take Robert to a place of peace.

"She's gone." The words caused the dust caught in the sunshine to swirl about.

"*Oui.*" Armand waited a moment. Two. Before saying, "Would you like to talk?"

Armand assumed the silence was the answer, but then . . .

"She was fine when we went to bed." Robert spoke to the Bible in his hand. "I gave her her meds, then I read to her until she fell asleep." He continued to stare straight ahead. "We weren't even halfway through the book."

It seemed a non sequitur, but Armand understood. It was no longer a book, it had become a symbol.

He remembered finding, at the age of nine, the book his father had been reading. It was on the bedside table with a bookmark where he'd stopped. Where he'd expected to continue. But never did.

Young Armand took the book into his own bedroom and placed it in a drawer. Safe for when they came back. So that his father could pick up the story where he left off.

It had taken Armand more than forty years to finally open the book. He'd sat on the bench above Three Pines, day after day, holding it but not yet daring. And then, one day, he dared.

Armand, a grandfather by then, read to the end, finishing what his father had started. He hoped that one day Robert would too. But the minister did not have forty years to wait for the bridge, or the boat.

Jean-Guy got to the rendezvous location much earlier than planned and pulled into a small opening where Monsieur Godin, or Fleming, could not see him.

After confirming that Annie, Honoré, and Idola, along with Daniel and his family, were safely at the lake house, he opened an email from Reine-Marie.

Attached was a photo of the clock from the original *Paston Treasure*. All around the face there were lines, markings.

"Oh, *merde*," he said. His heart was beating fast, in excitement or dread or both.

Curator just found this on original painting. Not there before.

Beauvoir forwarded it to Dr. Brunel to decode, copying Gamache.

"I remember the day I came home and told Sylvie I wanted to enroll in divinity school," said Robert, smiling.

Armand listened. He wondered if the minister remembered he was there, or if he was talking to himself.

"She didn't argue. Wasn't surprised, though it meant a complete change in lifestyle. No more private clubs, no more business class travel. No more fine meals in ridiculously priced restaurants. We'd have to sell the business, the house, the lake house at Manitou. We'd have to watch every cent. But she didn't argue. I think she was relieved that I'd finally seen what had been obvious to her for years. I was miserable and making everyone around me miserable."

He turned slightly and looked at Armand. Studying his face for something. Then he looked away again.

"This's our first posting, you know. I wanted a church in Montréal or Québec City, so the bishop sent me here." He chuckled. "Took us a few days to even find the place. I kept calling the diocese to make sure they got it right."

Robert shook his head. Lost in the past. Where Sylvie was beside him in the car.

As Armand watched, Robert reached out, palm up, then slowly closed his hand over hers as they searched the countryside for the place that seemed more myth than real.

"She'd decided to stop treatment by then. She wanted to just live out the rest of her days. That's really why I wanted a city, so we'd be close to a hospital. But she wanted the countryside, where she'd be close to nature. She loved going for walks around here. Every evening after dinner, we walked, though recently we just sat in the garden." He fell silent, remembering. And then he remembered. And lost her again, the island drifting farther out to sea.

For Robert Mongeau there would always be a before and an after. All events would henceforth be dated from Sylvie alive and Sylvie dead.

As Robert squeezed his eyes shut, Armand felt the sharp thrust into his own heart.

"I know, I know, I know she's with God," said Robert. "I know she's at peace. But oh God, oh God."

Armand reached out and took his hand.

He was aware of time ticking by. Aware Beauvoir was waiting for him. Aware Fleming might be too, just outside that door.

But this was important. He hoped, if something happened to Reine-Marie, someone would hold his hand.

"I'm sorry. I'm so sorry," repeated Robert, crying openly now.

"It's all right," Armand whispered. They were, he knew, empty words. But he had to offer something.

Mongeau gathered himself, sat up straighter, took his hand from Armand's, and wiped his eyes and nose with a handkerchief. Then unexpectedly smiled.

"I can't imagine what Claude thought. I practically ran him over when I backed out of the drive on my way over here. After they'd . . ."

It took Armand a moment to understand what he was saying. "The driveway? At your house? Claude was at your place this morning?"

"Yes. I pay him extra to do odd jobs around the place. He was weeding the drive. In my hurry to get here, to get away, I didn't see him. Thankfully he managed to get out of the way. He's far more agile than he looks."

"Was he there yesterday too?"

"Yes, but only after he'd finished work here."

Armand stepped carefully, but Robert seemed grateful for the change of topic.

"Can you tell me how you came to hire Monsieur Boisfranc?"

"Claude?" The minister paused to think. "I thought I told you. He was recommended. Some woman staying at the B&B came to service one Sunday." He paused. "I remember because Sylvie was too weak to come. It was a bad few days for her. First service she'd missed." He reflected for a moment, then continued on. "The woman stayed for coffee and cake after and must've overheard Gabri and me talking about the search for a caretaker."

"What did she say?"

"That she volunteered for a group in Montréal, a halfway home for former convicts. Claude was one. Convicted of petty crimes. In and out of prison. I interviewed him and decided to hire him."

"A former convict?"

Robert shifted in his seat to look at Gamache. "You're the last person I'd expect to deny someone a second chance. You have, after all, a convicted murderer in your home. The worst Claude did was steal some clothes."

"I'm not blaming or accusing you of anything."

"Are you accusing him?"

303

"No." Not yet. Though this did explain Boisfranc's loathing of Gamache. Almost certainly of all cops. And who could blame him?

But alarms were going off for the Chief Inspector. "Do you know the name of the halfway home?"

"No, but I can find it for you. Does it really matter?"

"Do you have Claude's address?"

"Here? I let him stay in the church basement. Why?"

"How about the name of the woman who suggested him?"

Robert laughed. "You're kidding, right? That's almost two years ago." Then he stopped and tilted his head. "Actually, strangely, I do remember. It was—"

Before he even said it, Gamache knew.

"—Mountweazel," said Robert. "I know that Claude's a little odd, taciturn. But he's been a godsend."

"Yes, I'm sure he has. Listen, Robert, Reine-Marie won't be back until tomorrow at the earliest. Come over for dinner. Stay the night. Please."

The minister considered for a moment. "*Merci.* I'd like that. I'm not sure I could sleep at home . . ."

"Yes."

They were silent, Armand aware of the need to leave soon.

"I hope Reine-Marie's enjoyed herself," said Robert. "Sylvie and I used to love visiting galleries and museums in London. And Paris, of course. Her favorite thing in Paris were the flea markets. The big one, what's it called again? My mind isn't working."

"Les Puces."

The minister gave one short laugh. "Of course. Les Puces. The Fleas. You must miss Reine-Marie when she's away."

"I do."

"You must tell her that, Armand." The minister turned and looked at him directly, for the first time since Armand had arrived.

"She knows."

"Yes, I imagine she does. But you can never say it too often. You can never let someone know too often that they're precious. That they're missed." He paused. "Believe me."

And Armand did.

"Did anyone visit Sylvie yesterday?"

"No. We were at Clara's briefly, but no one came to the house. Why?"

"Think, Robert. Anyone?"

"What is it, Armand, why're you asking?"

"I'm just wondering."

"You're more than wondering," said the minister. "Tell me."

"Occupational hazard, I'm afraid."

Mongeau stared at him. "Occupational? You're not thinking she was . . . That's insane." His voice was rising into the hysteria range. "Why would you say that?"

"I'm not saying anything, Robert." Armand's voice was steady, calm. "I'm just asking."

"She had cancer, for God's sake. What're you suggesting?"

"I'm sorry." And he was. But still, he had to ask. Again. "Did anyone come to the house yesterday? A delivery, maybe?"

"No." But now there was a hesitation, a slight shift in the minister's attitude. "Actually, something was delivered. Sylvie said she didn't remember ordering it, but I think the cancer had gone to her brain. She was forgetting things, getting more muddled."

"What was it?"

"A clock."

"Clock?" Armand thought of the photo Reine-Marie had sent of the detail from the real *Paston Treasure*. "Do you know what time it was set for?"

"Of course not. Who notices that?"

Gamache was almost afraid to ask the next question. "Was there any writing on it?"

The minister looked at him as though he'd lost his mind. "Writing? What are you talking about? Sylvie's dead. Don't you care? For sure, let's talk about clocks now."

"I'm sorry, of course I care." He leaned forward. "I wish I didn't have to do this, but . . . Robert, where was she taken?"

The minister looked perplexed, then his eyes widened. "Good God, you're not suggesting an . . ."

"Autopsy. Not yet, but we need blood and tissue samples. And I need to see the clock. I am deeply, deeply sorry, but if someone did something to Sylvie, we need to know. It might help us find the person and stop him hurting anyone else."

Appealing to the minister's sense of social responsibility might have been manipulative, but it also happened to be the truth. They had to get possession of Sylvie Mongeau's body before she was embalmed.

"But it's ludicrous. Why would anyone hurt Sylvie?"

"I don't know, and she probably died peacefully and naturally. But we need to be sure."

"No autopsy?" said Robert. "You promise?"

"No autopsy. Not without telling you. I promise."

Mongeau gave him the name of the funeral home. Armand got to his feet.

"I won't be able to come to your home after all." The minister's voice was cold, formal. "I'll have Claude drop the clock off at the Old Train Station."

With that he turned his back on Gamache.

"I wish you'd reconsider, Robert." The minister didn't move, but Armand had one more question. "Does Monsieur Boisfranc have a key to your home?"

But Robert just continued to stare ahead. Though Gamache was pretty sure he knew what the answer was.

Instead of heading outside, Armand went down into the basement, where he found the caretaker's room. It had a single bed and dresser. Armand stood at the threshold and looked in. He had no right to search the man's place, and anything he found could not be used as evidence.

He considered. Weighing the consequences. The legal and the moral.

And then he entered the room and searched. Quickly, expertly.

But there was nothing there. No photographs, no letters. No handwriting of any sort.

This was the modest room of a man without roots. Then Armand looked behind the door and found a poster. It was from Clara's first solo show at the Musée d'art contemporain de Montréal.

The museum had chosen the extraordinary portrait of Ruth Zardo as the abandoned, forgotten, embittered Virgin Mary, clutching a blue shawl to her scrawny neck and looking out at the world with contempt.

Except, except, except. For those who did not hurry by, there was a reward beyond imagining. It was the tiny dot in her eyes. The tiniest hint of hope.

Did this man lie in bed at night and stare at it? And if so, what did he see? The despair or the hope?

Was this an insight into a man trying to right his life? Or was it another sign from Fleming? Of all the posters Boisfranc could have chosen, he'd pinned up one unique to this village. One that spoke of an enraged mother of Christ.

Yes, it was just the sort of image a fallen worshipper might choose. And exactly the sort of image he would misinterpret.

As Armand left, he looked for the caretaker, but Claude Boisfranc was nowhere to be seen, though the scraper was lying by the clapboard wall.

As he walked to his car, he thought about his exchange with Boisfranc. While not particularly pleasant, no alarms had been set off. He'd looked into those eyes and had not seen John Fleming. But then even eyes could be disguised with colored contact lenses.

As he considered that, he realized he'd just left another man who, roughly speaking, fit the description of John Fleming. Add weight. A trim beard. Put in contact lenses . . .

Armand paused by his car and placed a call. After being transferred a few times, he finally got through.

"Bishop Hargreaves? My name is Armand Gamache, I'm the—"

"Yes," said the man. "I know who you are." It was said with good humor and even warmth. "How can I help you, Chief Inspector? Not a crime, I hope." His voice grew grave.

"No. I'm not sure if you've heard, but Sylvie Mongeau passed away last night. She's the wife of one of your clergy, the minister who's assigned to my village church in Three Pines."

He waited for the Bishop to recall.

"Robert Mongeau. Yes. Oh, dear. We knew it was coming, but it's always a shock, isn't it? I'll call him and say prayers for them both."

"Can you tell me a bit about him?"

There was a pause. It was clear the Anglican Bishop wanted to ask why but restrained himself.

"Well, his records are private, of course, but I can tell you that he graduated from divinity school just a couple of years ago and applied for a position in Montréal. I was going to assign him to one in Westmount, but Sylvie came to me privately and asked for a posting in the country."

"Why Three Pines?"

"She asked for it specifically. Said she'd heard from a woman friend how nice it was. Peaceful. With a good community feel. A place that would be supportive."

"Of her, because of her cancer."

"No. She was thinking of Robert. That he'd need that support, one day."

Armand glanced toward the church and the man he'd just left, even more devastated than when he'd arrived. He let out a long breath and continued.

"I don't suppose she told you the name of the woman friend."

Now the Bishop laughed. "You must be practiced at praying, Chief Inspector. There's no way I'd remember that, even if she told me, which I doubt. I looked up the village, and sure enough, Three Pines had had itinerant ministers, as you probably know, but no permanent one. In fact, we rotate responsibility for the care of the souls between priests, ministers, and rabbis. I asked my colleagues, and they all agreed to let Monsieur Mongeau minister full-time. I wouldn't normally assign a dedicated minister to such a small congregation, but I sympathized. I'd lost my own wife a year before."

"I'm sorry."

"*Merci*. But it does tenderize a person. I'm sorry about Madame

Mongeau. I liked her. I like them both. Robert is extraordinary. But then people who find God again, after wandering in the wilderness, often are."

"*Merci*, Your Grace."

He hung up, relieved. He hadn't expected any other answer from the Bishop, but he had to be sure that Robert Mongeau was who he said he was. He then called Correctional Services, for the file on Claude Boisfranc. And, most important, a photograph.

As he drove to the rendezvous with Jean-Guy, Armand pledged to try to stop seeing ghosts, or Flemings, behind every tree. There were a lot of trees. And a lot of ghosts.

Jean-Guy looked down the dirt road. Again.

Gamache had texted to say he'd be a few minutes late. It was all Beauvoir could do not to get out of the car and pace. Finally, he saw the Volvo approach.

Beauvoir was there almost before the vehicle had fully stopped.

"I went over Fleming's file," he said, clutching the dossier and getting in the passenger seat. "There's a list attached to the back of the last page. It's of places he lived and dates. John Fleming was in the same town as Clotilde Arsenault twenty-six years ago. I called up the Arsenault file and compared. And get this, he was in the next village over when Clotilde was murdered."

Gamache stared at Beauvoir, stunned. "It's not in the file I have."

He took the paper and put on his reading glasses. He'd spent hours and hours at that desk in the little room in his basement, going over and over, over the years, the thick dossier.

There were huge holes in the timeline. And in those holes, Chief Inspector Gamache was convinced, were buried more victims. In those holes he might find the name of an accomplice, still out there.

In those holes he might now find the escaped madman.

The list of places and dates that Beauvoir handed him was scribbled on paper torn from an exercise book like the ones his granddaughters brought home from school. All that was missing were the little pony stickers.

"This's information he gave them while at the SHU," said Beauvoir.

Gamache took off his reading glasses and looked out the windshield at the sun-dappled dirt road. His mind worked quickly, going back to that November day by the shore of the iron-gray lake. To that house. Those children. The videos. Could Fleming be on one?

Could Fleming have somehow been involved in Clotilde's murder?

"It could be more lies," he said. "To confuse us, have us running off in the wrong direction."

"Thought of that. I called detention and spoke to the warden. He admitted lots in the file was faked. The ID, the fingerprints, DNA. But not that list."

"I'm not saying the warden necessarily fabricated it. I'm saying Fleming lied to them about where he lived and when. We only have his word, and we know what that's worth."

The list might as well have been written on toilet paper. But still, Gamache didn't dare dismiss it outright. It was certainly more manipulation, but that did not make it untrue. And it was certainly strange that, if he made it up at random, he'd choose those towns and those years.

"We need to find out if his name was in Clotilde's ledger."

"Will do."

"In that file"—he nodded to the dossier on Beauvoir's lap—"is there mention of a wife? Children?"

"No. But that's something else, *patron*. I did the math. If what's in here is true, John Fleming was not only in the same town as Clotilde twenty-six years ago, he was living there when she gave birth."

"To whom?" Though he could do the math himself.

"Fiona."

There was silence for a beat, two, as Gamache stared at Beauvoir.

"Are you suggesting that Fiona Arsenault is John Fleming's daughter?"

"Yes. Maybe. It's possible. There's no father listed on her birth certificate, and Fleming was gone by the time Sam was born. We can get her DNA records, and once we find Fleming's, we can compare them."

Armand felt like someone had just struck him hard on the side of the head.

Could it be even worse than he had feared?

Not Sam after all, but Fiona, as Jean-Guy had always maintained. As others had maintained. But he'd ignored them. So sure of himself.

Fiona. The young woman whose release he had secured. Who was released into his custody. Released into his home. Into his family.

"You couldn't have known, *patron*."

"You knew."

"I guessed. I didn't know and still don't."

And yet, for all Armand didn't want to believe it, one of his strengths was seeing the truth, no matter how awful. And this looked like the truth. And this was awful.

Jean-Guy reached for the door handle, but Gamache stopped him.

"I have news too."

He told Beauvoir about Sylvie Mongeau.

"I called the funeral home," he said. "They're sending her body to the coroner. I've alerted Dr. Harris to just take blood and tissue samples for now and get them analyzed quickly."

"You think Madame Mongeau was murdered? By Fleming? But why would he?"

"I don't know. Maybe she wasn't. Or maybe she knew something, saw something. I think she met the Mountweazel woman. She specifically asked that they be assigned to Three Pines because some woman had told her it was a peaceful place. I think that woman was Mountweazel. Maybe Fleming was worried that Sylvie would recognize her."

"So you think she's here too?"

"I don't know. Maybe she hasn't arrived yet. Maybe that's why Sylvie needed to be killed now, before she does."

Maybe, maybe, maybe. But there was one more, and a big one.

"Sylvie asked Myrna to bring a book, even though they were only partway through the one they were reading. I think the book was an excuse to talk to Myrna. As a therapist, perhaps, but maybe it was as Harriet's aunt. Maybe she recognized Sam from somewhere and wanted to warn Myrna."

"Maybe," said Jean-Guy, but Armand could interpret the look, the tone.

He thinks I'm unwilling to accept Fiona's the one we need to watch, not Sam. And he might be right. Maybe it was Fiona she recognized. But then, why speak to Myrna and not Reine-Marie or me? No, it must be Sam . . .

He was desperate to believe that the monster in their midst was not the one he had released. Not Fiona.

Not Fiona.

Not Fiona.

But Sam.

Dear God, maybe it's both.

"Maybe asking to see Myrna has nothing to do with her death," said Jean-Guy. "She just liked books and wanted her company."

Gamache nodded. It was the simplest explanation, and the most likely.

"Maybe."

"Poor Mongeau," said Jean-Guy.

"*Oui.*" Armand would try again to see if the grieving man would come over for dinner and stay the night.

He flipped through the file once more, his eyes coming to rest on the list of Fleming's victims.

Armand, of course, knew them all by heart. Their names. Their families. Their communities and jobs and friends and faiths.

The Hudson's Bay clerk. The fisherman. The bridge builder.

"Oh, my God," Gamache whispered.

He stared at the list. Then, getting out of the car, he walked away. In the opposite direction of the Godin house. Jean-Guy was about to go after him, but knew enough to let the man just think. He watched as Gamache turned and walked back. Then turned again and walked away. His hands clasped behind his back, his head bent as though leaning into a whirlwind.

Then he stopped, turned, and stared at Jean-Guy.

"What is it?" asked Beauvoir.

But Gamache was on the phone. It rang and rang, then went to voice mail.

"Nathalie, it's Armand. Can you send me that list?" When he hung up, he walked quickly over to Jean-Guy, talking as he strode. "Fleming's fourth victim, Connor McNee. He was a bridge builder."

"Yes." Beauvoir's eyes opened. "Is that why there was the picture of the Québec Bridge in the painting?"

"I think so. Those engineer's rings are made from the remains of the bridge. I think Connor McNee was an engineer. I think that was his ring."

"But he's dead. He couldn't have left it there."

"No, but Fleming could have. The bodies were never found. Just the heads."

"Oh, fuck me," muttered Beauvoir. They'd gone way past palaver.

Gamache checked his messages in hopes Nathalie had already sent the list of people who'd worn that ring. She had not. But there was one from Jérôme Brunel.

"What is it?" Beauvoir asked, seeing Gamache's expression.

"Dr. Brunel has decoded the message on the clockface of the real *Paston Treasure*."

Armand turned his phone around for Jean-Guy to see.

Time's up.

"Oh, dear," whispered Beauvoir.

CHAPTER 34

Myrna was getting more and more worried. She'd texted Harriet and called. Emailed and sent a WhatsApp.

But no reply.

"I'm sure she's fine," said Clara. She was on the stool in front of her easel. Myrna was on the sofa, her bum on the floor and her knees up around her ears. "She's just ignoring you. She'll calm down eventually. Give her space."

"Yeah, maybe. I'm going over to the B&B." She groaned in an unsuccessful effort to get up.

Clara sighed. "Did you hear a word I just said?"

"I did," said Myrna, finally rolling off the sofa. "I don't agree."

"Look, why don't you call Gabri. Ask if Harriet's returned. She's staying there now, right?"

"Yes." It was a good idea. As the phone rang, she looked at the painting Clara was working on.

It was a swirl of giddy colors. It looked like a hot mess.

After speaking to Gabri, she hung up and sighed. "She's back. Harriet and Sam returned to the B&B a few minutes ago. They ordered an early dinner from the bistro."

"Good," said Clara, turning back to the canvas. "See? Safe and sound."

Though Myrna was far from certain that was true.

* * *

Harriet stirred. And threw up. Her head felt like it had been split in two, and she tasted blood, mixed with the vomit.

She tried to move, but couldn't. It took her fuzzy brain a moment to realize she was tied up.

That can't be true, she thought.

Her vision was blurry, but she could see enough to know she was in the forest. Darkness was closing in again.

This can't be happening, she thought.

Just as she lost consciousness, she saw something on the ground a short distance from her. It looked like a body. It looked like . . .

"Sam?"

"Got it. The information on McNee," said Beauvoir, standing outside Gamache's car. "He worked in northern Québec, building bridges. Married. Two daughters. Born and raised—"

"Yes, yes, I know all that. But his schooling. His training?"

Beauvoir skimmed. Then looked up. "He was a civil engineer."

Gamache called Nathalie Provost again and this time got through.

"I just sent it off to you," she said. "Is everything all right? You sounded stressed."

"Just fine, better now that I have the list. Thank you."

He hung up, then clicked on the list. And there was the confirmation.

"Conner McNee was the last person to wear the ring," he told Beauvoir.

The full horror of what Gamache was saying struck Jean-Guy. John Fleming had kept the ring, for years. And dropped it there, like a land mine for Gamache to step on.

It was a message, a warning. He could go anywhere. Do anything. He could get deep in Gamache's home, into his life, and Armand could not stop him. He moved, seen but unseen, through the community, through their lives, with impunity.

The engineer's ring, a symbol of what could happen when mistakes were made, was now used to taunt Gamache with his own mistakes. And the deaths that resulted.

315

"We need to arrest Godin," said Gamache, striding through the late-afternoon sun toward the old farmhouse. "Take him in for questioning. We can keep him for twenty-four hours before having to charge."

"You think he's Fleming?" asked Beauvoir, running to catch up.

"I don't know, and we don't have time to find out. We have to get him off the streets."

But Godin wasn't there, and neither was his car.

"Damn," snapped Gamache. "I should have had him under surveillance." He turned to Beauvoir. "We need to send out a province-wide alert. And get local agents out here. We need a ground search. And, Jean-Guy, get up to the lake house. Make sure they're safe."

"You don't think—"

"I think Fleming has had years to plan this, and I don't think he'll stop at me."

"I can send members of our own team, and I can stay with you."

"No. Fleming has too much information. I have no idea how he's getting it. If he bribed the head guard and the warden, it's possible he also got to someone inside the Sûreté."

Inside the homicide unit. Gamache was loath to think that, but he had not grasped quickly enough exactly what was happening, who was behind it, the lengths he'd gone to, and the size of the threat. So far at least two people had been murdered, perhaps more.

Now was not the time to underestimate. He needed to assume the very worst.

Matthew 10:36.

"There are members of our team we can trust, have trusted with our lives," said Beauvoir. "I'll call Isabelle. She's vacationing at Mont-Tremblant. That's close to Manitou. I'm as anxious as you to protect the family. Annie. My own children. But I also know that the best way to do that, the only way to do that, is to catch Fleming. And he's here."

He stood rigid, his arms taut at his side, fists in balls, staring, glaring at Gamache.

"All right," Gamache conceded. "Call Isabelle. Then you lead the search for Godin. I'm going back to pick up the caretaker."

As Gamache drove, he whispered, "I'm coming for you."

Then, from inside his own head, he heard the sneered reply.

Time's up.

Gamache went directly to the church, but there was no sign of the caretaker. Just the scraper still lying on the landing. He placed it in a tissue and put it in his pocket. Then he carefully entered the chapel, standing with his back to the door, allowing his eyes to adjust.

He could see Robert Mongeau sitting where he'd left him, his head bowed in prayer.

Taking a quick look around to see if he could spot the caretaker, Gamache walked quietly up to the minister.

"Robert?" But he didn't move. "Robert?"

When he got close, Gamache noticed a dark patch on the side of Mongeau's head. He slipped into the pew, just as the minister slumped. Gamache caught him and laid him down, feeling for a pulse.

He was alive, but there was a lot of blood. Mongeau's eyes opened but seemed unfocused.

"It's all right, Robert. It's Armand. It's going to be all right." His hands moved swiftly over the minister's body, looking for other wounds. "Everything will be fine. Stay with me."

But Robert's eyes had rolled to the back of his head, and his lids had closed.

Armand tore off his jacket and pressed it to the minister's head wound, then he quickly considered. He could call an ambulance, but that would take too long.

Lifting Mongeau, he carried him out of the church, down the stairs, and to his car. Seeing this, Gabri and Olivier came running out of the bistro, and Ruth limped quickly across the green.

"Help me," said Gamache as he struggled to gently lay the minister across the back seat.

Mongeau groaned as Gabri crawled in the other side, took his shoulders, and pulled him across.

"I'm coming with you," said Ruth. "I know first aid."

Gamache did not protest. As much as Gabri liked to refer to

the elderly poet as the Labrador on the leg of life, she was indeed trained.

Besides, she was already in the car, cradling Robert's head.

They watched in surprise as Gamache ran back to the church. Once inside, he quickly searched between the pews. Then behind the curtains at the altar. Then downstairs he raced.

But Claude Boisfranc was gone.

Returning to the car, he waved off their questions, then drove as fast as he could to the hospital. When they arrived at Emergency, Mongeau was wheeled in semiconscious, protesting feebly that he was all right, before throwing up and asking for Sylvie.

"You okay?" Armand asked Ruth.

Ruth was looking unwell too.

"Yes, I suppose." She looked at the swinging doors through which the emergency staff had wheeled the minister. "What happened?"

"I don't know. I found him like that."

"That's why you went back to the church, to see if you could find whoever attacked him."

"Yes."

"But why would anyone want to hurt the minister?" She turned her rheumy blue eyes on him. "And so soon after Sylvie died. A coincidence?"

It was clear she did not believe that for a moment.

"I don't see how." But he had a pretty good idea who. "Can you stay here and wait to see how Robert is?"

"Where will you be?"

"I'm going downstairs to the morgue."

"Is that your happy place?" Ruth called after him, but he was already through the door, showing his ID to the orderly who'd stepped forward to stop him.

The coroner looked up. "You didn't have to come here, Armand. I could've called you. But no results yet." Sharon Harris looked at him more closely. "Are you okay?"

"Why do you ask?"

318

"You have blood on you."

He looked down and realized his shirt and slacks were stained from when he'd carried Mongeau to the car.

"Someone else's. I brought a friend to Emergency."

"Jesus, looks bad. Hope he's okay."

"Head wound. They bleed."

Dr. Harris glanced at the deep scar by the Chief Inspector's temple and imagined the blood from that.

"Can you tell me anything at all about Sylvie Mongeau?" Gamache stepped to the other side of the autopsy table where the woman's body lay.

"Well"—Dr. Harris glanced down—"given the mottling and the dilation in her eyes, I'd say it looks suspicious, but we need to wait for the blood and tissue tests. After that, I would have to do a full autopsy."

"If I got you DNA samples, can you compare them?"

"Yes, of course. It won't be official, you'll need forensics for that, but it will be accurate. For this woman?"

"No. One's for a Fiona Arsenault. I'll have those sent over from her files. Another is also on file now. A man named Godin. I'll have that sent to you too. The other one is here."

He brought the scraper out of his pocket.

She put on gloves and took the scraper over to her workbench. "You think they might be related, or the same person?"

"Definitely different people, but yes, they might be related."

"This's to do with this woman's death?"

"I think so." He paused, but the clock was ticking and now was not the time for discretion. Besides, he'd need the coroner's help. "I'm looking for John Fleming."

Dr. Harris turned to look at him. "Fleming? The serial killer?"

"*Oui.*"

"You do know he's in the SHU, right?" When the Chief Inspector didn't answer she repeated, her voice strained, "Right?"

"He's out."

"Out? Out? Someone let him out? Out?" Her mind was snagged on that word.

"Sharon, were you involved in the case?"

"He's out?" Her voice was now barely making it through her constricted throat. "How the hell could that happen?"

"Were you on the case?" he repeated.

She took a couple of breaths. "I was in training, so I wasn't the lead coroner. Never testified. But I saw . . ."

"Yes."

". . . what . . ."

"Yes."

". . . he did."

"*Oui.*"

She looked at him. "You did too."

"*Oui.*"

It was a small club. With a horrific entrance requirement. Armand quickly patted his pockets. The photos from the file. He'd put them in his jacket. The one he'd used to staunch Robert's wound. It was still upstairs.

He'd have to go back up and get them before anyone else joined the club.

Gamache sent the DNA results from Fiona's and Godin's files to Dr. Harris, then he called Jean-Guy and told him about Mongeau.

"I can't find the caretaker," said Gamache.

"And I can't find Godin. Fleming can't be both of them. He's fucking with us. What do you want to bet he's killed one of them, and just wants us to waste time and effort looking for both. Who do you think is Fleming, Godin or Boisfranc?"

"Look, at this stage I think I might be Fleming."

Beauvoir laughed. "I'll organize another search for Boisfranc and send out an alert. Can we get Boisfranc's DNA?"

"I have it. Dr. Harris is doing a swab now. We just need to get Fleming's real DNA results to compare."

"I've pushed the prosecutor's office, but they just laughed when I told them Fleming might've escaped. I've sent them the warden's confession. I'll call the head prosecutor. Why would Fleming want to kill the minister? Why then and not when he killed Sylvie?"

"I questioned Robert this afternoon about Boisfranc. Maybe Robert decided to give Boisfranc a chance to explain. If the caretaker is Fleming, Robert would've inadvertently warned him."

It was like the minister to do that. And he'd led Robert right into it.

And yet, even that didn't ring quite true. As Beauvoir had said, why not kill both the Mongeaus? Fleming had never been squeamish about a body count.

The croquet matches in summer, the handshake, the cough, the kiss / There is always a wicked secret, a private reason for this.

There was, Gamache knew, a reason for this. But he'd have to go deeper into the cave to find it. And the wicked secret.

"I'm going back up to Emergency. I left Ruth there."

"Ruth? Jesus. Like those people aren't suffering enough. I'll continue the search for Godin. It'll be too dark in the woods soon, and we'll have to call it off 'til morning."

Armand was just leaving when Dr. Harris called him over.

"I have the results, but there's a problem. Look."

He leaned into the microscope. As head of homicide, he'd studied innumerable DNA results and had a practiced eye. "Which is which?"

"The one on the left is Godin. The middle slide is the woman's DNA profile. On the right is, well, the men."

He turned his head from the slides to look at her. "Men?"

"Yes. The scraper thing was contaminated. There were two sets of DNA. Both male. Maybe yours. Maybe someone else's. Someone else handled the scraper."

"Damn," he said, and went back to the microscope. "Looks like Fiona and Godin aren't related."

"Agreed, but I need to look more closely. There are similarities between hers and the contaminated one. But with the cross contamination, it's impossible to tell. I will say, just my guess, that the person who handled it last is probably the relative."

And that, Gamache knew, was the caretaker. Claude Boisfranc.

"You can at least eliminate me."

She did a swab before he left to go back up to Emergency.

Once there, he was surprised to see Robert Mongeau sitting in a wheelchair, beside Ruth. His head was bandaged, and he was pale. Armand's bloody jacket lay across his lap, and on top of it were the photographs, facedown.

"Robert, what are you doing? You should be in a bed."

"What are these, Armand?" the minister asked, his voice weak and small, but determined. It was obvious what he was talking about.

Gamache held Robert's eyes and saw something deeply troubling there.

"You looked at the pictures," he said.

"They fell out of your jacket. I wouldn't have looked, had I known."

Armand's eyes traveled over to Ruth, and his heart dropped. "You showed them to Ruth?"

"What are these? What's it of?" Mongeau asked. "Why do you have them? What . . . ? Why . . . ?"

Armand reached out and gently tugged them out of the minister's hands, picking up his jacket at the same time.

"They're from a long time ago, Robert." He looked at Ruth. "Are you okay?"

"Yes, yes, of course. I've seen worse."

For some reason, he believed her. Though he could think of only one thing worse than those photographs, and that was the man who'd done it.

"Can you excuse me?" Without waiting for a reply, Armand walked through the swinging Emergency doors. As he did, he stuck the photographs in his slacks pocket.

"What are you—" the doctor asked, but then her eyes traveled to the blood on his shirt, then to his face. "Chief Inspector? Are you all right?"

"I am. The blood belongs to the man Mongeau you just treated."

"Yes. Head wound."

"It wasn't an accident. Can you tell me what the weapon was?"

"I wasn't sure what had caused it. I asked him, but he didn't remember. I thought maybe he'd tripped and hit his head." She'd walked over to her desk. "I picked these out of the wound."

The doctor handed him a small sterile plastic bag.

Gamache took it. He was shocked and yet not surprised. It felt as though elements were both falling apart and falling into place. Their rightful place.

The bag contained tiny pieces of what looked like brick.

"You released Monsieur Mongeau?" he asked, tucking the bag into his pocket.

"Yes. There's no skull fracture and I don't think there's a concussion. Looks like he turned his head at the last moment, so it became more of a glancing blow. Enough to knock him out and cause a lot of bleeding, but not enough to seriously hurt him."

She paused and stared at the head of homicide. "Was that the intention? Did someone try to kill that man?"

"You'll obviously keep this to yourself."

She nodded. "I gave him a dozen stitches. He'll need watching, and someone to change the dressing. I also gave him some antibiotics and painkillers."

Armand returned to the waiting room. "Did you see who did this to you?"

"I'd have told you if I had," said Robert. He looked drained.

Ruth was looking at the minister with concern.

"I'd like to go home," he said. He was weak and wilting. "Please. Do you mind driving me?"

"You can't go home, Robert," said Armand, wheeling him out. "You're coming back with me."

"Armand?" Ruth touched his arm and motioned him to step away.

"Are you sure he's okay," she whispered, glancing toward the minister, who was staring into space.

"The doctors have released him. I'll take good care of him."

She nodded and seemed distracted by some thought.

"What is it?" he asked.

"I just . . . be careful, Armand. That's all."

He knew what she was saying. Whoever did this might try again. Almost certainly would. That alone was reason enough to bring Robert Mongeau back home with him. Where he could protect the man. And maybe, maybe, catch the assailant when he did try again.

Fiona put the tray on the table.

Grilled salmon, roasted cauliflower with orange and dill crumb, and baby potatoes for Harriet, and piri-piri chicken thighs with roast parsnips and sweet potatoes for Sam.

She'd brought it over from the bistro, putting in the order with Olivier.

"Young lovers," she said and saw him smile.

Once in the room, she locked the door, drew the curtains, mashed up the food, and then flushed it down the toilet.

Harriet roused. Her head still felt like it had been split open, but her eyes were clearer and she felt more alert.

The forest seemed in perpetual twilight, as though the sun were afraid to drop into the woods. But one thing that was dropping was the temperature.

A chill went through her, acting as a bucket of cold water to the face. She was no longer in any doubt. She was tied to a tree, her ankles also bound.

"Sam?" she whispered. It looked like he was lying on his side, a few feet from her. Still. Too still. Raising her voice a little, not wanting to alert her captors that she was conscious, she repeated, "Sam?" But the body didn't move. Finally she shouted. "Sam!"

Nothing.

And now she just screamed. Not his name, not anyone's. No words. Just a shriek. Startled birds took off, and squirrels scampered away from this new beast.

Her heart pounded, her head pounded.

Fuck, fuck, fuck, fuck, fuck.

After what seemed hours, she'd exhausted herself. No one answered. No one came. But they must have been looking for them. A search party? Someone would know they were missing.

Myrna sat in the bistro with Ruth and Clara.

They were silent. Ruth had told them what had happened to Robert.

"Something's wrong," she now said, her voice uncharacteristically quiet.

"I'd call murder and attempted murder more than wrong," said Clara.

"I need to find Harriet," said Myrna. "I need to make sure she's all right."

"She is," said Gabri, joining them. "Fiona came and got them some dinner. They're eating at the B&B."

"I guess she's not ready to see you yet," said Clara.

She glanced over at Ruth, who was staring into the fire.

"Well, they're not starving," said Gabri. "Chicken thighs for him, roasted cauliflower and grilled salmon for her."

"That's not right," said Myrna. "Must be the other way around. Harriet hates fish."

"Guess so," said Gabri. "I must've heard wrong."

"You need to eat," said Armand.

He'd warmed up some broth and cut a slice of fresh bread for Robert, placing a slab of aged cheddar on the side of the dish. All bland, but nourishing.

Robert picked up the mug of soup, then put it down again, as though it were too heavy.

"I'd like to get some sleep if that's all right with you, Armand."

He helped Robert upstairs to one of the guest bedrooms, the minister leaning heavily on his arm. After getting him showered, Armand put Robert into fresh pajamas, then tucked him into bed. The meds had kicked in, and the minister had become groggy.

Armand had read the doctor's instructions. He was to waken Robert every couple of hours, to make sure he was all right.

Armand checked the windows. Where normally he'd have opened one for fresh air, now he made sure they were closed and locked.

He then went through the rest of the house, checking and double-checking. Turning on all the lights. He was not sure if it was for strategic purposes or because he knew, from childhood, that monsters hate the light.

He suspected the latter. He also found himself singing softly as he went.

"Hooray for Captain Spaulding . . ."

Jean-Guy had texted. He was on his way back. While the early June sun was still just over the horizon in the village, it had gotten too dark in the forest to continue. The searches for Godin and Boisfranc would have to pick up at first light.

Once every room had been searched, every closet opened, the underside of every bed inspected, every window locked, every light turned on, Armand returned to the living room.

Reine-Marie and Amelia's flight would be landing soon.

He wrote both to say an agent would meet them at the airport and drive them straight to the lake house in the Laurentians where the rest of the family was staying.

He then wrote separately to Agent Choquet.

Do not leave Madame Gamache. You are to guard her and the family. Confirm.

Twenty minutes later Jean-Guy returned. They did not eat dinner. Neither was especially hungry, but there was another reason. Both knew if there were injuries, if surgery was needed, it was best to have an empty stomach.

Messages came through twenty minutes later, from both Reine-Marie and Amelia. They were on their way to the cabin.

Armand's shoulders dropped a little. One less worry.

He and Jean-Guy spent the early evening going over and over the evidence. They discussed, but mostly they waited.

For Fleming.

And then, at almost nine p.m., there was a knock on the door.

CHAPTER 35

Chief Inspector Gamache stared at Agent Choquet in disbelief. "What're you doing here?"

"I came back to help—"

"You disobeyed orders," snapped Beauvoir, striding over. Blood was traveling up his cheeks, like a cartoon thermometer. Half of her expected his head to explode. The other half was aware that blood was also mounting her own cheeks.

Beyond Amelia, Armand saw Fiona and Sam walking to the bistro. His mind worked quickly.

"Come with me," he said to Amelia, then turned to Jean-Guy. "Stay here and make sure Robert is all right. We'll be at the bistro. You're armed?"

"*Oui.*"

"I won't be long."

As they walked down the path toward the road and the village green, Amelia could feel the Inspector's eyes boring into her back.

"You promised," said the Chief, not looking at her as he strode across the green.

"*Pardon?*" she said, jogging beside him.

"You said you'd protect Madame Gamache, but you didn't. You left her." His voice was soft, calm. It was this very calm that chilled her core.

"*Désolée,*" she said. "But Madame Gamache—"

He stopped abruptly and turned to her, on her, as she skidded to a halt. "Is not the head of homicide. Madame Gamache does not have the information I have." The effort to keep his voice down, and keep his anger in check, made the words raspy. "Madame Gamache does not give you orders. Madame Gamache"—he paused, marshaling himself—"must. Be. Protected."

The Gamaches' feelings for each other were plain for anyone to see, but in that instant Amelia saw more. She saw into his soul. And there, smiling, her arms open, was Madame Gamache.

And Amelia almost burst into tears, so painful was the thought of one losing the other. And it being her fault.

Madame Gamache had told her to return. To protect her husband.

And Amelia had done it. Partly because Madame Gamache had insisted, and partly because of what she owed this man. But now she realized her great mistake.

If "*Désolée*" ever described anyone, it was Amelia Choquet at that moment.

"I'll leave right now," she said. "I'll go back up."

"You'll stay right here until I tell you to leave."

Gamache stepped away, turned away, and brought out his phone.

Robert Mongeau was right. While he often told Reine-Marie that he loved her, he hesitated to say that he missed her, out of fear she'd feel guilty when she left to visit family or friends.

He never, ever wanted her to feel that. And so he'd kept that last bit to himself. But now he saw he'd been wrong. Whatever happened, and Armand knew that it would be soon, he wanted nothing left unsaid.

I love you, he typed. *I miss you. Terribly.*

He erased the "terribly." Then put it back in and quickly hit send before he spent half the night erasing and adding, erasing and adding that one word. And never sending the message.

Then he turned back to Agent Choquet. "Let's go."

Myrna and Clara were standing by their table, and Myrna glanced at Gamache and Choquet when they arrived in the bistro, but her eyes were drawn to Sam Arsenault, who was sitting with his sister.

"Don't," said Clara. "You'll just make it worse."

But it was too late. Myrna was already on the move.

"Where's Harriet?" she demanded when she was only halfway across the room.

Seeing her weaving between tables, patrons lurched forward to protect their wineglasses and plates from the juggernaut.

Sam stood up, looking confused. "She's at the B&B. I thought you knew."

"Why isn't she here?"

"She didn't want to come over. She was afraid to see you. You know her. She hates confrontation."

"I've been texting and calling."

Fiona stood beside her brother. "She just needs time. We've both encouraged her to reach out to you. No one knows better than we do how important family is."

Myrna glared at Sam, hesitated, then turned to Fiona. "Please, tell her I'm sorry. Ask her to just send an emoji, anything."

"I will," said Sam. "Don't worry. She really is fine."

Harriet yanked her sweater off the tree limb and plunged on. She'd freed herself, though her wrists were raw and bleeding.

And now she ran. The faster she went, the more convinced she was that she was being chased. All the horror stories told over bonfires on the village green had come to life.

The boy who was murdered and now hunted other kids. The zombie cheerleaders with burning coal eyes. The ghosts and monsters, the alive and the undead. The lunatics with chainsaws, the madmen with axes. The wild beasts. The demons.

All took chase as she plunged through the darkening forest, tripping over logs and roots and running headlong into trees. The bundle she'd thought was Sam had turned out to be a rotting log.

So where was he? She'd screamed for him. Screamed for anyone. Just screamed.

Her face and hands were torn and bloody, she'd lost a shoe.

And still she ran. Faster and faster. Pursued by all that was unholy.

The last vestige of her sanity screamed that she had to stop. Had to regroup. Had to come up with some sort of plan.

But still she ran, with each step turning into the lunatic she was fleeing.

"How's Robert?" asked Clara. "Ruth says he'll recover."

"Yes, he was lucky," said Gamache. They were standing by a table for two that he'd chosen not far from Sam and Fiona. "He's staying with me until he feels better."

"Would you like to join us?"

She pointed to the table by the fire, where Ruth and Rosa were waiting.

"*Non, merci.*" Gamache's tone was abrupt and she got the message.

While Clara left, Myrna lingered. "I'm worried about Harriet."

"Yes, I gathered. How long since you heard from her?" Armand so obviously just wanted to get on with his own business, but could not ignore Myrna, even if he wanted to.

"Since the fight this morning. I know, I know. She's an adult and can't be considered a missing person."

"True, but we can trace her phone at least. Do you have her number?"

"Yes." Myrna felt relief for the first time in hours. She sent it to him, then embraced him, whispering, "*Merci.*"

Before sitting down, and afraid he'd forget, he sent off a message to one of his agents asking him to trace the phone.

As he did, he noticed a message from the coroner.

Ran samples again. Godin DNA definitely not a match for Fiona Arsenault. Second contaminated sample, Boisfranc, does not contain your DNA. Belongs to someone else.

Armand replied.

Can you stay there? I'll send over three more items to be tested. He paused, then added, *Official records for Fleming have been compromised. Can you find his DNA in Coroner's Office records?*

Dr. Harris replied immediately. *I'll stay. Doubt it re: Fleming, but will try.*

"What is it?" asked Amelia when he put down his phone.

But Gabri had just arrived to take their orders. Armand, after pausing to think for a moment, pointed to the menu and said, as though asking a question about one of the specials, "Can you take Sam and Fiona Arsenault's utensils when you clear their table? Don't touch them yourself, and make sure you know which is which."

He looked up at Gabri and smiled. Gabri, to his credit, caught on quickly. He wrote something on his pad, and said, "And for dessert?"

"Put them in unused plastic baggies, seal them, label them, and bring them to me, please."

"Good choice," said Gabri.

After he left, Gamache told Amelia what had happened in her absence.

"But why the cutlery?"

Armand glanced over to the siblings, then told her their suspicions.

"You mean one of them could be related to John Fleming?" she said, her voice low. "But didn't Inspector Beauvoir say it couldn't be Sam because of the timing?"

Gamache looked at the young woman across from him, inviting her to think harder. He believed she had it in her to get at the answer. He believed she had it in her to do just about anything.

He'd recognized that as soon as he'd read her application to the Sûreté Academy.

And yet, knowing that, he'd still rejected her. For the greater good, he'd told himself. Or maybe it was the lesser evil.

But as he'd sat on the bench overlooking Three Pines, holding his father's unfinished book, Armand couldn't escape the truth. He'd rejected Amelia Choquet not because of her, but because of what lived in one of the files he kept locked in the basement.

At the age of seventeen, Amelia's father was drunk when he'd fallen asleep at the wheel and drifted into the oncoming lane. A car, heading in the other direction, swerved to miss him, ran off the road, rolled, and hit a tree.

The occupants of the car died at the scene. The occupants of the car were Armand's parents.

The young man at the wheel had gone on to marry later in life and have a child. Just one. He gave her the same name as the woman he'd killed.

Amelia. After Amelia Gamache. Mama.

It was, Armand knew, an attempt at atonement. Though it was so feeble it had enraged him. That the man who'd killed his parents thought such a tiny gesture could even begin to right the balance.

Reading her application, he had recognized that the Sûreté Academy was almost certainly Amelia Choquet's last hope.

Knowing this, he'd turned her down. Tossed her, and her file, into the rejected pile. Tossed her back into the sewer that was inner-city Montréal, to sink slowly below the surface.

He'd ultimately changed his mind and given her that chance. He'd done it for his mother. For his father. For the man they'd hoped he'd become. *A brave man in a brave country.*

The fact he'd initially turned Amelia Choquet down still haunted him. It was an act of very slow, deliberate murder. Armand was shocked, appalled at himself, and deeply ashamed. But it had an unexpected benefit. It forced him to go deep inside his own cave. And look at what stinking, putrid, rancid creature was curled up there. Watching and waiting.

It gave him insight into the evil that decent people could do. John Fleming was a monster, without a doubt. But Armand Gamache had his own monster. He'd seen it. He'd fed it.

He'd put it back in its cage. But he still had the key.

Armand had had no idea that Amelia knew this connection until they'd been at the airport and she'd pledged to protect Reine-Marie. It was an acknowledgment of what her family owed to his. She grappled with the sins of the father. Even as Armand confronted the sins of the son.

He knew now why she'd returned to Three Pines. It was to protect him.

Their meal, chosen by Gabri, arrived at that moment. Armand was about to tell her not to eat, but Amelia didn't seem to notice it was even there. Her lightning mind was going over and over the facts, considering, dismissing, honing.

Until she had it.

"The dates Fleming gave the warden for when he was in the same community as Clotilde Arsenault years ago could be lies. Probably were. Otherwise, why would he volunteer that information? He wanted to shift the focus to Fiona. And away from Sam."

She glanced over to where Gabri was clearing the siblings' plates. And cutlery.

"If so, then the fact Godin's test was negative is meaningless," she whispered. "It would be if he was Sam's father, not Fiona's."

Armand smiled, unjustly proud of this young woman. Amelia.

Gabri arrived a few minutes later to clear away their untouched plates. He bent down to wipe the table and placed two sealed baggies, wrapped in linen napkins, by Gamache's hand.

"*Merci, patron*," said Armand.

"I wish we'd never found that damned room," said Gabri, straightening up. "Ever since we opened that wall, things haven't been the same."

Armand agreed. But he also knew they were always going to find that damned room, exactly when and how they did. This chain of events had begun years earlier and was inexorable.

If not fated, then preordained by some rough beast.

Once Gabri left, Gamache turned to Amelia.

"Now, Agent Choquet, you're not getting out of here without explaining yourself. You ignored my orders." His voice was clipped, and while still at a normal level, there was a force to it that made other diners glance over.

"You're not supposed to be here." Apparently realizing others were paying attention, he lowered his voice, though it still carried. "You were ordered to leave."

"I know. I'm sorry. I made a mistake."

She was confused. They'd already been over this. She could see he was angry, his hand was trembling, his agitation so great it kept striking the table. But still, it wasn't like him to go back over past grievances.

"That's not good enough. You're an agent with the Sûreté. Your mistakes can cost lives."

He made an effort to stop the shaking, balling his hand into a fist. But the gesture only made the shaking more obvious. He took a deep breath, but as soon as he released it, the trembling became even worse.

That was not a good sign.

"Let me be clear, Agent Choquet." His voice had risen again. "You will leave here immediately. You will stay away until recalled." He glared at her. "Is that clear?"

"Look," she heard herself saying. "If you'd been clear in the first place, I would've stayed away. This's your fault, not mine."

She clicked her tongue post angrily against her teeth, knowing it annoyed him. Annoyed everyone within listening distance.

He got up. "That's enough. Leave. We'll discuss this later."

"Fine with me, *patron*." The last word said with more than an edge of contempt.

Sam and Fiona had just left, and she wasn't far behind.

"Well," said Olivier, giving Gamache the bill and their meals to take away. "That went south fast."

Gamache paid, leaving a larger than normal tip for all the disruption. "I'm sorry. That's been coming for a long time."

Once home, he called the dogs, who joined him for a walk around the village green. The night was dark, the stars and moon hidden by a thick layer of clouds. The forecast was for rain, though it wasn't expected until the morning.

As he walked, he tossed the tennis ball and looked up at the light in the second-floor window of the B&B. He waited, and watched, but saw no one moving about.

Stopping in front of the bistro, he tossed the ball again, then checked his messages. There was one from Reine-Marie.

I miss you too. Terribly.

He smiled and gazed through the mullioned windows. Friends and neighbors were there, enjoying dinner. He imagined Reine-Marie among them. Imagined going in, ordering a meal, and joining the conversation. Joining her.

Then they could go home, together.

He imagined not having a worry in the world.

Just then the old poet turned in his direction. The look on her face brought him back to reality. The light that Clara had painted in those eyes was all but gone. Leaving behind just despair.

And though he knew she could not possibly see him in the darkness, still he had the impression she was looking right at him. And asking, begging, him to do something.

As Armand walked home, he prayed he could. Prayed he would be enough. Prayed he'd be a brave man in a brave country. Prayed he'd be able to stop whoever was out there in the dark. Waiting.

Though, once again, he was wrong. "Out there" was not the problem.

Jean-Guy had been upstairs checking on Robert Mongeau and so he hadn't seen Fiona let herself in.

And he hadn't seen Fiona let her brother in.

CHAPTER 36

~

"How's Robert?" Armand asked a few minutes later when Beauvoir joined him in the living room. A vantage point from which they could see both the front door and the French doors into the back garden.

"Last I looked his pupils were slightly dilated, but he roused and knew his name. Oh, and Fiona's home."

"You saw her come in?"

"I heard her and checked. She went upstairs to her bedroom. We said good night but that was all."

Armand had considered telling Fiona she had to stay at the B&B but had decided against it. It would be difficult to justify without giving away their suspicions. Besides, while having her under his roof might be dangerous, not having her there was worse.

At least he knew where she was.

Instead of running the risk of being overheard, Armand and Jean-Guy sat a few feet apart and exchanged texts. Like teens.

We need to lock Robert's door, in case she tries anything, Armand wrote.

Already done.

Armand looked up and smiled at his second-in-command. Of course it was. Though both knew an inch of wood would not stop Fleming if his goal was a second attack on the minister.

When Mongeau woke up, Gamache would have to have a serious

talk with him. What he'd seen or heard. What he knew that had put him and Sylvie in the crosshairs of a killer.

Typing again, Armand sent, *You saw the message from the coroner?*

Yes. We need a clean sample for Boisfranc.

Agent Choquet's taking care of that.

Armand's phone pinged with the message from his agent back in Montréal. The pin showed that Harriet's phone was in the B&B. Armand forwarded the message to Myrna and got a heart emoji reply.

Sam used the flashlight on his phone and swung it around. There were no windows in the basement of the Gamache home. No danger of being seen.

He examined the preserves on the shelves. The pickles and jams and infused oils. He saw the skis and snowshoes and hockey equipment neatly arranged along the far wall. He found old and tattered cardboard boxes of Christmas decorations in another corner.

Opening one, he picked out a length of tinsel. Doubling it up and wrapping it around both fists, he pulled it taut. Yes, it would do. Better than the twine he'd used on Harriet. Still, the girl was weak. She'd never get free. He'd go to her in the morning, and . . .

He spent a few minutes fantasizing about what he'd do to her. He'd seduced her to taunt her aunt. To piss off Gamache. But she'd become far too cloying, moving into the B&B. Expecting to stay with him. So he'd had no choice. She'd brought it on herself.

He dug deeper into the Christmas box and found a large glass ball with *2000* stamped on it in glitter. The millennium. If he broke it, the shards would do the trick. Sam Arsenault took pride in reusing found objects. Like bricks. And glass.

He'd brought along a serrated hunting knife, but the idea of using Christmas decorations, ones that were visible in the background of that family photograph, appealed to him.

Harriet's breathing came in short, sharp gasps.

She was crouching on the ground, her arms clasped tightly around her knees, making herself as small as possible. Her eyes were wide, though she could see nothing. If she hadn't been able to feel the ground beneath her, she wouldn't know which way was up.

But what her sense of sight lacked, her hearing made up for.

Every snap of a twig became a gunshot. The claws of chipmunks running up trees became monsters approaching. All around her there were howls as one creature chased another. And shrieks when they were caught.

But the loudest sounds were the pounding of her heart and the chattering of her teeth as the cold settled into her bones.

Above her there was a cry and the scrape of sharp nails.

Harriet got up and ran. And ran.

Amelia gave the cutlery and glass to the coroner.

The cutlery was labeled, *Sam Arsenault* and *Fiona Arsenault*, and had come from the bistro. The glass she'd lifted from the caretaker's makeshift bedroom in the church basement.

It had taken Amelia just a moment to realize that the Chief Inspector's fingers hitting the table wasn't involuntary. He was tapping out a message. One he knew she'd be able to follow from all the times she'd used her tongue stud to send some Morse code message.

Generally *Fucking liar*. Sometimes *Shithead*. Never directed at the Chief Inspector himself, often about some suspect.

She hadn't realized that he'd understood. Now she did, and she'd clicked out her reply.

I understand.

Amelia had left the bistro, gone quietly to the church to do as he'd ordered, then driven directly to the coroner to drop the items off.

"Do you want to wait for the results?" Dr. Harris asked. "Shouldn't take too long."

"*Non, merci*. You can message them to the Chief."

Dr. Harris looked over, but the young agent was already gone. She shook her head. What Gamache had been thinking admitting her into the Academy, then into homicide, was beyond her.

* * *

It was just after ten p.m.

Beauvoir was upstairs, keeping watch on Mongeau, while Armand settled into his office after checking and double-checking the doors and windows. Again. All were locked. No one could get in.

And no one could get out.

Sam Arsenault wondered if he dared risk breaking the glass ball but decided against it.

It would be more fun to do it in front of Gamache. So that the cop could see. Could slowly grasp. Could understand what was about to happen.

He looked at his watch and settled in.

Not long now. Time was almost up.

He tossed the Christmas ornament back and forth, then bobbled it and reached out. But it slipped between his fingers.

Armand heard a sound.

It seemed to be coming from the basement.

Getting up, he cocked his head. Listening closely. He looked toward the wall safe, hidden behind the bookcase, where he kept his service gun.

Should he?

He, better than most, knew the dangers of a loaded gun in a private residence. While he knew how to use it, and how to defend himself, Armand also knew how often even cops were disarmed. With catastrophic results, and not just for the cop.

Still, this wasn't just any night. He stepped toward the safe, then paused.

He looked over at Henri, who'd been curled at his feet and had lifted his head, his prodigious ears now folded against the underside of the desk.

Gracie was snoring away on the sofa in the living room. Fred was nowhere to be seen. Armand smiled. This had happened before. Fred, being considerably smarter than Henri, which was not actually difficult, had long ago realized the stash of dog food and treats was kept in the basement. Albeit well beyond his reach, but still there.

It was, for the old dog, his sacred place.

If the basement door was left even slightly ajar, Fred managed to get down, but being arthritic and almost blind, could not get back up.

That must be it.

Armand left the gun locked in place and headed for the basement. Sure enough, the door was open, Fred-width wide.

"Fred?"

Sam froze.

Fuck. He turned off the flashlight app, took out the hunting knife, and got into crouching position.

Armand started down, flicking on the lights.

Sure enough, there at the bottom was the old dog, smiling up at him. Front paws on the lowest step, his tail swished back and forth, back and forth.

"Silly boy," said Armand, going down.

Sam gripped the knife and pressed his back to the wall, ducking beside the huge box of Christmas ornaments. It was an imperfect hiding place, but the best he could do.

In the dark he hadn't seen the dog. Hadn't even heard him. Which was a good thing for the dog.

Now he made himself small, compact, coiled. Ready. Steady.

If Gamache turned in this direction and saw him, Sam knew he could get across the space before the cop had a chance to react.

It would be over in seconds.

Please, please, please turn.

Armand got to the bottom and scooped up the old dog, holding him securely in his arms. Then he turned.

Sam braced.

Armand's eyes went to the closed door at the far end of the room.

It was still closed, but was it locked?

He considered going over to check, but his arms were full of Fred, and he had no reason to believe the door wasn't locked since he was the one with the code.

Armand turned back and walked up the stairs, using his elbow to turn off the lights.

Sam exhaled, though he was disappointed.

He'd imagined plunging the knife into the man. He'd done it before. Felt the knife go in, so easily. He'd seen the shock in the eyes. Not pain. Not right away. Just surprise, as the man, the woman, had looked at the handsome young fellow they'd trusted. Who'd just killed them.

He'd remove the knife and strike again. And again. Feeling the breath, the life, leave.

He'd done it to strangers and near strangers. But never had he killed anyone he actually hated.

Until tonight.

Sam knew it would be far more satisfying if it didn't come as a complete surprise to the cop. If Gamache knew, for a while, what was going to happen.

Still, he could not help but be disappointed.

Armand returned Fred to the living room, lowering him onto his favorite place at the other end of the sofa from where Gracie lay snorting. Then he kissed Fred's smelly head.

When he returned to his office, he found a message from Amelia.

She'd dropped off the items and was heading up to Lac Manitou. She'd be there in twenty minutes.

Armand then went back over the reports, the photographs, the conversations. He considered returning downstairs and consulting, yet again, the files in his private archive. But decided that wouldn't get him anywhere.

He knew them by heart. Wished he didn't. But did.

He sat back and stared out the window. Three Pines was going to sleep.

Time's up.

He glanced at Myrna's bookstore. Then lifted his eyes to her loft.

Gabri was right. It all started when they'd opened the wall and found the room. Found what was in there.

Found what Fleming wanted them, him, to see.

There is always another story / There is more than meets the eye.

There must be something he'd missed. And if that something was anywhere, it was in the painting.

He told Beauvoir he was returning, briefly, to the Incident Room. Then, just before he left, his phone buzzed with a message from Dr. Harris. The coroner had the results of the DNA tests.

Sam Arsenault's DNA was not a match for either Godin or Boisfranc. But there was a clear match between the caretaker's DNA off the glass and Fiona Arsenault.

There was no doubt. Claude Boisfranc was John Fleming. Fiona was his daughter.

CHAPTER 37

The worst had happened. Harriet was being eaten alive. Not by animals but from the inside out.

Fear, her lifelong companion, had finally consumed her.

Her body still functioned as she raced wildly through the woods, but she'd lost her mind. She'd become the Tin Man, the Scarecrow, and the Cowardly Lion, all rolled into one.

And now even her body was giving up. Soon she'd stop running, stop walking, stop crawling, and just lie still. Waiting for death.

She did not have to wait long. A moment later, Harriet Landers ran right into it.

She fell to the forest floor and stared up.

Death hung suspended above her, arms out, wrists bound. The man's feet slowly swinging like some gigantic clock pendulum signifying that time was up.

From deep inside Harriet Landers came every shriek she'd ever swallowed. All the fear, the frustrations, the anger and buried resentments. The wounds, the pain, the losses and humiliations. The times she'd been ignored, marginalized, diminished. Judged and found wanting. The parties not invited to, the boys who'd mocked her. The girls who'd left her out.

All her insecurities, loneliness, hurts, and rage from birth to this, her last moment, came rushing out.

* * *

Amelia Choquet had parked the car so as not to alert anyone of her presence and was creeping carefully along the dirt road when she heard a scream. It was deep in the woods. She'd never heard anything like it and couldn't figure out if it was human or not.

But she couldn't take the chance.

Checking the compass on her phone so she could get back and putting on the flashlight, Amelia ran into the forest.

Harriet stopped screaming. She had none left. She had nothing left.

Harriet Landers was finally gone. The last sound that came out was a whimper.

A pathetic little moan as she lay in the fetal position on the forest floor.

In that moment she heard herself. She saw herself. Reduced to a tiny, filthy, weeping and sniveling mass. The world, her world, really would end with a whimper.

Numb. Silent. Paralyzed. Hollow.

As she'd lived, Harriet would die.

Though in that void, something stirred.

A small fuck-it. Then a fuckitfuckitfuckit. Louder and louder. Fuck it.

She got shakily to her feet. If death was coming for her, as it came for this man, she would not die sniveling on the ground.

She heard a sound. Something plunging through the forest toward her. The creature had finally found her. Harriet's newfound courage withered.

She fell to her knees, and as she did, she felt beneath her torn palms a thick branch. Clasping it, she stood back up and turned to face it.

Fuck it.

The light in her hand swung wildly as Amelia ran, so that she only caught glimpses of something horrific up ahead. A nightmare image of a body suspended between trees, as though crucified.

All her instincts told her to stop, or at least slow down. But she kept running toward the creature.

Something equally horrible was standing in front of it. Holding a weapon. A rifle.

Now Amelia did slow down and brought out her gun.

"Drop it!"

The creature, who looked like a part of the deep forest come alive, raised the weapon further. It was not, as Amelia had first thought, a rifle. It was a tree branch.

She walked forward slowly, gun still out and pointed.

"Drop it," she said, in French and then in English. "I'm with the Sûreté du Québec. Drop your weapon."

And Harriet did.

Amelia recognized her now. "You're Harriet Landers."

"Yes."

"Are you okay?"

Harriet didn't know how to answer. She was hurt and bleeding. But . . .

"*Oui*." Yes, she was okay.

"Who did this to you? To him?"

"I don't know."

Amelia shone the light on the body. It was eviscerated. Gutted. Amelia grimaced, then she lifted the light to the man's face.

It was the caretaker, Claude Boisfranc.

Her tongue stud clicked out, *Fuck me*, while her mind worked fast. She had to get a message to Gamache. He thought that the caretaker was Fleming. The coroner had told them that. But clearly that was wrong. It was Godin, and he was still out there.

"Shit, shit, shit," she muttered.

Finding the phone icon, she went to hit it, but her hands were trembling so badly she dropped the phone into the dead leaves. Falling to her knees, she scooped it up and, taking a deep breath, she steadied herself.

"You've seen worse, you've seen worse, you've seen worse," she muttered to herself. Harriet wondered if that could possibly be true. It was also a strange, though oddly comforting, mantra. One she knew she could use for the rest of her life.

Nothing could ever be worse than this.

Though she was wrong.

Amelia hit the icon for the Chief Inspector's number.

Nothing. Nothing.

"Fuck." No signal. They were too deep into the woods.

She composed a text and hit send in the hopes that as soon as even a weak signal appeared, it would go.

"Come on," she said, checking her compass. "We have to get out of here."

"You think?" said Harriet, clutching the club and racing after her.

Armand stood in front of *The Paston Treasure*.

John Fleming was everywhere in this painting, a world not of curiosities but of grotesque bits and pieces of a madman's mind.

Here were the carved faces of John Fleming's seven victims. The Beast of Babylon.

Here was the reference to the Québec Bridge, the tragedy that formed and informed the engineer's ring.

Here was the sheet music. "By the Waters of Babylon." The song John Fleming used to hum.

And there was more. Things he hadn't noted before. The small unicorn stickers, like Fiona had had as a child. Like those used in the terrible ledger. There was the model. Like the ones he'd mistakenly thought were Sam's, but again were Fiona's.

Were they put there not just to point him to Fiona, but to taunt him with earlier mistakes?

The clocks worried him. They were all set to the same time.

Eleven thirty. And the clock sent to the Mongeau home the day Sylvie died, and left at the Old Train Station by Boisfranc. It was also set to half past eleven.

He looked at his watch. It was ten past eleven.

Then his eyes went back to the painting. And the face, bright, almost illuminated, of the little girl. She looked familiar, but Armand didn't know if it was just because he'd been staring at the painting for three days now.

Then he had it. He stepped back, as though shoved. The face was Reine-Marie, as a child. From the photograph taken at her first communion. She never looked at it, but he did, sometimes. Marveling at the resemblance between his wife and their granddaughters.

Then, like a building collapsing, everything fell. But instead of falling apart, it fell into place.

Les Puces. Lac Manitou. Mountweazel. The DNA. Sylvie. The God-fearing man. The Fallen Angel. The book. The blood, so much blood. The timing. Three years. The time.

Eleven thirty.

"Ohhh, no," he whispered.

He dashed off a three-word text to his entire team. Just as he hit send, he heard the Incident Room door open. And a hum. A hymn.

"Armand?"

He turned so quickly he almost fell over the corner of his desk. Standing a few feet into the Old Train Station was Reine-Marie.

And behind her someone, something, else. Something dreadful had just walked in.

John Fleming. But not Boisfranc. And not Godin. Though Armand already knew who it would be.

It was Robert Mongeau. The minister.

Fleming's eyes, unshielded now by contacts, were unmistakable. The manic energy, the hatred, filled the space, threatening to blow out the windows, the walls, the roof.

But all Armand really saw was the knife at Reine-Marie's throat.

For a terrible moment Armand thought he might pass out. His heart had suddenly gone into overdrive, his head swam. His eyes blurred.

He steadied himself against the desk, then moved forward, but Fleming tightened his grip on her, and Armand stopped. Never taking his eyes off Reine-Marie's.

He whispered her name.

She didn't reply, couldn't for the blade at her throat. He could barely breathe, barely think. For the blade at her throat.

Calm, calm, calm, calm. He repeated it to himself. The word hardly registered above the shriek filling his head.

He needed to stay calm. There was a way out of this. There must be. If Jean-Guy got his text . . .

Reine-Marie's eyes were wide with panic. And apology.

"Ahhh," said Fleming, watching Gamache. "Now that's the look I've spent years and years dreaming about, Armand. Have to say, it's even better than I imagined. Your terror, tinged with nausea. The dawning horror. You're not going to pass out, are you?"

"Let her go," Armand rasped.

"Well, since you asked so nicely." But Fleming gripped Reine-Marie tighter. She gave a small gasp.

Armand reached out. "No."

"No." Fleming loosened his grip again. "Not yet. Hands where I can see them, Armand."

"I'm sorry," Reine-Marie whispered.

Armand held her eyes. "No, no. Not your fault. It'll be all right. It'll be all right."

"Your idea of all right must be different from mine," said Fleming. "You do know it's your fault she's here. She came back because you wrote to say you missed her. As I knew you would. As I knew she would. So easily manipulated. Don't blame yourself, Armand. Actually, blame yourself a little."

Armand felt himself being dragged into the cave. Deep into Fleming's mind. If that happened, they were well and truly lost. He had to close his mind to what Fleming was saying.

Jean-Guy was armed. He must have gotten the message by now. But Mongeau had gotten past him. How? Though he suspected. Jean-Guy had gone in, on Gamache's request, to check on the minister. And Mongeau had surprised him.

"Jean-Guy?" he asked.

"You'll see soon enough. Of course, had you recognized me earlier, none of this would've happened. That was part of the fun. To give you enough hints, a sporting chance to get out of it. To save yourself and everyone you love and care about."

Fleming tilted his head and stared at Gamache.

"You're wondering how you didn't recognize me earlier."

He was wrong, of course. Armand was well beyond caring about that. His mind was solely occupied with how to get out of this.

There was a way. There had to be. Think. Think. *That's right, keep talking, you lunatic. Give me time to think.*

"I'll tell you, Armand. It wasn't just the weight gain, the lifts in the shoes, the beard, and slight hair dye that fooled you. It wasn't even the contact lenses."

All Armand heard was blah, blah, blah as his mind worked out logistics. Distance to Fleming. Chance of distraction. Would a loud sound do it? What if he fell? Faked a heart attack?

With lightning speed Gamache grabbed at options, examined them, then tossed them aside, while Fleming showed off his brilliance.

Blah, blah, blah.

But then Fleming said something that penetrated Armand's thoughts.

"You didn't recognize me because all you really saw when you looked at Robert Mongeau was the fact he loved his dying wife. It never occurred to you that John Fleming could love that deeply."

With horror, Armand knew he was right. He'd been blinded by the love Mongeau felt for Sylvie. And out of that blind spot came this monster.

"I did love Sylvie. With all my heart."

"But you killed her."

Fleming sneered. "Well, you love your wife, and you've killed her." Now he smiled, seeing the effect that had on Gamache. "*Go now to your dwelling place to enter into the days of your togetherness.*"

With a jolt Armand recognized the quote from the prayer they'd had at their wedding. "*And may your days be good and long upon this earth.*" Fleming smiled. "Amen. We're going to go now to your dwelling place, though I can't vouch for the rest of the prayer."

But Fleming didn't move. Instead, he looked at the painting. His mercurial mood now changed to whimsical.

"That was my companion in the SHU for months and months. Painting." He laughed and shook his head. "It was therapy. It did help, but not in the way they'd hoped. When Sylvie showed me photos of *The Paston Treasure* from the exhibition, I immediately saw the potential. It came to me fully formed. An act of God, a gift from God. I could create my own World of Curiosities. Put in all sorts of items you alone would recognize. So with the help of that greedy, stupid warden, I had them bring in art therapy, and use *The Paston Treasure* as one of the exercises. I already knew how to escape, the head guard and warden were so deeply compromised they'd do anything to avoid exposure. But I needed to know what to do once out. And so I stayed in that hellhole. For you. And painted. And waited. And thought of you, all day, all night. For years. Time and patience. Whoever said they were the strongest of warriors was right. You gave me both, dear man. I might've died in prison, but you gave me purpose. You made me strong."

He actually bowed. Armand leaned forward, about to leap, but Fleming raised his head, raised his eyes. Met Armand's eyes.

Armand stopped cold. Fleming was trying to provoke him. He wanted him to try it.

Not yet, thought Armand. There'd be time. Time and patience.

Once again, as though reading Gamache's mind, Fleming glanced at the large clock on the wall.

"I wonder if you've figured out the significance of the time. Put your phone and gun on the desk, please."

Armand took out his phone and glanced at it. No replies yet to his text.

"I'm not armed."

"Bullshit. Gun on the desk." Fleming's manner went from hyper-courteous to enraged in an instant.

Armand put his arms out wide. "Really. I never wear one."

"Turn your pockets out." Armand did. "Take off your shoes." Armand did. "Roll up your pant legs." Armand did. Then stood up straight.

Fleming glared at him. "I thought you were many things, Armand, but never a coward. What kind of cop doesn't carry a gun? What kind of cop expects others to protect him? Just one more mistake in a litany of them."

Fleming shook his head, while Armand thanked God he wasn't armed.

"Come along, little coward. Back to your home. The walk'll do you good. It'll give you a chance to clear your head and come up with a plan. Think, think, think. I'm sure there's a way out of this. I've had years to plan, you have about fifteen minutes. Better think fast."

They walked slowly through the cool evening, over the Bella Bella, past the three huge pine trees. There was still a light on at the B&B, but the bistro was in darkness, as were the other buildings. Though a weak light shone through the ragged curtains in Ruth's home.

All the way, Armand's mind was working.

Think. Think. Think.

If all Fleming had was a knife, there was a chance. Armand knew most people who held weapons on others at close quarters eventually lost concentration. A moment was all he needed. That and a sliver of daylight between the blade and Reine-Marie.

At their front door, he paused.

"Open it, Armand."

Even before stepping inside, he heard the dogs barking from behind the study door.

Then he saw Sam standing over Jean-Guy, who was slumped against the wall. His hands and legs bound up in Christmas tinsel. Blood streamed down his face, and a brick lay on the floor. But he was alive.

Sam was holding a gun. Beauvoir's Glock.

"Jean-Guy," said Reine-Marie, and tried to move forward, but Fleming held her fast. Sam cocked the gun and placed it to Beauvoir's head.

Armand stared at Jean-Guy, who stared back. His eyes were bleary as he tried to focus.

"*Désolé,*" Jean-Guy whispered.

"Welcome home."

Armand turned to the voice. Fiona was standing by the fireplace, holding the framed picture that had hung on the wall. It was done by his granddaughter, Florence, during the pandemic.

The little girl had drawn a cheerful rainbow and beneath it the words *Ça va bien aller.*

All will be well.

"You know my daughter," said Fleming. "I want to thank you for looking after her. Making sure she was safe in prison. Getting the École Polytechnique to admit her into distance learning. People are kind. And then you vouched for her and got her released on parole. I am grateful."

Fleming's eyes flickered to the clock on the mantelpiece. As did Armand's.

It was 11:21.

"And while Sam isn't my biological son, he is family in every way that matters. I recognized that early on. I think you did too." Fleming looked around. "I've always liked this room. Cheerful, welcoming. Filled with your treasures. A microcosm of a life fully lived, as the historians would say. Books. Family photographs. Art. That's a Morrow, isn't it? Some of this stuff no doubt picked up in galleries and flea markets on your travels together. Les Puces? You didn't pick up on that, did you?" He nodded toward the framed drawing that Fiona held. "Done by one of your grandchildren, I imagine. I'll be meeting them soon."

"Don't you—" began Reine-Marie.

Beauvoir shouted an expletive and struggled against his bonds. Sam placed his boot on Jean-Guy's chest and pushed him roughly back against the wall.

"Ahhh, careful now," Fleming whispered into Reine-Marie's ear. His breath hot. Moist. "Best to learn from your husband. If you do nothing, there's a possibility I'll lose focus and then you'll have your chance. That is what you're thinking, isn't it, Armand. What you're waiting for?"

Armand was silent and Fleming sighed.

"I've planned meticulously. No piece out of place. Nothing extraneous. A purpose for everything. It took me years, but finally I knew

I could predict your every move. Suspecting poor Monsieur Godin. He had to go, of course. Hiring poor Boisfranc. He was so grateful. Even the attack on Mongeau in the church. Sam did it, of course. A glancing blow, but enough to draw a lot of blood. I knew there was no way you'd let me go home alone. Not after that. I knew you'd have to invite me here. Into your home. Kindness kills. Remember that."

Gamache felt physically sick. If it really was that well planned, then . . .

"Sylvie was Mountweazel, wasn't she?" he finally said.

He'd at first thought their only real chance was to engage Fleming long enough for the Sûreté to arrive. Now he knew he didn't have to. And he saw a tiny glimmer of hope.

The very thing that brought them to this could help them get out of it.

John Fleming was not only a planner, he was an overplanner. The details he was so proud of had allowed him to escape from the SHU, had brought them here, to this moment, but they also imprisoned him. He would not deviate from his plan.

Armand knew that John Fleming could have already killed them many times over. That much was obvious. But what was also now obvious was that he was waiting for the perfect time.

The right time. Eleven thirty.

Armand shifted his eyes to the carriage clock on the mantelpiece, by where Fiona was standing. Her hand was resting on Florence's drawing as though she enjoyed sullying one of their treasures.

Eleven twenty-two.

Eight minutes.

Think, think. Think.

Fleming's eyes followed Armand's. Then returned.

"All will not be well, of course." It took Armand a fraction of a second to figure out what he was talking about. Fleming thought he was looking at Florence's drawing. Not the clock.

Fleming didn't realize Gamache knew the significance of the time.

"For you or, sadly, little Florence," said Fleming. "Or Zora. Or Honoré, or even Idola."

Jean-Guy shrieked, struggling, flailing against his restraints. "Fuck you. Fuck you!" he screamed. "I'll kill you!!"

Fleming was smiling. Clearly fed and made plump by rage and terror.

"You didn't think I'd stop with you? I'd hoped they'd all be here, but you were smart enough, Armand, to send everyone to the lake house. Lac Manitou. You didn't pick up on that either, did you? In our conversation in the chapel I mentioned Lac Manitou. And even intimated I knew that Reine-Marie was in London. You'd sent out word that she was in Gaspé with a sister, so how could I possibly know she was in England? I wondered if I'd gone too far. But you didn't notice. You were blinded by my grief, my sorrow at losing Sylvie. And so you missed the very clues that could have saved your wife. Your whole family. You were too slow."

Armand was silent. Thinking. Thinking.

"If you loved her, why did you kill her?" asked Reine-Marie.

"I bet you can guess." When Reine-Marie was silent, he turned to Armand. Who also remained quiet. "Guess!" Fleming shrieked.

The dogs set up more barking, throwing themselves against the study door.

Fleming's restraints were weakening, Gamache could see. The outbursts coming more frequently, with greater and greater force.

Whether this was in their favor or not, he didn't know.

"Release Reine-Marie, let her come over here, and I'll tell you."

Fleming grinned. "Really? That's your idea of bargaining? Telling me something I already know in exchange for a hostage?" He looked at Reine-Marie. "Did you know you married not just a coward but an idiot? I'll tell you what, Armand. I won't slit her throat right now if you tell me. But make sure you're right. If you're wrong . . ."

Armand stared at him for a moment. His mind working fast. "You killed her because she'd invited Myrna over for tea."

He'd considered this before, but with all that had happened in the meantime, he had to recall the details. The theory.

"Sylvie made it sound like it was for the book, but you knew you weren't even halfway through the one you were reading together, so why would Sylvie ask for another? You were afraid it was about something else. You were afraid of what Sylvie was going to say to Myrna. A therapist." As he said that he could see that it was wrong. Regroup. Regroup. "But more than that, she's Harriet's aunt. You were afraid that Sylvie, so close to death, might be trying to make amends. It wouldn't be much, could not right the balance of what you and she have done, but it might save at least one life. She would warn Myrna about Sam."

He looked over at the young man, smirking.

"Did you kill her?" Armand asked. "Harriet."

"What do you think?"

Reine-Marie groaned, and took several quick, shallow breaths.

"You were afraid that, doped up on painkillers, she'd even confess who you really are," Armand continued. "And so you killed her."

Fleming's face had grown hard, his grip on the knife had tightened. Armand had to do something. Say something.

"But finally, you did it out of love and kindness. As you say, kindness kills."

Sam, Fiona, Jean-Guy, Reine-Marie, and even Fleming all looked at him, astonished.

"Sylvie was facing a long, painful death." Armand glanced at Jean-Guy, then continued. "It wasn't murder, it was a mercy killing."

"It wasn't a mercy killing," Jean-Guy shouted. "It wasn't love. It was the cold-blooded act of a lunatic."

Sam made a move, but Fleming stopped him. Recognizing what Jean-Guy was trying to do. Perhaps even seeing the collusion between the two Sûreté officers.

Beauvoir was trying to provoke one of them into hitting him. And that would be the distraction, the moment Armand needed.

The focus would shift, and in that split second he would make his move.

Armand had worked it out. Everything that would happen.

Fleming would be, for just a moment, distracted by the attack on Jean-Guy. Allowing Armand to rush forward, grabbing Fleming's hand and yanking the knife away from Reine-Marie's throat.

Run! Run! he'd shout.

By then Sam would have turned the gun on him.

Fleming was older. Smaller. If he could just reach him, Armand was confident he could easily overpower the man and use him as a shield. Sam would shoot, but the bullet would hit Fleming. Armand would push the body forward, onto Sam. That would give him the seconds he'd need to tackle the younger man.

Sam was fitter, younger, stronger. But Armand had the great advantage of experience. And desperation. He would subdue Sam.

But none of that happened.

CHAPTER 38

⌒

There was no reception. No signal. No signal.
Amelia kept stopping to check.

She had to get to the Chief Inspector. She'd seen the message from the coroner telling him that Boisfranc was Fleming. But he wasn't.

The caretaker, now disemboweled, was one of his victims.

She knew what must've happened. The glass she'd picked up from the caretaker's room had someone else's DNA. The only other person who used the basement kitchen was the minister, Robert Mongeau.

Could he have done it on purpose? Handling things in the caretaker's small bedroom so his DNA would be on it and forensics would mistake it for Boisfranc's? They'd see the match with Fiona and assume Boisfranc was Fleming.

That's exactly what had happened.

Shit. Shit, shit, shit. Robert Mongeau was the escaped serial killer. He was in Gamache's home and the Chief Inspector had no idea.

No signal. No signal.

She and Harriet raced, then stopped. Raced forward through the forest, then stopped to check her phone.

No signal. No . . .

One bar.

"Oh shit, oh shit, oh shit," said Amelia, her hands shaking so badly she could barely hit the right icon for Gamache's number.

357

It rang. And rang.

No answer. No answer.

"Fffffffuck." She called headquarters and spoke to the duty officer. Giving him the information even as she ran.

He already knew. Had received a message from the Chief Inspector minutes ago saying Robert Mongeau, the minister, was John Fleming. Amelia then found the same message on her phone.

Gamache knew, so there was a chance . . .

But the message said no more. If the Chief Inspector could, he would have issued orders. Instructions. More information.

But there was nothing beyond those few words: *Mongeau is Fleming*.

Fortunately, Agent Choquet knew exactly where John Fleming was, and she told the duty officer.

"His home?" said the agent, unable to conceal his shock. "The serial killer is in Chief Inspector Gamache's home?"

"Yes."

"Oh, shit. I'm sending every agent down and alerting the local detachment. I'll trace his phone and let you know where the Chief is."

But Amelia feared it was already too late. Feared what the silence from the Chief Inspector meant. Feared what they would find once there. Not just Gamache, but Beauvoir and Madame Gamache as well.

As soon as she'd gotten to the lake house, Amelia had been told that Madame Gamache had returned to Three Pines. Amelia had immediately rushed back.

Now she could feel the panic rising, threatening to overwhelm her. She tamped it down.

"My aunt," said Harriet. "We can call her. She can go over."

"And then what?" They were running again. Tripping, helping each other up. Holding each other's arms as they ran through the forest toward the car. "If she goes over there, she'll be killed."

She'd almost said "too." *Killed too.*

* * *

358

Six minutes.

A phone rang. It was Beauvoir's. It was lying on the floor where it had fallen when Sam hit him.

Sam picked it up. "Amelia Choquet," he read on the screen. "There's a text from her too, and an earlier one from"—he turned to Gamache—"you."

Fleming raised his brows. "Now, what could you have said? Open it."

Jean-Guy shook his head.

Fleming grabbed Reine-Marie again. "Open it," he shouted.

"You'll have to untie me," said Beauvoir.

Armand held his breath. *Do it. Do it.*

He tried to keep his expression blank. His body unchanged. Even as he prepared to move.

Do it.

Fleming nodded, and Sam walked over to Gamache, holding the phone out.

"I hope you have the code." Fleming needed to say no more.

Resigned, Armand took the phone and punched in the numbers. He'd hoped and prayed this wouldn't happen. But there was nothing he could do now. They had one chance and now it seemed even that was gone.

Sam grabbed the phone back and read the two texts. Amelia's first.

"Well, looks like they found Boisfranc. They must think Godin is you," he said to Fleming.

Then Sam's face grew hard, his eyes narrowed, as he read the next text. From Gamache.

"What is it?" said Fiona.

Sam turned the phone around and showed the message to Fleming. It was—it should have been—the distraction Armand needed, but Sam was blocking his view of Reine-Marie. He couldn't see the knife. Couldn't see, or get to, Fleming.

He had to let it pass. Time and patience. He was running out of both.

When Sam stepped aside, Armand saw Fleming's eyes drilled into him. "Seems, Armand, you were slightly smarter than I thought. You figured it out."

"What did he figure out?" Fiona demanded.

"He sent a text to his entire team telling them that I'm Fleming. They'll have alerted the local Sûreté."

"Shit," she said, heading for the door. "They'll be here any minute."

"Where're you going?" demanded Sam.

"To look out for them, where do you think?"

They both looked at Fleming, who nodded to her. "Go. Warn us when you see them."

This was unexpected. The first wrench in the works. And the meticulous Fleming hated wrenches. He had very little ability, or need, to pivot.

Until now.

Gamache's body tingled, every nerve jangling. How would Fleming react? Would he slaughter them all now and run, like any sensible lunatic? Or stick to the plan?

"Fuck," said Sam. "We have to do it now. Then get out."

"No," shouted Fleming. "Not yet. Four minutes. But"—he stared at Gamache—"we can make a start. I believe you have those photographs in your pocket. Take them out, Armand."

When he hesitated, Fleming screamed, "Take them out!"

Armand took a deep breath, then put his hand in his pocket and brought out the pictures. Used in court. The ones that, like Medusa, changed anyone who looked at them forever.

"Put them on the table."

Armand did.

"Back up. Further."

Armand did.

Fleming nodded to Sam. "Give them each one."

Reine-Marie took it but didn't look. Instead, she kept her eyes on her husband. She saw in him a profound sadness, and apology.

"Look at it!" Fleming screamed, tightening his grip until she could barely breathe.

"Fleming," shouted Armand.

"Stay where you are. Look at the photograph. Look at what's about to happen to you."

And Reine-Marie did. And Jean-Guy did.

Armand watched their faces pale. Watched fear turn to terror turn to horror. Watched as the size of the monster in the room with them became clear.

Agent Choquet and Harriet stopped, gasping for breath, at the top of the hill that overlooked Three Pines. A message had come through.

"Gamache's phone is in the Old Train Station," said Amelia.

Harriet took off. Maybe this, she thought, was why she'd spent her adult life running. She'd thought it was to get away, but maybe she'd been in training to run toward.

Amelia chased after the wild woman, who was still clinging to the tree branch as though it were a club. It looked like Amelia had stumbled across the missing link in the forest outside Three Pines. There was something primal not just in Harriet's appearance, but in her being.

Her lifelong flight response had turned to fight.

"Three minutes. I, of course, will be the one to finish what you started, Armand, so many years ago. When you broke your promise to me. But I promised young Sam here that he could help. And I keep my word."

He nodded to Sam, who tucked Beauvoir's gun into his belt and approached Gamache with the hunting knife.

"I've hated you from the first moment you came into our house," said Sam. "When you ruined everything."

Armand kept his eyes on Reine-Marie, and she on him. But he could see Sam getting closer.

Come on. Come on, Armand begged. *Come get me.*

"Look at me!" shouted Sam. His arm shot out, bringing the blade to Gamache's throat. But Armand did not move his eyes from Reine-Marie.

Closer. Come closer. Come on, you little shit. Just one more step.

Another few inches and Armand could grab the gun from Sam's belt.

Come on. Come on.

He could shoot Fleming before the man knew what was happening. And he could overpower Sam. He knew he could. The adrenaline was rushing through him. His senses in overdrive. True, the knife might slash his throat, but Gamache knew there'd be a few precious seconds of consciousness. And that was all he'd need.

He didn't drop his eyes, didn't want Sam or Fleming to know what he was about to do.

Come on.

"Wait, stop," commanded Fleming. "Step away. Give me the gun."

Sam did.

Fleming held it up and looked at Armand. "Well, that was close."

Armand knew then that Fleming had done it on purpose. Allowed Sam to get within inches. Allowed Armand to hope, hope, that there was a chance.

Only to take it away.

Seeing this, Jean-Guy began to flail. Struggling to get his hands free. But he could not. The cords were tied too tight. In knots, he realized, he'd taught Sam after the boy had been kicked out of Scouts.

Jean-Guy had asked Sam why, but hadn't asked the Scout leader. If he had, he'd have discovered that it wasn't because Sam wet his bed during a sleepover, as Sam claimed. It was because the boy, all of twelve, had killed a cat, and the Scout leader had found out.

Had the Scout leader not taken pity on the boy, knowing his background, had the Scout leader warned the authorities, had the authorities warned the foster home. Had the foster home looked in the crawl space, they'd have found the other creatures Sam Arsenault had eviscerated.

Then none of this would have happened.

But none of that happened.

Instead, Jean-Guy had taken it upon himself to teach the boy some of the things he might have learned in Scouts. Like tying knots.

Armand had warned him not to get too close. But Jean-Guy did not agree with Gamache. He knew that Sam was the victim and Fiona was the dangerous one. The psychopath.

They were both right, and both wrong.

Jean-Guy rolled and thrashed, fighting to get loose. Honoré, Idola. Annie.

Annie. Honoré. Idola. Jean-Guy bucked and fought and struggled.

Tears of frustration and rage and terror blinded him. He howled his outrage.

Henri and Fred and Gracie were barking and scratching and throwing themselves against the study door.

Armand's eyes fell on the picture his granddaughter had made when all seemed so dark, so hopeless, during the pandemic. When something as simple as going to the grocery store was a life-and-death act.

When something as simple as an act of kindness by children could give hope.

Ça va bien aller.

There was always hope. If he was right, if he was right. If . . .

It was a huge "if." He feared it was magical thinking. But Armand Gamache believed in magic.

Amelia's phone rang.

"Where are you?" the voice demanded.

The person didn't identify herself, didn't have to. It was Isabelle Lacoste, Inspector Lacoste, who shared second-in-command duties with Inspector Beauvoir.

"Almost at the Incident Room in Three Pines."

"The local Sûreté is still seven minutes away. I'm right behind them. Are you armed?"

"*Oui.*"

"Wait for backup."

"*Oui.*"

"Eleven thirty, Armand. You know the significance."

"*Non.*"

He did, of course, but wanted to shove Fleming closer to the edge.

To give him the impression that something so significant to him meant nothing to the man he hated.

It also kept Fleming's attention on him. Away from Reine-Marie. Away from Jean-Guy.

Think. Think. *Come on.*

Gamache's eyes now gripped Fleming's.

He could see this insult was working. Fleming, wildly unpredictable, was becoming more unbalanced.

Come on.

"You fucker. You do know. I know you know."

Gamache just shrugged. "*Désolé*, but that time means nothing to me."

He saw Fleming's eyes narrow. The risk, the terrible risk, was that in pushing Fleming so far, the man would first do harm to Reine-Marie before turning on him.

He could see it in Fleming's eyes. In his grip on the knife. His grip on Reine-Marie tightening.

"Oh, wait. Is that the time when you left the SHU?" he asked, pulling Fleming back from the cliff.

Fleming glared at him and loosened his grip, slightly. "It's the time you dragged me back in."

"Right. But for a brilliant man, you must've known I'd never let you out."

Gamache was scrambling to keep Fleming focused and occupied. And just off-balance enough.

Push, recover. Push, recover.

"The very fact that you thought I would proves your insanity," Gamache continued. "And now you think you've bested me? Do I look like a man in despair? You know, somewhere in that lunatic brain of yours, that there's something you've forgotten, John."

The room had grown quiet. Beauvoir had stopped shouting. Even the dogs were silent. Time had suspended. The earth had stopped moving.

Armand could see it in Fleming's eyes. Finally. Finally.

If Fleming could get into Gamache's head, and he could, then Gamache could get into Fleming's.

And he was. Finally.

Gamache could see the piles of garbage, the sewage, the rot and decay and filth. The hatred and jealousy, the loathing. The madness.

And the fissure of doubt that had let him in.

He could see Fleming's mind working. Going over and over what he had spent years planning. Building. Was it possible, he was asking himself, that there was some detail, some miniscule item he'd forgotten?

The sort of tiny mistake that could derail a train, collapse a building.

Bring an entire bridge falling into the St. Lawrence. One small miscalculation. One tiny, missed calculation. And catastrophe.

"His files," said Sam. "In the basement. The ones Fiona told us about. There must be something in them. Something he found. He knows even if we kill him, his people will find it."

"That's impossible. There is nothing."

"Then why does he keep it locked?" demanded Sam, his own voice rising with anxiety.

Gamache could see Fleming's doubt growing by the second. He was tempted to push in further, but resisted. He knew that his silence only made it worse. It spoke of confidence.

Which he did not actually feel.

Though the Chief Inspector was confident of one thing. His days, months, years as an investigator had proved that everyone had secrets. Things they kept from the world. Often from themselves. But they were there. Buried deep. Festering.

Even a psychopath had things he never wanted to admit, even to himself. Secrets that might be locked in the room in the basement.

"You're fucking with us," snarled Fleming.

"You're right. There is nothing there."

Fleming glared at him, his eyes scanning, digging, tunneling deeper. Trying to find the truth. And the beauty was, Armand had just told the truth.

There was nothing.

"Tie them up," said Fleming, and Sam quickly bound Reine-Marie's and Armand's hands behind their backs.

"You stay here," he said to Sam, handing him the gun again and taking the huge hunting knife, always his weapon of choice. "If we aren't back in three minutes, shoot them."

As he pushed Gamache toward the basement door, Fleming looked out the window. Still no sign of cops. No signal from Fiona. He had a moment of doubt, but then he saw her standing on the front lawn, looking up the road out of the village.

Gamache saw her too. Still, he clung to hope. Though he knew that when the clock on the mantel struck the half hour, no power on earth could save them.

Fleming flicked on the lights and Armand started down, his mind racing. He'd managed to separate Fleming and Sam, but he was far from certain that was an improvement.

As he walked down the stairs, his eyes traveled around the familiar space, for something, anything, he might use. This must have been, he realized, where Sam had hidden. He'd obviously gone through the box of Christmas ornaments. Finding the tinsel to tie them up with. A big glass ball lay shattered in the dirt.

Daniel, just a child at the time, had bought it with his allowance to celebrate the millennium. It was now a curiosity. And a family treasure.

Was that the sound he'd heard earlier in the evening? Not Fred, but Daniel's ornament breaking? Could all of this have ended then had he only looked closer when he'd come down?

He thought of his grandchildren, his children, at the cabin, and what would happen if this lunatic and his apprentices escaped.

"Hurry." Fleming gave him a shove, and Gamache lost his footing, tumbling the last few steps. Unable to reach out to cushion the fall, he twisted and landed on his shoulder, then rolled a few times, ending up on his back, winded. Gasping for breath.

"Get up," Fleming commanded. "You have two minutes now to open that door, get the files, and get back upstairs before Sam starts."

Gamache rolled onto his knees and knelt there for a moment, head down, gasping for breath. Then he struggled to his feet and staggered to the metal door to the room where all the secrets were kept.

Amelia and Harriet were almost at the stone bridge over the Bella Bella when a voice came out of the darkness.

"Stop. Wait."

Not a shout, but an urgent plea.

Amelia drew her gun. She recognized the voice. It was Fiona Arsenault. She was running toward them, waving her arms.

"They're in the house. Quick. We're almost out of time."

Amelia hesitated. This could be, probably was, a trick.

Gamache's phone was in the Incident Room. There was every reason to believe he was too, and Fiona Arsenault, John Fleming's daughter, was luring them away.

"For God's sake," pleaded Fiona. "You have to believe me."

Amelia Choquet, who'd seen terrible people do terrible things on the streets, had also seen acts of immense, immeasurable courage.

But which one was this? She stared at Fiona. Stared. Stared.

Then she changed direction and ran after Fiona, Harriet hard on her heels. The three young women raced across the village green, past the pines, toward the house.

"What's the code?"

Fleming was standing in front of the keypad.

"Zero, zero, zero, zero."

Fleming turned and glared at him. "You're lying."

Armand's head was lowered as he struggled for breath, his shoulders heaving. Raising his eyes, he met Fleming's.

"Would you have ever guessed it?"

Fleming smiled, shook his head, then punched in the numbers. There was a clunk. Fleming reached out and turned the door handle. But it didn't move.

"You dumb f—"

That's as far as he got. Armand launched himself forward, knocking Fleming against the wall.

* * *

Hearing the struggle in the basement, Sam lifted the gun to Reine-Marie's head.

"Stop," Jean-Guy screamed. "No!!"

Amelia skidded around the corner of the house and onto the back patio.

In a flash she could see what was happening.

Armand heard the shot.

The shard of glass he'd picked up from Daniel's broken ornament had cut the tinsel almost all the way through. Now, with all his might, Armand wrenched his wrists free.

There was a second shot.

He yelled, a roar of rage and anguish, even as he crushed Fleming against the wall. His hand shot up and grabbed Fleming's wrist just before the knife could reach him.

It flew away as both men fell to the ground. Gamache's hand closed around something, and he lashed out, hitting Fleming squarely on the skull. Once. Twice.

He heard a cracking but didn't stop to check. He knew the man was down. And wasn't getting up.

Grabbing the knife, he ran up the stairs, two at a time.

At the top he rammed into someone, knocking both of them to the floor. Gamache scrambled to his feet, his eyes wild. Brandishing the knife.

"Chief," shouted Amelia, her hands up in front of her.

He took her in, then looked around. Around. A—

And there she was. Coming toward him.

He dropped the knife and went to Reine-Marie. They clung to each other. Rocking and sobbing. Then Armand reached out and grabbed Jean-Guy, bringing him into the embrace, as Amelia and Harriet looked on.

And Fiona knelt by her brother.

CHAPTER 39

⌒

R abbit, rabbit, rabbit," said Harriet, as she greeted the month of July.

She got up, stretched, then went for her early-morning run before the day got too hot.

By the time she got back, the villagers had gathered on the bistro terrasse for a late breakfast.

"Happy Canada Day," said Harriet, kissing her Auntie Myrna on the top of her head.

"You stink," said Ruth when the young woman sat down beside her.

"*Merci*," she said. "And you look like crap."

Ruth laughed. Then, lifting her middle finger, she waved to Armand and Reine-Marie, who were just stepping off their front veranda, Henri, Fred, and Gracie tumbling after them.

"Welcome home," Clara called.

After greeting everyone, Armand and Reine-Marie sat down.

"Who's that?" Harriet pointed to a young man, shirt off, placing logs in a teepee pattern in the firepit on the village green. Ready for the Canada Day bonfire that evening.

"My nephew," said Billy. "He's just started working with me."

They all looked over. The young man was glistening in the mid-morning sun.

While the others turned back, Myrna noticed that Harriet had not.

Myrna and Billy exchanged glances. Ahhhh, to have that many pheromones again.

Olivier placed French presses on the table for the Gamaches, along with jugs of hot, frothy milk.

"*Merci, mon beau Gabri*," said Reine-Marie. She plunged, then poured the coffee while servers took their orders.

"How was the cabin?" Gabri asked.

It was a delicate way to ask how they were. And, just possibly, to dig for information.

As soon as they were able, after the siege at their home, Armand, Reine-Marie, and Jean-Guy had gone to the lake house. To spend the rest of June with their family. To swim and canoe. To sit on the dock and watch the early-morning mist rise from the lake, then burn off as they drank their coffee and did their sums and welcomed a fresh new day. One that, for a while that long night, they never thought they'd see.

The best sound ever, Armand decided, was the slamming of a screen door. It meant the children were awake and racing out to play.

It meant all was right with the world.

It meant that all was well.

He and Reine-Marie and Jean-Guy went for long walks in the late afternoon. The others, Annie, Daniel, Roslyn, left them to themselves. Understanding this was time they needed. Alone. Together.

At first they just walked, in silence. Each lost in their own thoughts. Then, little by little, they opened up. About what had happened.

Through the sunshine, through the woods, up and down the hills, over the wooden bridges, along the dirt road, they talked. And talked. And walked. And listened.

Sometimes they'd stop as one or the other halted. Overcome. Unable to go on.

They'd wait. And when the person was ready, they'd walk some more. Moving forward. Slowly. But always forward.

On clear, warm nights a bonfire would be lit. Marshmallows and hot dogs would be burned. Florence and Zora would crawl onto their grandfather's lap, nestling into his open arms, while Honoré would curl up next to his grandmother, sharing a Hudson's Bay blanket.

Jean-Guy always held Idola. Keeping her warm against his chest. Rocking her slowly. Back and forth. Back and forth. He'd push his chair back a little from the light so that no one could see his tears.

But rainy days were Armand's favorites. They'd sit on the screened porch watching the warm rain on the lake, listening as it drummed on the roof. He'd get out the Monopoly board and, with Idola on his lap, he'd play all day with his grandchildren.

When they tired of Monopoly, he taught them cribbage and always, always, always cheated. Counting his cards to a ridiculous point total, to howls of protest.

And then it was time to leave.

If Armand's and Reine-Marie's embraces were a little tighter, a little longer, than normal, no one noticed. Or, if they did, they didn't say anything.

John Fleming was dead. His skull crushed by the brick. Though Armand was honest enough to know it wasn't the brick that did it. He did it. The brick just happened to be the tool at hand.

Sam Arsenault survived the gunshot wounds and was recovering in the prison hospital. He was charged with the murders of Claude Boisfranc and Monsieur Godin. Though Gamache suspected he was also responsible for the death of Madame Godin. Or was at least an accomplice.

But it was someone else's case. He was now a witness.

He'd been interviewed, of course. And twice agents from his own department had traveled to the lake. He, Jean-Guy, and Reine-Marie had insisted the interviews not take place at the cabin, but in the detachment in Ste-Agathe. So as not to upset the children.

And now they were home in Three Pines.

Both Reine-Marie and Armand had wondered, as they'd driven back, how the place would feel.

Would they walk into their home and be overcome with terror?

Would those ghosts come out of the walls, the floorboards, down the chimney and attack?

The place had been cleaned professionally, of course, in their absence. Several times. Then Clara and Myrna, Ruth, Olivier and Gabri, Monsieur Béliveau and Sarah and other friends and neighbors had gone in and scrubbed it down again.

What worried Armand and Reine-Marie as they got closer and closer to Three Pines weren't the physical traces of what had happened. It was what could not be seen. That there was more in their home now than met the eye.

Armand unlocked the front door and reached for the handle, but Reine-Marie stopped him.

He looked at her, wondering if maybe she was about to say she could not go in. The place was not theirs anymore. John Fleming had taken possession of their home.

They would sell it and find a place somewhere else.

But instead, she laid her hand on top of his. "Let me."

As she walked in, Reine-Marie was met with the familiar aromas of coffee and wood smoke and pine. The scents were embedded in the home.

But there was something else . . .

She turned and saw the huge bouquet of fragrant bee balm on the coffee table. And through the open door to the kitchen, she saw vases overflowing with roses and lavender. All from gardens around Three Pines.

Perennials. That never failed to return each year, no matter how harsh the winter.

She closed her eyes and dared the monster to do his worst.

Come on, she taunted. *Come and get me.*

She waited, but all she sensed was peace. And calm. And safety. There were spirits here, yes. But no demons.

Opening her eyes, she noticed a new painting. It was Clara's latest.

The wild, exuberant, vibrant swirls of colors seemed to spill out past the unframed canvas and tumble into the room.

Reine-Marie couldn't help but smile. She knew immediately what it was. Who it was.

She turned to her husband. Armand was searching her face. She reached out and placed her palms on his chest so she could feel his heartbeat.

"Welcome home."

A few minutes later, as she embraced Clara, Reine-Marie whispered, "*Merci*. The painting is magnificent."

They sat down and enjoyed breakfast together as the friends brought the Gamaches up to speed on village life.

The play Gabri was organizing.

The cooking course Olivier had decided to offer.

"I need to show you the new bedroom," said Myrna. "Harriet's room."

"It's finished?" asked Armand. "So quickly?"

"We all helped," said Ruth.

They looked at her. Rosa had been more help than the old poet.

"There is one more thing we need to do," said Clara. "But we've been waiting for you."

"First, though, I have some questions."

"For God's sake, Ruth," hissed Gabri. "We agreed not to ask."

"You did. I never agreed to anything."

"You did so," said Clara.

This went on for some minutes while Reine-Marie finished her Croque Monsieur, the melted Gruyère and béchamel sauce dripping out of the crispy croissant and onto her plate. Armand poured more maple syrup over his blueberry pancakes until they looked like islands in a sweet sea.

"Just one question then," said Ruth. She turned to the Gamaches. "What happened?"

"Oh, for fuck's sake," said Olivier.

Armand opened his mouth, then started laughing. "That is the question, Ruth."

With that, the levee broke.

Clara leaned forward. "It started when we realized there was a hidden room, right? What would've happened if we hadn't? I mean, it's been there, bricked up for more than a century."

Armand was shaking his head. "It all started—"

"With the letter," said Billy. "From Pierre Stone. Was it real, or did Fleming forge it?"

It was one of the first questions Armand asked too.

"It was real, and you're right. That's where it started. John Fleming was in the SHU, but determined to get out. He knew how, and he knew he'd pay me back for what I did to him. What he needed was a plan. He spent years researching me, researching all of us. Working out our desires, our triggers, our core beliefs, our fears. All those details became the building blocks—"

"The bricks," said Harriet. She'd been staring at the young man building the bonfire, but now turned to meet Armand's eyes.

"The bricks," he agreed. How she'd changed, he thought, as he regarded the self-possessed young woman. "But what he needed was the structure. Sylvie's job was to find something that would act as a catalyst. It took a long time, but finally, on searching the local historical society archives, she came across the Stone letter. She recognized the potential."

"But how did something that important go unnoticed for so long?" asked Gabri. "It's been around for a hundred and fifty years."

Reine-Marie sighed. "It's our fault. Historians, archivists, researchers, professors, biographers. We look to the so-called important figures. We value the papers left behind by Premiers, Prime Ministers, Presidents—by the most prominent witnesses to history—and forget there are other witnesses. The people who actually lived it. The First Nations. The farmers. The cooks and cleaners and salespeople. The laborers. The immigrants, the minorities."

"The women," said Harriet.

"Yes. The Stone letter was among the papers of a stonemason. A bricklayer. No one thought they could be of value." She shook her head. "It is a terrible flaw in written history."

"We were also wrong to assume Pierre Stone was next to illiterate," said Armand. "The fact is, he went to university, but had to drop out when his parents died. He needed to find a skill to support his family."

"The most obvious one was as a stonemason," said Billy. "Like his father and grandfather. He discovered he was not only good at it, but liked it."

"Sylvie found the letter and gave it to the head guard to give to her husband," said Armand.

"So they knew there was some hidden room," said Olivier, "but how did they know where it was?"

"Sylvie had all Pierre Stone's papers," said Armand.

"There were more?" asked Myrna.

"Oh, yes. All his letters to his fiancée, who became his wife. Whenever they were separated, he wrote her. Every day. He told her everything, including where the room was. Sylvie stole the letters. We found them in their home."

The "we" of it wasn't completely accurate. The investigators, led by Inspector Lacoste, found them while Armand was cheating at cribbage with the children.

"As soon as he saw the Stone letter, Fleming recognized the potential," Armand continued. "From there he built his plan. It sounds, when I talk about it now, as though it all fell into place easily. It didn't. It took years to put together all the elements."

He stopped and took a small breath, suddenly visited by that voice. *Time and patience. Time and patience, Armand.*

His friends waited for him to recover.

"All right?" said Ruth.

"All right," he said.

"Fuck, fuck, fuck," said Rosa.

He looked at the duck, and the duck looked at him.

"You got that right," said Armand, nodding. But then, he often did. "The next big breakthrough for Fleming was when Sylvie sent him a photo of *The Paston Treasure*. He knew he could use it as a sort of Trojan horse, hiding within it all the items designed to alert but also alarm me. The art conservator from the Musée called it offensive, and that's what he wanted."

"But, but," sputtered Gabri. "The room. If the Stone letter is real, why was Pierre hired to brick it up?"

"He doesn't say in his letters. I doubt he looked into the room. Probably frightened." Armand turned to Ruth. "But I think you know what was in there."

"I think I do. What was the one thing that didn't really belong?"

"The book," said Myrna.

"Yes," said Reine-Marie. "The grimoire."

"We'll never know for sure," said Ruth in a rare admission of uncertainty, "but I think it was dug up when they were first excavating for the building, back in the 1870s. The guy who was putting up the buildings realized what it was, and it scared him. As far as he knew, the grimoire was a book of the damned, designed to raise demons. He tried to destroy it. There're burn marks on it. But then he changed his mind, either because the leather wouldn't catch, or he was afraid of angering the evil spirits."

"And bricking them up wouldn't?" asked Gabri.

"Out of sight, out of mind," said Olivier.

"Well, he must've been out of his mind," said Ruth. "I'm no expert, but I suspect demons can get through walls."

They suspected Ruth was, in fact, an expert. She did have the ability to show up unexpectedly, and uninvited.

"It's hard to get rid of—" Clara began.

"Ruth?" said Gabri.

"—beliefs. Think about what we're planning to do later."

"What are you planning to do?" asked Armand, half afraid of the answer.

"You'll see," said Clara.

It was the answer he was afraid of.

"Did you say it?" Myrna asked Harriet.

"Of course. It's the first of the month. Did you?"

Auntie Myrna nodded. She'd taught Harriet to say *Rabbit, rabbit, rabbit* when her niece was just a child.

"It brings good luck," she'd explained to the wide-eyed girl, who seemed to need luck. "But you have to say it first thing, before anything else, at the beginning of each month."

And Harriet did. Even as a rational scientist, she still did it. Because . . . because you just never knew. It did no harm. And Harriet Landers was beginning to understand that believing something was even more powerful than knowing it.

I've seen worse, I've seen worse was her new mantra.

Fear no longer had her by the throat. She would always be afraid, but she'd come to realize it was not so much a matter of less fear, but of more courage. And Harriet Landers had that. Now.

"So, the owner put the grimoire in the attic and commissioned the stonemason to brick it up," said Billy, guessing the rest. "He chose Pierre Stone because he hadn't worked on the original building and he wasn't known in the village. He couldn't tell anyone about the commission, even if he wanted to."

"But he did tell one person," said Reine-Marie. "His fiancée."

Armand nodded. Each of Pierre's letters to her, and there were many through their lifetime together, ended with the same thing.

I love you. I miss you.

The letters had sat, in a box in the basement of a rural historical society, buried and dismissed. The unimportant memories of a stonemason and his wife.

Or maybe, thought Gamache, they were waiting. For Sylvie Fleming to find them and set all this in motion.

Part of Armand railed against the notion of fate, preferring to think they had at least some control over their lives. But another part of him found comfort in the idea of predestination.

So far the Fates had been kind. Though not everyone, looking at events in his life, especially recent ones, would agree.

But any agency that allowed him to spend a month by the lake with his family, then return home to this village, to have breakfast with close friends, his beloved wife by his side, was kind indeed.

"Armand?" said Myrna.

"Wake up, Clouseau," said Ruth.

A car had stopped at the crest of the hill down into the village. The driver got out and stood, staring down.

The one investigator Armand had invited to join them at the cabin by the lake was Isabelle Lacoste.

"You know, *patron*," she'd said as they strolled down the dirt road, the sound of laughing and screaming children fading into the distance, "this isn't a social call. I'm here to question you, as part of the investigation."

"I know. It's all right."

The last time she'd seen him was very different. She and her team from homicide had arrived in Three Pines, afraid of what they'd find.

What Inspector Lacoste found was Agent Choquet working on a badly wounded young man in the living room, another woman kneeling beside him, holding his hand and rocking back and forth. Whispering that it would be all right.

Chief Inspector Gamache was holding a bandage to Beauvoir's bleeding head.

And a wild woman was standing in the middle of the room, clutching a tree branch.

"Oh, Isabelle. Thank God," said Reine-Marie.

Lacoste scanned the room, making sure there were no threats, then turned to Gamache.

"Ambulances are on their way, *patron*," said Lacoste. "Are you all right?"

Armand didn't know how to answer that, so he said nothing. Isabelle understood. She went over and bent down beside the wounded man.

"I shot him," whispered Choquet, trying to stem the bleeding.

Lacoste took her bloody hand and adjusted the pressure. "You were told to wait for backup."

"Sorry. Next time."

As Lacoste got up, she whispered, "Well done, Agent Choquet."

Isabelle Lacoste had taken charge of the situation. Issuing orders, coordinating the collection of evidence. Placing the victims and witnesses in the kitchen, away from the shambles.

"John Fleming's in the basement, Isabelle," Gamache said to her quietly. "I killed him."

It was a simple statement of fact that gave the man no pleasure. At all.

She'd gone into the basement and found the body. John Fleming was clearly dead. Still, as she'd approached him, Isabelle had slowed, then stopped.

The eyes, open, glassy, glaring, seemed to be inviting her closer. Trying to create an intimacy, into which he could place all the horrors of the world.

She did not back away. She did not blink. Isabelle Lacoste did the one thing she knew was a defense against this monster. Not prayer. Not singing.

Isabelle Lacoste smiled.

Then she stepped forward and closed those lunatic eyes for good.

Days later, she drove up to the lake house to debrief Beauvoir, Madame Gamache, and the Chief Inspector again. They'd been through it once, that night. But often the second time through was more useful, when the shock wore off.

She was just about to ask the first question when the Chief began to talk. His hands behind his back, his face forward, Armand told her what had happened. It felt a bit like he was relating a Grimms' Tale, or a fable de La Fontaine.

A tale of demons and witches, hidden rooms and unexpected saviors.

Of Fate both cruel and kind.

Armand left his friends on the bistro terrasse and walked past their home, past the church. Up the hill, to greet the young woman he'd invited down.

Amelia Choquet had parked the Sûreté vehicle and was now standing on the grass verge, looking out past the village, to the forests and hills. To the endless expanse of what seemed wilderness but was not.

To find the wilderness, they had to look inward, not outward.

Amelia knew that. Had learned that on the streets. Here, now, she felt only peace.

"I'm glad you came," said Armand.

They sat side by side on the bench in silence, warmed by the July sun.

Below them the villagers had gathered on the green. Armand and Amelia watched as Ruth and Rosa, Olivier and Gabri, Clara and Reine-Marie and Harriet formed a circle around Myrna. Monsieur Béliveau and Sarah the baker left their shops to join them.

Myrna lit something and passed it around.

"Looks like a huge joint," said Amelia and heard the Chief Inspector grunt with amusement.

They both knew what it really was. A sage stick.

Each villager took the thick bundle of bound-up sage and sweetgrass and wafted the smoke over themselves. Smudging themselves. Cleansing themselves of any ill spirits, in a ritual as old as the hills and forests and streams.

"Well, that's just weird," said Amelia.

"Glass houses," said Armand and saw her smile.

They watched for a little longer before he turned to her.

"Thank you. You saved our lives. My life. My family's life."

She looked at him. Saw the terrible scar at his temple. Saw the lines down his face. Saw the hurt, the pain, in his eyes as he thought of what might have been.

But there was something else in those eyes. A bright spot. Maybe from the sun.

Below them, the villagers were just making their way to the little chapel. Once there, Myrna wafted the sage toward the white clapboard building, taking extra care with the stained-glass boys.

Only when they disappeared inside did Amelia speak.

"I know it doesn't make us even. But maybe it helps."

"You're right. It doesn't make us even." He turned to her again. "I am indebted to you. And I owe you an apology."

She cocked her head, confused, but said nothing.

He took a breath. "When you first applied to the Sûreté Academy, I turned you down. Not because I didn't think you'd make a good, even an exceptional, agent. But out of revenge."

Instead of rushing his words, he spoke clearly, precisely. "I wanted to hurt you, to hurt your father."

"Because of the death of your parents," she said. "Because of what my father did."

He exhaled a long, long breath. "*Oui*. I suspected if I turned you down, you'd remain on the streets." He paused and gathered himself. "You would die on the streets." He held her eyes. "I'm sorry. It was a terrible thing to do and I'm ashamed of myself."

"Are you asking for forgiveness?"

He nodded. "I am."

"I don't see why. You did save me. You admitted me to the Academy." She thought for a moment. "If you hadn't, I couldn't have saved you. Funny how that works."

"Yes." He watched the procession walk back across the village green and into the bookstore, where they would cleanse the loft. "Funny that."

He looked down at his hands. He was clutching a book, and now he offered it to her.

"It belonged to my father. I want you to have it. I think he'd want it too. As thanks."

She hesitated, but finally took it.

"*Merci*. It will be treasured. And for what it's worth, *patron*, I forgive you too."

The procession below them was now heading for the Gamache home, trailed by Henri, Fred, and Gracie. Harriet disengaged herself and approached JJ, the shining youth.

"Will you join us for Sunday dinner?" Armand asked Amelia. Who nodded.

* * *

The home had already been smudged by the time they got there.

Everyone was now in the living room.

Ruth had stuck the sage stick into the vase of bee balm and sweet pea and was pouring herself a scotch.

"Ruth," said Reine-Marie. "It's only . . ." She looked at the clock on the mantel. "Oh, what the hell."

She poured drinks for everyone, while Armand stared at the framed picture Florence had made. The one with the rainbow. The one Fiona had taken off the wall and held that night almost a month ago. Her finger had been pointing to the words his granddaughter had written in her careful hand.

Ça va bien aller.

Armand hadn't known for sure, but he'd thought, wondered, hoped, prayed that Fiona was sending him a message. That yes, she had helped her brother, helped her father. But unlike them, she had limits. And had reached them.

She would not help them murder the Gamaches.

All would be well.

That was Armand's last hope. The one he clung to even as time was running out. Ran out.

When Fiona had left the home, he knew it could mean one of two things. Either she was, as she said, looking out for the police to warn the others. Or she was going to flag them down, guide them to the house. Which was what she'd done.

The three women together—Fiona, Amelia, and Harriet—had saved their lives.

On their way home from the lake house, Reine-Marie had asked Armand to stop at the women's prison where Fiona was being kept. She would spend many years behind bars for her role in what had happened.

Armand knew he would speak, once again, on her behalf. On behalf of John Fleming's daughter. Though he wasn't ready to see her. Not yet. But Reine-Marie wanted to. Needed to.

When she returned to the car, she was pale. But calm.

"What happened?" he'd asked.

* * *

Armand went over to Myrna.

"Drink?" she asked, lifting hers.

"Please. Scotch, neat. Can I borrow this?" He'd picked up the still smoldering smudge stick from among the flowers.

"You can have it. It's done its job."

"Not quite."

He went downstairs for the first time since the confrontation with Fleming. As he descended, he could smell the musky sage and sweetgrass. Here too had been cleaned and cleansed. Washed, sanitized. Exorcised. But he needed to be sure.

Armand knew that ghosts could be stubborn.

Walking around the room, he wafted the smoldering sage stick toward the walls, the floors. The boxes of Christmas ornaments. He spent extra time on the pile of bricks, the ones he'd meant to get rid of. But had not.

The head of homicide for the Sûreté du Québec went through the ancient ritual, solemnly smudging every corner of the room.

Then Armand turned to the bolted door and punched in the code: 1206. December 6th. The date of the shootings at the École Polytechnique.

Standing in the middle of the little room, surrounded by secrets, he closed his eyes and wafted the sweet smoke over himself. As men and women had done for thousands of years.

Then, noticing that Fred had followed him down, he picked up the smelly old dog and carried him upstairs.

That night a bonfire was lit on the village green in front of the three huge pines, celebrating Canada Day as they'd also celebrated, a week earlier, St-Jean Baptiste.

"Whatever happened to the women?" Harriet asked. "Anne Lamarque and the others."

JJ, Billy's nephew, was sitting on the log beside her. His name, perhaps not surprisingly for a family that had produced a Pierre Stone and a Billy Williams and a Mable the Maple, was John Johnson. JJ.

"The witches?" said Ruth. "Many years after being exiled, they each returned to the places that had banished them, just once, to confront the people who did that to them."

"That must've been a shock for their families," said Olivier.

"For the priests," said Gabri. "Imagine seeing the witch return? Must've scared the shit out of them."

Reine-Marie thought of the painting Clara had left in their living room. The bold swirls of vibrant colors had coalesced into a face. An old woman's face, with blue eyes and sunburned skin and wild white hair.

And a surefire cure for warts.

"Did they go back to curse them?" asked Olivier.

"*Non*," said Ruth. "To forgive them. That was the magic."

The wizened Anne Lamarque in Clara's painting was smiling. Happy and free.

"What happened?" Armand had asked Reine-Marie that morning when she'd returned to the car after confronting Fiona.

"I think you know." She smiled. "Let's go home."

ACKNOWLEDGMENTS

~

I'm often asked where I get my ideas from. It's a very good question and one I always feel I should be able to answer. And yet, I struggle.

How can I not know?

I think it's because there are many ways, some clearer than others. I walk around with a notebook, and for many months before writing a book I observe and listen, taking down turns of phrase, single words, quotes from poems or books, snippets of conversation, or clipped articles from magazines and news reports. I often liken it to a pointillist work of art. Putting a dot of an idea here, another there. Some large, some tiny. Some to do with characters: Armand and Reine-Marie, Jean-Guy, Clara or Myrna, etc. Some are plot points. Some practical, some silly, some intuitive, some nutty. Some destined to become major themes, many destined to be ignored or used in another book. Or used as unexpected inspiration in later drafts.

For *A World of Curiosities*, I could not tell you exactly where the idea began. Where the major theme of "forgiveness" emerged. I have the feeling it wasn't really until near the end when I realized how often, unconsciously, the characters struggled with it.

How often I've struggled with the need to forgive. To let go.

I've loved exploring that theme in this book.

I can tell you exactly when the idea for the painting, *The Paston Treasure*, hit me. I was in London reading a feature in one of the newsmagazines where prominent people talked about their favorite work of art.

This particular personage said, *"The Paston Treasure,"* then proceeded to say why. It was a revelation. I'd never heard of it, but what a wealth of ideas for a writer! I knew then it was going to be my Trojan horse that would allow all sorts of clues, all sorts of ideas, themes, references to past books, to enter into the lives of the Three Pines characters.

I'm not sure when the idea came to look at the case that first brought Armand and Jean-Guy together. Until I started writing those scenes I actually had no idea what that case was.

From there it was natural to also consider Armand's "origin" story. At least, how he came to be in the homicide department. Again, I did not really know how it happened, until I went for a long, long walk. And the idea came to me.

To be honest, it was troubling. To use a real, tragic event—the murders at the École Polytechnique—and fictionalize elements?

I was a young journalist working in Québec City that day. December 6, 1989. I remember going into work early the next morning. I hosted the current affairs program for CBC Radio and needed to try to get clear on what happened at the École Polytechnique before going on air. The reports were still garbled. The researchers did amazing work, and through the morning I interviewed police, students, teachers, politicians. Trying to make sense out of a senseless act.

Fourteen young engineering students murdered. All women.

To my shame I initially believed, and gave airtime to, the politicians (all men) who insisted that this was the work of one lunatic, and not an indictment of society. There was no need to look at institutionalized misogyny. To examine equal rights, or lack of them. To have stronger gun control.

This was sad, a tragedy, but the targeting and murders of fourteen women and the wounding of thirteen others held no greater lesson.

It took me several days to hear, beyond their shouts, the quieter, more insistent, more thoughtful, far-more-compelling arguments of the families of the victims and the survivors.

To believe them when they said that the act was made possible because of hundreds of factors over hundreds of years that diminish, marginalize, sexualize, stigmatize women. It was an act of misogyny, as were the angry denials of the politicians, journalists, and gun advocates.

Yes, even as a woman, a journalist, I was so used to the status quo, it took me far too long to believe what these families, these women, were saying.

The deaths of those young women changed Canadian society. It brought about much stricter gun legislation (though it could be tougher still) and forced a long, hard, often painful examination of equal rights. Of human rights.

In deciding to look at the mass shooting at the École Polytechnique, and the reverberations that have changed Canadian society, I faced another issue.

How to write about this event without turning a tragedy into entertainment?

Before I began, I contacted Nathalie Provost.

Nathalie is one of the survivors who became—along with others, including the remarkable Heidi Rathjen—a passionate, indefatigable proponent for tight gun control, as well as an advocate for human rights that extends beyond equal rights for women.

I asked Nathalie how she felt about me including her and what happened at the École Polytechnique in a Gamache novel. And by necessity, since Nathalie would become a character in the novel and meet Armand, fictionalize elements.

Fortunately, she reads and likes the books. That helped. We corresponded about boundaries, and I said I would send her the final draft. If there was anything she objected to, I would change it. If I got facts wrong, I would either change them, or make it clear here in the acknowledgments where I chose fiction.

The day came when I sent Nathalie the book. Have to admit, I was afraid.

It took a few weeks for her to get back, partly because the École Polytechnique was giving her an honorary doctorate for all her work. An honor well deserved, at a terrible price.

Nathalie was beyond gracious in her comments. She wanted me to make it clear that the first calls for gun control, the first insistence that this was not the random act of a lunatic but the natural and grotesque consequence of widespread and often subtle misogyny, came not from her but from the families, for the most part. Nathalie herself, along with other survivors, was far too traumatized at first to be able to collect her thoughts.

That came later. And when it did, it was seismic. Nathalie, Heidi, and others brooked no dissent. They were articulate, passionate, and unrelenting in their calls for gun control. For equal rights. For human rights. For Québec, for Canada, to take a long, hard, fearless look at itself. And change.

Nathalie also wanted to make it clear that, for her, one of the horrors was when the media blamed the young male students for leaving when the gunman told them to. I remember how those young men were pilloried. Hounded. As though there was anything they could have done. As though the journalists would have rushed an armed man. It was a public hanging of innocent young men.

Nathalie also pointed out that many students stayed behind, hid, and when the shooting stopped they were the first to rush forward to help the wounded and dying. And yet, they got no mention, no credit.

They are heroes.

She also wanted to say that while Canada has strict gun laws, they should be tighter. I agree. Not surprisingly, so does Armand.

And, while the story of the engineering rings in Canada is true, Nathalie said they are actually given out at a special ceremony later. But I decided, for plot reasons, to go with the fiction.

Thank you, Nathalie, for helping me with the book, for being so very gracious, and for so much more than my story. For saving hundreds, perhaps thousands, of lives with your work with others on gun control.

If I have offended anyone in my use of the shootings at the École Polytechnique, especially the families of the murdered women and the survivors, I apologize. Profoundly and unreservedly.

On the issue of fact versus fiction, I want to point out that Anne

Lamarque was a real person, tried as a witch, and accused of owning a grimoire, which she defended as a book on herbs and medicine. In real life she was acquitted and never banished.

Many, many others helped with this challenging book.

I want to thank my assistant, Lise Desrosiers, for always being there for and with me. She has not only made the writing life possible by lifting so much off my shoulders but she makes it huge fun!

Thanks to Linda in Scotland. To Shelagh Rogers. To Danny and Lucy at Brome Lake Books.

Kelley Ragland, my editor at Minotaur Books, along with Andy Martin, Sarah Melnyk, Paul Hochman, and the CEO of Macmillan, Don Weisberg. Thanks to Jo Dickinson and her team at Hodder in the UK; Louise Loiselle, head of Flammarion Québec; David Gernert, my agent; and all the great people at the Gernert Company, especially Rebecca and Will, who do foreign sales. Thank you, Jamie Broadhurst, and the fine folks at Raincoast Books.

Thank you Rocky and Steve, The Hovey Gang, Kirk and Walter, and all my friends and family, who are so generous in their support. What would any of this mean without you?

And I want to thank you, for not only reading the Gamache books but for embracing the characters, the village. Me. I feel it, and it means the world to me. You have given me the most amazing life.

I do want to say that Nathalie Provost is not the only real person in the book.

Inspector Linda Chernin is inspired by Michael and my close friend Linda Chernin Rosenblatt. Linda, I love you.

Agent Hardye Moel is based on my amazing friend, Hardye—you guessed it—Moel. One of the wisest, kindest, funniest, and bravest people, along with her husband, Don, that I know.

Hardye, being a therapist, also helped me with some of those issues in the book. Thank you, Hardye, my love.

Finally, I want to return to the question of where I get the ideas for the books. I mentioned being magpie-like in picking up thoughts, articles, quotes, etc. But there is something else.

I honestly don't feel I can take full credit for the books. There is, finally, an element of magic, of inspiration that seems to come out of nowhere. I have my own theories about where it comes from. I wanted, at the end of this, the eighteenth novel, to make it clear that in writing the Gamache books there is more than meets the eye. And always has been.

1. In the beginning of *A World of Curiosities*, we meet a young Jean-Guy Beauvoir—a very different Jean-Guy than the one we've come to know in recent novels. What are some of the most significant changes you noticed in Jean-Guy from his first case with Armand Gamache to the most recent one? What are some ways he's stayed the same?

2. In the first case Armand Gamache and Jean-Guy Beauvoir work together, they meet two children: Fiona and Sam Arsenault, who both grow up to be important characters in *A World of Curiosities*. How do you feel about Fiona? About Sam? How do you feel about their relationships with both Armand and Jean-Guy over the years and over the course of this novel?

3. *The Paston Treasure*—a seventeenth-century painting showcasing a wealthy family's collection of curios— plays a significant role in this novel. When Reine-Marie and Agent Choquet visit the original in England, the curator mentions that he plays a game with himself imagining which objects or treasures he'd add into the painting if he could. Which elements of *The Paston Treasure* fascinated you the most? If you could add any of your own mementos into the painting, what would you choose?

4. *Before I was not a witch*, wrote Ruth Zardo in a poem memorializing the terrible events of the Montréal Massacre. *But now I am one.* Knowing what we do now about the events of that day, why does Ruth incorporate imagery of witches into her tribute to those students? Where else does Louise include references of witchcraft and magic in *A World of Curiosities*?

MINOTAUR BOOKS

5. Early in the novel, we meet two new residents of Three Pines: the pastor Robert Mongeau and his ailing wife, Sylvie. Armand mentions that "he could see why Robert and Sylvie had fit in so well." What about them makes him say this? What other qualities do you think it takes to "fit in" in Three Pines?

6. In one scene, the villagers gather for dinner in the Gamaches' kitchen. Louise writes that "the final guest was Anne Lamarque, very much present, if only in spirit." Discuss the relevance of Anne Lamarque to the village of Three Pines. Where else is her spirit present in the novel?

7. During a confrontation, Fleming accuses Armand: "I thought you were many things, Armand, but never a coward. What kind of cop doesn't carry a gun? What kind of cop expects others to protect him?" Do you agree with this statement? Why do you think Gamache regularly chooses not to carry a gun?

8. Soon after Armand joined the homicide unit of the Sûreté as a young officer, his first mentor gave him one short, cryptic piece of advice: Matthew 10:36. *A man's foes shall be they of his own household.* How does this verse relate to the events of *A World of Curiosities*?

9. We're used to Gamache keeping his cool during tense moments, but during his conversation with the warden of the SHU, he reacts "beyond anger, beyond rage, into a territory Beauvoir had never seen in the Chief Inspector. Gamache was losing it." What is it about John Fleming that provokes this type of reaction in Gamache? How does his loss of control make you feel?

10. *Ça va bien aller*—all will be well. Readers will certainly recognize this phrase from *The Madness of Crowds*, but Louise uses it throughout *A World of Curiosities* as well, including once as a disguised message. Where else does Louise incorporate secret codes, or hidden messages, into this novel?

11. Louise refers to a quote by W. H. Auden throughout the novel: "There's always another story. There's more than meets the eye." What does Gamache miss in this story? And why? What role does the blind spot play in events in the book?

12. In her acknowledgments, Louise writes about exploring the idea of forgiveness, the major theme in this book. Discuss some examples of forgiveness in *A World of Curiosities*. Are there any characters you wouldn't be able to forgive?

MINOTAUR BOOKS

Mikaël Theimer

LOUISE PENNY is the author of the number-one *New York Times, USA Today*, and *Globe and Mail* bestselling series of Chief Inspector Armand Gamache novels, and coauthor with Hillary Rodham Clinton of the number-one *New York Times* bestselling thriller *State of Terror*. She has won numerous awards, including a Crime Writers' Association Dagger and the Agatha Award (eight times), and was a finalist for the Edgar Award for Best Novel. In 2017, she received the Order of Canada for her contributions to Canadian culture. Louise lives in a small village south of Montréal.

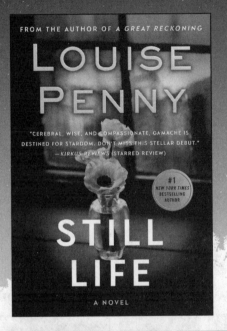

LOUISE PENNY'S
INSPECTOR GAMACHE SERIES
ON AUDIO

READ BY AUDIE AWARD–WINNING NARRATOR RALPH COSHAM

"My only quibble is that the Penny-Cosham team kept me listening past my bedtime."
—*AUDIOFILE* on *BURY YOUR DEAD*

READ BY AUDIE AWARD–WINNING NARRATOR ROBERT BATHURST

"Robert Bathurst is just about perfect delivering the sixteenth Chief Inspector Armand Gamache novel. . . . Listen to all the Gamache audiobooks for maximum satisfaction."
—*AUDIOFILE* on *ALL THE DEVILS ARE HERE,* Earphones Award winner

Visit MacmillanAudio.com for audio samples and more!
Follow us on Facebook, Instagram, and Twitter.

 macmillan audio